METROPOLITAN BOR

Please return this book to the Librar
before the last date stamped. If nc
by letter, telephone or in person. Fines will be charged on ....
books at the rate currently determined by the Borough Council.

ALLENN, T.M.

Lease of Will

LEASE OF WILL

T M Allenn

JANUS PUBLISHING COMPANY
London, England

First published in Great Britain 1993
by Janus Publishing Company

Copyright © T M Allenn 1993

**British Library Cataloguing-in-Publication Data.
A catalogue record for this book is available
from the British Library.**

ISBN 1 85756 096 5

Cover design David Murphy
Printed and bound in England by
Antony Rowe Ltd, Chippenham, Wiltshire

Log of Length

Preface

Edmond Rose is not a myth, he merely exists in various lives, all at the same time. He is the product of the misconception of liberal minds and unyielding people. He refutes any asserted credit and responsibility for changing the world, while complaining of the change taking place without his active participation. He is a free spirit trapped in the clothing of the modern man; his manhood is a tribute to his desire to do his best to experience the world before the final clamp of regenesis; his understanding of it is exciting and dependent on circumstance, as his appreciation is worthy of none of the Greek philosophers. The decadence of all society is a joke, never to be told in public or over a drink. His confessions are loud thoughts on paper, given the title of experience, compiled as telepathy and coloured as everyday posture of time. He requires no judgment, believes in few restrictions and dreams of nothing that indulges in the claim of possible reality. He is a simple man of simple needs and diets on daily friendships and long-harvested grains of understanding. He does not feel obliged to explain his love of life to himself or to anyone else. He is justly tied to the silky nuance of words in textures unusable to anyone for whom life is either a short-lingering trip or a passage through the barbed wire of self-confinement. Therefore, utopia to him is a thought of self-enhanced visual imaging, enjoyable to the extent of believing that it is definitely there across the line dividing one fantasy from another.

Edmond Rose was born under a different name. He agrees with me in keeping the original description of himself taken from the paper-biographed sequence of events. The others whom he inscribes onto paper have also been surgically implanted here with re-disclosed new names. All events detailed, however, carry their accurate fullness of description and emotions undiluted in their true length.

1

Birth and Ascension to Reason

When I was born, I was given three things by birthright: a name, a promise into a certain religion, and the duty to be. The name promptly identified me from others, including my two sisters and the world of other boys, a tag of kind. The promise into my family's religion I was expected to bear cut and engraved unto my flesh several days after my birth and required of me to carry throughout my life as the second dimension of the name tag. The duty to be was more intricate and was not explained to me until I was seven, when religion was tanned on my soul and the fear of God was imprinted on my expression as more important than honesty or basic duty or full kindness; all shall come from the fear of God, I was firmly told.

This duty to be had many branched points that appeared in care, in relationship of conscience to my family and my people and, in a lighter respect, to the rest of the world as the third dimension of the birthtag, it had to be nurtured and did not simply affiliate itself to me at birth. My duty to myself consisted in those early days in sleeping and complaining when I was hungry or in discomfort through wetness or thirst.

Yet in none of these dimensions of after-birth matters was I consulted, required to agree or allowed realistically to change, even after my puberty. I was to grow into them, live with them, sleep and wake in them, accept their infallibility of fate and refrain from the slightest whim of questioning them. I have to admit that these given criteria, for many years felt normal and most natural, starting as they did from the knowledge that all people had similar sets of markers, unique to each and yet common to all, edged by the ease of personal identification, discussion, understanding of the pattern motives and behaviour of others, to the point of expecting or categorising their mode reaction and possible reasoning.

The wisdom of people before us, who seemed to have devised these markings in time-scholared inheritance of experience, looked natural for the first ten years of my life. Then my ease of acceptance of these markings grew hard to sleep with, tough to forge through without daily dispute and the assumption of some guilt or other improper design.

Sometimes, in my teens, the argument was solved through pure reason; at other times the deduction smelt of greed, vanity, dark possession beyond mercy or simply to cover immorality, an assumed purity, deduced barely from the apportioning of such and such a name and colour, all with the tint of conformity to the rule and majority of society. Those who held tightly to their name may have taken inheritance of mere materialistic opinion and wealth as the best reason to divide people and bar them off. After all, the possession had to pass to particular people and not as indiscriminately. Others simply saw it as pride in belonging to particular fathers and mothers, unstained by possible illegitimacy; the latter was shameful and unbearably ground into us as a stigma for an unforgivable flaw. Others again saw their name as a requirement in carrying on the tradition of family work and a guarantee of future quality in that work.

To some of us our name was simply an acknowledgement of warmth and duty to parents who had taken it upon themselves to endure us, care for us and shape our dreams for us and in us. I thought of my name in good faith always, respected it for reasons of pride and sanity of logic and for thirty-seven years of my life accepted it as I accepted my looks or achievements and failures simply as me and as being there. At the end of the day, everything had a reason, be it or not believable, plausible or ridiculous and in spite of the description put on it, existing and possible. This was true for me the rest of my life. I use a different name now, often for anonymity.

As I recall, the first two years of my life must have been contented, as I do not remember being unhappy and the definition of unhappiness was not in my vocabulary. I was not born a mal-minted child or super-intelligent, but a simple child with wants and don't wants like many children by instinct and later training of senses. Any contemplation of my being but a normal, noisy and demanding child must be speculation. I required abundance of time and I must have obtained it, until at the age of three I was informed of the arrival of my new baby sister.

The prospect of total domination of my mother's time became an illusion of which I had to find the fallacy. The baby was fat, fatter than I remember myself, quiet and totally uninteresting, one could pinch her and yet she would not complain, she would not utilise her voice loudly even when she was hungry. She was my sister, yet completely alien to me. She did not resemble my pattern of how to be a child and get everything one wanted.

I was still drinking from a bottle, always liked it as if the milk or other liquids would not taste the same if not flavoured with the taste of freshly boiled plastic. In a way, it was the earliest form of possession. My mother tried weaning me off it, but come bed time, I found it difficult or unacceptable to drift into sleep without it. One day we were late returning from an outing. I had some fruit but my baby sister had had nothing for long hours. My mother looked for my sister's bottle to feed her but could not find it and proceeded to feed her using my bottle. The experience of losing possession of that bottle hurt and horrified me and I refused to use it again come bed time. The bottle had suddenly lost its magic as it became a communal property.

At the age of three I learnt the facts of inevitable loss of personal property of a child, as with the feeding bottle or when other children were equally entitled to the same privileges or made play with things allocated to me alone. I found sharing would devalue my affection towards things. I cannot explain to this day the reason that made me relinquish that bottle simply because my sister used it.

During the following years, I was happy to play with things that were valuable to me away from the eyes of visiting friends and only when other children were not there, although I was happy to share other toys that were not of great value to me with them. But I was consistent in one thing all along: I did not lend anyone anything unless temporarily and the object was given back to me almost immediately. I had one other habit, I did not break my toys in fits of

temperament or boredom and I resented the other children breaking things simply because it was something they did anyway.

I had a keen interest in how objects were constructed and spent
hours dismantling and assembling them in great care. Those that I
could not re-assemble properly used to haunt me at night time in
nightmares, begging me and frightening me in their deformity. I
used to demand that they were fixed before I slept, out of fear. I
also had another peculiar fear: anybody playing with my toys
would break them eventually and I would feel responsible and
guilty. For this reason, my selfishness in hiding my toys when
visitors were there seemed quite devoted, rational and really
unselfish in nature.

My mother was a quiet woman whose voice had the authority of
true command in gentle warmth. Her eyes shone like the stars in
the midsummer clear sky night. She treated both of her children
then with equal devotion and care. I somehow, always had the
feeling that I was her favourite, although it was not anything she'd
do for me, such as granting my every wish, no matter how small, in
spite of the demands of my little sister; it was the way she looked at
me when I said something that sounded funny or new that gave me
such a clear idea. Her interest was radiant and wordless.

My father was to me in those years a man who spent most of his
time at work. He spent most of his leisure periods with me and his
lifelong friend, Drake. This man was as familiar to me at that age as
my father was and I liked and loved him equally. I used to enjoy
their laughter and spend stretches of time in such wonderful
company while they drank, told jokes and reminisced of youthful
days and the storms they had weathered. I did not need to understand their jokes to feel the warm, joyful resonance of their contentment.

When I was four, another sister was brought home from a place
first noted as the hospital. It was a new usage of the place's versatile
definitions, a new utility of the word that I was proud to have
discovered and added to my understanding of such a place. The
new sister was noisy, more demanding and always hungry. She
was thinner, smaller and more helpless when compared to the one
I had last year. When she was asleep, she looked like a toy baby
which I had seen in my neighbour's house of four girls, a boring
place where the children spent their days dressing and undressing
plastic babies with great care. I tried to do it once and a leg, then an

arm came off as I tried to dress them. I was worried it would be permanent, but luckily the mother of the girls was experienced enough to make them look fixed.

I kept away from the new baby for a long time afterwards. She was different, the minute you touched her, even when she was asleep, she would wake and start crying. I hated babies that easily screamed, when I did not know what to do to make them stop. The loudness of her voice was a nervous deterrent, uncomfortable and unpleasant to my ears. I was surprised, somehow, in those days how my mother could by looking at a baby, tell us immediately if it was a girl. I couldn't at that stage. Although I had a deep feeling that she was different from my other sister, I could not foretell the reason for that feeling and I did not take to her as I heartily did to my first sister. With the passage of time, she did not repel friendship or vogue for squabbles, she proved to be just like any sister and I to her like any brother. We could be nice or thorny to each other, depending on the event and our age at the time.

In July of 1958, when I was five, winds of grave consequences blustered over us. We children were unable to ascertain their grave and deep-rooted temper, nor how close they came to scorching our lives and destroying our simple childhood. We had just moved into a big house, newly built, and although the garden was but of young shrubs, not much younger than ourselves, the high walls of the house, about six feet as I remember, were compensated for by the open space and the winding concrete walk-about. We resented for a while being not allowed to go and play on the street, haunted by the sound of happy and playful children, by the palpable excitement of others talking and shouting across lower barriers as we played in our garden, strictly discommunicated of all those friendly-sounding voices that flowed over the height of the multi-brick isolation.

A few months after moving into this fort, the sounds became loudly different as they crossed over in the heat of July. There were fewer that seemed friendly as before. Sometimes foul, strange language and terms were communicated; we learnt a new vocabulary that we were forbidden to repeat. Some of the children seemed angry with us, called our parents those names and often threatened us with the fate of being dragged on the street by passing cars, towing our bodies by a rope. These voices, mostly young, encouraged us children to open the gates, confront our tyrant parents, live above something called the decadence of the day and become purified. Other voices sometimes came, warning the first league of voices, not to associate with these prisoners across the wall, not to be friendly to them and without delay to be true sons of what was described as 'the revolution that was being made there everyday by the new army chief'.

As children we were tempted by anger to open the gates and defend our parents, explain that they were not as bad as these voices thought, invite them to play with us, share our garden space and tricycle rides over the tremendous and enchanting concrete paths that were like miniature roads and alleys. I was the only one of the three children who was tall enough to attempt to unlock any of the solid metal gates. The decision had to be mine, but I was not sure I should.

We had an old chef of about sixty years of age. His name was Mercury, after the element, not the planet. In his spare time he would line up the three of us and tell us stories which had a mythical inaccuracy as he told them over and over again. He was a man whom we could trust greatly, in front of whom we could make our mistakes, without fear of ridicule or punishment, a man who built for us other castles to enchant in times of play and sleep.

He was also unique in that he could not read or write, but his vivid knowledge of people and of the world was that of someone who told us we could only be as knowledgeable as he if we were good in school and did our studies properly. He could be asked any question and would not hesitate to advise, judge or navigate through the world if he wanted to or had to. I mentioned to him in passing the matter of the whispers and the shouts, the invitations and the threats, the dilemma of proving to the world our anger as well as our goodness as children of this house and for the first time in my memory that solid confident man seemed disturbed.

I did not at first welcome his advice. He told me not to listen to those voices which were like the forty thieves of Baghdad and went on from advice into the punch-line of the story of Ali Baba, which I had memorised at that stage. I liked the story, as I usually did any of his, but could not understand his reservation over the phantom voices, I wanted a sight of their faces, to know what at least one of the forty looked like. Why be afraid when we had him, two dogs and I in front, to defend the house if trouble broke loose?

I had neither any conception nor visual figurement of death at that age, nor did I think bad people could win a fight against the good. When you are five years old, reality has not yet differentiated itself from the utopia of made-up and well coordinated stories. Some seven or eight years later, you may find them very different.

Two singularly important and totally unrelated events, which happened in the right sequence a few days later, after this conversation, made me realise that the old man had actually saved my life and was true in his warning to keep the gates intact. As I was walking in the garden one morning, I found a dead cat, which the dogs must have killed. At the age of five, I had only seen cats in colouring books and immediately identified the animal as being like the one in my book, although it was stiff and without any movement.

I took a stick as a sword and prodded it in its side. It refused to move and I prodded it again; again it seemed undisturbed by my action. I hit the cat on its head and as before it refused to show any defence or interest. I went and called the old chef who unmistakenly announced it dead, showing me the signs where the dogs had bitten it and proving to me that it was not moving in reaction to any provocation. He also informed me of the civilised attitude on such an occasion: the rituals of burial and prayer (for something called its soul).

As he went to get a white-flour canvas bag, I was left watching the stiff animal, I refused to move until he got back, in some hope of revival or suspicion of play-acting on the part of the cat. Someone at that instant had let the dogs loose, both came directly to the spot that I and the cat were sharing. One dog smelt the dead cat while the other tried to drag it away. A fight broke out between the two dogs as my favourite of the two, a German alsatian only one month older than I, tried to remove the dead cat to another location.

I had never been scared of the two dogs, whom I had previously regarded as playmates or children. But now their angry nature was revealed to me in a single-second sequence, as they tore the dead cat apart in their fight over possession and control of its body. They were uncompromising in their voracity. The stench of the torn limbs is in my nose to this day every time I think of it. The two dogs were eventually controlled and the body pieces removed through the authority of the old man and my father who came running at the call of my screaming.

Two days after this, another tense event took place in the house.

The telephone rang, my father answered it and sharply slammed it down. Two minutes later the same happened. He then called in my mother from the bedroom and told her that he wanted to talk to her in the absence of the children. We were ushered into another room and were told to stay with our grandmother. I was too curious and stubborn to comply. I pretended to my grandmother that I had to go to the bathroom and proceeded quietly towards the sitting room, its door deleteriously and excitingly left ajar. I heard my father telling my mother that the men who had called several times that day had promised him that he would end up, anytime now, dragged from the bumper of a car, tied to it by a noose.

The noise on our street was loud; chantings came of hard cure from the decadence and corruption of the age and the ruling families, the thing called revolution was on the move. I went to an upstairs window, still failing to understand the connection between the two happenings. An old man, thin, well dressed but his clothes muddied from the surface of the road, where he must have fallen and got up, was being pulled behind a slow moving lorry.

As the crowd chanted louder, the lorry began to gather speed. Before the march reached the end of our road, I heard a loud cheer and the lorry was now speeding away, it turned and came back even faster, dragging the old man behind it. It almost knocked down a few of those gathering round on the return journey. As it passed under our window, I could see the old man had already lost one of his arms, wrenched away by the tugging crowd as his body looked like a dark piece of cloth separating them from the lorry in an uneven tug of war. A trail of blood drew a line between the point where the arm had been torn away and the point where the lorry was dragging the rest of the old man's body. For a moment I saw the dead cat's stretched body torn apart and then quite unexpectedly the body of the old man with a face much like my father's. As the lorry stopped, his eyes were fixed, open and colourless even from a distance.

For a moment I thought it was my father who was lying with half his face covered in blood-wet dirt, while the other half was as pale a colour as I had ever seen. I must have been screaming; suddenly my father slapped me in the face to quieten my anguish, fear and loudness. It was the first time ever my father had struck me.

I was sobbing in loud contention of fear, but no one on the street seemed to have heard me; no one look up or seemed interested in looking anywhere than at the body that was now being kicked all along the street's dusty pavement.

In a matter of two days and an afternoon, I seemed to have reached some kind of puberty at the age of five. It took six months for the images of that afternoon to fade from close recall and two years for the nightmare live-show to cease its nightly recurrence. In partly accepting fate and even more so through my warmth of regard and appreciation of my father's courage in disputing the incredible odds of living through the following two years, I came to remember that afternoon less as time went on.

I did not play near that high wall and would not touch the trees that overlooked it, until the age of ten. That wall had well-justified its existence and allowed me the security of sanity and logic after that. I never asked to be allowed to play or even liked to be outside it for six years after the onslaught. None of my friends at such a comparable age or time had encountered and known the real dimensions of the word 'death' as I had.

2

Gains of Concepts

At the start of the school year in September 1958, my father resisted the request of the headmistress of the school he had chosen to keep me in kindergarten for another year. His evaluation was partly based on my progress in home-driven study and on my comprehension of the first year school material, (the material that the primary schools required their students to grasp freely in attention in the class and expected their students to pass their exams in).

My father knew the local school programmes coordinator in the department of education. It would have been enough if the latter man had put in a good word for me with the headmistress, but because of her objection on the basis of my young age and her insistence on going by the age regulation, my father suggested I should sit oral and written tests to determine my application. She could not refuse, although she was probably trying to gain an extra year's fee out of my parents, as the school was privately run. She was sure that I would not make it through and went about arranging the test on her own ground.

On that intense day, my father's friend called by the school on a random inspection. He found a small boy sitting in a cold room awaiting his oral after finishing his written kerb. He sat through the oral at his 'own' request. I had never seen the man before in my life and indeed the idea of his being there or the purpose of his visit was not confided to me by my father. On doing quite satisfactorily, I was told before the end of that day that I would be sitting in the big class, starting the next day. I was very happy with my achievement, although the idea of going into a strange class, where I did not know any one, was disturbing. More or less, new friendships had to be struck and old ones ultimately thinned out as the opportunity of spending time with my old friends during the day was going to be somewhat restricted.

The new class had two male teachers who shared the schedule of seven subjects and the blame for the longer homework between them. We had five hours of teaching, a subject each hour and half an hour of sports everyday, together with an extra hour of learning how to be a scout every third day, six days a week. It was a hefty schedule for such an early class which required at least two hours of homework every night, five nights a week.

The two longest fifteen minutes in each day came at the beginning and end of each school day, when we had to stand to attention, while the national flag was raised in the morning and lowered in the afternoon, with accompanying music from the sixth graders. The disciplined silence during those two periods was hard, but the solemn obsessiveness of the procedure was stifling. Respect for the flag was enforced with fears of detention in an old cellar which was known to everybody as the rat room. Other punishment such as being struck with a sharp-edged solid oak ruler on the hands, was also common for a series of misconducts and unprepared homework or misattention in class.

The hinted threat of the cellar always disciplined us more than the pain of injury by the thick ruler, no matter how hard or frequent the assault was. We were children, under guard-watch, during the ten-minute breaks between classes, but other and different people, silent and obedient in all the remaining time. We were, now, different from the little people of kindergarten, who were watched children all the time, except for the ten-minute periods of transporter-embarked or -disembarked troops.

There were thirteen of us in the new class, nine boys and four girls, the latter seated in the first two rows of the class, watched more suspiciously and punished less. They were the privileged few who never knew the manly experience of the rat room. They were threatened by being reported directly to their fathers, if they misbehaved or fell back on their homework.

Punishment, irrespective of penance or duration, was administered and defined centrally by the headmistress. A big-bodied woman of forty-five, she was never seen smiling, except when handing us notices of quarterly invoice of fees, destined for our parents' humour or attention. There were, on the other hand, rewards for being the monthly knight of the class, honoured by the same mass of firmness as the best student of the class for that period. The chosen pupil in each class would be obliged to wear a four-inch-wide long sash of soft cloth which had the name of the class marked on it and was draped cross-wise from the right shoulder to end in stitched-together tassels at the left of the waist. Those chosen and honoured from any class had, for a month or so, to wear this acknowledgement throughout every morning and afternoon ceremony involving the flag rituals.

Fairness rarely counted for more than the occasional true pupil evaluation for the best in the class. For more times than we could remember, the declared best was a nephew of the headmistress. Although he was not inattentive or stupid with his studies, there were others who did better in exams and understood better all round; yet at the end of the day the famous nephew was declared the best of us, in spite of his good, bad or indifferent performance for that month.

This trend was to continue for nearly six years, until the sixth and last primary class, when the exams were conducted by unified questions and marked by a board of examiners from the government education department. When the aunt could not interfere with either setting or correcting the questions, the pampered nephew came the very last of all the class. It was a fine vindication for all of us, but not even ridicule was sufficient compensation for our hard efforts and defiled trials.

Most of the parents had a feeling that such a practice occurred, but had little proof and less intention of further aggravating the situation for their children. The battle raged, many were disillusioned, a few lost all incentive but some of us forgot the daily grind and went on in spite of it, passively.

The summer of 1959 came with much change and the first long break from the harsh confinement of routine days. The end of June was welcomed by me with an honesty of good humour. I had come second in the class, second to the nephew, naturally.

In the long summer days of intense heat that followed, I was allowed to play freely for the first month of that summer holiday. Early in the ensuing August, my father brought home a box of books, next year's texts. I was asked to set aside two hours a day to study them and was questioned regularly about the daily requirement and intake. I did not complain at first, but as the summer got effectively shorter, I found it hard to summon the required drive to continue, thinking of the oncoming school year, the threatened punishments and the rigged rewards.

My stubborn and increasingly persistent failure to attend after instruction and my fading interest in my summer study troubled my father and my mother equally. Neither of my parents could appreciate my unwillingness in this regard. When my father asked me why, I told him about the nephew and the preferential appraisal he received in school, how he did not perform as well in class, failing to answer questions properly, yet still coming on top nearly every month. I told him what the older boys, two of whom were repeaters, had said in amplification of the nephew's offences and the fact that all of us in the class shared the common belief in the rigging of the monthly test results. I went on to tell him how I missed the old class, of my fears of the cellar and other unfair punishments.

He listened and although I could clearly detect signs of his anxiety, his calm voice reflected no indication that I would be excused from continued endurance the summer's plan. He went on to explain to me that I had to do what I did not like sometimes, especially if he or my mother thought it was the right thing. As far as the punishments were concerned, he told me that one had to do what was asked of him, nothing less, or one may receive the penalty for not doing so. I was not hearing what I wanted to hear. He asked me if I had been sent to the school cellar and I had to tell the truth: no I had not been, but others had.

He then asked me what a rat looked like, and I was able to describe the horrifying, fat, dirty creatures that spent their time in that place waiting for those who made mistakes or were unfortunate enough to get caught while they were enjoying their bad behaviour. My father did not say that he did not believe me; at the same time he was offered neither explanation nor apparent sympathy for those who were sent there. I had seen the rats from a little window on the ground-floor landing of the room downstairs. My excessive use of adjectives was probably my doom in making the issue deemed unbelievable. I got some comfort later, when I heard my father discuss the rats with my mother, to her disgust, his quiet

anger and my good satisfaction. But any hope I had of the burden
of study lightening during the remainder of that summer disappeared the same day as I was told to carry on regardless and that
the situation in the school was irrelevant.

I studied hard in the summer to gain the satisfaction of my
parents and I understood that I must do it to please them, not for
the school as such. A system for home rewards was implemented
for me that summer, a toy at the end of every hard two weeks and
ice cream at the end of every near-impossible task. These rewards
convinced me that I was studying for my parents, as these were
purely signs of their appreciation and joy for my good performance
and compliance. I did not mind so much for those reasons and my
interest flowered considerably, aided by the all-wonderful conviction of being good and the warmth of achievement.

By the end of that summer when school started again, a new
subject of focus slightly offset my apathy. The new class had seven
girls and only four boys. Some of us from the last class had been
transferred, new pupils had joined and the resulting mixture was
different again. Most of the girls were noisy and kept to themselves
in a gang-like conformation, while the boys were intimidated by
the outspokenness, physical size and temperament of this new
majority.

The year started slowly, but about a month later one of our male
teachers was promoted to teach a higher class and a new female
teacher, called Rose, was appointed. She was a slim, delicate
woman of thirty, recently arrived from the capital with her husband, also a teacher but in a different school, to take up house in
Basrah. She commanded the class with vigour and logic, none of
us found it demanding to obey and outdo each other in study,
preparation, attention or mere quietness in her class. She taught us
history, art and magical science.

Rose was a new-generation teacher; she spoke to us as children
or like adults, depending on our resistance or compliance and
accordingly won every time. When history was the lesson, she
taught it not just from the book but out of finding reasons for actions
taken and motives for inaction. Every happening was debated as
if the book was not true or was heavily masked in an untrue texture
of dilemma and cover-ups. To prove her final points, she often
produced history texts of years gone by, mouldy books that looked
and smelt of forgotten interest and neglected attention.

Sometimes, the contradictions of content in the print-stated facts were almost absolute. It took us nearly a month to comprehend the difficult, unreconcilable fact about written history: each outlook had its motive and revealed only the superficial intent of ideas of those who had written it. We were confused and haunted with a new factor in study: what to choose as the right answer for the test every month. Rose knew this somehow. She told us one morning that in tests we should exhibit our belief in what we held to be true and be ready to defend it. A direct quote from a book was not sufficient and indicated that memory rather than logic and understanding would be at fault.

Lessons were just beginning to be exciting, when suddenly she was removed from us and another, older teacher was assigned. It was hard now to accept the written context as absolute; yet the replacement teacher was only interested in following the autocratic rendering of facts. No discussion or highlighting of opposing opinions was advocated, whether or not the latter existed. Another respect that intruded on our interest in study was that he was not infallible as she always made us believe teachers to be. She was a goddess of some undefined mystique, he was a plain teacher who filled the time jar with sand and pressed down diligently as we all watched the crystals accumulate downwards out of gravity and a shallow passage of time. Science also, with its wizardry of achievement, became once again sets of unquestionable cold facts and art became copying something on paper from the dust-plagued blackboard or follow-colouring an already outlined shape on a page, with him.

The imagination of possibilities that Rose invoked in us in science, or the freedom she gave us in choosing our colours and leaving us to define shapes of objects, over-painting them with a picture that our minds saw after moments of looking intently into our designs, where our eyes started to see shapes or colours unseen in the first look: all such things were readily ridiculed soft minded by him, the teacher in command. He would mark our tests with the same guidelines and assured firmness. We, the newly oppressed, indoctrinated to reality without a vision, eventually conformed to the drive of present ways. Lessons were again a show of inflexible will, a stretching of control.

An astonishing discovery was made during that year by the boys: the girls were happier with the male teacher than they were with

Rose. We, the boys, were the opposite. Furthermore, the male teachers were more respondent to the girls, accepting any of their excuses but did not do the same with us when homework lacked finish or was not produced the next day. This unprovoked and daily partiality was not a difficult matter to see, but almost impossible to explain for the time being. As a result, the boys worked harder but progressed as lesser equals.

We were asked once to write a composition about some historical event. I decided to engage the help of my father, I knew he had a large collection of books in the house library and thought I could do better than the rest by finding out more details and writing it from more than the school text book source. My father was enthusiastic about my idea and went with me to the shelves of stacked books in his study.

I was shocked to see the small number of books my father had on the shelves, much fewer than I ever remembered them to be. On the floor next to the shelves there were about ten or more boxes of books, some neatly arranged and some thrown in as if in a hurry. I picked up a book from one of the boxes, which I recognised as one of the books that Rose had brought once into the classroom. My father was swift in taking it from me and putting it back in the assigned box, without volunteering any explanation. From the available selection remaining on the shelves and the ones which I was allowed to take up and open, there was not any that suited the required subject of the composition. I ended up writing the essay from the approved text and for such effort getting nine out of ten to my surprise and delight.

The following weekend I went into the study again. The boxes had disappeared and the number of books on the polished shelves was unchanged. I smelt a strange odour, strong and distinct, coming into the study through the window that captured a wide view of the back garden. As I approached the window, the smell became stronger and I saw my father standing by a high-flaming fire, which he was observing closely. He was throwing things into its multi-coloured smoke. I ran down the long marble stairs in fast coordinated movement to reach the fireside hastily. It was exciting to watch the flames so readily eat up the food they were given.

My father asked me to stand with my back to the afternoon breeze, so as not to feel the intense heat or choke on the smell that was making the colourful sight repugnant. Despite that I stood facing the burning close to my feet.

He said nothing more and would not answer me when I asked why he was doing that. He just stood there with his eyes fixed on the flames while watching me stand motionless as instructed. He just looked in silence, threw on more books and tidied the wind-sailed papers and photographs that tried to escape total charring with an old piece of raw iron poker.

My mother came out to the garden, probably attracted by the smell of smoke. She stood at a short distance from the fire as her expression changed to one of sorrow. She simply asked him why he was burning piles of his books and her photographs, but was afforded the same silent answer I had received. She waited for a response before she started getting angry. My father attempted to explain, without looking at her and in a single breath his words were in short, incomplete sentences, as if badly rehearsed: they were raiding houses, mobs, what do they think they would do if they broke into our house, found these, think of the children.

She did not understand, he tried again: lynching mobs are breaking into houses of the known and old political families, they are looking for an excuse to catch any reactionaries as they call us, with the slightest evidence of unreformed thought or documents, what do you think they will do if they found these old books or these photographs of the past, of our family members standing, shaking hands, welcoming, eating or conferring with the deposed or hung monarchists, would they understand what they don't want to see, except as probable cause for infliction of pain and death? Think of the children, think of me, think of what can happen to us all, he pleaded.

She began to understand his motives, but it was hard for her to see the flame advancing through the two-tone colour and time-stiffened boundaries of her past world, her past forty-four years, what she could identify as the world in old shapes and geometrically non-aligned buildings and people who had long ago left these photographs as the undisputed proof of what they were or were like. It was harder again to fell the shadows of those past years as they slipped into black and grey, into a thin film of unrecognisable and blended crumble, into misidentity from the charring edges or the flame-swept content into nothingness. Yes, she would still keep them stored in memory, a storage that would fade with time and become as blended with its edges as the burnt photographs. Some images were too valuable to entrust to one's mind without the conformation of the paper-soiled record.

She began to cry, whimpering alternatives, such as discreetly hiding things where no one would find them or other similar possibilities, but the man was adamant; they would be found, and without looking at her face he kept throwing more on the fire as he murmured again and again the possible consequences and the price for keeping such evidence in times like these, mentioning that the children came first and above all worldly promise to keep faith with the past. He was solid in his fatalistic conviction of having acted in the best and safest manner.

As I stood in silence, my father's words gave me an uncomfortable feeling: suddenly I was looking at the fire and could actually see the man tied to the car that dragged him down the street and the mob cheering on. Moments later, I visualised the flesh of the torn cat, gripped beneath the dogs' fangs, I could even smell it, the smoke had a smell similar and just as sinister in its striking effect.

My mother went inside with a minimum of protest. I followed her with sorrow for my mother's sorrow, silence for my father's silent grief; but most of all I was filled with sickness for the corruption of love between my parents for each other, their aperture in fear and all in favour of us, their children who had become less than the joy of being children and everything that is life's vulnerable risk and prize.

More days went by in silence. It took nearly a month before my mother accepted her loss and my father came to derive more joy out of his garden than in cancelling memories of consequences. It took until next spring, before the circle of ash in the ground ceased to disfigure the soil. He stayed longer in the garden then each consecutive day, pruning trees, re-rooting more shrubs, checking that each band of small shade-dwelling plants and high datepalms alike received their proper quota of irrigation. The garden was his commune of silence, a crossing point of sanity and humour over a threshold of disillusion.

The school year came to an end with a few casual words from the headmistress and less enthusiasm from the teachers and pupils at the end of the last day in school. The object was to get home as soon as possible to start the summer holiday, once we had all got our passing marks and were invited to occupy the higher grade class the following year.

It was by the most humble of standards a year dedicated to paradox and the least of achievements in the lightest of tones in school. It was a year to inch us forward by a couple of thoughts, towards our early puberty of decision and judgement of our lives, in total partiality although in ultimate soul strife.

The summer before the start of the new decade was quite ordinary, the first month spent like the last in play, the second month in trial, studying the text books for the next class. Two things were different in their apparent eventfulness and context, both giving joy in a new fashion of concept. The first happened quite arbitrarily one Thursday morning when my father brought my tricycle into the house and started dismantling the two back-balance small wheels, without cause or warning.

I thought first I was punished for something, as it was obvious to me that I could not have it to play on that morning in its present state. To my delight, the tricycle was transformed into a bicycle, one tyre in the back, similar to the one at front.

I was given it to try, but without practising my balance it was impossible for me and the bicycle to stay erect, no matter how I tried. My father took me and the bicycle in the company of uncle Drake to a long stretch of newly tarred road, not far from our house, held me while I got on the bicycle and pushed me into motion while he maintained my balance. The fear of falling was intoxicating, but I was warned that once the bicycle had gathered what was termed by my father as adequate speed, I had to manage it on my own.

He ran after me pushing hard, pretending to let go once or twice, with me achieving imbalance the minute the announcement of being let go was made. After few rounds, my father finally did it, I steered the machine successfully until I realised I was on my own, then I hit the pavement's high kerb. My knees were spilling their red colour onto the peeled skin, I was lightly hurt but felt the injuries more like amputation.

My father was not deterred, he insisted I try again, instructing me with two tones of appraisal, one for nearly mastering the balance, the other ordering me to get on and try again. I tried again. This time he did not warn me that he had let go. I went on for a longer distance before realising that he had withdrawn his hold; then when I realised it, he started to shout at me not to mind his being so far away and to drive the machine. It came to me without trying too hard. I was able to maintain a vertical posture while riding and it suddenly became naturally easy.

When we got home, my mother was furious but I was pleased. I could ride the bicycle as a grown-up person, not like an infant on three wheels. The next morning, I tried the bicycle in the back garden on my own. I was surprised that it was still easy to do it again and without supervision. This achievement gave me more than the simple pleasure of riding faster round corners, which was difficult with the tricycle. The feeling that I had grown in years was infectious and with pride exhaled hard the excitement in speed of breath and words.

The second event was even more exciting, although at first it was just an experiment. I was in the garden, arranging small pieces of dry caked soil, some in a straight line, others randomly, with the intention of going over them with the wheels of the bicycle. This was to prove to myself that I could control the bicycle in a decisive contest with myself, by pretending that I was an air force pilot, the bicycle was my aeroplane and I was bombing enemy troops. If the cake was crushed, it meant it was a direct hit; otherwise a near or total miss.

I went on doing this for hours when we were called in for lunch, I was tired and hungry and the sun's heat was encouraging me to abandon battle anyway. I was totally surprised to see a second cousin of mine had arrived from Kuwait on a visit. I did not remember meeting the man before, but he seemed to know me well and he called me my first name without hesitation. I was quite astonished he knew it.

After lunch, he went to his room and came out with a huge carton box which he laid on the table and told me was mine to take. I advanced with caution towards the dusty box, opened the top with as much slowness and reluctance as if it had contained snakes or rats and looked inside. I could not believe my eyes. It contained about fifty or more pieces of miniature army sets, scores of cars on wheels, tanks of different sizes, artillery on wheels or carried on top of armoured vehicles, shells of different sizes that could be loaded and fired from guns and tanks, but really most beautiful of all: five sets of different jet aircraft, all with the names of their make

(I was shown) in English, engraved in clear letters to distinguish one from the other. It was a dream.

The afternoon was spent in identification of the different set-pieces, sorting them by their respective sizes, functions and test-firing the range of missiles and shells from many different angles and distances.

It was then time to build cardboard castles from my boxes of the playset and to spend time firing at the newly constructed fortresses, improving designs of double and treble carton thickness as barriers and roofed troop accommodation, to achieve total resistance to the ensuing shells as well as to camouflage the defending forces from any of the attack units. The immediate imagining of situations was fantastic and yet so real, so effectively real as to be easily plausible.

Either of the two sides had the chance of winning when I played against myself, since victory was immaterial and I was often undetectable and equitably impartial. The often demonstrated idea was that one side can have the upper hand in battle as a result of sheer chance and not skill was baffling, as the same skill was affected for both sides by the same impartial gunner (I) and an exchange of guns did not bring about a reversal of the result.

When one of the neighbours was visiting, and one of her boys played with me, each of us taking a side, I made for the first time two important conclusions. One was simply that I was euphoric in winning. I had the advantage of knowing the range of the artillery and tanks as well as the force of impact. All of the enemy's armour was hit halfway from their launching pad and all his buildings were ablaze shortly after the start of this swift and hastily acclaimed victorious war.

Cheating, which was not welcomed in other games, was vital to winning in this one. As I pretended to go to the toilet in the middle of the game, I passed by most of his defences as if I were a high-flying plane on recognisance. The enemy commander did not seem troubled by my obtaining such information and was totally amazed at how I could focus my firepower onto his correct line of attack. The added factor that I did not feel guilty for cheating was a new experience. My action justified itself and took nothing from the feeling of absolute joy in winning.

The second round was more difficult, but I also won it. This time the air force was involved. Again my practice bombings were effective in that my planes dropping their bombs (rubbers, pencil sharpeners and so on) on their targets more accurately than his air force did. Moreover, I linked two mission objectives: bombing the enemy positions as well as using the raid for reconnaissance. A genius of an idea came to me instantly: rearrange my troops after the enemy had made his air raids, so as he could not use his information for bombardments. This last step ensured me total surprise and coverage of plans. He wasted his shells on my unoccupied positions while I was able to recycle his shells and hit him with them in return.

The thought that he had worked out my deployment and important positions from his air raids and had used them in reconnaissance, like me, showed me that the enemy learned as fast as I did. This was not a comforting thought in war and I had to move my armour around the battle field. His surprise when he did not hit any armour in his follow-up shelling was apparent on his face. None of his shells was heard to convey the usual sound of hitting metal on impact. This he understood and interpreted correctly, as missing the target. He lost again. After the second defeat he retired from war and refused to engage me ever again.

These and such war games were to change my outlook on people's motives and actions as well as understanding their reactions, I suddenly became some kind of a two-fold thinking person. Now, in my new class in school, which followed after that summer of military strategy practice, I could fantasise when some one said or did anything. I would try as a matter of course to think why that person did it. If the person was some one whom I disliked in school, I would think of him as the attacking enemy in one of my limited version war games, try to think how to overcome the situation and satisfactorily win the current confrontation.

This positive approach was not the only side of this newly learnt strategy of reaction. I found out to my surprise that not all the information was given out correctly. Sometimes it was disinformation, lies, sometimes it was a purely innocent misinterpretation of the facts. Some of the boys in my class might seem to imply something in the form of questions which were in fact meant as small talk and not as tactics to affect or win a situation, I would take them as an underlying statement of some action to follow, but sometimes the measure almost deduced and anticipated, did not happen. My waiting was not always rewarded.

A boy once asked twice where I had got my new pencil sharpener.

When that item became missing in a matter of an hour, I complained wholeheartedly to the teacher and after an analysis of the situation accused the boy of stealing it. As the boy was found innocent and the sharpener later found in the possession of another, I was harshly reproached for my accusation by the teacher. I lost that battle.

On another occasion, one boy asked another in front of me about his homework, which was correct when most of the class got the answers wrong. The second boy told the first the truth: his elder sister had done it for him. While he was confessing his mastery of cheating and showing off his plan for attaining easy, high marks, I began to feel uneasy about the nature of the questions. I thought the boy with better marks was walking into a trap; and going even further, thought that if I was asked such a question, I would not have told the truth. I would have not have lied but simply would not have told the truth.

Within ten minutes, the teacher called the cheating boy, confronted him angrily and struck off his mark from the homework grade book, without hesitation. This time I was correct in my analysis of the situation and although it made me more cautious about what I might say in the future to anyone, I took pride in being able to anticipate the likely outcome. Being right and knowing one was right gave a fresh feeling of growing into the domain of elders and adults.

Important though this discovery of weighing up a situation may have been, it was not until a few years later that I could predict beyond doubt or miscalculation the action or reaction of others. For the time being, such a concept became like a game, enjoyable when I was right or when I was only an uninvolved spectator, purely experimenting with a theory. For others it may have been instinctive questions of being dealt the cards early, when they played all the time on the street with others or had their share of being deceived out of their marbles until it was their turn to do it to others, as part of the learning process of competitiveness and survival, gains and losses. But for the boy isolated within high walls and enjoying only partial contact in school hours, such realisation of the world and its being only came through gradual deduction, the monitoring of others, indirect appraisal and the progressive establishment of rules of combat.

Another game was widely played that year in school until it was discovered and banned. A new type of pencil sharpener was sold in the school kiosk. It had a three-inch round mirror on its back which hid the ugly shape of the pencil-sharpening groove and was the fashion for smart pupils. We bought it first because everyone was using it to reflect the sunlight onto walls or as a gun with which we would chase each other. If one of us directed the light reflection onto somebody else in the game, it meant a direct hit and that person would be dead, be out of the game.

This new toy was also the means of betting on a new thing, quite out of the ordinary. In this year, a new female teacher was now scheduled to us, teaching us art and religion. The repeaters and older boys in the class utilised the mirror-sharpeners in hushed-up betting, in a fashion which was new to us. The rules were first of all explained to us newcomers and younger members of the class. When the meaning of the word betting was understood, we were encouraged to play our pocket money. Bluntly worded the bet was: what colour of underwear did the new female teacher have that day? We would bet on a colour prior to her arrival in class and at least three mirror-sharpeners were laid mirror side up at the feet of the first row of desks. The teacher would stand briefly at the beginning of class near the first row to call the attendance. As she read the names, her wide skirt would reveal the colour of her panties, reflected onto one of the mirrors. The result of the bet would be announced at break time, at the end of the first period. The colours our teacher wore were black three days a week, green two days a week and red once a week in an unbreakable pattern. After three weeks from its initiation, we got tired of the game when it was restricted to the teacher.

This game was then extended feverishly to the girls in our class. At first the scheme was a boys-only secret, but the girls eventually found out about our little game and informed on us. All the sharpeners were gathered in and confiscated, never to be restocked in the school shop again. As the girls were considered a separate species, with whom we mixed only slightly, their underwear and any significance related to it did not mean anything to the majority of us. It was a means of embracing them and joyfully watching them blush as we told each one what colour panties she had worn that morning. Any one of us would have blushed if told the same and in a similar way. The game was humorous, innocent in its gesture and unrelated to sexual comprehension or later wonderful discoveries.

3

A Storm of Tenderness and Loss

In the following year, when I was nine, something happened which felt illogical to me and drove me in my silence and bewilderment into torments of promise and madness in an attempt to understand events without asking the obvious, without asking questions that would make others know I knew about certain things, those things I was not supposed to know at that age. It was a candid answer that was offered to a naive inquiry, that radically made me aware that there are sides to adulthood that were considered the ultimate taboo, considered much worse than mere bad manners. I became aware that although some topics were rigidly ignored as if they were ordinary, were boundlessly unmentionable or not to be spoken of. It happened quite accidentally and without any contemplated slyness or plotting on my behalf.

A distant cousin of mine, introduced as Tamara, was visiting us, we were told. She came to stay with us in September. I was puzzled why she was not in school. She was fourteen. I was led to believe that you can be in school to the age of thirty-five; my father was in the biggest of schools (which they called college) until that age. But my cousin did not seem to be going to school, she was there when my school bus collected me in the morning and she was there when I arrived back after school. She also did not seem to do any homework, either when I was doing mine or at any other time. She used to read magazines and spend the day in faraway places, as she confided in me and without the need of physically being there. She was in a state of continuous dream, she claimed often, in trances of incoherence. Her presence made me aware of many details on the surface of existence and within.

She was the most beautiful girl I had ever seen, with golden-tanned velvet skin, a soft voice and gentle brown eyes, so gentle that warmth shone through them when she looked at you or touched you with her slender fingers and caressed your hair to make you sleep without your needing to ask for such a loving portion of tenderness that was her soul. Her body was immaculately slender, topped by black, straight-cut hair that separated into single strands whenever she bent her head and brushed it out. The sun penetrated the strands of brushed hair with magical glitter as she stood between the mirror and the sun-drenched window. She was a mythical creature of dreams.

I often used to marvel how wonderful she was and why we had not seen her before. I could not put forward any explanation or reasonable possibility that satisfied my mind. She quickly became a friendly and comforting companion, to all three of us children in the house, a model adulthood with her ravishing calm, melancholy silence and tender logic, in expressed thought as well as in reason that derived her will and her hope.

She always seemed as if she was in-waiting for a purposeful change in life. At the age of plain fourteen, she seemed to be a complete adult and more a woman than a mere adult in personality. She guided my early puberty with its sincere observation and its slender citadel of thought within me towards simple happenings and complex choices that lay at each step of modest observation and beyond, through attempts to chime with understanding fully the worlds of others different or dissimilar to ours. She pointed to an understanding that was free of prejudice and bare of malice, but fundamental of acceptance without prior judgement or later condemnation. Before her, I had looked upon the world as a series of events, without observing the colour of the sky or any distinct depth of thought. All I remember of my life before her is still with me, but exists only as an abstract formula, without background details, description of things in black and white, unblended into other details.

I had not met anybody like Tamara before. My mother, who was a simple woman, saw our world, the children's, in two reasonably modest and unadorned portions that blended together simply and complemented our thinking as childish beings. We were to play and enjoy ourselves for the time being; we would be ready for the world when the moment came. My father, on the other hand, saw us as beings of potential, but did not feel obliged or compelled to bring on our adolescent thought before its time either. I was just over nine years old and he judged me by his own measure of achievement in wakening to a hard life on his own, at the age of fourteen or more; it was far too early for me to start conversing or acquiring the necessary seriousness in either interpreting or evaluating life. He could leave that until such time as he felt he needed to and had to.

In a sense they agreed, without formal debate or intent that we would be left blindfolded until we ask for the blindfold to be lifted, or at least until we realised it was there. Both my parents allowed us to keep our innocence about many matters, our inquisitiveness dormant and our childhood prolonged for such time as it was essential for us to maintain its texture.

I was in bed one night, drowsy but not fully sunk in deep sleep. My room was next to my parents' bedroom and they were talking in bed. I could make out parts of the sentences but not all that was said.

I suddenly heard my mother ask my father: what if Tamara was not still a virgin. It was a word I did not really understand; neither the implication of its loss or virtue of its maintenance to a girl. We lagged behind in biology lessons in the late fifties in Iraq and even if such a word had been added to our biological vocabulary, I doubt whether in such a decade we could have made the important imaginative connection between the cocoon-butterflies and the acts of man.

My mother went on: Tamara had been feeling sick in the morning, without a high temperature. To any mother, the guardian of a fourteen year old girl, in full bloom physically, such symptoms were only the underlying manifestation of something she could not bring herself to characterise or categorise in detail.

I sensed she was anxious and her voice was mixed with some enforced sadness. I could not see the direction or understand the practical deductions to be made form such sadness. My father dismissed what ever it was she thought possible in his usual way when he did not want to believe something or favoured an end to its discussion.

I thought that Tamara was ill. Then I thought of the big room she had been given, the open-ended and unspecified period my father told us she might be spending with us and the sadness in my mother's voice: all things indicated preferential and kind treatment.

The thought of our guest being unwell fitted ill with my assessment of Tamara. She looked healthy and in no way drained of vitality, unlike any of us when we were ever sick. My friend, the mystic chef and story teller, told me once the legend of the beautiful princess who died suddenly when she ate a poisoned-unwashed-apple, given to her by a witch. That princess did not look ill but died suddenly afterwards. When I mixed all these thoughts together, I felt such sorrow, I was sure Tamara was dying and that my parents were making sure she was comfortable in her last days. When my mother suggested taking her to see our doctor, my father neither objected nor agreed.

For the first time in years I was crying, tasting the familiar salty taste of flowing sorrow; it must have been strenuous enough to put me asleep at the same time. The next morning passed slowly and without incident. I was too tired to get up early, too disturbed to concentrate on school lessons and the bus journey home which normally took about fifteen minutes felt like a month of miscomprehending senility that had to be endured.

When I got home. Tamara was out with my mother, at the family doctor's clinic. They arrived soon after I had got in the front door. I neither inquired about the outing nor pretended to have known its destination. I sat down to do my homework quietly, waiting for the news to break, as both my mother and Tamara looked as if they had been crying, together or separately.

I was at my little desk facing the door of my room, trying to look busy with questions we had been given for work out. I did not stir as I heard light feet coming up the marble stairs. I knew from the hovering sound that it was Tamara; she never wore shoes in the house, unless she was compelled to. Her eyes had dried a little by now, but were reminiscent of sadness encountered not long earlier.

She asked to check my homework, although I had a feeling she sensed some irregular silence in my manner. I always used to hug her when I came home form school and today I offered neither my arms nor my usual closeness.

She had always astounded me with her unique sensitivity. She could always tell by casually looking into my face if there was anything wrong, if I was sad or angry or if I had had a bad day at

school. She always guessed the nature of my trouble without asking
or probing, more accurately than my own mother. She looked at
the paper scribbles, muttered noises of amazement and for a long
while made no comment. She kept looking into my eyes, as if her
assurance was sufficient to change my silent stealth of purpose into
stares of encouragement and warmth.

I kept to my silence tenaciously, afraid to ask and find it true. I
could not imagine the void in my life if her eyes were shut forever.
She was puzzled, her eyes were changing expression as her
thoughts, intrigued, endeavoured to identify the cause of change
in me. After a long spell of silence, she asked me what was wrong,
holding my head against her abdomen, as if extracting the warmth
of my face, avoiding the look in my eyes. She had felt my sadness
but she could not deduce either its plausible reason or my hollow,
misunderstood pauses that made me look suspended between
truth and fallacy of madness.

I murmured: You were at the doctor's, half-hoping she would
deny or contradict my assertion. Her eyes were filled with tears and
an incommunicable silence. I know you're ill and near death, I
added, almost powerless to articulate my thoughts and reluctant to
say anything further. She stopped sobbing and tried to smile,
betrayed by the stream of tears that, too late, still flowed down her
cheeks. Her left hand left my right side and instinctively wiped her
tears with an upward swoop to her eyes.

I am not dying, your mother took me to the doctor for a check-
up, I am fine, she assured me with a smile. If I die, I know you'll
always remember me, it's enough to ease anyone's death to know
you cannot be forgotten, she added in her usual strong logical
tone and convincing words. I was not happy with her simple
demonstration of assurances; I still felt she was either lying to
prevent my sadness or that she did not give full expression to her
problem.

After lunch, I decided to sleep that afternoon, a preference I had
not expressed for the past few years. I always adored the silence of
the mid-afternoon slumber, when the energetic people of the
house, now tired, took to their sheets in a slow procession, in
deference to the custom of the country rather than out of the heat-
ordained boredom. As I lay in my bed, I could hear my mother
report to my father the happy news: Tamara was alright.

That was all that was said. My father showed his relief by

accepting the fact without any discussion or expression of suspicion. The matter had been settled and both were happy to fall
asleep promptly, without a cause for delay or worry.

In the next room, I was baffled. The chain of events and words of
the past two days emerged in my mind as an ongoing puzzle or a
strange gift that was neatly, strongly wrapped but tantalisingly
difficult to resolve. After twenty minutes, I was tempted to get out
of bed. Ten minutes later still, I got up and made my way towards
Tamara's room. The door was ajar, the curtains were nearly drawn,
with a trickle of light filtering to the foot of the bed from the almost
veiled window.

The cool temperature of the room was refreshing. The bed was
tidily made but for a bulge in the shape of a body in the middle, a
crease that had hair spread openly and evenly over its top. Tamara
lay with sheets up to her bust; bare shoulders extended to the
slender arms that were keeping the folds of the sheets in place,
weighting them downwards like designs for paper weights, in
anticipation of a breeze.

I stood at the door and watched her open her eyes in fine slits,
wondering whose short shadow was on the shiny-tiled floor. A
smile crept over her mouth as she went closed-eyes again. I came to
her bed, reached with small hands to a strand of hair that seemed
to have separated itself from the neat rest and felt it with my
fingertips. She opened her eyes again, looked at me for a moment
and whisked her sheet upwards in a wordless, timid gesture of
request, far enough for me to get in; not as far as her erect arms
would have reached, but sufficient to displace enough of the sheet
to ease my occupancy without either disturbing the other half of
the sheet or moving herself deeper into the other part of the bed.

I got in, without thinking of what I was doing or of my movements, without resistance or active decision. Her body heat and a
faint fragrance of some time-weakened perfume, were delicious
and hypnotising. With her eyes remained closed, she reached with
her right hand and held the tip of my forefinger on the left hand. I
responded to the wetness of her palm and the gentleness of her
soul by a slight folding of my thumb over the back of the hand
holding mine and my face nestling upon her sheet-covered small
breast. We fell asleep contentedly together without further movement or words, in an accelerating lapse of consciousness and the
slow cast of dreaming.

She woke me up an hour or so later; someone is awake, she said. As if I knew it was not allowed, I went into the next room, where my homework was awaiting my attention and started writing, conscious that I needed to finish the allotted proportion.

She came into the room and asked me if I had had a nice sleep. I started to say I had but I was interrupted by her again. She asked me not to tell anyone I had slept in her bed. I promised immediately and without hesitation or asking why I must not speak of it.

In the evening and shortly after supper, Tamara said she was tired and went to bed early. I, too, went to my bed at the stroke of eight, announced by the small pendulum-wagging clock in the hall of the house. My two sisters were already in bed an hour before. They always seemed to sleep early, something I never felt unusual or out of the ordinary for them. It was a habit I remember both of them observed, as a matter of course throughout the summer and until the weather got a bit colder for most years in the past.

In the day that followed I spent the morning playing with my armies in the garden. My father was either watering the trees or digging holes to take the new transfers the next day. On Friday, the last day of the weekend in Iraq, I sat down and listened to a story read to me by Tamara from one of her randomly piled magazines. The story started when a girl wore her mother's pearls pretending they were hers and put on lipstick, pretending she was her mother. The story went on to describe what happened to the little girl who defied her mother's instruction in leaving the house alone with the pearls and the make-up on her face. She was stopped on the street by someone who stole the pearls and hit her, being of the opinion that the little girl was really nobody's gentle and respected ward, but looked cheap and worthless because of what she had on her face. The little girl was saved from abduction by a man who was passing by and who knew her father, a strong man who was able to retrieve the pearls and bring the girl home.

The story concluded that morals are learnt only through difficult situations and every instruction on how to behave in society was justified as it was based on the wisdom and experience of years. A good life was a product of living within the realm of rules and appeasing human society, for the simple reason that in the absence of rules or non-conformity, one would encounter tragedies, as inevitably as the sun would rise.

I asked if such a warning or example was always true. Tamara was hesitant in replying immediately. After a slight pause, she nodded in confirmation. Her hesitation diluted the strength of my acceptance of her reply. I stared in her direction and found her not looking at me. I asked again, in a different manner: 'I know not to go out on the street alone; I am afraid of someone dragging me away; my mother told me that it might happen. I am still small and cannot fight off big people.' She agreed with my mother completely and instantly. I asked then if all that was in that book, that magazine, was true.

She did not want to confirm, disagree with, discuss in detail or dismiss the magazine out of hand. I was not satisfied with her answer, I asked again: 'My mother puts on red lipstick, she's not cheap.' I was sure she was not. Tamara agreed with me, explaining that a woman who was married and had a husband, was allowed to freely put on lipstick. Tamara added: unmarried girls, like me, could be thought of as cheap women if they were seen on the street with a lot of make-up. I asked what actually was the difference between the two sets of women. She summed up her answer hurriedly in one word: 'virginity.' There was that word again, I thought.

I tried to make her explain further, but she left me, making some excuse or another, to continue the discussion another time. I wondered which of the two types of women had virginity and which had not. I could not decide readily. Furthermore, speculating what it was and how one could lose such a thing, I reasoned that may be if I knew exactly what it was, I need not ask how it could be lost.

A few days followed where I felt Tamara was avoiding staying with me to inspect my homework or to talk to me if we were alone in the room. I did not think widely of it at first, but on the third day I missed our closeness and being alone with her, when we could talk of anything, nothing forbidden, misplaced or wilfully hidden from our discussion and mental exercise. Before this, I could ask her anything and she'd answer to any demand for information on my part. She always promised not to lie as I likewise promised. It was a candid exposure and exchange we always practised with each other.

Freedom of this sort seemed always evident when we were alone. In the presence of others, even of my mother or father, we always seemed either shy or afraid of punishment or anger if a wrong question was pursued or an allowed question was improperly worded. This mutual ease, this secret pact, naturally and unintentionally designed, came into being from the second day after she arrived in our house. I was smacked that day rather harshly for mouthing something I was not allowed to say. In a fury of pain and anger I said something worse about my mother for hitting me and also about my father for not defending me after my mother had left the room. No one heard me complain as I was sobbing and Tamara and I were alone together. She comforted me and made me stop crying. I expected that she would run and tell my mother what I had said, a familiar situation with my sisters. It did not happen.

She earned my friendship that same day. I earned hers another day. She was upset because she was caught talking on the phone to someone. When she was questioned about it she refused to give his name. She was imprisoned in her room for the day, eating alone and we were not allowed to talk to her through the closed door. Somehow I could not sleep without talking to her. I went down in the middle of the night, trailing both my fears of the dark and of being found out. I was amply rewarded for my brief bravery. We both were able to extend a binding strength to each other, nearest to love and furthest away from loneness.

As we were both guests of our elders and pointed to proverbs which trailed the rash faith of our young age, our unwillingness to accept advice and rigid rules was always to others a proof of inexperience and of a fragile but more evidently necessary passage into a coming of age. Purity was our best asset in protecting both innocence and incredible guilt. No one could believe that children can be calculating, when their errors were easily forgotten and erased from memory with a smile or a tear.

My mother did tell my father about the mysterious phone call, but both of them resisted taking it as a serious overture for what was to come. I did not ask, never intruded or insisted on a clear explanation, I too was one who erased the consequence of it in immediate forgetfulness. This secrecy was to prove fundamental to the assertion of all that was sensitive friendship. Like a vein cut with the jagged rusty edge of a knife, you might stop the bleeding with a miracle but required a harder one to clean the wound.

One afternoon when I came home from school, the house was unusually quiet. All the rooms seemed filled to some degree with still tragedy. A smell of unrestrained grief hung over everyone, as everyone suffered in his or her own way. My father was more angry than sad, my mother was more stricken with blank-faced shock and sadness than with disgust; my grandmother, who always had a fine-cut black-or-white view on the seriousness of life, did not indicate she knew much, except to point that there was a serious problem, a thought the extent of which she either wished hard not to entertain its dark shadows or was fearful of its evident outcome.

The mixture of sentiments was explosive, though silent it was finitely a discourse to the minds of those present, a loss of unity of opinion and a diversity of individual uneasiness. I was afraid to ask a question or hint at a feeling of curiosity. It was a minefield in which to attempt a true evaluation of the gravity was apparently a total risk of the situation.

I went to Tamara's room; it was empty, the bed was unmade, garments of a soft texture were scattered all over the clean floor, leaves torn from a writing pad were barely visible where they had been swept under the untidy sheets that hung in the careless improvisation of a hurried clearance. I picked up the torn store of marginally legible messages, lines bent on the unlined pages.

It took me two hours to stick them together on clean sheets of paper extracted from my homework book. There were three pages, one written with a clear hand and strong pressure, which looked like the effort of a person older than sixteen, though I was guessing. The other two pages were covered with sloppier, lightly pressed pencil markings, elegant despite the haste and the apparent uncertain way of explaining a detail or stating a fact. Many words were written, crossed out, re-written and crossed again or kept in, showing an indecisive inclination.

The first single sheet had four words on it: eight o'clock, morning, here; and a signature below: D. The other two pages were addressed to me and signed: T. These started with: dearest boy, I must go, don't judge my escape as a loss of judgement, this is what I want, uncoerced and undeprived of will. The next two lines, though crossed out, were still legible and read: All of us whose will is mere conformation sanity, waiting for the passage of time, must be escapees or perish in stress of pain and loneliness. The next two lines were incomplete, blackened from erasure and crossings-outs: (something) will my departure – or I shall – bleed broken – destined – path – unto self – regression – and – .

The second page seemed a milder or better construction of the lost paragraph. It read: Love, and you will know its stress of insanity that pushes us into leaving to be with those we want. If I don't try hard to leave and be with him, my deprivation will make me regress in being a self unworthy of sustaining its purpose of existence, bleeding on cold marble and white sheets of dishonesty, into paths of dark and unlit hopelessness. I needed and obtained your truce for my ill judgement, I would like to keep this unchanged and for ever.

A new paragraph started: Forget me if you must, but never reject my memory if you can. It ended abruptly in the middle of the page.

She must have changed her mind over leaving me a message or an explanation, as if she had first thought I was owed at least a statement of her purpose, but on reflection had decided to leave me on a fence of barbed wire rather than let me remember the loss with sadness. I thought of her being in the grasp of temptation, unsurviving its impulse. She seemed to be like a cutting edge, to attempt to erase everything completely, dimming her bright soul, trying to produce a complete severance of memory: a good tactic, I thought, if it was, to reduce loss and diminish sorrow.

It would have worked readily if I hadn't found the torn pages, I would have decided to forget easily, driven by the sharp pain of betrayal and abrupt abandonment on the cold marble of winter nights. I found the letter apologetically truthful in the face of the loss of all that was warmth. I accepted its unforgettable and tender form.

In the sitting room, which was declared a theatre of operations and forbidden to us children for the afternoon, my father made four phone calls serious in tone: one to Tamara's brothers in Kuwait, one to a chief of police, a third to someone else; and one of serious, threatening and angry nature to someone's father. The latter lasted over ten minutes. Its loud content was not calmed by the apparently apologetic replies and pleas of ignorance from the other end of the phone. The excuses, as my father called them, were not valid. He neither accepted nor believed them in his frame of mind. The offer to talk over the situation calmly was turned down as my father demanded that the man did something easily possible from one point of view and unrealistic from the other. My father did not believe the man was sincere.

At four in the morning, a loud shouting and sobbing filled the downstairs of the house. Tamara had been captured and escorted back to us by the police. There was no evidence of D. or mention of his having existed. Tamara was locked again in her room. This time I waited until after six in the morning to go down to see her, as my father was awake. A few minutes after the hour I walked down the stairs, as dawn was forcing its gradual bright light through the fly-meshed windows.

I stood at her door like an injured animal awaiting the opening of the gate to a secret burial ground. She did not answer the soft words of an anxious friend asking for her well-being.

I fell asleep after an hour or so at the gate where I was refused entry. I woke up just before my mother. I was in the bathroom as she came in, easily putting up the pretence that I had just awakened, I was shivering from the cold and the sleep in my eyes still obscured them. I asked about the noise late in the night and was given to believe that Tamara had been brought home from a safari where she and her brothers had been on, in the marshes; they were late because the car had broken down unexpectedly, as I think the phrase was. I queried the matter no further, it was a forsaken attempt.

The new day had started unpromisingly distressful; it slowly progressed into insanity and sickness. I was ill, feverish through lack of warmth and sleep, in thrall to my desire to talk to Tamara, yet obedient to the quarantine of her soul away from my hard craving for an exchange of words and the touch of her comforting will. I stood redeemed and she destitute of her will to escape her bondage. My temperature raged that night and my fighting soul was rendered worthless as if broken and sold.

The following morning, I woke up to Tamara's voice calling me into consciousness, I opened my eyes, smiled to the thought of dreaming and closed them again. A warm hand touched my lips, I opened my eyes again, it was her in the haze of the morning sun reflected off the dressing table's straight mirror, as the light curtains were dislodged from their inertia of the last two days.

I opened my eyes fully and hugged her instinctively, without prior intent, in indecision to offer her body my warmth or her face more than a glued-on surface where her tears extended their free-flowing course from her cheeks onto mine in a quite unexpected sharing of the salty produce of longing and the last chance to speak of such things as remembrance and the slow-fading pressure that was intimate of pain and hope. Within all that is possible and most of that which is impossible, both were disguised as an impermanent goodbye and temporary leave of separation.

She was explicit in her promise and I was adamant: never, forget, never forsake and above all never dispute each others' remembrance. She kissed me on the lips and slid her hand away from mine in gentleness of intention and warmth of promises made to be kept. I still remember them of her.

I got up and went to the cold-fogged window, that would not yield to the strength of the sun and watched as she got into a car with her elder brother, who supervised her getting in and locked the door, pretentious in his fear for her safety, ensuring she did not fall out of the door when in motion. My parents neither waved goodbye nor went to the door.

The high gates once again became a wall of insensitivity, a bold and unmoving barrier, respectful of the lock and silent in its unyielding. My hands collected the dew that dropped when I opened the window to see the dust of the car. It left something hanging in air of desolate resolve as if kin was cut away at the cord like an unwanted birth.

In some hours of longing, her kiss resides within me, a dull pain of faint regret in loss. Unwilled remembrances seem harder on the thought and wetter on the eyes.

At an age that was aching for friendship, when love was yet undefined, felt as a breath of strength or a deforming twist on a green twig, bruised beyond reform, wisdom came as a poor assonance of patience and tolerance.

4

Early Puberty of Intent

Far away from the disposal of undealt-with pain, a child is a man uncontrollably indifferent to the world and mistrustful of himself. Past failures have a strong impact during youth and grow more bearable with age.

For all those we lose when we cannot measure our pain, we climb a single step of anticipation at a time, weathering the storm with forgetfulness and healing. For the lesser number whose loss we remember when our age has passed into two digits, the loss somehow refrains from haunting the mind that had its share of memory, passion or pain. It is one more for the casual or discarded diary, one less for long remembrance, one less to revisit in the depth of the night or early morning sleeplessness.

Most of the time I begrudge the two months I knew her, I envy that year, the warmth of which still holds my memory in the soft textures of clothed closeness. I condemn the hopelessness of my age of nine, wished always I had been at least fourteen then, wished I had her opportunities of belonging. Aided by my innocence, I wished and wished again she could have lasted all my life, my life.

I will wonder for the rest of my life: will I see her again?.

I thought in shallowness of mind for the best part of a year and a half. Tamara's disappearance was anticipated but, not so soon and never left devoid of feeling. It was a period of silence and superficial thought. The days passed at school ordinary, the afternoons after-wards were bland times of homework and squandered time, the nights that followed dreamless were spent quickly and without reluctance. I have not forgotten her but I pretended not to think of her, keeping my effort directed towards the sustenance of my sanity and the occasional smile. It's hard to greet pain with the anarchy of suffering, it's simpler to avoid the footbridges of trouble-ridden streams.

When I was eleven, a set of plastic flat squares and self-supporting bricks was given to me on the occasion of the school's spring break. I spent days assembling buildings I had never seen but quite clearly visualising their occupancy and use by many people. These were unsymmetrical at first and fell apart as I tried to move them from one room to another, to show my father or mother. After a week, I realised the strategic strength of symmetrical or properly shaped boxes which contributed rewardingly to their stability and power to stay intact. My father used to watch me assemble, dismantle and re-assemble the variety of construction units, different only in the number of rows of plastic bricks in their width, length and height.

He drew my attention to something small but quite important in nature: by moving the hollow-framed doors and window-like pieces to different positions or numbers in the brick arrangement, a great variety of buildings resulted, each unique or at least different in outward appearance. It was a very deep and astonishing revelation: anything in existence which was different from anything else, could in reality be only slightly different and was not necessarily different to the core.

On showing off the acute observation to a couple of playmates, it became evident that I was, as my father had told me, right. As I got a second, bigger set of the same building blocks, I continued investigate the number of different possibilities of buildings of the same size and shape, keeping every one I made and comparing it to the ones already built. I reached a stage where whatever arrangement I made, it resembled one that already existed.

I consulted my father on the problem in hand. He confirmed after a long examination of the assembled units and studying further possibilities that the limit of potential had already been reached and thus concluded could not be surpassed. My enthusiasm and hope rebelled against this new rule in life, which ultimately left me unhappy. My father gave up quite readily, while I was not ready to do the same.

I tried more possibilities and came to the same conclusion eventually. He then asked me to sit and listen; I complied. He went on to tell me about this friend of his who would not accept what was called reality. His friend was trying hard to outdo himself in something (I cannot remember now what it was), but ended up disillusioned and broken hearted. Father went on to tell me what he called his philosophy or way of thinking on such matters in life: when one reached the limit of potential, there was only one of two things that could be done: either accept you had reached the limit, be happy about it and move on to doing something else; or dismantle everything and start all over again, in the hope of doing things differently so as to reach a better level.

He tried to explain that the latter approach was always a gamble, an option you call out. If it was as you called it, you'd win more, but if it turned to be not as you called it, you'd lose all. My mind was getting in a maze of thoughts, I understood little, a few scattered details, but the full puzzle refused to hang together, although I nodded in total confirmation of understanding when I was asked if all was clear. It sounded so close to the betting of pocket money in school, to trying to confirm a belief in the colour-of-the-day underwear game we had played two years ago with our mirrors.

A few days later, we were in the garden. As I watched my father trim the rose trees, I noticed there was one rose bush that he had planted away from the other rose bushes, in a small shaded space near the house wall. I asked him why that was so. He answered my inquiry with a confident and simple answer: that particular one was too delicate a plant and would wither in the strong heat of the sun. He was trimming it at midday so as to judge and cut at the full height of the bush, to keep it from being in the sun. I asked him why the plant was growing so far into the sun if it knew that the intense heat would damage it. He answered me, with a logic that seemed to be similar to that which he applied to my building design, that the plant was trying to overcome its limit of potential. I did not believe that the same logic applied.

He saw I was not convinced and agreed to leave one tall branch, already outside the shade, uncut, for me to see the result. A week later, the branch showed signs of starting to dry up, while the others that he had trimmed had already started to grow new shoots, horizontally and away from the sun. The plant had two choices, to grow in a different direction, or to take a gamble and try and grow upwards over its limit of potential and built-in tolerance. He pointed out the clear test result to his satisfaction and my amazement.

He added that there is a force in the world, the universe, which made us and gave each of us a certain capability and potential. This being, whom we called God, knows what we can do and what we cannot, as he had created each of us differently, although some of us are more alike while some are more different. He asks us to do our best and utmost every time, added my father. I suddenly realised that this great force was masculine and not feminine, but said nothing. I found it really difficult to accept and harder to understand how God would allow us to try something beyond our ability, especially when he should know that we can't do it and might end up breaking or withering as a result of it.

One day and without asking, my father brought this thin booklet entitled: One God, many faces. He called me over to him, after he was sure I had finished my homework, handed me the booklet and asked me to read it whenever I had time. He emphasised, twice, that I should read it and give him my opinion or consult him if I had any queries regarding the terminology or the basic content, which he thought should not be very hard. He informed me that he had already read it.

I was asked to read it and analyse it. His original motive may have been closer to censorship and to vetting my thought rather than to screening difficulties, but at that age I was not suspicious and was deeply happy with his equable behaviour and the hint of testing responsibility, even when constraint was portrayed as guidance and trust.

The booklet was a surprise to me. It did not favour any single religion, but concentrated on balancing all of the five main world religions, taking as the common ground of all concerned a general promotion of religion. The differences between varying views and banner categories were swept aside as being vaguely unimportant and were avoided at all costs by the author (whose name I cannot remember now) on the grounds that they were of the present book.

The first page – the preface – defined religion as the attempt to make man (and presumably equally woman) perfect in character. The first question was, therefore: what was a character and how would one know it was perfect? Furthermore, could one achieve perfection with evident success? The answer was mystical and incorporated a common and essential balance: good is rewarded in most religions by an ample vesture of gains in another world, if needed to be a terminal world called heaven, where an undefined and great entity called a soul, was the format of all bodies, existing totally beyond the physical body. Once this out-of-body liberation had been reached immediately after death by the majority of consensus; or by a minority of consensus, when it was re-routed into living another life, in a perpetual recycling of one's life in this world, through taking up another body: then and only then, after either liberation or re-incarnation, a person's previous life was judged. This judgement could be either instantaneous, resulting in occupancy of a lower-level life, or at a later date, as decided by God. One particular religion averred that all its followers are judged throughout their current life, rewarded or punished before death.

This balance of any consequent punishment or reward according to all opinions seemed dependent on reaching the perfection or failure of character. The balance seemed delicate and continuous, but thankfully was not so strictly required of children. This was comforting, as the divided territories had yet to be exactly established and the demarcation lines strengthened. What was or was not allowed had yet to be defined.

When asked, my father made the terms of reference quite simple to list and define: steal not, lie not, hurt not, delete vanity, meanness and doubt of another's good will. All this was later summarised in honesty with a conscience. He further added: a conscience was a pure facility of perfection of character, a silent hand that guided one unto good, but slapped your hand before it committed evil. The hair-fine line between good and evil was marked now with warnings and encouragement; shiny, two-sided labels faced you, depending on which side of the fence you stood at.

A man must think of his actions. If he realised he was doing evil, or was sinning, he must pay the penalty, purge himself, repent, but most of all must remember not to repeat his sinning again.

The next set question was more difficult to answer: What were the driving forces that made us sinners or pure? If we all knew the guidelines, why were there sinners? Most importantly: God knows what we think and our abilities as well as our shortcomings, why would he not have made all of us pure? He had the power to weed out evil; why did he not do so? Father did not apply his ease of answer, his usual powers of word and deduction to lay my fear aside. He asked me to write the questions down on one page and write my best conclusions on the page facing it, as clearly as I could. He also asked me to write the date on the answer page and show it to him, as if it was an exam paper. His request also detailed that I keep the query book for some time to come, repeat the same exercise the following year and compare the two answers after one or two long periods of shelving all thought on the matter. His plan seemed detailed and extraordinary. I could not envisage the message as an evaluation of opinion over time.

I stared at the page of numbered questions, stared at the empty page facing it, the latter void, the former crowded with difficult misapprehension and unresolve to the point of disturbance and fear of failure. I decided to write some comment on the unpencilled lines: 1. Don't know. Numbers 2 and 3 were equally empty handed. So far I could not will or even discover any alternatives. Their existence was a shadowy-pale nothingness of thought. I was disappointed.

The next day in school I went to see Rose. In the quietness of her office, away from the noise of playful children in the yard. I explained about the booklet, the drawn-up plan and my fear of failure, my unsettled feeling and loss of ambition to understand and unravel the problem. She smiled, as she always did in sign of appreciation and positive admiration of a budding thought.

Rose suggested that I divide the problem, placing each question on a separate page and writing a list of all the background information surrounding the point encountered in the question. On the facing page, she asked me to write again possible answers, but in line with the available detail on the opposite page. The summary of known information and division of the questions as if they were truly separate, seemed ingenious and promising, as practical and positive ideas.

As soon as I got home, I started implementing this strategy of evaluation. In respect to why sinners sin, the note read that we were all of us aware of the guidelines. One possible answer was that it must be because sinners chose not to follow the guidelines. Another possibility was that these sinners were unaware that they were committing sin. Is such a thing possible? Yes, especially for children, I wrote boldy, and probably in self-defence. A third answer lay crossed out: Maybe these sinners had to sin, as part of their character. The last option seemed less logical.

The compelling urge to do wrong, as superficial a motive as it looked and as far removed as it was from logic, did pose an interesting question: What did really make us commit deeds unacceptable in thought and unworthy of our consciousness? Was it something bred and formulated in us since childhood, where recognition of wrong was not enforced? I discounted that notion lightly as a product of ignorance and boldly as an impossible belief. Yet I was getting things down on paper and that was pleasing, even if they were pure possibilities, rejected outlines of correspondingly irrational thoughts.

For the question of why God let us sin. Why he denied his divine effectiveness and refused to will the end all sin and to erase it, the answer page remained blank, while the detailed background was full of affirmative adjectives that related to God's power, creativity and generosity in allocation of senses and thought. One possibility seemed plausible: We had the choice to depict our behaviour freely and without divine intervention. After some thought on this point, it seemed a possible answer to the two questions of why God let us sin and why he refused to erase sin. I tried hard to sustain this conviction, but I failed, unrewarded with any comfort.

I went to my father who was in his study, busy reading a thick book and writing notes on paper in neatly arranged lines. I showed him what I had written. He was astonished as much as he was pleased. His pleasure in my logic was more credible to him than it was to me; I was of the opinion that I had scribbled untrue or unreasonable explanations.

But my father, the adult, the expert, the logic-curate, was happy with it. I was delighted. When praise and encouragement had been dispensed, I had to query some aspects of the composition. Firstly, were people blameless if they sinned unwittingly? My father paused for a minute and then answered me in short sentences of alternating tone. There are two laws in the world, he said: one is God's and the other is called 'civil', or man made. In the latter, ignorance of the law does not excuse breaking it. The solicitor had taken over the father-voice. In God's law, he said softly, ignorance may excuse sinning, if it was for the first time, but after that it is not excusable, he affirmed in a suddenly stronger voice.

God is always compassionate, my father went on. He forgives our sins if they were not premeditated, he knows when it's innocence or evil, the forceful thoughts of which were to blame. No one can deceive or lie to God; he can read our minds and judge thoughts easily. I was silent, the two-fold idea of laws was new to me. The difference in judging merit was also new and fascinating in its principles.

I accepted the points put to me. They were unprepared but satisfactory. I then asked: what do you think about God letting us sin, why does he not eliminate sin from all the world? He is powerful enough to do it and since it was against his wishes, why does he not do so easily? My father smiled. God gave us a mind so that we can use it in making decisions and present choices to serve ourselves. In both cases of the two types of law, he added, we always have a choice, it is always up to us to make the right choice, that's why I showed you the other day what to do and what not to do to achieve perfection of character and good name. Do you remember the five things I listed to you? I answered that I still did. I had not forgotten.

He went on: God does not force us to do the right thing. One must do the righteous deed in recognition of it being right and by our will, not simply because we have to or are afraid of punishment. If one did good without the goodwill for it, it'd be meaningless. It would be pure deception and God will know it, he concluded. I was quietly unhappy, surely obeying the law was sufficient, whether or not one did it in total acceptance or with the urge to comply with the strict instruction of the latter. I needed to study my reaction before hastily showing partial understanding and faith.

The following morning, in the first interval between classes, I went to see Rose. Firstly I showed her my written script, which she read carefully. I then summarised my father's verdicts and explanations, together with my own reservations and asked her for a second comparative opinion. She looked at me in a long moment of silent consideration. She must have seen the riot of doubt in my presentation of my father's reported sentences. 'I will tell you my opinion', she said, suddenly exhibiting an unreserved caution I had never seen in her before.

Rose was seriously considering the wording of the opinion she had promised. She hesitated before asking: Will you promise not to attribute my opinion to me? It will be between you and me, won't it? I promised as required, heartened by the extreme trust implied in the request. She touched her lips briefly and went on. God wants us to try and become perfect. He has laid down guidelines for such a transformation, but does not offer us any additional strength.

Instead we have to realise our own and use such strength effectively. He always stays impartial in the struggle; his condemnation of evil is as far as God goes in forcefully backing those on the side of goodness and virtue. This is my personal opinion, I do not wish it to be repeated in public, she added.

Firstly I had to ask why this opinion should be kept a secret between us and not openly discussed with others. She looked as if she was about to deny her words, but suddenly changed her mind. 'What I expressed was my personal opinion. It does not comply directly with the general view of religion as it stands, to criticise God lightly. None of us are supposed to criticise God or make any question marks about religion that stand out in bold letters, she concluded, softly. I thought that such criticism of God was not intended to lessen his divinity.

I firmly believed that in order to understand, one had to ask. I expressed this point in one form or another to Rose. She said that not all people were open-minded; most of them had already made up their minds about certain matters and had either closed their notebooks or thrown them away without feeling a need to reconsider their stand, irrespective of change of circumstance. It was an intentional intransigence; those people sometimes would not understand others who held either different or changing views. 'So what', I asked innocently. She warned me not to express any opinion without knowing if the person I was talking to was open or strict in accepting the views of others.

She explained how angry or harsh some people can get if offended and offered me an example: two years earlier she was taken off our class because she wanted us, the pupils, to have an open mind about history and question different interpretations of it. I remembered how our enjoyment of lessons with her had been abruptly cancelled, without explanation. We thought at the time that she had been promoted, as she was moved to teach a higher class. I understood that this was more than just a simple example. I realised that there was a division of power and that the underdog had to watch his tread carefully, or be punished.

I had to ask: 'If we confront God, disbelieve in him or merely question his wisdom, would any of that be as bad a sin as letting evil rampage?' She smiled and said: 'It's acceptable to question God or his divine wisdom, if and only if one advances from that into total believing and into strengthened acceptance. If instead one regresses from that into more doubt or less belief, then God shall judge us and condemn us into hell. That is already explicit in many of the instructions laid down on God's behalf'.

I was horrified at such revelations: it seemed so harsh of such a gentle God. I was speechless. If God was so resolved to steer us into righteousness, would it not be more logical and easier for him to will all sin to vanish, without the hardship to sufferers, the difficulty of choice and the retaliatory punishment, I was anxious for clarification. Rose was silent again. She was thinking solemnly. She then reached out and held my hand unexpectedly.

'If there is no evil in the world, there would be no need for righteousness. Both seemed dependent on each other to be. Would we admire colours if there was only a single colour or if we could only see a single perspective', she asked me. 'Difference in perception and variety of options or choices are essential for life, essential for us to enjoy life and feel its worthiness in living', she concluded.

She further asserted: 'Reward and punishment is a delicate balance that makes people desist from evil and enhances the chances of virtuous victory'. She further confided in me: 'I do my best and try not to trespass unto shades of darkness. I offer my advice when I think it worthwhile, I do not force anyone or coerce anybody into a decision. Choices are personal and they are not designed to stress gambling as much as strength of conviction'.

I arrived home understanding more than I had expected to in the span of a short conversation. I went to my notebook and wrote what I understood, the facing pages were full of comprehension and I was happy with my conclusions. My father inspected my notebook. He seemed further surprised than the day before and asked me where I had got these ideas.

Remembering my promise to Rose, I had to lie to keep my word to her unbroken. I told him that the religion teacher had raised a discussion on a subject related to hell and heaven. I had understood it and had related some points discussed to my questions and that was how I could put up some answers here. I remembered the delicate balance Rose had enshrined in me; telling a small lie was not as bad as breaking a promise and causing trouble for Rose. Partly selfishly, I was afraid she would not trust me or might not discuss anything seriously with me again. God would understand my choice, I concluded personally.

I had enjoyed and for the second time, keeping promises and other people's secrets. It seemed a part and an important articulation of being grown up, of being trusted and worthy of confidence.

If I had a twinge of guilt, it was not directly due to secrecy but indirectly emanating from it: to keep a promise I had lied, I had unintentionally strayed unto a sin. Whether it was small and forgivable or technically and eventually punishable, was quite irrelevant and bogus. Such was the consequence of truth, if in keeping faith with one thing, I broke it with another. I asked my father if everything in life or faith was as clear as a contrast of black against white. What was the status of grey if it existed, was it borderline illegitimacy, to be condemned? Unethical and parasitic, taking its existence from bare reasons of survival and appeasement regardless of price, a goal to achieve irrespective of cost and morality?

This different stance was not encouraged by my father, who shook me by saying half in disappointment and half in anger that grey was the colour of cowardliness and born of weakness. He would rather be scarred than back away from his fear of the fire and I should be the same. I was not convinced and noted with displeasure that I was being lectured when I had asked for a pure, short opinion. I did not dare to contradict my father or investigate the matter further; rather I decided openly to lay down my arms and the front of my questioning put to silent truce.

My spiritual enthusiasm dampened. I felt disappointed and hurt; I had not expected my father's reaction, neither its severity nor its rigid and solemn restriction. I had merely been assembling the possible ingredients for a solution. His assumption of my dissipation of virtue and crookedness was not valid, neither in its false estimation of myself nor in its fallacy. He had reacted harshly and dishearteningly to a simple inquiry that derived from wanting to understand rather than straying into a dishonest and conscious discounting of values.

I found myself, as I had many times before in days of hurt and confusion, in the garden, solaced by the heat of the day's quiet and its solitude, comfortably alone under a big and old date palm tree at the end of the garden, where no one could see me slump on the dry soil and let tears flow unhindered.

That tree, which I had christened Bertha a long time ago, was the only tree found in the grounds of the house when it was built. My father had refused to cut it down when the garden was being planned and the concrete paths were being laid, as if he could tell it would be needed. She gave me coolness of shelter from many days of searing heat and accepted my confessions as gladly as those tears that seeped unto her base, hugged and swallowed almost immediately.

My other friend, the month-older-than-me alsatian, which we had christened Kessler, always seemed to find me on days of play and confessions alike, the minute he was released from his rusting bondage. The dog hurried to the base of the tree, sprang to my face and licked it with a compassion exceeding sometimes any of that shown and expressed by any of my family, only surpassed by that of Tamara. Where was she now, where can she be, I sighed hugging the dog who was confused by my tears and silent mouth.

After drying my torment, I stroked the thick hair of the dog, who distracted from crying seeming to ask for a cooling shower. I brought him to the usual water mains and sprayed him with playful jets that he in turn shook back with quick, contented movements of his head and body. I went inside and tried to sleep restfully during the afternoon, refusing to think even unintentionally of hurt.

The attitude of taking faith as laid down, without question or dispute with a solid, hard conviction, troubled me. The thought that forsaking one's suffering, sacrifices and pain might be cowardly or even immoral and that one must realistically weigh the consequences for reward before forging regardlessly ahead, seemed illogical. Rose was right, infallible again; one must be careful of displaying one's opinion. The backlash might be costly. I went again the next day to her. I repeated my opinion and told her of my father's indignation. To my surprise, I was also indignant and did not like being so. Rose, proud of me and my analysis, proposed a compromise: 'Your father esteems to inspire correct thinking in you; you should regard your honesty as an achievement, but if you start with a doubt of humanity as the core of all motives and fail to see the good in people prior to analysis, pronouncing your judgement before study of the case, you'll end up one of two things'.

She stretched out her first finger: 'One; you'll be fatalistic and see nothing good in people'. She aligned her second finger with the first: 'Or you'll acquire a closed minded to the progression of life'. She paused a little and then continued: 'You and all your future friends and close acquaintances will become like a gang in your thought, a lynch mob to anyone who differs from you'. I was startled by that warning that inflexible theory could lead to so much severe inhumanity.

She warned me not to misjudge my father's motives and that I should be lenient in accepting to differ with people. It was certainly not my intention to criticise my father. I loved and feared the man to the point of pious divinity. My father seemed in some sense to resemble God: He was pure in his instruction of virtue and as swift in showing his wrath. Still, there were distinct differences between them: God seemed unmoved in his conception of truth and the way it should be, implemented unchanged. My father looked as solid in his conception, but was not as solid in his deed.

I remembered clearly how he burnt the family photographs, yielding to the evil rule of the mob in the intention of saving the children and the family from their wrath.

Furthermore, I remembered how despite all he had accepted the street lynching of that old man outside our door, dragged behind the lorry to suffer a deformed and undignified death. He should have protested louder than with silence. Is that not appeasing evil, is that not immoral? I reached my silence in discomfort. I could understand his fear and ultimately his motives. But wasn't that precisely a form of sinning God had asked me to abdicate, when he advocated virtue regardless of consequence?

In one way I realised that he was trying honestly to enshrine truthfulness and conviction in me, to instil straightness of belief and attitude, and to discourage a taste for compromise. I understood his sacrifice of principle to earn us an escape from harm. It must have been uncomfortable for him. I could not condemn his action though I was not happy with the instruction he forced upon me. It was a point or flaw in his character, which I now consider uncomfortable, as I became aware of it and firmly questioned it.

Rose advised me not to convict my father harshly yet, to leave the matter lay its own course. In a year's time I should re-think it and compare my notes again on how to accept my father's good intentions along with the momentary unsettlement.

She led my pride to overtake my troubled inspiration: 'Aren't you a bit young to decide such grave concepts about others, so soon in your young life?' she said. Her words made me feel that she had regarded my mind as older than my body, I was considered grown-up, advancing into adulthood, although I had fewer years than I needed to have to qualify for it.

It was a handsome reward for intentionally freezing a discussion on the designs of others in life. It touched my life with the contentment of self-appraisal. It also left me calm in deferring decisions on fate of my reason and the explanations I offered myself of how things happened, the motives, those theories I had claimed I deduced or understood their correspondence with honesty and span of reality. I accepted her suggestion, partly because it made me happy to feel amongst adults but mainly because it left my vision of my father as a good man unaltered. I could be indifferent to his newly-discovered faults and discontent. I still loved the man and not any less than before.

5

Ingredients of Slender Friendship

Such acceptance of love in its blindness of perspective was new and exciting. It was another self-proven point of puberty, I thought quietly to myself. Whatever designs people express or disguise, our ultimate judgements illogically hint at our appreciation for such people and reflect strongly the way we refer to them.

It did not matter after the original shock had passed, as the relationship between father and son had survived the budding fear that its fallacy was more dominant than its binding terms. I had to lie again when my father asked me what I thought of his opinion regarding the matter of bold righteousness. I had to tell him I knew it was correct. I had no intention of reopening the subject and risking his disappointment and hurt, as I might have to question his virtue of action. I felt it was not worth the risk; he was happy and I had accepted his stance as necessary for the benefit of us all, before as well as now.

I was called into the sitting room one afternoon from my bicycle ride in the garden. With the advancing autumn, the brightness of five o'clock in the afternoon was not what it was a month before. I wanted more time and was not happy to be called in early. In the sitting room, my father was talking to a man, a friend of his, I supposed, from the warmth of their conversation. The man, called Vern, greeted me with a smile although I had not met him before.

My father informed me that his friend had just rented and moved into the empty house next door, where he was to live with his new bride. This trivial information was not of any importance to me, the man looked old enough for marriage, I thought, he was about twenty-five or thirty years of age as I estimated. After a quarter of an hour I asked to be excused. The two men were making jokes about things that did not seem humorous to me, such as soft flesh and young, virginal touch and so on, all discussed with laughter and an absence of malice.

I neither understood the things they said nor were they a matter of immediate interest to me. The code was effective. I found it impossible to break.

In the next room, my mother and the girls were entertaining the man's wife. I passed the half-closed door, intrigued by the joyful serenity of loud laughs and the happy bride. I looked in, curious to see what she looked like. She was so beautiful and elegant, sitting cross-legged in full adulthood of manner and courtesy.

For a moment, as I caught her eyes, her brown eyes, for a moment she resembled Tamara. My heart pounded, drumming with impatience and longing. I shook my head, as if to awaken my mind. As I looked again, I could see she did resemble Tamara, except in height: she must have been six inches shorter than Tamara, and oh, her breasts were slightly round and a slight slice bigger. Her waist was as slender as my phantom beat of thought.

She was nicely mannered too: she shook my hand when I was asked to come in and say hello. Her eyes were fixed on mine as if she had seen a ghost friend in me, as I momentarily had. She stopped talking and in her silence her eyes shone with an iridescent glow. My mother was watching us both and I blushed childlike without the intent of doing so.

The visitor introduced herself as Rhea, explaining that she did not realise how grown-up I had become and assuring me it did not matter if I did not remember her, since she had left our street some six years before and especially as she had not been to us since then. She asked me if I would like to visit her sometime, she had a huge stamp collection, a hobby I enjoyed whenever I could, she remembered from past years. I did not myself have any organised stamp collection, I had to admit.

The next day in school was ordinary. Rose stopped me in the crowded corridor and asked briefly how I was. Feeling awkward, I confirmed that I was alright. The warmth in her intention and the crowds around us made it difficult for words to express other than the immediate hollow denial and assurance. I was in a better mood than the previous days, but it would not have taken much for depression to encroach on me and I tried in all honesty to forget that such sorrow was there. Rose apologised for delaying me from going into the next class, which was physical education. Basket ball was fast becoming the relief from self-imposed thought control. I would lose myself within the excitement of the game, although I was not as good at it as the football but better than at gymnastics that we all hated. The latter was categorised by most of the boys as a time-wasting feminine sport; an arbitrary but strong belief.

Late one afternoon after school, I thought of Rhea. I left the house and crossed the nearly empty street. I had finished my homework and wanted to see her stamp collection. A teacher in school had asked us to write a short descriptive composition about collecting stamps, showing the different aspects of forming a collection, what to look for in a stamp, what makes it valuable or worthless. I was looking for advice and additional information, new words to fill out my composition and increase its authenticity.

When I rang the battered electric bell, a face I did not recognise peeped from a dust gathering windowsill. The door opened with a grating noise that betrayed the age of its wood. It was Rhea, covered in a large bathtowel, her hair glistening in the orange sunlight that reflected its wet, tight coils.

I was asked to enter quickly. The door shut behind me hastily and with a slight warning. I asked where Vern was, he was on his late shift, (he was a policeman). I felt embarrassed and was about to make a gesture of leaving when she asked me to have a coke. I fondly accepted. When I told Rhea what I came for, she was happy to help. She disappeared into her bedroom and, bringing out a deep box, asked me to inspect the stamp albums as she got dressed.

I took the first few albums out of the box and started examining them. The stamps were fabulous. Some seemed older than the albums had implied. The collection was extensive but showed signs that it was not looked after, as if it had been neglected for a while.

Rhea emerged from her quarters, dressed in a thin slip that barely covered her body. She sat next to me and asked me what I thought of the collection. I was anxious to exhibit my full enthusiasm, which pleased her. We talked about different stamps and colours and identified countries of origin. Afterwards and without warning she asked me if I would like to take all the stamps home for myself and keep them with me. I was surprised: she had spoken with such keen interest of her stamps that I could not understand why she was giving them away, especially as she had expressed such sincerity in her voice and offer.

She was explicit: she was about to become a mother, that's what was expected of her. No, she was not pregnant yet, but soon, even at the age of seventeen she was not going to have enough time for any hobbies. The house work and the baby, when it came, would all actually mean her hobbies would be neglected, she had no time already, so what would it be like later? No, I should have the stamps, I would take care of them, she knew it.

I was more than grateful, I was so happy I gave her a hug without implying anything other than gratitude. I promised I would always take care of the stamps, promised to bring them over when I had new additions to them, solemnly swearing.

She asked me if this would mean that we were friends. I agreed without thinking. I was flattered. I really needed a close friend, I wanted someone in place of Tamara, I missed having someone I could talk to and feel the closeness of friendship with and for. Also, although I was less than thirteen but more than twelve, I wanted to look as if I was over fourteen and past the verge of acclaiming my coming of age. I sought to demonstrate this by agreeing in a natural fashion to the obvious and showing myself devoid of reluctance, mature in my substance and intellectual in my behaviour.

The adult in front me was impressed with my gullible fast appreciation of friendship. I preached values of friendship, believing them truly, handling complex words, planting them here and there, at the ends of sentences and the beginning of opinions. I was happy to concede the shedding of my childhood skin with the vigour of at least a fifteen year old. She accepted me as such readily.

I brought the box home and unravelled it in my bedroom, one album at a time, neatly piling the one I had finished with, back in its previous resting place. The room was half-occupied with my mother's own things, the cupboards sheltered her collections of clothes and items dating from different times. I thought for the first time of a room of my own. There was an unused one in the house, three doors further from my parents' bedroom and two doors down the hall from the one I was in.

When I asked if I could have it as my own, my mother agreed with unexpressed reluctance, whereas my father agreed immediately. It was a gesture of leaving the nest, of reaching out for the first time. I was asking for something that meant only more space for me, they understood it as a budding bill of sale for independence, a mental receipt.

My small homework desk was not moved with me; instead a real metal desk with three side drawers was purchased for my new room, to house the private valuables that I might start to collect. My father handed me its keys with great pleasure, his pride was evident in the way he asked me not to lose them as they were the only copies, irreplaceable.

There was a old wooden bookcase in the room where I moved, which I seemed to have inherited as well, without asking. I was glad of it too. It was not empty, since it sheltered a few booklets, which my father informed me he would reclaim another day. I immediately put the few books I had in it, to assure myself that it was my possession. After properly dusting the remainder of its shelves, I rested the stamp collection on a shelf all on its own, with no other contender for that space.

I was now within my realm, where I could stay up late without being found out easily, especially in the coming holidays that were a month away. Rhea visited us the next day. I was delighted to show off my newly acclaimed space. I took her to the room, showed her my desk, commenting on the key access to the desk drawers and where I had kept her albums safe from any dust and disintegration, neat and valued. She expressed her admiration for the move, especially for having a personal place where I might keep what she called possible love letters, expected soon, to her mind. I replied I hadn't had such and probably should not expect any such confessional material for some time. She laughed, expressing her difference of opinion with a muted 'we shall see'.

After some five weeks and in the midst of the spring holiday from school, my father received a fat letter from Turkey, bearing large stamps. I was given the envelope to add the stamps to my collection. I soaked the whole envelope in water, to detach the tight-gummed patch of interest. I was watching it with impatience when I realised that some of the ink was starting to stain the stamps. I removed the envelope in hurried anxiety from the water bowl and washed it under the tap. The stamps were still stuck and somehow had changed their natural colour slightly.

I ran over to Rhea's house for advice. The stamps were spoils about to lose their value. It was eleven in the morning, Rhea was still in her bed. After a determined ringing she answered the door with her dressing gown on and eyes that seemed as if they hadn't closed for a few nights, were hungry for more sleep and not fully awake. I apologised for the intrusion and mouthed the urgency of saving the fate of the newly attained jewels. She understood, but looked faint of spirits. I was let in, welcomed irrespective of the motive.

I gulped the glass of coke I was offered, breathing anxiously. She calmed me: 'Let's cut the piece of envelope to the size of the stamps and then try to soak it again in a large amount of water with some hand soap, it should work'. It actually did. The stamps retained their original colour after the effort of patient waiting. She further explained: 'you should always cut it to size to avoid ink discolor-ation, then heat a kettle of water and put the edge of the stamps to the spout of the steaming vapour. The stamps should peel off cleanly and easily, maintaining their paper texture. To submerge stamps in water a long time, may thin the stamps', she claimed expertly.

While she was demonstrating this, we stood close to the kettle, the steam condensing on our foreheads mixed with our own per-spiration. Holding the disfigured paper in one hand, she reached with her other hand and wiped the droplets off my forehead, in the silence of a warm smile. I wished unintentionally that the moment would last a lifetime. I was regaining a feeling I had with Tamara, except it made me stir in a way I had not felt before, I was fighting my wish to hug her. Her closeness was riveting, I could feel her heart beat, pulsing against my shoulder with a loud and persistent rhythm. I glanced at her face but could not keep my eyes off hers.

Her lips reached my face slowly in time with my calm surrender, intimate and unresisting. She planted a kiss that was lovingly moist of breath and length of hold. I let my lips feed on her warmth, unprepared to let hold of her body, in hope of lasting heaven, a greedy suspension of time.

The steam from the kettle caught her fingers and she pulled her body away. For a moment I did not understand why, I looked at her, awaiting a scolding for my surrender. She licked her forefinger with a justifiable complaint. I suddenly understood and took her hand into my palm, licking her finger intently and slowly.

The gesture was rewarded wordlessly and with passionately with continued kissing that started at the side of the mouth and crept to displace the burnt finger which seemed to have recovered from its pain, deliberately. Her hands moved to stretch from my waist to the top of my thigh. I felt something expanding within me, inconsistent with my body. I looked down, surprised, at this newly discovered change. I was in a state of hazy confusion, enjoying the transformation, although I was full of exclamation.

She took my left hand and inserted it into her dressing gown. She must have undressed in her passion earlier, there was nothing clothing her body underneath the dressing gown.

I felt her underarm, smooth and soft as she stretched. She had tender skin that became more tender as she guided the hand towards her left breast, stopping at the point of the nipple. The sensation was an intense emancipation of will. I hugged her more tightly without intending any further action.

Her hands crept back to my thighs. She quickly unzipped my short boyish trousers and entered the virgin domain of my rebelling sex. I pulled away in slight embarrassment and total surprise. She chased my mouth with hers, kissing me in spite of the strength of my resolution to ask her what she was trying to do as she held my breath for me. I stayed silent, taken, fully willing my slide into passiveness in a momentary lapse of decision.

She took a part of me outside the trousers zip, exposed it to the growing heat of the room and seemed to contemplate playing with me. She handled it gently and with an excessive exhibition of passion. Suddenly, I felt an eruption of pressure inside me, which she felt too, clothing my urge with her hand. This sensation lasted for a few seconds that seemed longer, until it subsided suddenly and peacefully.

She unfolded her hand slowly, examining it lightly, pretending either she was not doing so, or that the examination was, somehow, immaterial. Her eyes exhibited a query, questioning the emptiness of her hand. She felt the dry texture of her skin, maybe expecting a timid viscosity to have resulted from the pressure of my inner surge, the utter draining of my will and my surrender of soul. She did not dare ask, but rather questioned her own instinct that the spillage had occurred earlier than she had thought.

She kissed me again and brought my face to touch her in between her breasts, intoxicating me with the sound of her slow breathing and the stickiness of her skin. I held her as she held me, in total appreciation of tenderness. We let go as if almost in agreement on the timing of release. She asked me if the experience was new to me, if I had enjoyed it and, with equal uneasiness, if it had surprised my innocence with its joy. I was unable to answer her inquisition instantly. I agreed with all her points in a soft and tamed voice. She then asked me about my truthful age and I had to confess. She seemed happy to reach a conclusion in believing my virginal youth.

When I asked why she wanted to know my accurate age, she started explaining to me the facts of seminal fluid and sexual puberty and the reasons for her indirect inquiry. She asked me if I knew of these or of the female cycle, conception and the birth of babies. I was truthful, I did not have such key knowledge. The instruction continued, barring some aspects, with ample explanation. I was left open mouthed and riveted with curiosity in half-disbelief at the complexity and detail. I instinctively looked at her pelvis, trying to imagine the process of a baby coming out of such a small area.

She commented, dismissing my worries that all women have to overcome that hurdle, as she would have to soon. She and husband were trying to initiate the process presently. She added: 'It's the hidden reason for any marriage and sometimes the overriding reasonable aim of it'.

I suddenly smelt something burning. It was the stamps. Their backing paper had curled up with the heat of the cooker, where they had fallen from her hand, near the kettle. It was too late to save the stamps, which saddened me. She apologised with a kiss for the result of her inattention. I accepted her good without further discussion or blame. The result was irreversible and I accepted it as such, as I did my closeness to her, as I bade her a short farewell full of gratitude.

The week that followed was hard, as I searched for a repeat dose. The new addiction had gripped its consenting devotee. From the window of my room I watched the street, which I had clearly mapped out reconnoitred. It was early afternoon as I saw Vern leave his house. I waited for five minutes before I decided to go over to see Rhea, full of enthusiasm for an experience that promised to overcome my acute withdrawal. She opened the door, pulling me inside before I had a chance to greet her. Her kisses confessed her sudden awakening from withdrawal that intertwined with mine in long, hard embrace interrupted by our slow, gradual undressing of each other. We lay down on the cool floor, our bodies touching on all points, sharing warmth and moisture without thought.

Our mouths touched and in the intervals we offered each other a look of deep friendship and love, as our slow breathing confirmed the heat.

For a long while, her legs were closed tightly over me. She pressed her neatly trimmed pubic hair over my corresponding area, rocking her body left and right, up and down, forward and backward, trying something of which I could not imagine the purpose. Without declaring her intentions, her legs opened fully allowing part of me to sink into a space of which I only recently understood the function. She pushed harder, pressing her body closer, as if to swallow my whole body inside.

I opened my eyes feeling the same inner pressure I had felt the last time with her, but now I was melting inside her. She responded by closing her legs tightly, squashing me forcefully. Her cries made me worry that it was I who was inflicting her with pain. I watched without comment. As the cries seemed to diminish in frequency and vigour, her mouth left mine for the connecting flesh between my neck and left shoulder, which she kissed repeatedly.

Then suddenly her clamour started to mount again, accompanied by relentless movements around my pelvis. The ritual lasted for a few minutes until the final hard tug and squeeze finalised the movement within her mouth and her teeth bit the flesh she had been tenderly kissing moments earlier. The grip of her teeth was matched only by the force with which she clung to my body, her hands buried in the back of my shoulders.

I was speechless under her besetting. My skin looked bruised but felt numb of corresponding pain. I closed my eyes and drifted into sleep. She raced ahead of my intention with eyes closed before mine. Hours later we awoke, stretched against each other, filled with contentment in the sacrifice of time. My virginity was eroded, forever lost, forever discounted.

At the discontinuation of innocence, the dark blindfold was slowly lifted, gentle colours displaced the darkness with brightness at first as light and habit were accommodated, then I proceeded further into acclaim, defining all past shades of life of which I was conscious. They crowded lightly, past each other, still recognisable, driven by the thought of previous deprivation of longing and belonging, driven by the appetite of greed, trying to stall the moment in the hope it was forever and under the threat of a self-made fear that it was the last second of a fleeting present.

That was the way I felt about Rhea. That's the way she left me feeling forever, that was the way. Days passed me in a turbulence of craving. I wanted her even when I did not think of her. For those who think that a woman you do not admit love towards, yet feel the ache for her body in an addiction of the flesh, is a woman who would disappear with less hardship once the hunger goes; I say you're shallow of passion and much less of self. Even the women who give their flesh as an investment of means more than time, would remain like a fold in the skin you're bound to remember.

A casual meeting is not less aesthetic than a planned rendezvous, neither the first word of love more easily forgotten than a dedicated two-page poem, nor the first expression of touch less meaningful than years of heat and long lifetimes of climax and dependence. Yet it was love with Rhea and at the same time it wasn't. The time yielded to us was as happily distributed between the strength of borrowed companionship and the weakness of aching for the oft-nursed flesh.

After we had first taken each other, we had met twice to talk and to aggravate our heat-dependence. Each time, then, we shared slumber entwined with each other. After a few months, I became one day officially of age. I flooded her sheet with what she feared had seeded her the time before that. At the end of the same week she knew otherwise as she flooded her own sheet with wasted eggs, as she termed her pain and bleeding. The process brought me nearer her inner hidden wishes and reasons for living, as a woman of hope, not disappointing herself as a true woman.

She was in her front garden, sitting out in the brightness of the sun one late morning in April. I knocked on the door, but my knock seemed drowned by the loud music of the radio. I knocked again, harder. As I was about to turn away from the door, she appeared in the sitting room. I saw her shadow through the fine fly-mesh on the window, I knocked once again. She opened the door. Her breath seemed to have a sweet smell, which I caught from the short distance separation us. I went in, lent my mouth to hers; the smell was stronger than its taste.

She was drinking in the back garden and asked me if I wanted to join her. I agreed for the sake of her company, but not for that sweet sauce of delusion. I did not like the taste of alcohol in those days. I was still boyish and acquiring a taste for anything but that which smelt as horrible as it tasted.

She was in a state of depression that at first seemed random, but which ran deeper, I discovered later. Such melancholy recurred in cycles in a pattern I had not seen in her before. She had not told me about it nor had I caught her in it before that day. I tried strenuously to find excuses that would give me a reason to press her for an answer, a muddled sentence or a simple projection of words, if I could not aim high for an explanation of her depression, its depth and its sources. She had had her period again, the seventh period since she had married Vern. Her use of such a monthly event as a calendar by which to view her marriage was unusual and bordering on the morbid.

I sat looking at her in confusion, not knowing how to restore her self-awareness, without mishandling her emotions, tinged as they were with cynicism, or hurting her sense of being. I had to endure her self-abasement and waited until she was nearly unconscious before I could persuade her to go to bed. I stayed with her in bed, fully clothed and awake.

After three hours she woke up with a headache that seemed worse than her complaint of its size. I made some coffee for both of us, strong brewed.

She apologised when I told her bluntly what had happened. It was hard for her to explain and when she did, the whole obstacle to sanity seemed as unimportant to me as it was life-threatening and vital to her. The doctor she and Vern had consulted for advice, had confirmed that day that she was not capable of conceiving, or rather more specifically of ever carrying children. All her periods, as she thought, fewer, as I thought, had been actually miscarriages, lost babies.

Although it was not easy for me to see the significance of conception as a prerequisite for a purposeful and useful life, the essential degree of its importance was evident in her voice and vocabulary as she blamed herself, as much as God. He had endowed her with a body that refused to support her ambitions of motherhood. She felt her body was God's wrath for the clear sensitivity of her soul and the durable cleanliness of her mind. She could not accept God was merciful or had intended his order of the universe to be founded by wonderful faculty.

I was a bystander who had felt her pain deeper than I had felt her loss. The latter I could neither evaluate, nor quantify. I had to watch her for hours, days and weeks in turmoil, without being able to alleviate her suffering more than a little at a time, without replying, merely listening, rewarding her with a surrogate gesture of value and warmth of touch. It took us three months before we really touched again. Our later themes of conversation became sparse and faint of interest.

With the passage of time, but yet further pain and less comfort from the old sentences of consolation, it became gradually clearer, though less agreeable to contemplate, that I was useless in her eyes and powerless to dissolve her mental barriers. The taste of flesh melted into an ordinary coming together of different kinds of closeness. The need for spoken companionship evicted the selfish drive for sex, without striving to consider her fulfilment of soul. Her encouraging cries of climax seemed fainter and lower; she never refused but seemed less affected and eventually I became more hesitant to ask and less insistent in trespassing on her.

It was unusual to regress from a point of inseparability to being nearly estranged bodies, although what separated us were thin layers of skin. The trend was restless, disorganised and increasingly in an aid of the charity for the mind. Although neither of us had the intention of losing the need for being with each other, we were meeting less frequently, at a diminishing rate, week by week. The transformation was ominous in its warning of probable change and loss.

At the end of that school year, I had to move to a new school, further away than my first fields of experimentation. To my sadness, I had to wander away from the watchful eyes of Rose and the few friends I had. I was least happy at being fully exposed to the expected new environment of unthinking boys, whose lives rolled against the football post and whose almost claustrophobic number per class gave the school the air of a market place, heavy with the stench and the heat of summer, the decay of discontented study and learning.

It was also the summer when Rhea was to move to another city, her husband being reallocated to a new station. She was as helpless as I was, we both had to follow the course of events with an acceptance of tranquil devotion to our slow, compliant friendship.

I missed her body and our delicate, miniature world. We were already outgrowing our habit of mutual dependence, but to our appreciation of time spent. We were already true friends and much lesser lovers. In the wake of the parting morning sun, we had to be entities, separated by each residing within a memory of existence, indestructibly passed.

For the few months that followed, I stayed within the confines of my room listening to a new radio that I was awarded for the excellent grades I had attained in the last final exam. It always surprised me how in deepest of affliction, I could still do well in exams at the end of term, as if I had two minds that never intruded on each other's domain: one thought for feeling and passion or worry and sadness or joy in one side of the brain; another thought for study for school awards and learning materials in a completely separate sphere of the brain. No explanation. One voice said: Losing valuables is fair punishment for sins committed; sin is always a harder concern than innocence.

6

Lease of Will

At the age of thirteen, the world seemed at my feet. Within its own fields, my vision was bold and my understanding acute. Rhea had travelled away more than four months now. I received a letter from her; she seemed happier where she was now. The problem of her futile attempts to conceive had lightened its burden, as a consequence of parties and new acquaintances and acceptance of her inability to change something that was beyond her control.

I missed her at some times more than others. Lately, time elapsed when I did not think of her more than in passing. Through her gradual coldness in sex, though not so much in conversation, I seemed to have drifted slowly away from the shores of longing, driven by winds of an acceptance of eventual ending and floating on thin planks eaten away by the waves of distance and endured separation. It seemed painless and serene in its message. I did think sometimes that I had lost her because of my willingness for her flesh. A sinner expects a hard penalty. After my loss of innocence, the pain was a payment in kind, lesser always than one deserved.

I now greeted her past gentleness and warmth to me with gratitude for her fondness, lavished with appreciation of her breaking me delicately and her tolerance of inadequate training of my senses. In her tendency to treat me in an equitable purpose, she had trusted my unexaggerated inexperience and was pleased for the growth of my word and feeling towards her without judging or condemning her. She had found me as her companion, her latitude and her soul-consort.

If I had been so close in body and soul to Tamara and had been of a similar age to her, I would not have been so uncomplaining; I would have been heart broken, I would have told her I loved her and probably promised her my life and thought eternal. With all that was of Rhea and I, the term friendship dominated all other deeper and dormant affection. Rhea was the mistress of my blossoming, regardless of how we started and how both of us faded together.

My younger sister, now eleven, started bringing some of her new girlfriends home to play with her. She broke my isolation as she was allowed to break hers. One particular girl, named Jessica, a Jewish girl of twelve, was a wonder of a girl of at that age. She could make boys treat her with true camaraderie, as if she was one of them. She was the same with the girls: equally popular.

One could tell Jessica was special, even at that young age. As the months went by, I became more than a boy in heat as I was the first time I saw her. I became as fond of her as I could be, wonderfully nearer to the point of love than to participating friendship and furthest away from fleshly thoughts of acquiring her body by storms of touching.

Jessica soon became the past love I always imagined and wanted to have. She leased most of me to myself. I recognised this feeling early on, as different to my will to have her innocence, which with Rhea had taken me into puberty of pure flesh. It took some time to characterise, but finally surged freely, with a purity of its own. It was fair, honest and flawless.

Our relationship gave us a passionate togetherness in conversation and wandering aspirations, aims of living and discussion of plans in life; it was a profound admiration of mind unrelated to body. I have overworked my thought to the point of slavery, without complaints over the rattle of chains and beyond the fear possible loss.

I wrote her unsigned love letters, which I never sent. The pencils had an aroma when sharpened that I had never noticed before, only surpassed in clinging and warmth by the scribble of heart-foolish verse, a fever most logical when it carried the dream to the limits of what I thought was its reality and to the breaking point of hope. Her lips pressed better than any biblical dispensation of truth, far warmer than any divine passion could be imagined, softer than all youth and more respondent in dream than being in love.

Although being in love was fashionable at that age, a bequeathed fortune, the heart was foolhardy and the breath was clean and short but of a fervent echoes of heart-beat.

Restless like a butterfly trapped between the fly-mesh and the glass of a window, she was acquainted like the sun at break of dawn, capable of all moods, resembling a wave that changed its mind in the midst of flow and opted to ebb, guided by the gentle look and the wordless glance, peaceable and appeasing appeasement itself when she so wanted. For natives like me, the sail of her boat was like God's message of power and fear.

Her reaction to suggestions I may have made at moments of slackened concentration was almost always unpredictable; the firepower of her ship was strange and strict, depriving the savages of their habits. I was taken like those previously untamed shore inhabitants.

The politics of love were not a retort to power-sharing at first. The shine of the blade had enlarged its cutting edge, intensified its effective penetration of the skin. Fear allowed it be more effective than pain. I wanted love exchanged freely, but was hesitant to declare my intention, which resembled the shadows of tall trees that give an impression of space within the shade, uncertain over time, reclaimed by the hardy sun to awaiting either the worry of rejection or a bold declaration as it trails its beams to familiar or newly drawn horizons. I was quite happy at thirteen; visual touch and soft glances were sufficient.

Jessica's maturity was evident, noticeable in not going bra-less, although the water easily covered her skin, forbidden to the sun, when we swam in mixed company. She was exhibiting something that was not as we knew it at her age: the realisation of an accepted change from childhood, relishing the knowledge that a point had been reached where the innocence of self-unawareness was a boat that had finally lifted its weight off the golden sands of fine simplistic immaturity. She was not as I once was at such a point: finding my hand waving happily to the occupants of that boat, before realising I had been left behind.

Being beached was not for her; not for her a declaration of bright-green grief that may not always make you manifest an escapist passion for raft-making. Far away and beyond the free coconut drink, the sand asked shamelessly more of the naked foot and the salt-driven foam. She made an opinion expressed or exchanged over any matter look complex in its drift of discussion.

Sometimes I felt so unsure that I held my breath as she thought along or against my view. I felt as if my shopping items were being counted. (with the excuse of neatly arranging them in a carrier bag), fearful that I had miscounted my heart beats or left behind my wallet of words before approaching the pay till, where I would be found penniless or with insufficient backing in the exchange of thought.

One could not tell at thirteen if the next birthday was to be lucky or ordinary. Darkness of thought visited me often at fourteen, alternating with hope or dreams. It was not like the condensation on the glass of a window, where the fog is cleared in the confrontation with shattering sunlight and the powerful air of trees and corrosive daylight. Zany awakenings were often hard, convincing you of failure. I had kept an attitude of fatalistic surrender in my wait for positive happenings, an attitude independent of any wish for its reverse. I wanted her, but could awaken my bold demands.

I sat some evenings blaming myself for imprecise wording or adjectives with which to test her confessions on sex and love. After all love was clear in its purpose, but its existence had come after a short year to require a flesh-sacrifice at this stage of its journey in me.

Sometimes, love pronounced its frailty in her with an absence of declared passion and want and of any need in her to give away her body. I was unsure she loved me truly. At other times, the matter could be judged differently: it was unimportant; thought was the currency of love. The relationship was adequate, depending on the intensity and frequency of time spent apart.

A sudden realisation at fourteen easily accounted for the apparent failure of the past year, in not being comprehensively sure she loved me or that she actually wanted me: it must have been an enforcement of virginity with uncertainty. Love then was a glance, a throb, a touch, a gesture. Unexpectedly and for some time now, I seemed somehow to be different to her from last year. Nothing I did made a wrong impression, nothing I spoke could be misquoted, scrutinised or dismissed as irrelevant, although my behaviour over the twelve months past towards her had remained stationary. I was not aware of any change I had instigated. Whether in deed, thought or word, I was still the same.

Her sudden, overextended warmth in word and look was now a thriving worry in me. Did she think that I ready for the sway of the world after a long wait, or was she braving a humble urge in submission to my plea for a physical affair of heat? I could not decide the growing motive that seemed to spurt out of control.

I was sitting one afternoon in the garden, thinking of her. I was on the ground, my legs doubled in front of me, my back leaning against my self-purge tree, Bertha. She came into the garden. She knew where to find me, as I was always in that place when I was alone or wanted to be alone. She knew that and very well. She sat facing me, kneeling back closely between my legs, inspecting my silence with her own.

Her hand reached my face, in slow, friendly thought. My lips kissed the inside curve of her hand as, speechless, she lifted my face. Her face followed her hand immediately after she had withdrawn it from my lips; the mouth-to-mouth kiss, long awaited, had happened. When I realised I had said I loved her, though she gave me no answer, the sun was setting and we had been kissing softly for at least an hour, probably longer.

She left, shivering with cold and surprise at this incursion into both our wills. She again repeated none of my words as she stopped for a last look, brief in recognition of the hour. It was a moment for silent, serious reflection, for glances that asked a formidable question: is it fate?

The next afternoon, I sat in the same place, clouded by hunger for the body; I could erase all that was blending into confusion and start again. Love seemed to have two faces, two needs: the spirit longs for hours of hugging, exchange of souls, a wordless measure of piety, fingers enveloping each other, endorsing its next stage, the face of love: the sovereign and irresistible merging of flesh, classical lust; or was it a sharing of bodies after souls had been twined together?

The purer versions of love, as revealed, did not reject the sordid shadows of need and hunger. How could the ultimate purity lead itself willingly into sin, accept it and encourage its upbringing as a matter of course? Confusion loomed, stopped only when the method analysed was rejected. What seemed real was illogical; it was natural to accept it as feeling and leave it inside as feeling, to forget about that which condemned it, wind up the net, rather, and be comfortable with the day's product.

Depth was intellectually brutal: lease it to nothingness, be happy, I kept telling the rebellious pressure. Take the offer lightly and easily, feel its warmth and forsake the coldness of its retraction.

I had just made up my mind to resist any act of judgement, to bend the branch of love into any shape it required. Sanity should be respected and hung up high; sanity, a gut feeling of righteousness, guiding itself towards affection, care and trial. If the day came when a man had to coerce his instinct, it'd be a day for the disparate man to release his inhumanity and lack of will. Flesh would be another form of wood, feeling would rest itself out of the rain, away from the sun, to rust contented as a forgotten thin piece of iron, breached.

She found me under the same tree, swimming in a total loss of words. I emerged in a single-minded mood, determined to press my decision, resisting the temptation to sink below my need to be correct in ethics and manner. I wanted her, yet mostly told her, without asking, how I wanted her, how I wanted her and now.

I looked into her eyes, those that harboured lingering fear, candid acceptance of the sacrifice of virginity and the motto of saving one's self until taken, pre-arranged by parents and precise, social arrangement. She held my hand: her silence said yes; her lips said now; stress said gentle, gentle and slow; love said before she changes her mind; her head bowed said closed eyes, an open mind, a half-awaiting wish, half fearful of disillusionment; the fear of hurt and pain overwhelmed with uncertainties, youth and inexperience; teeth-bitten lips said exotic flow.

We laid on the soil a bed, gently removing our clothes in the heat, under the shelter of the pious tree of my youth. I could feel my heartbeat rippling inside my ribs, in contrast to hers, skin-amplified a thousand times. All was forgotten: the honest, generous purity of a year; the pain of the distance close enough to touch, far enough within the will; the lengths of deprived waiting in want and fear of refusal; flashes of footage from the moment of love when it was levied with fate; all was forgiven, all was immaterial, all worthwhile.

I took her by the hand past her innocence of the body to final experience. Between consecutive flushes of desire, there was that pain and tightness, unusual from my experience. For my body, it

felt like the first time too. Everyday, afterwards, was measured by
the health of this love's touch, by the length of its hesitation before
a response came and by the religion of its bodily worship. A
different addiction was in the making. I remember those days even
now, the purple shade of pink she wore in a thin garment on top of
her skirt, the red bandanna as a sign of strength, the yellow of her
underwear, the sign of openness in that velvet-textured blouse that
restrained her breasts; all in a combination of colours that was not
yet in fashion for the mature woman of the day. The shades and
colours she wore, on reflection told me she wanted the experience,
she wanted its passion on her undressed skin, freely and consciously.

Thus armistice and solace of demands which might be thought of
as a desecration of the soul, passed to us, children aged in love,
whose manner of growing up was unsuspected or considered
only lightly by our guardians and pets alike. Kessler accepted her
presence as did my parents and hers, with me in a momentary
lapse of suspicion and the expected puritanical reaction. The flesh
soon became an addiction as in thought we undressed each other in
the presence of others, when we were fully clothed. It became a
colourful truth, ever more dependent on the next time. The dream
possessed the dreamers, beholders of the bright glow and smooth
offerings of all that is warmth and promise laden.

As we lived apart for most of the day and all of the night, the wait
through sunset and sunrise betrayed our affliction in long strides of
patience and denial, evincing endurance as on cold cobbles, testing
one's breaking point and appreciation of reward. Dust, sharp stones
and inner pain were all alike: instruments of perfection in word-
patented journeys and anxiety for a speedy arrival.

Lit candles earn their place: destruction of fear, when we are
small and caught in a power cut; a soft glow and frozen tears at
their burning, now in adulthood; an appreciation of soft light in
later adult years; at last in old age, when the least bright light boosts
confidence and competes with the confusion of weak sight or the
fruitless passing of age; or at death to brighten the anticipated,
unreal darkness as we approach its restless, damp passage, a
caravan on the move, biased of old camp fires and their welcome. A
little light to help us at those points where we hopelessly cross to
where being is defined, earned by mere past deeds or thoughtless
repetition of movements on the already laden track, by forceful

change in the affliction of self-enlightenment; nothing short of either extreme constituted reward at the end of such a day, that day at least. And now candles reminded me of her eyes, always shining in reflection of a strict smile.

I looked upon a world animated by a new light, as she looked at me, by new philosophies: breath always hid excitement and denounced exhaustion after an eruption of passion or expressed want from a distance. The curtains she had drawn across her room as it was lit, were shut away: the cloth had no part to play, no objectiveness or loyalties.

When she was not known to me, when she had lived behind the curtain of time, a powerful hand had aligned the loyalty of the cloth for the moment, drawing it across with soft bars of shadow, less fond of the spotlight that exposed its inhumanity. A touch conveyed more tenderness than an illusion. Such was the religion confirmed by prophets of belief in totally unspoken declarations of their intentions.

I, the philosopher, was born out of reality and myths of pleasure, out of tenderness and a bold acknowledgement of need. At such a time all the stars in the summer sky served as proof of our existence dismal, in comparison to the universe, a reminder to keep us awake at night, teasing tiredness with colours of dreams. I had made up my mind, after a short discussion with myself: this was the love of a lifetime, nothing could make it any less or be greater than it. The little experience I had of love and of abundance of feeling, showed they were intimate friends of hard bark, deep roots and multi-coloured petals. The softness of our eyes, stringent of shy, serene passion, made the risk a tolerable commitment of binding.

The gentle musk of her skin in closeness of touch, awakened a vision of a forest at sunrise, as its trees turned into an enchanting fete. At the point of darkness the same day, imagination allowed each disfigurement to release a shadow behind and beneath every branch. Twilight may bring either an encounter all shadows or an exhalation of relief, depending on where you stood at either edge of the magical forest, where the sun struggled to assert its fledgling light as a token of its continued dominance. The gentle musk of her skin bequeathed all that to me. It was unsettling at times, even threatening, to feel the disbandment of past sorrow and loss, and so easy, too easy now.

Lately her thought had followed two planes.

She adored butterflies. Once she once felt sad when she saw
painted butterflies in repose on flowers imprinted on a vase of
delicate bone china. The gentle creed left any scars on the plain
orange surface of their hosts. She said once, as an afterthought:
'When we're happy, the fields are full of butterflies. Sorrow comes
when we see the wind-broken wing and last breath of a butterfly,
desirous of everything, yet kept short of burial. Have you ever seen
anyone burying a dead or paralysed butterfly, trapped in the wire
of a fence, an unfluttering miniature rainbow?', she asked.

'We may leave our silence and sorrow, preferring to move on',
she continued. 'When we are happy, the glazed look lasts briefly;
in sorrow, we dwell in a house of ill thought, helplessly sleepless,
in vast sentimental demise'. 'We're always more sensitive to sadness than we are to sunlight', I thought.

Watching her articulate her thoughts, I reflected sometimes that
the maze does not look difficult, a puzzle, until one is sufficiently
far in from its entrance, close to its inner core. A hedge could be a
butterflies' burial ground. In the morning frost, wings are marked
with crisp stillness. It may seem cruel, but is credible and close to
life. Entangled butterflies in a hedge look part of the puzzle, a small
point in the making of the maze.

I woke up one morning with a sense that something was different.
It was not yet bright outside. The darkness surrounding my eyes
seemed like a blindness in its restless confusion, incomprehension
and unexpected disorientation.

All those words saved to be said this day, felt inappropriate,
worthless and devoid of will. The feeling of being half an hour
late for something authentic and irreplaceable overcame all the
goodness in life.

A deep sense of mourning drove my ignorance towards weary
anger and distaste, grievances that folded a row of unbudded,
unopened button roses into a shrivelling space. I thought of sur-
prises in life, how they always seemed more memorable in their
sudden, swift unexpectedness. I thought of the rapid thrust of a
new, shiny blade that cut deep and as it did so, it made the force of
feared severance wholly unforgettable.

Without probable reason, I was mourning someone, a faceless
person. I thought of Tamara first, then Rhea, but both faded, they
did not bridge with my thoughts. Then I thought of Jessica, her

eyes were fixed on the sparkle of the thin edge of a blade. She, unlike the first two, refused to fade away. She stood erect, facing the mirror, unresponsive to my calling, I stood behind her anxious and in confusion.

I was seeing her room further: on the bed a blade lay unfolded. She moved towards the bed slowly, focusing on the blade; nothing else in the room, not even I, was evident to her.

I yelled at her, my voice thin, as if the words were voiced but lost before reaching the edge of the mouth unheard. I was dreaming, awake, yet as if asleep. I stood at the mirror as she approached the bed. She felt the soft sheets, skimming its surface, as if she wanted it cause a ripple on the surface, as if the sheets were the despondent face of a stagnant pond; not extinct, rather motionless, motionless for long periods. She stopped about few inches from the blade, recognising its shine and authority. I imagined further: stop, stop, please stop. I pleaded silently. She stopped as if she had heard my thought or knew I was there all the time, or was about to say a few words before, unopposed, she did what she was about to.

She released a smile that was full of thought, but devoid of passion. She turned back, away from my face and towards the blade. Her right hand reached to touch it; her left hand remained hidden. She shrugged quickly, silently in indecision, slumped back momentarily, then strengthened to stand upright. She remained, her face turned upwards, inactive, ignoring me. I could smell a new fragrance advancing as I stood awaiting some movement of her body.

This thought prompted my curiosity: I could hear something dripping onto the uncarpeted floor, strong and abundant in its rhythm. I looked downwards, her unshod feet were firm on the ground, a red stream of viscosity was casually travelling to the floor, surrounding her small toes and soles. Motionless, I seemed unable to inflict my will on my body. She turned and smiled again, overcome by a longing to undo the flow, her right hand folded tightly over her left wrist, as if denying any consequence to me. Her mouth assumed the shapes of letters, spelling what seemed like a solemn farewell, final and eternal. I rushed forward, eyes fixed, towards my own bed; she was a ghost of my thought.

It was a moment of blindness and restless confusion. A handful of hours earlier she had confessed in a soft voice: 'I do not want to drift apart from you, from here', (she hesitated between the first and second parts of the sentence); 'I'd rather die'.

She was discussing with me a decision which was being considered by her family; they seemed to have an option of migrating to Israel.

I was shocked, not in the ordinary sense or reflecting as some people did, that Jews were renegades if they preferred to leave their homeland (Iraq) and emigrate to another and opposing country (Israel). I was not politically aligned, I could not care where a man lived, it would not make him a lesser patriot or liable for condemnation. It was a personal decision, I always thought. I was deeply concerned, somehow, at her leaving.

I had tried to postpone the discussion, ridiculing her worry as mere anticipation of an event. Selfishly, I was hoping that that day would not dawn or rather, was hoping that I would not have to face it if it ever happened. I could understand her people trying to live with their own clan, if they wanted to, as long as it did not mean losing her. She was too precious to lose or mislay. If they decided to move away, it was unlikely that she'd be left behind. Where would she live and with whom?

The next improbability followed shortly: do I want to marry her in order to keep her? I could not marry her, even if I wanted to. My parents would not approve of such an impossibly young marriage, while on the other side, her parents, who were more religious, would not allow her either. I was not Jewish and worse than that I was not religious at all.

The next aspect was more worrying: it would be found out if they moved away that she's not a virgin. As far as I knew, irrespective of religion, people in such society would kill their daughters rather than be disgraced, I had heard it done to another Jewish girl and to that other girl whose father my own father had got acquitted in court the year before. Although I could not estimate the gravity of such reasons or motives, the act seemed unethical, unreligious, pure insanity.

If a girl was sincere and clean-minded, would it matter if she was a virgin or not? It seemed such a high price for pleasure and warmth, impossible to pay after one mistake (if it was that). If that should happen to Jessica, I would die; I could not resist the easy penalty compared to living if she was killed because of me. I asked her: would you blame me for making you stay, giving me yourself?

I was sweating while she was considering her answer. She asked me then: 'Are you faithful to me and only me, do you think you'll always love, want and respect me?'. My answer: 'Yes', was easy for two of the three. Why should I not respect her, I wondered. I asked why. She retold me her myths of early childhood, how a girl who went with any man, apart from her husband when she was married, was considered cheap, unworthy of respect.

I protested that I did not think in such an illogical fashion. She replied: 'Any way, I came to you, you're blameless, you have not sinned. The Talmud is clear about that, as I remember'. I was not sure whether what was supposed to be my own religion was as partial, but my conscience was untroubled for having had her; I did not feel I had sinned, of that I was clear in my own mind. The idea that one set of behaviour might be required of men and another of women did not seem fair, but as she was sure of the verdict, it seemed unimportant to dissect the rule further or at least not certainly that day. I was able to still the renewal of discussion.

I held her, told her the truth of my hope that they would not move away, how I needed her and forever, asked her not to worry about it, assuring her that her father had too much at stake to dispose of his life as it stood and gamble everything all over again, in a new place and circumstance. The move would not be wise for him.

As I was thinking of all this, there was a hard knock on the front door, an energetic, loud and relentless knock. My father opened it, only half-believing it was happening. It was too early to expect a call. The urgent, barely separated knocks, frantic in their frequency, were probably warning of disaster.

My father came upstairs where my mother and grandmother were asleep. He woke one, went into the other room and did the same. The two women seemed in a hurry to dress and leave the house. I was behind the door of my bedroom, awaiting an explanation or news. My father telephoned a doctor, a friend of his, excusing himself for the early call by urgent nature of the matter and stressing the youth of the patient and the need for professional aid in maintaining a life.

7

Progression in Loss

I had come from behind my father. He turned around unexpectedly and saw me there, my face bare of emotion and wrapped in worry. He finished his call, pleading its urgency, came to me and ordered me to return to bed. I had been awake too long to be able to do so and was too distressed to attempt sleep easily. He repeated his order strictly, as an order, void of reason. I ran to my room, shut my eyes over my tears as I shut the door behind me. I was sure it had really happened and was not a dream as I had thought earlier. I was so sure that my sadness was too deep to imagine that I might be wrong. I could not explain to myself how I knew; it was not important now, it was more important why it happened.

Defeated from within, I was trying not to believe my concert of fears. My soul was paralysed and my eyes were unyielding, tearful. My body was shaking, before the futility of things. My loss, incalculable and vast, was impeding my hope that it was a nightmare. I stayed in my room in bed, trying to silence echoes, unintelligible echoes and quieten my shivering. In the distance I heard the outside door and the gate slam shut as my mother ran to Jessica's house.

After some unquantified passage of time, of which I was hardly conscious, I heard the gate and the main door open and shut again. My mother had come back, eyes overbrimming, artificially dried. She came into my room. She wanted to tell me, as if she knew the strength of bond between me and Jessica, or if it was a last chance for her to test it. She sat by my bed, starting off with a comment about what I was doing in bed at eleven in the morning. She knew I was far from asleep, my face showed it, my drained energy announced it and above all my silence made it clear.

She started undecided as to whether to say it out loud in one continuous sentence or to break the words into smaller groups of half-aggregated syllables, thereby making it easier for her to assess their impact bit by bit and adjust the next part of the sentence accordingly; she opted for the latter. Tina's friend (that's my sister's), Jessica, had died that morning, my mother finally breathed. She had become ill suddenly, in the middle of the night, she continued. My father had tried to get a doctor in time, but it was too late when he arrived. She was assuring me of our good will and care.

There was a silence. I did not ask how she died, but looked away towards the window misting over with the accumulated heat of breath. Was I alright, she asked, turning away from the subject. I answered with a nod or some other falsely affirmative gesture. We will have to tell Tina, she added, returning to the subject. I made no attempt to conciliation. She got up to leave the room, her face wearing a wig of worry and stupefaction.

At the door, she turned to look at me again. 'May be you'll able to tell Tina, gently, between you and her, softly, softly', she asked me. 'I do not want her to feel sadder, as I would cry before I had finished telling her', she explained. 'You're old enough to do this; do you want to?', she asked again. I agreed.

The feeling of being treated as a grown up did not seem as sweet this time as in other, earlier times. Maybe it was no longer an important sign of appraisal; or may be the duty was not clearly stratified into the trickle of her intention. I felt quietly uncaring, numb now. I went to my sister, who was playing in the room she shared with my other, younger sister and my grandmother. I asked her to come with me to the garden where I told her I had something to show her. She jumped up in curiosity and wonder. I walked out of the room with her, ordering my other sister to stay and watch the dolls or some other excuse.

We went to the garden, she demanding to know faster than I could walk, while I was thinking of a way to tell her. We finally arrived at Bertha, my sanctuary and private world. I had not intended to end my steps there, it just happened, without thought. She looked at the old date palm tree, inspected it, expecting to find whatever it was hidden there.

I started to tell her: 'You know Jessica, a few doors down from us, our friend?. She nodded. 'Well she had to go away somewhere this morning. It's a secret, we do not want to tell Aiken' (my youngest sister), 'about it, it's a secret', I repeated. She agreed to keep it from our little sister. 'I am only telling you this because you're bigger', I assured her of the reason. 'Well, Jessica is not coming back ever to see us, she is gone forever', I spouted it out, half-believing it myself and half-starting to weep. She asked why. I looked at her hard, tears streaming down my face: 'She's with God now'. I was saying the words without any planned sequence, but effectively gave them utterance.

My sister took about a minute to evaluate my last message before starting to cry herself. I hugged her, she hugged me harder, we both cried on each other's shoulders, for the lengthiest part of an hour. I observed that the pain was flowing more easily but was of less magnitude when I cried with her. She was sobbing while I was imagining Jessica in the same spot, smiling back at me, refusing to confirm the message I had just conveyed. My tears belied my imagination and showed my acceptance, while my mind was the opposite, undecided.

I confessed to Tina, that I had liked Jessica a lot. She was somehow not surprised, but turned to me with a brief comment: 'I know, she was your special friend'. She dried her tears faster than me and ran inside to my mother. I stayed where I had first found my now lost Jessica.

Three days passed, quiet and reserved. The fourth day was different. It was the day of the burial, I was neither invited to attend nor was expected to. In the middle of the morning, I received a letter, which I took from the postman. I had answered the door, as no one else was in the house. I was surprised: it was addressed to me and carried no return address on the back. The writing on the front was familiar and at the same time unrecognisable, written in great agitation and hurry. I was surprised: who would send me a letter?. I opened it with little care and more effort, since it was glued tight, I had to rip its seam to liberate the five pages imprisoned within.

The letter was from Jessica, each page initialled, starting from page 1. It was dated: today and written on brown and green colour that mingled all over each page with, a purple haze where the two colours blended at random in an artistic effect. On the first line was a note: This is to be mailed by someone you never met.

The first paragraph read: Hello, Edmund. I hope you did not get a frightful surprise when you opened these folded pages. I write this note of explanation to say least of all farewell. I do not want you to feel obliged to read it today if you don't feel you want to, but do not throw it away yet. This is not a blaming note and in way relates whatever I decide to do tonight directly to you. It's a note saying what I feel, as I feel it.

I was stunned with the number of capital-lettered 'I's' I had already noted in the contents. I have always liked to use a small 'i' when I write anything. Rose once attracted my attention to the rule: 'I' is always in capitals. I replied that it was ignorant to assert one's self in arrogance and that I did not believe in it. Obviously Jessica had been told the same and had accepted it as a rule without such metaphor deeply analysed.

Anyway, I have always written it as a capital when quoting someone else. I have never presumed to exaggerate or downgrade their portion of such expression. Jessica is important to me still, she can comfortably write her I in capitals; I do not judge her prerogative.

The next paragraph read: Firstly, my family had decided to leave in a few days and emigrate to Israel. The decision was confirmed to us children last of all, tonight. I was asked to pack what I could in one suitcase. How much of my life can I fit in one suitcase?. It seems that we are not to tell anyone anything, except that we are going on a holiday. We might get into trouble if anybody knew where we were going, although I heard my father tell my mother that if people knew we were emigrating, he would get less for the sale of his business and house. Someone I have never known will be here, sleeping in my bed, a foreign skin between my sheets, giving them new loyalties and purpose. I refused to accept and comply to leaving here. My father spoke to me gently at first, but probably like all other fathers, when he felt he was losing the argument, he slapped me, for the first time in his life, shaming me with our whole purpose of being, the promised land and *our* duty to our own people. I abstained from speaking, as always.

The third paragraph ran: My mother tried to comfort me when I told her I did not want to leave. She outlined the advantages and enticements that ranged from living in our *own* house, ours forever, to free this and cheaper that, more toys, going into the army when I was older and shooting guns, ('isn't that fun!', my mother asserted). I could be a nurse in the army if I wanted to. My mother also explained how my father was getting less and less business all the time; the political situation was getting hard, people are hardening their attitudes towards *us*, Jews. I do feel sometimes that my father comes home stressed in the middle of the day; someone has said or done something to him. I never felt anything like that, especially from your family; you were, no still, are still my best, most compassionate friend. I always thought you'd never be like those others. You were always special, very special. My family are going, there isn't anything to indicate a hope for the opposite.

Page two started with the fourth paragraph of the letter, short and more neatly written: One enticement, as my mother thought and dwelt on, was my cousin, waiting for me in Israel. He's two years older than me and in three years' time I'm expected to be his wife, cook his food for him, wash his clothes, raise his children and be the third most important person in his life after his mother and father. And, yes, inherit or share in his vast wealth. It was arranged when we were four years old. I don't remember, but I am assured it is true.

The next paragraph was not as long: I do not want to leave here, leave you and my life as it is. I am quite happy here. Adults have this urge to force unforeseen decision on us children, who must comply, even if it's not fair, who must neither disagree or question so firm a decision. I wish sometimes I was born older or not at all. I suppose you would willingly follow your family to hell if that's where they were going. But I am to go to unfamiliar fields, new people, a new ethos and a new existence, to be offered to some one I do not know or love, expected to offer my *virginity* as proof of future faithfulness and past purity. I cannot offer such a proof and you know why. No, no, I am not blaming you, *I* wanted it to be exactly where and how I wanted it to be. You may think it childish of me, but as I see it, I don't think I could be, ever will be happier with any man, for the rest of my life.

The next paragraph was shorter: I have two options, to go along with my family or to decide to stay here one way or another. Maybe if I told my mother I had been with some boy, not mentioning your name, she might understand and they might decide to quit leaving. I might get to stay or be left behind with my aunt's children. I have to let her know I am no longer a virgin. She must know how I feel about leaving, really, and about marrying the pre-assigned cousin, husband to be.

I was reading the sequence of someone's present, feeling as if I were in a revolving door, trapped, too afraid of chance stopping its pace.

The next page was smudged with the dried residue of pain. It started: Maybe I shouldn't be confessing this, but you were not the first, though you'll probably be the last. I have to clear you; it was not your fault, you're not responsible for my degeneration. I felt something other than lust, more than just being, lesser pain and loss, something more honest than promises, be it love as you confessed it, or warmth of heart, I feel all of that when I am with you. The point of proof is that I forget my world, the day's confusion and even the first boy I had, when I am with you. Life seems purposeful and whole, tender and colourful whenever we meet or share an hour. The obsession of pacing after the painted laugh, without a division between reality and fantasy, is in all of us, but I always found the fantasy real with you. Forgive me, please forgive me. You have given me times of joy and less guilt, apart from not telling you I love you. The words of such a confession are demanding and a commitment to eternity. I did not want to lie to you, I could not guarantee it forever.

The contemporary character of love did not surrender to my unleashed questioning. I was residing within short distance of her hurt, but with what seemed a temporary avidity of her feeling. I did think at one time that I had heard her respond to my confession of love, I observed it but never logged it in the course of our relationship.

The next paragraph was short: Whatever you think of me now, do not judge my statements in a simple reaction. Whatever I do next, I am doing it for myself, its good or bad outcome has no reference to your action or inaction, it's just the way my will will trespass on life. Again, I do not want to leave here. I cannot stand the anguish of stammered unfamiliarity at this stage of my life, not after the past year.

The last paragraph was written in a different colour of ink: I apologise for the glue smeared on the envelope but I had to open it several times after I had sealed it, to insert more and more. The inconsistent stickiness is to ensure its staying closed till you have opened it. I feel now I cannot offer anyone anything worthy of giving, although you always had a way of making life worth living when we were together. You may not agree with me, if I told you that songs, laughter and tears are all shallow reproductions of happiness and sorrow, as false as the feeling that does not last its duration in strength and goodness. Remember the butterfly on the hedge. Spare the prayer and the candles, sacrifice none for me. May He, God, forgive me. I am sorrier than you can ever know.

The signature read: Yours, always a butterfly, Jessica.

The day was nearly spent. I sat, sunk in apathy in the darkness of the room, in early afternoon, with the curtains drawn. The gentle light of the morning had already turned into the heat of afternoon, undignified by even the slightest, most superficial attention. The letter was there, in my hand, the knowledge of her death common and confirmed. She was the Sylph fleeing away in front of me, my eyes saw her and my lips whispered her name.

For the moment, I did not seek the absolution of detail and involvement. I did not consider it worthy of debate, excitement of thought or prejudice of feeling.

Yet there was anger at the world of adults that instructed children and made them orphans of their friends, that big world of a power sitting in judgement on small entities of beings, watching, unmoved by outcome or behaviour, entering deeds across the corresponding pages of net results, without inquiry, without amendment or reaction for future reference, logging a valuable loss nakedly and objectively as merely another loss.

The letter was simple in its instructions and its presentation of events. The rumour that she had died in her sleep was treacherously compromised. When I read the letter again two days after its arrival, her words lay unchanged and still unyielding. I would have accepted it in its plain contradiction of feeling if I had not been intimately chosen as the source of past happiness and present beneficiary of her confessions. One plausible explanation, that she was carrying a child, strung the soul tightly and overlaid its restless hurt with an agitation far more restless, if less pronounced, than a simple accusation of guilt or penance.

Like an aged animal anticipating deliverance and sleep, I waited two more days before visiting Jessica's family to usher my condolences into their lives and at the same time seek information and understanding. There were two other people in the house, Jessica's two cousins, a brother and sister. The male cousin, a man of twenty or so, was formal and cold in his speech. The other cousin, a girl of eighteen, was friendlier and her words as well as her manner indicated that we had met. Her familiarity with my name, pronounced without prior hesitation, with my age, school and my sisters' names, was almost puzzling; I could not remember meeting her before.

She asked me if I knew her name, Joan. I had to be honest and deny it. When her brother excused himself and went out, Joan decided to stay behind. We were left in the room talking of such empty topics as the changing season. I reluctantly ventured to express my sense of loss. I had planned not to expose my closeness to Jessica to her cousin and merely wanted to confirm how wonderful she had been as an impersonal acquaintance. Joan seemed surprised at the general tone of my condolences. She came closer to me, hesitated for a short while and asked me if I had received a letter recently.

I was taken by the surprise, Joan was the go-between. I immediately confessed everything, slowly and without omitting any fact or feeling. Again, she seemed quite familiar with what was between us and again I was surprised. Joan was a grown-up replica of Jessica, her mind was similarly moulded, her words as accurate in pleading or instigating her proof of opinion.

She confirmed that Jessica had felt closer to me than to any of her family and especially over the past year. Joan unfolded Jessica's earlier life freely, unprovoked by my anxious seizure of opportunity to know more of Jessica's tender existence.

Jessica had already tried to take her life, once before, a year and a half earlier. She had failed then. That was after she was on a holiday in Tunisia. Her uncle, (her mother's youngest brother), whom they were visiting, had insisted that she would taste some of his home-brew. He insisted on the same, with all those who had attended his house-warming party. After a merry start, dancing and singing, almost everyone was feeling drunk and taking-up what ever space there was on the floor and fallen asleep.

In the morning, they found the celebrated uncle in Jessica's bed, both were asleep, naked. He had taken most of her pride, he had slept with her. She was barely conscious when he had his way with her. Jessica had been stolen forcibly of her innocence and her purity for ever.

The bruises on her body and the bloodied sheets were slight indications of what had happened. They were inadmissible in defence of Jessica's and as proof of her opposition in face of her uncle's will.

The uncle tried to amend his sorrow with an offer of marriage, by an old, and now unpractised, custom of the clan as he was religiously allowed to arrange the marriage of his niece to his son if she had wanted to and if her parents had accepted his offer. Jessica, boldly, refused, she hated him now, hated the singular mention of his name and was not about to consent to carrying it for the rest of her life and extend it to any of her children. She had not experienced such hate or worded it as transparently before in her life.

Jessica and her parents stayed in the uncle's house for over two months, racked with indecision and suffering, often balanced between blame and anger. The family finally arrived home without resources and fearful of being exposed. The problem further sickened them all a month later, when they found that Jessica was carrying her uncle's baby, a baby to which she had a month earlier refused to give legitimate rights and being. It was such bad luck, her mother thought, that it should happen in the month in which Jessica must have got her first period and so young at that.

There was one way forward, out of shame: Jessica was brought to a (wise) old woman, a distant aunt of some sort, who devised the extraction of the child and erasure of any possible condemnation of its family's morality. With herbs, prayer and sharp needles, the quest for ignorance but also for secrecy was made.

Jessica was seriously ill for many months after that. Her doctor, another distant relative, probably knew when he examined her, but never uttered a word in discussion. He simply attended her and led her by the hand to physical recovery. Her mental recovery was not his concern. On his last visit he told her as a final opinion that she might never conceive again. Jessica was sober and undisturbed by the news. Joan thought it was hard on her, but Jessica never complained, sometimes even expressing her relief over it. 'Whether she meant it or not, we'll never know', Joan confidently concluded.

Jessica's family had convinced themselves, and more importantly Jessica that she had to have the abortion. It was the only way left open to them in the circumstances, as they knew that to force her to accept the offer of marriage would mean that she might try to commit suicide, again, and that she might succeed the next time she tried.

The letter, now, was simple in its explicit message after Joan's evocation of such a short life in turmoil. It's not what we could have done to change the world that catches us unawares, it's what the world has destined our action to be in our final digit on time. The complex nature of death was only simplified by its end result: hers. Even if I thought of its leading events in the simplistic progression of a child's mind, the scar could not lose the hurt inflicted by the long war that raged every time I turned my face to my past, aided by a song or part of a forgotten verse faintly read or remembered. Much later on I added alcohol to the list of such pre-requisites of pain. She seems now immortal, for as long as I breathe and maybe beyond, indestructible as those hidden reaches of illogical thought or wishes of impossibility.

Surprisingly, as I remember now, she always knew the sun would shine, irrespective of her life or death. It was as fatal an argument as to debate progress on the basis of a dead end. On fewer than ten occasions, anger was my ultimate solution for thoughts of loss: more than twenty times, it was the play of possibilities or alternatives, a hope to shut the gate tightly, against the random complaint of wind and leaves of autumn, forsaken by unmotherly trees. One fear or another always left us finally bound and sceptical, willing but never hoping further than the horizon, outcasts of a purple sky and a passing cloud, I seemed like that cloud.

I sometimes wonder if she had chosen to be remembered in the only way in which she knew she could not be forgotten. For as chapters close, it is not mere paradox that makes them memorable, but rather the implications of continuity in thought and in the stream of events.

A new paragraph seldom brings characters either defined or implied, a final edge of the cutting thread binding pages past and future, an umbilical cord where detachment means a second and far greater, invisible thought of substantial dependence. If she had left a red poppy behind, it would merely have been as she left it: willing and colourful right to the end of every summer. In every butterfly fluttering across the fields would have been the colour of her eyes; in every butterfly that fell her desire to flee, lamed, the unwritten; in every butterfly kept for show in glass cases the spirit of her words and thoughts of the past, immortal only in suffering. I do not expect to have a woman like her again, neither shall I ever reach into my soul so deeply or sprinkle the sky as I did longing for her.

She was, and rightly so, the woman who had slept with my soul and refused to age according to her body, whose love was mystical, always available and lasting longer than her life for all of mine. When our ribs counted each other's, hers knit with my own, I could conceive of no other joy demanding less; when she held my hand and melted my eyes, I was lost in my own soul; but when she fled into the time of impossibility, I was left hungry forever. I have never smiled as passionately, or fed as fully since then. When I hear my name called in the midst of my thoughts, it is always her moist lips calling.

Sometimes my anger at her loss told me that she was a quest that left nothing for me to reach, a quest in which mere death was unable satisfactorily to explain hers fully; yet I return with ease to my point of departure: she was, is, the only sorrow I cannot ever bear, a decree, that admits of questioning.

The harder part of all acceptance was always nearer to hand, to pull the knife from its point of impact in the flesh where the bleeding had started to clot. Thence come fresh wounds of an old cut, self-inflicted by a shining blade, unaggressive until the rust remains in the colour of the soft-grained skin. She lies within me, a dream in awakening within the self, a tattoo on the soul, grey-coloured breath bequeathed to the cold air. Her faithfulness lives on to me alone, untarnished and unyielding, forceful and unchanging in its will.

If ideas of mortality were unforgetfulness and fortitude, then life is a philosophy, a momentary regression into reality. After that, our dreams make up the play, we are only marionettes on string that can be bent to purpose, our fate lies behind the thick curtain of time, useful in the face of expediency and shadowy or bright for so long as the lightbulb's shine. After that comes darkness, futile regrets and the other face of reality.

Every soft heart deserves a white rose, every soft eye deserves a glittering return and every soft touch deserves another. In the light of day to come none is forgotten, like Jessica, like Jessica.

8

Consonants of Silence

For as long as we solace the day's brightness with dark passages in nights of deprivation, for as long as some element of surprise enlightens our docility made heavy with years, we may grow dull in our routine, willing and passive. Yet a shallow after-thought acknowledged the strong sense of absence prompted by Jessica, a failed blossoming, beyond the inheritance of memory and sadness. It seemed as if everything was ill fated.

A decision to resort to books in the absence of a lover lasts for as long as there is a need to hasten recovery from stammering words, those drums infinitely distant from the horizons of the intellect and dystrophy of the will; it lasts as long prevailing quiet prefers its lone contentment in re-discovery of the world in a clinical reading far from involvement of the flesh or the torture of thought in its survival to remain correct and undisputed as before. The submergence of past-emerged icebergs was a comfort to the mind in a truce of almost faltering self-preservation. It was a matter of the survival of sanity and life's causal participation.

There were these wonderful companions of classical plot and trivial presence, those one-time-is-enough acquaintances and those who had a new face each time they were encountered; but ultimately there were those that brought memory forward as easily as they had forsaken the reality of undeclared terms. I felt mine must have been the greatest drive to read since words were once experimental and exciting; a re-coinage of previous use. For two years after the departure of Jessica from physical life, these new and old premonitions of being, these books of every skin and allure created a world indifferent to the real world. I was happy or carried in contented emotion, tranced out of pain. Time had lost its urgency and its voice protesting against ageing waste.

At the age of nearly sixteen, I successfully tackled the new school for the intermediate certificate of (formal) education in parrot-like assembly of information and set books. I was easily accepted after their entrance exam. The result was satisfactory on paper, an artificial glow of success, a smile and a gesture of appreciation: my father warmly endorsed my mother's delight in the distinction grades which her only son had achieved with ease and without demanding his reward for his valuable effort.

It was also time to receive instruction from foreign teachers. I was moved to a private school, an American missionary secondary school. The teachers were still unaware of the transition. A boy like me had already endeared himself to them. A sixteen year-old was a child to them, ready for re-moulding. I welcomed the change from the local teachers I had had so far.

With it came an energetic, gradual and softly-requested encouragement to revere Christianity, to change thought, or to amend it from that comprehensive, Catholic way in others to the value-driven dependence of the structured lines of an universal church. I was not pushed into acceptance as were some of my Catholic friends, who were tried and wilfully compromised into submission through every kind of word and discussion of theology, through indoctrination without the thrust of the cane, but nonetheless scarring in what the mind was exposed to. There were five American teachers who were decisive in that drive, and one old lady teacher who was the only one of the band not to participate in the campaign.

Miss Prudence Walker was seventy years old, with the tenacity of a fifteen year-old girl. She taught us English and spent hours listening to us repeat lessons pre-recorded on large reels of intimidating tapes, quite happy at the way we made and retained mistakes. One approach I fondly remember was her differentiation of the degree of aspiration in reading 'p' and 'b'. She aligned a piece of paper with her face and pronounced 'p' to make the paper sway away from her mouth. When she did the same with the letter 'b', the paper hardly quivered. The demonstration was effective in persuading those of us who found a problem in grasping such a difference of sound between the two letters; one particular pupil argued he required time to adjust to this differentiation in the absence of the letter 'p' in Arabic. Previous teachers of English had not had sufficient enthusiasm for the language to correct this obvious deficiency in pronunciation.

Miss Walker had other qualities besides the patience and the perseverance expected of her. She had books to encourage reading of the prerogative that others had assumed to express near-criminal views of the world. Her belief in the freedom of self-opinion had its visible barriers, limiting that freedom to art and enclosing thought and philosophy in closely-watched fashion; communism was not on the agenda and socialism was a disease, whereas capitalism was freedom to itself away from the topics on which discussion was refused. Politics was more than a sensitive subject: it was forbidden.

Miss Walker saw my enthusiasm for the language and the origins of those phrases that summarised wisdom, indignation and indifference. She lent me Othello and Macbeth, offering them in terms of the required essay and in answer to an already formatted question: What was the definition of their life? I found Othello giving superficial assent to life and Macbeth enduring it to reach something that in an undeterminant way was better.

My verdict was made difficult by quotations, in support of claims. The language seemed opaque, made up of a lumpy aggregation of terms of reference. The common ground of both their lives set values that veered away from religion and at the same time were entwined by religious controversy. The compromise seemed unethical, yet every word of expression was a compromise of opinion, each character had his own concept of the sacred instruction.

I was asked what my religion taught on particular points of life, what were we supposed to do here or there. I was ambiguous, not out of bigotry or ignorance, but out of a discreet non-alignment with it or any religion. I still had my problems with accepting God's impartiality on power and the fate of his subjects. I was, also, not in favour of damning any other person, committed as I was to the quiet flow and homogeneous equity of all religions. I was not interested in overhauling or glorifying any existing format, since all seemed equally sanctioned.

I would have preferred such discussion postponed until there was some interest, would have preferred to explore perceptions of religion rather than the strict confines of labels. Miss Walker asked me to stay behind after the last class and visit her in her house, one of two houses in the grounds of the school. I accepted. She asked me in, her voice informal now after hours, mixing with and masking the dryness of the hinges on the light wooden-framed fly-meshed door into the sitting room. There were other people in the house, meeting in the sitting room with its few pieces of furniture. She brought me into her room which looked the opposite, congested with books dealing with every colour, race, creed and concept.

As I consumed her homemade lemonade she sat on her bed. I was sitting facing her, in her reading chair. She asked me in some form or another what I thought of the school and of its name in particular. I hadn't really paid any attention to that although I had written it so many times on every book and note pad I had. The school was called High Hope secondary school for boys. The Arabic translation of the school's name was not so strong, pertaining as it did to a more delicate hope than the bold hope of its English version. In Arabic it was called Rajaa', which also meant a request. A better and closer translation to its English name might have been Amal.

I thought of the name in its dual possibility and I was about to explain my thoughts when Miss Walker's new voice, speaking Arabic in an almost alien, Egyptian accent, surfaced to interrupt me and make the same point. I was shocked at the pitch of her voice and her knowledge of Arabic. She seemed delighted to have found me full of analysis and meriting her interest. I responded with gratitude and much appreciation.

Her opinion of every word, in any language, was unique. There were similarities and correspondence between words when travel-ling from one language to another which predicted a degree of conformity in all languages, although they did not portray its strength. When more than one word expressed the same or similar meaning in different guises, the correspondence with other lan-guages becomes harder to conceive of. The thoughts of a man thinking in Hebrew may reflect softness or harshness that another thinking in Arabic may find unexpected or unacceptable, she asserted.

I was of the opinion that such a discrepancy might reflect ways of thinking rather than the actual correspondence of similar words. She seemed happy with our difference of opinion, since it gave her an opening for her next foray into my mind: What do you feel about the Jews, she asked hastily, making good the possible loss of a line of inquiry presented by her first example and my passive reaction to it. I was honest: 'I think of them as maybe a special people intellectually. In one sense they probably have had to be, to survive as a minority', I added, amplifying my short-worded opinion.

She had been in Egypt during the tri-national assault in 1956, when the British, French and Israelis had attempted to take the Suez Canal. The good offices of the Americans, which had helped to halt the assault, had resulted in a show of good will by both people and authorities towards her and her colleagues, she was happy to say. It made contacts with the people on the ground easier and her learning of their habits and ways of thinking more practical. 'The Egyptians could never think like you', she announced smilingly.

I replied that I did not know what the Egyptians thought, but I that experienced no pressure of conflicts in deciding what I thought of the Jews; they were people with certain characteristics of thought, as any other people. Rights and wrongs were embedded in the nature of each one of us. She countered my opinion with germ doubt: what about detailed differences of religion?, how did it come about that God's absolute instructions emerged in different formulae?. One group must be right and the rest wrong, she asserted. I was not sure what she was asking me to exhibit and caution inhibited the expression of my opinion.

Could it be that the difference in God's emphasis on essential matters of importance to each group is indicative of the change in his thought, progress and curbing of his own manners, I asked in reply. She smiled again. Was the use of weapons in the propagation of religion an indication of increased civility or an of greater extremism in the process of man's advance through time, she put forward, raising yet more doubt. Nearly all religions seemed to have advanced, to have conquered more ground. Their followers had the same sense of duty and the same determined understanding of the violence required to achieve an effect, she said in conclusion.

I protested gently that every religion teaches compassion, the core of all godly intention on earth. How could any one ignore it?. Her eyes were lit with that look of how naive, how warmly childish and honest you are. She looked away for a minute, to hide the remainder of her thought. She returned to face me with her lightly worded caution: this is the second face of human nature; we mean what we do not imprint with our deed, we often do what we are not supposed to think of. Religion sometimes channels other undesired flaws: people may look for conquests of profit and send expeditions against barbarians to bring them into the light; yet those same powerful people exchange that gift for the certainty of often reaping the barbarian's worldly goods for as low a price as possible. The immorality of war is neatly packaged with religion and the duty of conversion to righteous convictions. It was never a fair trade, she concluded, her honesty exploding.

I was surprised: it made logical sense, but from the mouth of a missionary (the school was supposed to be a missionary school) it was illogical.

The possible achievements of reaching new audiences, of opening up to learning all those native minds, who of necessity had to be taught to read so that they could read the Bible, thereby unleashing their ability to travel to other worlds and different times, did not, in my opinion, seem so unfair a trade for acquiring the new religion. If any man had that chance and took it further towards discovery, he would have achieved something for himself. If he did not, he was not worthy of thought; what difference to humanity would it be in that case if he was of the old religion or the new? Nothing at all, I concluded.

She was not quite happy with my line of thought and impartial indifference: 'That means that a worthy man is compromising his intention in acquiring the new religion, he is using it to go further away from simple acceptance, he is opportunistic in his aims', she said unhappily. 'I only thought it was inevitable, without judging the man', I asserted. She seemed disappointed: I had arrived at the wrong conclusion, she readily confessed. I ventured then: 'Maybe if there was no religion, just a mere conscience, we'd all be happy, in eternal peace, unthreatened by wars'. She became angry: 'Now you're talking like a communist! No, no matter how imperfect religion may be, one can not compare it to being suspended in mid air, without godly guidance. Always remember that, a conscience is not enough on its own without religion', she instructed me.

I thought: How could anyone accuse me of being a communist? I have to correct that. I told her briefly of the old man, torn and bloodied by those who promised protection to the people from their greed, those who proclaimed the equality of all men but practised killing men's souls and even their bodies if they did not possess the popular perspective. What those people had done in the absence of law, in its empty courts, in this country for the first three years of the revolution could not be erased, forgotten or forgiven; it was inhumane. She was silenced by my rage and cutting words.

It was time to leave. I asked to be excused and was allowed to, with a smile. On the way home, I stopped on the tiny bridge that separated the school block from the street where my house stood. The nearly-dry river had carried with it an umbrella for a distance I could not determine. The anti-rain device seemed implanted top down in the mud, beached by the shallowness of the mid-stream flow. I gazed at the abandoned object, useless in the heat of September. I felt some common ground, for it seemed to share my reflection on the passage of the afternoon so far.

Miss Walker had not achieved whatever she was trying to. I felt it in her last instruction and the permission to leave she openly granted me.

I had emerged unaffected by my thoughts on the forms of religion. I seemed neither to conspire against it nor to support it. I decided to deny effective access to further religious discussion with Miss Walker, I aspired to please her and not antagonise her further, an action I seemed to have taken many times before in my life, when I really appreciated a person but was unwilling to be forcibly convinced by his or her opinion. It was an acceptable and practical compromise.

The house was abnormally quiet when I arrived home. I struggled to do my homework, my eagerness already sapped somehow by the length of my discussion and the points raised and levelled with Miss Walker. My father was entertaining a guest in the sitting room. I entered the room to greet the guest, as instructed by my mother. The man was familiar but not readily identifiable in the first instant. He was Tamara's brother, the one who had collected her from our house some five or six years ago. I felt delight in seeing him once I recognised him and greeted him warmly.

At some point in the conversation, I asked him how Tamara was. My simple question was treated with extreme caution by the two men and I received a muddled and evasive answer. The atmosphere changed dramatically to one of solemn faces and inquest-like trends. My father, who did not look comfortable talking to the

man, became more uneasy. I was puzzled and felt as if I had tapped
a pent-up vein of festering sorrow and hardship. After a little while,
my father asked me to go and finish my homework, without asking
if I had already done it, as he normally did.

I could feel that something was out of joint between the two
men, especially after my innocent inquiry. I was restless. I went to
ask my mother, but she was just as agitated. In the corner of her
eyes there was that shadow of sadness, as if another nudge would
bring the flood gates down mercilessly. I persisted in asking. She
was standing in the kitchen, her back turned to me, her hands
giving the impression of being busy while her movements over the
cooker were designed, at best, to hide her uncertain expression.

She told me not to pursue the matter further, not to disturb the
dust of long-stored archives of helpless consequences. I did not
know whether that meant to forget it, or wait for another, less
pressurising moment. I could not let the matter rest before I knew
what had happened. My intransigence arose not out of stubborn
teenage curiosity, but out of that partial devotion to memory that
had always stayed restless with longing for Tamara and that feeling
of lost contact with an elapsed time which sometimes had erupted
into anger with her for not trying to write to me. I had the notion of
being incomparably important to her as she still was to me, a
stinging regret at the deep pain that would not be eased by her
contrition for not corresponding with equal effort and sincerity.

The pain of deep longing I felt for her seemed unworthy of her if
she was trying to lead her life without the slightest concern for me.
She might not have cared as deeply for me as she must have known
I did for her: these thoughts of unreturned faithfulness were real
and destructive.

I went to bed, not to sleep, but to be alone with my soul, to cry
away the hurt of despondency and the pillage of hope in life. My
mother called me for supper. I did not want any; I did not feel
hungry and if I was I did not want to eat it with Tamara's brother.
My mother served everyone food and came up to my room. She
asked sternly why I was boycotting the guest. I claimed loss of
appetite, being tired, sleepy and so on. She was not convinced for
some reason or another, bade me good night and returned to the
guest promptly.

I could not sleep. At about ten o'clock in the evening, when
every one had either retired to sleep or left, she came into my room.

She could detect from my fast breathing that I was not asleep, although I had my eyes shut. She sat on my bed, her hand stroked my forehead in caresses I had not experienced for long, since she had convinced herself I had grown up. She called my name softly, as if wishing I was really asleep.

I opened my eyes, stretched my arms around her and hugged her, my face nearly hanging over her shoulder, hanging like a child in search of attention and a little more comfort. My voice was almost a whisper as told her I missed Tamara and wished she would come to visit. My mother's arms tightened round me, as if not to lost me before the tide that was about to dash spray in our faces and paralyse our touch with restless times.

She softly shaped her voice, absorbing the accumulated silence: 'She has passed away, she passed away over six years ago, she has passed away, my son'. My voice rose with surprise and as I lifted my face to face hers: 'How? when did you know? why did she . . . ? I could not find the appropriate ending to the question.

She quietened my rebellious outrage by pulling my face harder towards hers: 'Look at me. A girl makes a dismal mistake and she pays with her life for it. It's different for a boy. I never thought it more than murder, but for her brothers it was justified, more than that, it was acceptable, not just allowed by law as a common judgement', she thus outlined the matter.

'All of us women are briefed with such danger from the age of puberty, even from our aspiring youthful years of eight or nine', she added. I replied angrily that I could not accept the same happening to either of my sisters; it was like living with a death threat over one's head. Were purity of mind and sanity of compassion not factors to be taken into consideration in a decision as final as that when a girl's life was to be ended?, why should any act be so drastic as to warrant death, especially when the girl had not taken any one's life in the act? I asked and asked and asked, but my mother was not about to condemn society in an attempt to retrieve the irretrievable.

She commented by way of warning: 'The boy who asked her to run away with him knew the rules and the possible result. He's as guilty of causing her to lose her life as her brothers are'. She got up from my bed, moving towards the door: 'You should learn from this; every time you sleep with some one, think: "are these hours worth the costly loss of the girl's life tomorrow?" '.

She closed the door quietly behind her, leaving me to a torrent of sorrow and anger: I don't want to belong to these people, I raged, I don't want to tolerate their presence with its life-cheapening excuses, I want to be free from this heritage of indifference to anything but a set of penalty applications, this heartless inversion of despondency over life.

I want to be somebody else, I wished, someone with a different name and thoughts. I want to be different, born again without exposure to the real consequences if I fail to escape the cage of this invisible matrix of pain. I wish now I had already died, before facing such hard knowledge. Jessica was intelligent enough to leave life before this deluge of transparent inanities, of the absurdities of violent conformity to the rule of society. How I envied Jessica, such resolve and courage, such boldness. In the midst of my pain, my words could not cleanse my hurt, my silence coloured my consonants yellow. I looked at my wrists: I am a coward, I shall live.

9

Pen Pals in Interludes of Hunger

At seventeen, a few months after I had laid the foundation of my grave lack of interest in the world, I was back to reading books. I looked at the world perfunctorily through opaque lenses that reduced all bright colours to dull. The profanities of the world have acted like an instructive pumice on my life, delaying reaction and interest in its importance; time has then become a passage of inconsequential dust.

My former body heat now lived in houses of dimly-lit windows; sex was a hobby of the past, almost forgotten in a field of rust-coloured weeds of discontinuity of manner and thought. My dependence on nature, experienced for five years, had now been unfairly discarded as an unnecessary and pretentious activity of past era, a passage once lively, now cancelled because of loss of popular demand, a restriction laid firmly on the coming years that sought peace and silence, dreaming in delicate apathy.

Miss Walker, worried by these new trends, called me into her office: I was trailing in school and showed an almost general lack of interest and poor performance. I was not worried, I still had just enough interest to allow me to pass my exams, sufficient for my purposes of advancing to the next class. She thought it a waste of my potential. I disagreed mildly. She handed me a new book, one she had talked about in class, called 2001 Space Odyssey or something like that. She thought I would enjoy the mixture of science and philosophy, intermingled with future notions of travel.

I read its first three chapters, skipped the next two and went on to the seventh. The book was odd, I did not miss the middle, which I had deliberately avoided reading. After two weeks or so, I returned it, with thanks. She took it up the minute I placed it on her table and inspected it. She quickly spotted the pages still tightly packed in the middle and asked me if I had read it all, cover to cover. I denied such absolute interest in the book. She then proceeded to establish the reason. I had none that would pass her inquisition. When I pointed out that I did not miss the middle part of the book, that it seemed quite all right without it, she marked her surprise with an exclamation of half-belief and reluctant acceptance.

I decided to expose the central argument of the book, as I saw it: The man, the central character (I forgot his name), was facing this tablet, this solid manifestation of his destiny. This metal template was from some out-of-universe force, maybe even God. He was chosen although he did not know why. I explained further: After seeing it for a few times, it was only on the final time it appeared that the tablet seemed to have an important purpose in appearing (to the author and presumably) to the main character (I failed to remember his name again). I went on: Life with all its advancement in technology and rules was still, even at times imperfect. God still needed to manifest himself or his will (laid down on the tablet) to some people to effect the corrections necessary for perfection of this ever-sinning mankind. I stopped abruptly before making the final deduction, uninterested in its outcome.

She was surprised with such an interpretation. She had to interrogate, such was her reflex and sat up in her chair: 'If what you saw in the book was correct, what would be the final outcome of such interaction of thought and instruction between God and man?'. I was unwilling to contribute my ruling, reluctant to voice my verdict on common humanity.

After being asked twice, I finally decided to unveil a milder version: 'We shall conform for a few decades, maybe even centuries, before we re-interpret God's instruction differently', I said. 'God will then have to bring about a new prophet, start again'. She asked me how was I sure of this. I simply pointed to the tens of prophets we had had to date, too many, reflective of our failure if not of God's will. Sooner or later the message would lose its value.

I surprised her again. I decided to leave her office before she let the discussion get into its stride. I went out, distinguished by neither valour nor courage, nor by strength of analysis. I neither expected praise nor valued it somehow, now.

In the next class, Miss Walker proposed to us an interest with a new outlook. She brought the addresses of three pen-pal clubs, asked us to choose two of them and to start writing a noticeboard-like advertisement of ourselves to be sent to the clubs, outlining our interests and giving general information on our age and preferences. We were encouraged to write to the world about our ideas, about things in our lives. She wanted it done soon, so that some replies might be received after the end of the mid-term break.

I wrote to the two addresses I had chosen. One was in England, the other in the United States of America. Then wrote out the second address in full. She carefully examined our letters and the envelopes. She asked me why I had spelled out the full address and not simply put 'USA'. I replied smartly that the abbreviation could mean 'Union of South Africa'. She was impressed with my care, but I could tell from her facial muscles that she hated the comparison.

It was nearly three months, nearing the end of the school year before I received two letters: one from a city called Bradford, in England, from a twenty-three-year-old girl, named Claire; the other from a man of undisclosed age, called Robert, living in Washington State, on the Pacific Ocean.

Both letters were introductory letters, setting out general interests and the usual impersonal-sounding details, as clinical as a curriculum vitae, written to generate a strong impression and continuing interest.

I wrote back in faster time, enclosing a recent photograph and requesting one from each of my new pen friends. It was difficult to dissociate writing to someone whom I had not seen. I felt it would be more realistic and easier on the mind to look at the person to whom I was writing my thoughts. I was hoping to receive colour-prints of them, although I had only sent a two-tone photograph of myself.

The second letter from Claire was warmer, asking in detail about my life and opinions. She was appreciative of the photograph forwarded, repaying me with a colour photograph. The picture was of her standing up and in full body length, that left no need to describe what she looked like. She was bare-footed, clad in a thin cotton dress that was wet from the sea in the background. Her feet were a softer shade of white than her arms and face. Her expression was one of silky, healthy contentment.

She was a student, studying science, in her final year at university. She had labelled herself lightly as not greatly experienced in the world and its inhabitants. Her family she labelled as grossly religious while she was not. She came from a little island near by, Ireland. She had travelled to escape, to see a new world and unfamiliar outlooks, she was curious to discover the unknown. In her own opinion she was freshly optimistic.

Robert also replied with a colour photograph. He looked about thirty-five or so, thin but not underfed, of medium height and with short hair. He had just come out of hospital, having been in an institution for five years, after being shot in Vietnam. He was much happier and older now than when war had started some six years before. His interest in religion reflected his appetite for philosophy and the quantification of pain, of the world's infinite readiness to seek and destroy its human face. He seemed not ready to concede, but near-the-edge portrait of the world as he saw it, made it hard for him to smile for as long as he was unable to ignore the stitches growing in his flesh and past wounds. He always awaited pay day to test his aptitude in bouts of alcohol.

I asked him more than once, in the letter that followed: what being in the army felt like. In his early letters, he always seemed to avoid the subject, tactfully.

In his third letter he included an undated, stapled bunch of pages, quite detached from each other. He seemed to be responding to the light-hearted letter full of questions I had sent him earlier. Robert was revealing himself on paper, to the light and maybe to me. He had written an account of what he thought of the world; it was written in groups of different sizes, pieces of paper, as if it was collected over a period of indeterminate length. He named the bunch of papers as: 'Premonitions of Robert after Vietnam'. In the sequence they were put, they read:

My father, a four-star general, told me today: 'We're going to bomb China with nuclear bombs. If the 'Russkies' interfere, they will get it too. I want you to know that I love you, son, always.

He continued in the next page: In Vietnam, I had always felt that within the confinements of my heresy lies a bridge of hope, a poppy with red tentacles and a gasp of withering heat. Avid, more reluctant than the enforced pressure of will, the day always announced its fear, in total disinheritance of thought and infested with cloud-gathered gloom. Fragrances of need were fostered with lines of dispatched breath that were sandwiched beneath the pain and probabilities of failure, a bite on a future forecast of a lavish past and a present deprived of experience; almost all of us looked like John Wayne.

Invisibly, like a faint eye-shadow paint, time was creased over by lack of sleep and dismal daylight; just as easy, to be, the fun-women would ask for the two dollars an hour for body-rent. There was one I visited often first and then lived within her cubicle of heat. She laid her pleasing in dominant horizons of purple and red-orange crossings, dishonestly willing to relinquish the thin thread of another day, always overstretched to the limit of shrill-voiced complaint and a warning of her breaking, uncompromising, abrupt and defeatist.

In Vietnam, after the furious rhythm of the rain, the clouds would discard the pretentious flavour of dampness of the fields that is mixed with the slight abrasion of heat; we were all of us wet in our souls. In total disregard of the soft whisper after sex, the rice dies solemnly, but not in fear, devoid of aggression, bare, stiff, stripped of a gradual regression in the silence of sunlight, while we are boisterous in a gentle wave, shy without remorse, boyish of childhood heat and in sudden surrender to stillness that followed leave of seeding-purpose. Regardless of presentation, the hunger always laid our looks in that preempted silk-feel, allowing dehydration of our mouths, unwilled by moisture and motivated the full hand into a posture of seizure. This is always followed by sadness, immediate, but hesitant to shed further warmth, other than a request for pity. As in sex-forsaken friendship, we seem to let strength out of a narrow barrel as it dictates life. Their soul lies on its face, resting on a badly carved arm, eyes closed, muttering a well rehearsed phrase of prayer. Away from the slight-filtering light, through the hope-stained glass, the other arm holds the rumbling flatulence at bay, even when manners are not a pre-requisite to mercy, in lessening the impact of smiles of pity and floating words of encouragement, from all those who regard the routine as a mere exercise of gratitude, well past duty tightly bound to endurance and the pretences of such understanding; we were in hell trying to justify heaven, we were in Vietnam for an inspired and most valiant purpose.

I did not have the chance to record a vote of no-confidence for origins of the orange sky, yet my sorrow voted for me, in a passive defiance of their hunger, my words echoed the inner of me, sounding hollow after arriving here and my mind had left its restlessness to decay in laden prizes for the rats, on cobbles of grief and memories of glistening grandeur of strength. For the natives and in partial reflection, enlightened by the mercy of soap and tainted potatoes instead of rice, the softness of their degradation is crushed by the hardness of the bread on dry gums. The flair for words is replaced by the hummings of gestures quite inadequate for an honest uplift of grace and the ideology of self-respect, bases of freedom and the butterflies of the crisp morning-air, butterflies that leave no colour on the meadow weeds. None of us can regret fully missing those fleeting chances, nor re-address the day if yesterday came belligerence: both cases are exercises of the mind and seeing unworthy of the time spent due to lack of resolve and loss of will for change and undue aggressiveness. Time honours only that which is worthy of remembrance and that which can be defined as meticulous joy, anything in between is lodged in faint colours ensuing from silly habits of undistinguished interludes. Many words should also be forgotten: unfortunate, inappropriate, even: opportune and wilful, all at the top of a long list of language, unnecessary and uneventful. The latter two, after the orange blitz have been idly sanctioned, a major paradox, a theology of more must and a vast argumentative loss. Conformity of man seems to lie placidly only twice a day: in feeding and shelter, homelessness is within the lay of wasted land and the last uttered word of sorrow. Those with a measured relapse of conformity feel vigorous in spirit, but lacking in its presence. They are plainly fostered by plastic hope, a hope unattainable by swift generous deprivation of soul, self-made and self-hidden; those who do not placate gratefulness with Yes, are those for whom luxuries are bare necessities, broken only in death, unjudged by many as hope. Hope many times makes us dreamy and disloyal to all that is today, not far from erasure of all that was yesterday. Yesterday is only defended by those who can see colour in the closing of a jaundice-darkened eye and the feeling of warmth within the pity-eaten crust of what was naturally, gradually stone-milled bread. Sliced toast had become the delicacy of power and a thought of the popular realistic revolt, refuge an ensemble of tact and partial will towards the hour to declare its peaceable means of destitution. I often wonder whom they do feed and who does show respect to conformity, to the strength of words, shouted not as much in anger as in authority from the other side of the counter, when the soup bequeaths it stinging to the unforgiving face of labour and clean hands of mercy. The Vietnamese can tell the edge of their flesh quite distinctly from the soiled white nail pit: soap is always in contagious demand. It's a luxury bar, once a week, when the feeders demand that they, the fed, use it, so as not to inflict them with the hungry flies that live in irony of the day: they get fed, their hosts get fed too. The instinct, if it dwells in my will still, fails my instigation. Between meals, when the hostile-hearted dance halls close, we may find peace with luck. In a heredity of instant purpose, highly priced, we shall always find criminal predictions of slums and dire contributions with a matching non-self-unity and loss of choices, deleted from memory by act. An apathy of remorse always competes with the hard betrayal of self-confidence and the presence of the limelight allowance of need. The signs of Come in, we're open *always*, are useful then for making fires *only*, destitute of the window-panes that were sacrificed during the casual hunger for left-over sleep, when the owners left their strength for the lease of absence in desertion of relief. Many a time in my many detention-like life in the last month I have felt I wanted to die, but never so much as in this moment, reprehensibly insignificant. From early adolescence I have had an unshakeable belief, a foursome of premonitions, dancing, exchanging each other's arms, separated by an interlude of silence. Each of them is a death at break of dawn, masterminded, dedicated to a Friday, covered with the warmth of sharp, passive pain at a cold pale hour, following an act of diligent love and passion, yet alone before my conscience and naked beneath my soul. I ask not for shallow gluttony of words; when my mind lays its barbed wire breached or when my lips no longer express the life I had in fullness and noise. For a sudden and quite brief moment I open my eyes long enough to glance at the orange sky, overcast with the blue obstruction of a faint white light of helicopter-gunships.

P.S. (in pencil): I am sorry for the nightmare of the day's black reflection. This is my last letter to you and any one. I have decided to re-enlist today, I feel more real under fire than any where else; it is easier to die out there, almost guiltless. These letters may have been a waste of postage stamps, they will not change the sleeping world you live in. My nightmares are real, at least to me. You may, one day, have days like these; when you do you'll understand the reluctance of peace and the prevalence of war. Man can only find refuge in moments of conquering, winning or losing, imposing his will or suffer nightmares of intimidation and defeat. I choose the easy way, to die, under arms. Best of luck to you, a dreamer of sorts and a delicate of soul. (unsigned)

I disliked the letter to the point of harsh ridicule. I took it to Miss Walker, who read it with smiles that resembled only a nervous contraction of the mouth. She explained: 'Some of our boys have suffered more than in terms of physical injury. It is the hidden cost of war, no more visible than a healed bullet hole or a knife cut. It's one of the sacrifices in war.'

I asked her how could she, the compassionate 'Christian', justify war, the taking of life? She was not as supportive as I had expected, yet like my mother she did not condemn a natural phenomenon she could not or will not control.

I asked about the 'Blitz', she explained about the nuclear bomb and about chemicals sprayed liberally to kill thick vegetation, how they were used to limit military casualties even if it meant increasing civilian losses. It was the way to break a nation's spirit, she was almost proud to announce.

I was not pleased to hear her opinion. When she sensed my disgust, she advised me to forget about the letter and to be a boy again. It was a man's affair, she said, and I was too young to be so pessimistic about the world. I would not understand until I became a soldier.

The letter was new material for discussion with Claire, the soft soul of my epistolary friendship. I wrote to her, summarising the latter of that day of confessional, asking for impressions and ideas, for debate and opinion. She was late replying to me, almost two months late.

Claire was unhappy I had raised the subject. She had shut it from her mind since the day her brother, a newspaper reporter, was killed in Vietnam, a bystander driven to his fate by the belief that neutral civilians were safe in a war zone, holding a camera that should be easily distinguished from a killing gun.

Obviously, a gun battle inside the capital, Saigon, was indiscriminate in the treatment of civilians. The autopsy did not indicate whether the small portion of lead was friendly or was sent by

Charlie; it was immaterial then. I apologised in my next letter, saying that I had not thought people from Ireland were in that war. She replied faster than the last time, accepting my apology and crediting my ignorance to pure absence of partisanship. It was a stroke of bad luck, or maybe an innocent choice, that she was hurt and barely-healed wounds reopened.

As for Irish participation in wars, she seemed to have a belief that, whether deliberately or innocently drafted, the Irish were always fighting somebody else's war, with the same result, although they had no real vested interest in any of them.

We exchanged letters regularly. After a period of a year or so I started telling her of my past losses, my hunger for bodily contact, my sexual loneliness and how I had not thought about sex in three years. For an oddly unrealistic reason, I started feeling deep physical attraction for her, even when our fingers had not touched and any intention that they should remain loudly unproclaimed by either of us. Her heartening companionship had retracted my soul from solitariness. I enquired more and more prudently about her love life.

In her next letter she reported honestly: With happy songs and far acclaimed self-imprisonment, this day feels fresh and void of sorrow. She wore her words. The Claddagh ring on the right hand, lavishly polished, keeps its hands closed inward, available to none but the one specified by the heart, she explained. In contrast, a gold-plated wedding ring on the middle finger of the left hand announces loss of virginity in all forms other than in marriage. Although lovers were thin silhouettes of imagination, signets of hope, the heart is faithful, the finger rotates the rings in full belief of the myth (a ritual, practised to hasten the arrival of husbands), and the eyes wonder at every viable enterprise. Amongst the crowd of years in exile, many of which have a turned-up collar, most rival the moment with memory, in examples of solitude hinting at a great withdrawal. A gypsy soul sustains a line of lightly disheartened ballads, barricading in drunkenness and fleeing unhappy parity of clear vision and lost comforts. Her children are all like misty wraiths, non-existent and anonymous with every diligent miracle of the flesh and deep gasping at the end result. She has hard-pressed loyalty to the next gasp of dormant postures, all of her will to gain her need without promise, everything for the sake of independence. A strand of single hair, out of place and unidentified on an infrequently used sheet, indicts princely vanity in being left behind; it rarely provokes any anger but that of failing to remember who had carelessly abandoned it, docilely and passively. The hang-dried sachet of lavender leaves, still fragrant and photogenic in its purple colour and fresh smell, gives justice to enjoyment and future desire.

In a wardrobe of small delicacies, the touch of a fingerprint lived in the softness of the hold, the crave for bed, the delinquent oneness of the spent moment and the slowness of undressing; all were shelters against the cold, a cover amidst shyness and the will to have that which passes with time into anything but hidden warmth and the delicate shades of honesty wanting. Abundance is addictive and never gentle when balanced between a decline in supply and regular surge of demand. At the point of unforeseen withdrawal, it is unforgiving.

The hunger was autonomous, speaking in loud, ominous grumblings with echoes of lent at festive times caught in alcohol-full dragnet of dreams. The shine of the rings was comforting at times of happy disclosures in a shared intent, but less meaningful in the dim-lit passage of movement within the daily array of discarded, opulent and ever-accumulating age.

The laughter-years were mere decadence of chance, when most failed to rise to the sacrificial clearance of the next sabbath willingly. The change in colour-preference as time went by, had left little of doubt as to the thrashing of the conviction that one's body and mind qualities were fading, that age is not on one's side. The will, sometimes, overlooked the possible brightness of later days, as if disbelieving that they could be of value.

In the sequence of time, Claire's youth lay used, the hidden words of each thought disregarded and gently subtle. Her face with its burning will, was laid exquisitely lined unbroken by the sign of time and references of age, indifferent to the twenty-four years past birth; lines uninhabited by fervour, showing the mere passage of dried out tears and the hardened influence of simple worry.

The melodies of siege and insurgence were far from light-footed marches. The wages of experience had clean outlines and definite pleasures; wrapped in the time-coloured ending of exile and forecast probabilities of release if so desired, and cushioned by anxious, optimistic caution and a bellyful of cramped disappointments, mortgaged heavily to a bank of old advertisements and newly-hung possibilities of ownership.

Her strength was fashionably resolute, enduring most loss with ease of payment and long term willingness. Most interruptions were ironed-out: in neat pleat-like coverings of tare, in arrears of brightly-shone light of hope, unmasked by the tall corn of the field. All the smiles and tears that time had brought fitted like fragments into a mind of anticipation, full of boisterous attempt and feminine of warmth.

The still-unpierced ear was neither a sign of underprivileged age, nor a recommendation of sensitive skin above the torment of balancing insecure and flashing earrings. All nights travelled with either acceleration or care were prodigal in fortune and appease-ment, beyond the presence of fate and barely short of the length of a blind conversation.

In the midst of the love-revolution years, notions of not belong-ing, of being unlabelled and totally free were not so revolutionary. I wondered long after her last letter how she could opt for the suspension of entrapment, regardless of how one was opposing it. I was seeing a new species: independent of independence itself.

I had to ask her; I could not set my defence aside, for however long or short a time the intention may have been in good faith to implement it.

She felt it essential to allow a clear interpretation of her thought: 'I am a woman of the new age', she wrote, 'I marry deliberately and when loneliness exceeds the value of my independence. I marry to legitimise my children; I marry when the dialogue dements the point of discussion; when I plan to arrive home at the end of the year; when my parents expect it of me for their sanity of mind and to declare an end to normal treadmill of liking men. He should carry my religion on his soul, so as not to confuse those of our children who will ultimately condescend to accept the farm they inherit. Old, rediscovered boyfriends, especially those we slept with first are the ones we end up marrying. There is less thought and even less discussion about it.'

I distinctly thought: For a long time now, I had supposed women of my skin colour were the only ones who would think like that. The universality of a woman's way of thinking at that age was strikingly unexpected. Although not out of keeping with my judge-ment of womankind, it sat well with my conception of ephemeral relationships between men and women, in an age where love was the golden place that was Xanadu. Everything else was a mirage, unnecessary in thirst but superfluous in every trail, bar a few.

10

Directions of the Wind

It was hard having a destiny of warmth without achieving it. It seemed to lose the scent of all those women I had known in the solemn and dull abrasion of time. Internal fortitude and external irresolution doomed every laugh to be transparent, every deep joy transitory, every wish trapped in disillusion; all awaited their replacement and the alternative face of solitude, all minimised the effort to succeed and rule for ever absolute. Loss did not leave the path indignant, but made it unworthy, harder in the future, more miraculous and unbelievably ill signed.

With those unfortunate inhabitants of dogma there was room for self-conciliation: all pain shall pass, its eventual visits will take us to the dormant waves of new hope in the cycle of regeneration: will lose its sharpness, although it will be never forgotten.

A conclusion of peace within the storm, evading that which related a relapse of continuity to a new start of time, a preference of the eyes to seek new light out of the foggy dew of pain, the ribs to expand in excitement; they now forgot the recent suppression of energy and the mind to activate re-issued invitations to interest: all voted for the passionate potential reward of the leap across, the probabilities of lesser hardships and a better, newer surrender.

For the moment, however, the hunger was not so sharp to motivate a degree of preparation or participation in a new experiment. Arguments in favour of keeping a safe distance urged caution over moving faster than the speed of slow healing.

There were higher moats to jump, there were deeper moats to

cross, be it with the thin trunks of old trees, half-stationary at points of crossing and points of arrival. In January of 1968, I declared to myself: I have acceptable fulfilment in reading, writing and sober correspondence, the physical attenuation of want and need: can be left to another time. It will come, but for now it was not essentially advised.

It was a year of preparation for entering that big mixing pot, university, a pot where ideas would blend gradually and without losing their identity of origin and manner of application. The large numbers of individuals attending promised all that and more.

It was also a year of surprise in discovery: I was mature enough to accompany my mother to London where she was to undergo medical investigation for undetermined feelings of ill health. I had to be with her, comfort her and see that centre of interest, said to be so thriving in people and change.

It was happy news, when it was confirmed in March of 1968. I could not wait to pass my delight on to my pen friend Claire. I anticipated that it could be the last chance to meet her; it was her last year in college, she was bound for home, towards new variables of life that might be inconsistent with her thought and my attention. We agreed to meet as soon as I arrived in London. She was willing and enthusiastic for us to meet for as long as time and opportunity allowed.

At the end of school, in June of that year, I informed Miss Walker of the big forthcoming holiday in London. I kept repeating the name in every sentence as I told her about the purpose of the journey and our plans. She did not look enthusiastic. Her response dampened my eagerness and led me to ask her if she had any advice.

She took a long glance at my smile and the nervous attention I was paying to her reaction, before saying the absolute minimum: 'Just be careful whose bed you end up in'. I was left with my advice, so unexpected, yet as if it was a telepathic response to all of my reflexes. After a five-minute silence, I was given a lecture describing the effects of the unrestricted behaviour of those sex-animals, all the infections and self-demeaning attitudes they exchange, fully licensed as they were in irresponsibility and immorality. The worst species of the above animals were the money-motivated auctioneers of bodies and their diseased and sordid customers. The bordello houses of French literature were tried and judged in ten minutes of morality.

I could almost hear myself think: 'So you agree with Mao Tse-tung regarding this point, Miss Walker? What a coincidence!' I smiled instead of saying what I thought.

In early July, we arrived in London. The summer was already hot for most, but quite cool to those tourists who had yet to adjust to the weather. The journey from the airport to the centre seemed short. New shades of wilted green and grey concrete contrasted with each other in the drowning late afternoon sun. The centre was old, but looked indifferent to its decay: the more ancient the buildings, the more beautiful their design. We were all tired from the seven hours spent in a suspense of anticipation and the immovable seating of the aircraft cabin.

The next morning came quickly. Immediately after we woke, I went down in the coolness of the morning for a walk, armed with a ten-pound note for an emergency taxi back to the flat and a sheet of paper that neatly summarised name, address, passport and telephone numbers. I had written it the night before, before closing my eyes in sound slumber. I had everything planned and carefully executed.

After a short, one-hour walk I returned, the neighbourhood mapped in my mind. We all had breakfast and my mother, a cousin and her mother planned the day: shopping in some department store. I went for the ride and out of curiosity. We were barely two feet inside the door when a man came running up, calling out with great gaiety and joy: 'Arabs? welcome, please, welcome!' The notion of being so easily recognised and so warmly greeted was not so welcome to the shopping party. I heard my cousin tell her mother: 'Oh, that Jew, he did that yesterday to someone else.' I found it difficult to understand her hard reaction. If they knew who owned the shop, wasn't it unusual to declare disgust and still shop in the same place? Such was the face of the Arab boycott of the enemy, as ridiculous as the indignation and revolt.

I went outside, attracted by the loud sound of music, (we were in an era before noise pollution). The record shop was like a museum of honest intrigue and smelt of wax polish, a combination of vast collections of records, soft and fast music, listening booths one could occupy to test one's taste of records and the perfumes left behind in them, as well as the short mini-skirts: so many fascinating interludes of heart throb and animation. We weighed in, all four of us and the half-ton of purchases, into one taxi and were brought safely home. Television, multi-channel and in colour, brought the evening to a fine conclusion.

The next morning I went for a longer, two-hour walk, from Harley Street to Hyde Park. In the tunnels connecting the park, with nearby streets musicians playing slow songs amidst intermittent gasps of feeling: it was already a wonderful summer.

On an impulse before the end of the day, I bought a tan-coloured shirt. It was the surfacing of rebellious behaviour. The city and its people were contagious in their free flow of thought. One black speaker, in a corner of Hyde Park designated Speaker's Corner, was advocating the rights of the Arabs against the last Israeli aggression. The man was truthful in his defence of what he believed and was bound to reply with adequate and unwilting fervour. Facing him was a man, five feet away, just as adamant, holding a four-foot high, black cross and imprecating against the present-day immorality of the city and its people, especially the flower-people, with their fallible free-love dispersal of venereal disease and collapse of the rule of society and in death of its religion. In a far corner a small, solemn crowd gathered, their seriousness reflected in the way they overcame their poor ability in words: a man in their midst was showing photographs of Hiroshima, accompanied by very vivid descriptions of west-east power games and of the possible release of a doomsday attack.

I found myself in an ethereal existence that made me forget all my inhibitions of thought and restored me to sympathy with the world. The apathy of ten years or more was dissolving, shed painlessly; a second birth was regally on its way. I found a reason for ending my painful lack of attention of the ways of people and the unconditioned placid smiles. The freedom to favour a riskless forward view was awakened.

On Sunday, the third day after arriving, I called Claire from the flat. At nine in the morning, everyone was lying in bed still asleep, in conformity with the habit of the country. Claire, her voice anxious, wanted to meet as soon as possible, on the following Saturday. She had quit her job the day before and would be arriving on the Friday night in London to stay in her sister's flat for three weeks. She needed the five days from Monday to Friday to arrange the transfer of possessions she had accumulated during the last four years in Bradford. This journey was her last stay in Britain before going home finally.

My mother went into hospital on Monday. I accompanied her and stayed for the afternoon to make her feel settled. I spent the week visiting her daily as she underwent different tests. The doctor in charge had on the Thursday confirmed that it was stress and not any physical symptoms that had initiated her chest pain. At the end of the following week, on a Friday afternoon, she would be released but had to be kept now to reduce her weight. It was a burden off my mind and the news improved my humour.

I had a week of loose supervision then, to make the most of and enjoy. I was given a key to the flat, despite my mother's orders and was free to come and go whenever it pleased me. I met Claire at ten on the designated Saturday morning at the door of the HMV shop. She was half an hour late. She recognised me though I did not recognise her at first sight. She was as I had imagined, but prettier than her photograph. She was slimmer, with soft black hair, so shiny, so neat that was easily disrupted with the light breeze. She had wide glasses, framing dark brown eyes that promised the world with a single look.

She wore light moccasin shoes that defined the white skin of her feet and let her tread lightly and slightly. She had a light cotton skirt that was not in line with the day's fashion, being knee-length. Her half-sleeved blouse hid a pale, delicate skin that was lightly tanned about the face and the lower part of her arm, starting near the wrist and ending in her long, slim fingers that pretended somehow they were used to practise music and reflected the gentle nature of their owner. We went for coffee and doughnuts to a small coffee shop near Bond Street, not far from our meeting point.

I was consciously taken with her inner calm that radiated pure intelligence of thought and speech. The first sentence was awkward for her: 'how do you like it here?' She then admired my shirt, saying its colour was her favourite colour of the rainbow.

I questioned whether there was such a colour in the rainbow, reciting my hard-remembered physics. She smiled. She seemed to have a habit of smiling when caught unawares, in something she had said.

She agreed and suddenly asked: 'Did you bring your wife with you? How is she?' It was a ploy with a hidden meaning. I understood it: 'I am not married. I'm only seventeen and four months'.

She smiled again. Her smile had an added impression of accepting my answer faithfully. As the juke-box entertained us with 'The music played', a song I once heard Jessica claim as her own, I floated back three years, without noticing that Claire was watching my face with some fascination and a look of hard analysis. Her hand opened and its palm pressed the back of my hand that was nearest to her. I woke, a shiver had been in my soul and now on my face.

She apologised, asking, possibly a second time, if I was alright. I explained about the song. She had known of Jessica from one of my letters. She commented, with sincerity, that Jessica must have been really special and I agreed swiftly. She wanted to know in more detail all about my life, my favourite persons, the ones I disliked, the ones I knew peripherally and all about my family. We spent three hours, she listened while I summarised.

I spent the hour following in questions about her plans, but not about her immediate-past acquaintances, rather about her people at home, her parents, brothers and sisters. After she had given me a lengthy introduction to her early life and description of her family, I ventured to ask: 'do you have a boy-friend?', sounding, as I hoped, impersonally interested. She denied the existence of any serious or continuous relationship. I supplied similar information on myself regarding such relationships, identical in content and assurance. She seemed to accept my statement, whereas I was not as sure of hers, although it did not matter anyway to me.

I felt differently somehow toward Claire, now that that anxious impulse had disappeared, and made warm and comfortable accommodation to her as a friend. The illusion of almost feeling in love with her, my longing to kiss her seemed so childish, as if they were thoughts made out of hunger and not of purely devised sentiment. It was now more a feeling of closeness, without the body's craving, a quite unfamiliar sensation. It was difficult to justify its first tenderness whenever I looked into her face. There was that desire to be fully committed to her love, matched by an eagerness for candle-lit vows that warned me not to say what I felt, not just yet anyway.

Her eyes shone with recognition, as if she almost knew what I was thinking. She asked me, suddenly, if, in my overtures of kissing and enthusiastic close-contact with any of my lovers, I ever said I love you, either as a matter of routine or out of great feeling. I thought hard. My silence was not well received as my long hesitation demanded clarification and assurance. I softly worded my reply: 'I may have said it a few times, maybe fewer than expected, but one need not say what one can show in look, touch or silence of mouth and expression of eyes and slow movement of fingers. If one did not say it, does that mean it is not there?' I asked truthfully.

She agreed but with some hesitation: 'a statement like that is so important for women, so reassuring, so vital before being taken, both in the act and in itself,' she affirmed. I did not agree: my confirmation in thought was more important to me than a three-syllable sentence.

We went walking down Oxford Street. Midway between its two extremities was a small cinema. We decided to go in and see The Graduate. I was more impressed by the music than I was moved by the acting or the soft-content of the film. Claire seemed more moved by the softness of the bodily contact. She leaned towards me in the midst of the film and kissed my face, away from the mouth but not so far away from it, licking the corner of my mouth and breathing gently near my ear and eye. Her hand flowed unto mine and mine curled into hers. She had touched my soul.

In the darkness of the cinema, we looked at each other by dim glow of the aisle lighting. I looked hard into her eyes and she looked harder into mine. I was not ready; I was taken by surprise, I was not in control, as if I was being measured for a new suit without any input of will or choice. We filled out our silence with more of the same, until the lights were turned on to indicate politely that we had to leave, as the film was already over.

We walked out of the cinema together holding hands. It was a feeling as natural as the one we felt walking in separately: it seemed a simple and spontaneous decision, portrayed without thought and in innocence. The sensation of walking in public holding a girl's hand was as unfamiliar to me as it was exciting and wondrous.

She asked me if I wanted to go to a party. I agreed immediately. We took the bus to Chelsea, to a flat on the third floor of a building with an old exterior but newly decorated interior. The stairs gave the only signs of its actual age: the banisters were carved but their carving had thinned from use, the depth of each incision was barely visible and polished to the point where the original oak colour was smudged by layers of different strengths of stain and shades.

The door of the flat was a recent replacement: its paint presented itself fresh and shining to our eyes, its flat surface and bland design giving away its hidden youth. The door opened with a slight push to reveal a loud mixture of people and music. Someone greeted Claire and took her to dance in the same breath. I was guided to a table crowded with a cosmopolitan variety and choice of drinks. I poured my first beer, part of what it seemed a growing compilation of daring and curiosity.

After half a glass, the world was rose coloured in its anticipation of more sustenance and expectations, discreet and exuberant in promise. A girl with black hair, the shine of which was only comparable to that of Claire, attracted my eye. I caught her attention when she turned as she was dancing; she smiled. I took another swallow of this new, magical discovery and found a sofa with a small unoccupied space, which I took. The boy and girl who had hurled themselves into the other half of it were busy extracting each other's breaths and did not feel my presence. I did not want to be noticed either, I had a new fulfilment now.

It must have been half an hour since we had arrived. Claire was looking for me now, covered with sweat and thirsty. She found my occupation of the partly-available seat useful as I was trying still not to notice the couple to my left. The remaining one third of the glass of beer refreshed her. She took the glass from my hand, turned it and put her lips to where my lips had left a light mark, looking at me and without asking for permission. I felt as if I was watching a slow-motion film. I looked up at her eyes and suddenly noticed they gave off a warm reflection of mauve eye-shadow. It complimented her eyes with a degree of lust and dreamy seduction. I was enchanted.

She offered to get a refill and was back in seconds with two bottles of beer and my glass. She sat on my lap, again without invitation. The heat of her body found its way to my thighs without rejection or much enticement. She asked if I wanted more. I nodded my head with approval as she poured the beer into its temporary container. We took turns in drinking from the same glass, our lips touching the same space at the edge. It gave the feeling of sharing brilliant heat.

Without any introduction or discussion of the subject, she asked me if I was feeling homesick. I denied it, without making the connection between the question and its real motive.

She asked again: 'Do you miss your long-lost, past friends?' I comfirmed I did. She concluded without giving me a chance to reply: 'Then you must be homesick.' I inquired how she arrived at such a conclusion. 'Home is a state of the mind, it's a combination of familiar feeling and belonging, it's a consortium of people and events, meshed together by deep longing, dissolved into dreams with remembrance.' She finally confronted her words, still looking for my agreement.

I had to admit I had never thought of home like that: yes, people did contribute sharply to the picture, but were not as centrally important or as strongly favoured. It was the heat of the afternoon, the morning-fresh sun, the sunsets and the open-armed sky at night that I remembered; the word of existing people, not those exposed nakedly to their disadvantage as pure illusion of memory. But her description was also acceptable and for the moment seemed more true to life. 'I will be homesick for here', I voiced aloud a passing thought. She smile barely glimmered, indicating a greater measure of satisfaction than she was admitting freely. 'So you may miss me', she added in quietly phrased words.

I agreed fervently, although it was the first time I had thought of the end of my trip, still in so early a stage. A sense of sadness framed my next thought: am I in love? What could I do to prevent its dominance or deal with its consequences? what can I do if I want to ensure its survival? I was undecided between wanting love and hopelessly avoiding it.

The heading of a thought crossed my mind: I wanted to be with her longer than I might be able to be. I tried not to manifest it in my face, which always betrayed me in my intention of hiding a dominant thought or a current way of thinking. I asked myself loudly: could I not take the present and postpone anything else that was not in contemporary terms or relevant to the future in motive and momentary honesty. She seem to have heard me and smiled again. She re-adjusted herself on my lap, turning her legs to touch the side of my thighs at right angles. She stretched her right arm so as to press her right breast more closely against the ribs housing my heartbeat, sustaining her posture with her right arm at the back of my neck and her fingers resting on my shoulder, in a similar position as if I was to carry her over some imaginary threshold.

Her breath slightly tainted with beer, she asked: 'Is your past threatening to break out, as if it was a rebellious skin rash, painfully blotched? Is your past so unsettled that it requires little to erupt in anger or massive, cutting blame?' I measured my next thought in reply, trying to evaluate the question and integrate its demands with the feeling of the moment.

I tried to explain: 'All of us Arabs are governed by our past in a fashion unfamiliar to most of you westerners, I suppose. There is always an over-comparison of the present with the past, flavoured to some lesser or greater degree with an intrinsic urge towards sadness, even when the present is far happier than the past. It's something born or bred in us. If you looked at the present tense of any verb or format in Arabic, you'll notice a subtle type of forceful-ness as compared with the version in the past tense; the latter is more mellifluous, mellow to the extent of gentleness of the words burdened with the sadness of loss. It is probably a conviction that things will never be as good again. The past seems to be always sentenced for life to being better, I added in an almost intentionally gentle voice.

She was interested: 'You, and maybe your people, appear dis-abled by the past, by any past form of the word. It's astonishing to be identical to some North American Indian cultures, which are dissimilar to the core to ours,' she confessed.

I asked her what meant. She was very patient with my ignorance: 'Some Indian tribes in North America have something just as strange in their language; they do not use a past or future tense among their expressions or words,' she said, simply. It was almost unbelievable to me; my face said it was for me thoughtlessly, less passively than I had intended. It was not so much that I didn't believe her as the difficulty I thought it presented for their daily communications: 'What do they use for even a simple description of past experience?'

She continued with her explanation: 'With them, their past lives are immortal in thought. A day, a year or even a decade is only a minute ago and is disqualified from being spoken of in the past tense. They find a past or future format in their language quite unnecessary, in fact unusable for their permanent present. I wish I was like that, I would be fortunate in my fate and faith.'

The idea of a continuous present was delightful for the care of the moment, but to me it implied a certain unfaithfulness to the past, which became precious or effective once it was memory and the removal of offspring intimated, that is a loss of status and design, of being and purpose. I found the idea of such characters contradicting the birthright of each other. It meant that a total dependence on constant uniformity or dismal change in ensuing events is to be the only possible expectation. Part of me welcomed the idea. I wanted the moment with Claire to last for ever, but not at the expense of erasing the heavy or light tone of memory.

I agreed with her: 'I wish these times would last forever!' Her bold and present appreciation was evident: her arm curved in a bow over my shoulder, her hand flattening the curls at the back of my head. She kissed me without allowing a strong imprint of the mouth to tug my thoughts somewhere else. She announced almost suddenly: 'Let's dance!' We danced for the best part of three hours, in shadows of slow and fast beat.

At nine o'clock, every one broke for supper: sandwiches emerged from what disclosed itself as the kitchen, more beer emerged from what was noted as the store room. More music, more dancing and more beer followed. More beer and slower dancing followed much later.

At about one in the morning the crowd was thinning in the main sitting room, although not many were leaving. The corridors and inner rooms with lights dimmed for purely naughty intentions, were increasingly populated; thick coverings were carefully placed over light shades, to attempt an artificial eclipse of brightness. I passed many people stranded close to the walls and many more beached on carpets everywhere. No one was disturbed by anyone watching, everyone was in a world of ethereal, silky existence.

I made my way back from a toilet shared by at least two others: one brushing his hair to increase his chances of scoring, talking to a second man who was not sure whether he wanted to go or stay and try again.

I arrived to find Claire in a serious mood. She was talking to her flat-mate, a girl who procured the airwaves for her living. She was a 'disc jockey' who rode such wild horses as late night requests and music for those who could not easily find sleep. Her friend, Sally, was not in good form: she had just found her boyfriend kissing another girl who had crashed the party. Sally wanted to evict both of them on to the street, away from her hospitality.

Claire was less decisive in her reaction. Her manner and tone of voice indicated her thought: Sally did not own the boyfriend any more than he owned her. Claire was trying to show her friend the insignificance of the man's attitude as reflected in her own past devaluation of his worth: 'I expected this long ago, I'm only surprised it took so long for you to find out'. Sally was more upset than she seemed at accepting such advice.

She began to cry, her indignation and pain amplified by the alcohol she had already accepted freely before the incident. I stood and watched the friendship of the two women: strained, failing to alleviate the hardship of disappointment, brought to the point of breaking with a statement of 'I told you so' from Claire, only to be rescued by warm hugs, where the tears of the two entwined faces exchanged their content of hurt and sorrow, then dissolved into understanding and the comfort of having each other.

I stood before humanity in its purest form of exchange and containment of the sharp edges of the disappointment that existed in love and friendship that selfishly betrothed of itself and preyed on sacrifice: accepting the minimal when nothingness is the only other alternative.

After a wordless pause of about fifteen minutes, tears were dried and both women were laughing, accepting their silly habits and emotional deluge. I hugged them both in brotherly recognition of their solidarity and strength of co-existence. Sally, reconciled to the insignificance of her love in the long run, was now more disturbed by the soon-approaching loss of Claire, who might no longer spend those long summers and hours of chat, prolonged by the heart-to-heart trading of experience and life-related information of previous years. Sally had not found another mate during Claire's absence when she was studying and looked forward to her friend's visits every second week and at long weekends.

I was alarmed with this description of Claire's departure, as if it was tomorrow and forever. I asked when she was leaving: 'In two or three days, going home', she reported, with light emphasis on the word home. I was taken by surprise. Claire had said she was staying for at least two weeks more, when we spoke on the telephone first.

Was I again to discover someone critical to me, whom I would lose so soon after such discovery? The ominous horoscope was understating my loss, again. I could almost feel myself bewailing her in silence, I would not get to know her as long as I would have liked. She tried to comfort me: 'I will write to you, my letters will not stop, they will find you, even when you have returned home', she assured me. For the moment letters were not enough, I nearly asked her, in anger, not to write again, but in cowardly fashion did not dare say it.

Claire turned to my now evident discomfort of thought and hugged me tightly: 'I will give you something besides the promise not to forget you, maybe later this morning'. I was not in a mood to anticipate heaven after knowing the approach of hell sooner than I had expected. I felt alone in the midst of the crowd, most of them inattentive of the serious events already proclaiming the institution of my need and its progression.

I hugged her back, partially accepting the promise and the fate of her friendship to remain a long-distance one conducted by letter, together with an illusive hope of reunion, matched by the lyric of Tom Jones's tune that was playing in the background of noise: a song of his illusive dreams and mine. We danced half lamely and half wanting to go further than hope, mostly saying nothing that portrayed hurt or disappointment. Much of the time we held each other, interrupted by beer and the hiss of the worn out interlude between one record song and the next played, chosen by the ease with which they were found.

Holding each other we finally fell to the floor, appeased, at peace with each other in our exile of pain. At five in the morning the party's disc jockey was falling asleep, so we turned on the radio instead, to allow continuity of music.

At seven, amid the awakening of the morning streets, we left, seeking coffee and doughnuts in the delicatessen only two floors below. It was about to open when we appeared at the door, having timed our arrival well. The old woman knew Claire and did not show any surprise as she let us in, as if Claire was routinely at her doorstep this hour of the morning. We talked very little, harbouring a sense of intimacy, of looks shared between those cups of coffee greedily consumed and solemnly appreciated.

I said goodbye to Claire at nine, promising to meet later that day in the afternoon. I went back to my temporary abode, to change, shower, sleep for a few hours and have a late lunch. At three in the afternoon I found myself in Sally's flat again. Many faces were familiar from the night before. There were five or more new faces of girls, all the new participants in the continuing party.

The music was livelier and more persistent than when we had left it earlier in the day. A new box of records had now been lined up for playing on the uncomplaining record player. Claire was asleep in a bed shared with two other girls and a boy, all dressed as I had left them, in last night's clothes. I woke her gently with a kiss. She opened her eyes with a smile of recognition, in a happy, ticklish mood. I tickled her feet to the objection of the other occupants of the bed, who were not interested in Claire's giggles.

She woke up and went to the bathroom, talking to me from behind the door, which was left ajar to enable us to converse easily and hear each other's words clearly. She would open the door a little bit more whenever she was not sure of what I was saying. I stood at hand, surrendering a face towel she said she required before she announced indulgently that she had decided to take a shower. She was half-asleep still. I went and sat on the bed in the next bedroom, waiting for her finally to rout the remnants of sleep with the jets of water that I could hear loudly.

She asked for a bath towel. I found it and brought it within reach of her extended wet hand that had temporarily penetrated the flowery see-through shower curtain. Her shadow behind the porti-ère, set in contrast to the long stems of painted flowers, was an image of a butterfly in a field in the early hours of a frosty morning, when the sun was straining to melt the frozen dew, when the sunburst was dispensing its heat in colours, reflected in the spec-trum of each freed dew drop as it was released from stillness.

I teased her, trying to pull the curtain away, offering the towel and snatching it back, in a game of catch. She was playing along when she caught it in a sudden move, faster than mine. She lifted the towel and stretched the width of it between her two hands, letting its length become a second curtain re-enforcing the nylon obstruction of vision.

I pulled the curtain away. She stood still, as if anticipating I would do the same with the towel. I stopped at the new barrier, not knowing what I was expected to do or what the limit was to my game of intrusion. She pulled the towel closer to her body and rested one corner of its width on one shoulder, the wetness assisting her shoulder in keeping the cloth in place. She then freed the second corner from her other hand, put it on the same level with her mouth and bit its end with her uniformly shining teeth. Then she opened her mouth, without warning.

The towel sustained its position for few seconds before slipping as slowly as it had been put in that position. The green towel was unfolding, unstoppably, intentionally. Her wonderfully wet, white-stemmed body was unfolding, her eyes were level with mine. For a few minutes I remained looking at her eyes, then my gaze, attracted to her body, started moving downwards. Her breasts were firmly in place, crowned by light-pink nipples. She said: 'They are size fourteen', interrupting my trance and causing my head to turn up to where the warm voice was originating. I felt a shyness I thought I had misplaced a long time ago in my past.

I bent down towards her knees, bypassing her naked sex. I picked up the absorbent towel from where it had fallen around her feet and handed it back to her, looking her in the eye and nowhere else. She took the towel from me, clasped in one hand and moved it away from in front of her. Unintentionally, I looked; she had short auburn hair, on proof of her established puberty.

'Take it, it's for you to take, I promised you last night, I promised you, I want you to take it', she whispered without moving from where she stood, in stillness of the offer and in confirmation of its seriousness and openness of billing.

I turned away, again surprised. As I pulled the wet nylon curtain slowly to her, I wanted her so much I could have flooded my trousers, already wet with water. I wanted her so much that I was impotent to make the attempt. She stayed in the semi-darkness of the restraining yet gentle barricade. Afterwards, she opened the curtain and stepped out wordlessly, wrapped in the towel.

I stood with my back to her, facing a foggy mirror as she moved into the other part of the bathroom. I could see her in the mirror; she was staring at a point in the middle of my shoulder. We stood in a stalemate of heartbeats and silence, of want and confusion, short in word and long on inquiry, in disobedience and reference.

I tried to explain: 'I do not want to take you; I want you but am afraid of taking you. Any girl that I had, I lost, lost irreparably. I feel this fate following me throughout my life. I want you to the point that I am afraid of looking, afraid I would weaken with a single look. I would surrender with a single gesture of love. Don't make the pain bear more strenuously on my will and my hard-found adjectives, on my expressions of illusion and ill-fated reality'. I added: 'You will never know, ever, what it means to have you, it's like a secret promise of sober intuition and fearful wanting.'

She stood, reaching out to the nape of my neck, fondling its hair and overturning such control as my mind had over seeping intention. She brought her lips forward, kissed me on the skin between the shirt and the hairline where her thumb lay. She was so close to me I felt her wetness left on the back of my shirt. She said nothing.

I walked out of the bathroom, destination: kitchen. Someone was making a civilised afternoon tea, brewing it in an old, much used ceramic pot. I was offered a cup without asking. Sally came into the kitchen and asked me where Claire was. I informed her she was in the bathroom, changing after a shower. Sally smiled, pointing at the wet patch on my back. I gave her the information that nothing had happened. She smiled again, probably in disbelief.

I spent the next half hour or more talking to anyone who came into the kitchen and I volunteered to be tea-maker until the end of the afternoon. Claire came in too. The conversation was wide, various and unlimited to any particular topic. At six-thirty I asked Claire if she wanted to go out for a bit of tea; she agreed.

In our snack bar downstairs, we had a light meal. She did not question me about the afternoon's events and I did not offer any explanation or open discussion on the matter. We went afterwards to the cinema to see Dr Zhivago. She cried when it was warranted, she was aroused when it was obvious, but was largely silent until the film ended.

After four hours' viewing, she was no more articulate or filled with any apparent hope. The moving account of the disillusioned idealist seemed too close to her immediate character. I avoided talking about the politics of the film. I felt that it would be inappropriate as I saw her dazed and incoherent manner. We walked at eleven from the West End all the way to Chelsea, feeling neither the need for tired legs to rest nor the urge to stop on the way to interrupt the long walk and the scheming silence that was brewing into desolation after the film.

As we reached the door of the flat she turned and kissed me on the lips with a passion unequalled by and incomparable to any kiss of any other lover I had ever had. The sweet gentle imprint had a radiance of warmth and innocent want, it was as if I was twelve again or being kissed for the first time. The voice inside my caged ribs wanted more, the voice beneath my eyes was demanding more, the third voice echoing my touch cried for more. I stood in the coolness of the ageing night, searching for the word that encourages the smell of spring and delays the setting of autumn, the long whisper that randomly declares: yes, now. Our hands grasped each other's hands, holding us mounted under the light that alternated from darkness to dimmed brightness with the finger-push.

We kissed until our breath required us to space our mouths apart just sufficiently to allow essential air to sustain the next wave of warmth. Our hands inspected each other's lips, cuffing words and stretching the silence into further non-speech and unexpressed will. Our words were orphaned by the irreversible need, where the eyes broke the golden rule, only closing temporarily within the span of every kiss. None of us complained, nor did we speak.

Finally, we said a casual goodbye, it was four-thirty in the morning, an ill-foreordained hour, I thought, as I looked at my watch, on the steps of the flat's front, heavy door. I remembered Jessica of all my past days and dawns of sleepless hours.

I called by phone the next day. Sally was sorry that Claire had already left for home. She gave me her forwarding address and telephone number in Ireland, in a small town somewhere out of physical reach and spiritual proof of existence. I understood without asking: the departure pained her, as it did me.

I lost myself for a week. For seven days, I went for long walks and short visits to places I wondered through fleetingly. The days passed evasively in thought, dragging their hours aimlessly.

After two weeks to the day, I rang Sally again. She had received a letter from Claire and a note for me. I went to Chelsea to collect it. When I entered the flat, a party that looked at least two days old was still devising reasons for its survival. Newcomers were replacing lethargic or mood-depleted participants in a constant pant for alcohol and the fast, unrelenting initiation of sex, moved by likely opportunity and the prospect of a mass orgy. Nothing had changed in two weeks, neither did it look as if it would for the next century or indeed forever. It was as if the party life of that flat was immortal, without halt or stoppage.

The note was brief: two photographs and a single paragraph. It read: Dear Edmund: Do you still think of me? I think of you every day and every sleepless night that has to be negotiated. Did you decide not to take me in order that I might remain remembered and viable in memory? I feel you were more decisive than you let on to be. Still, if ever in Ireland, you have my address. Oh, yes, try to ring me before you leave London. I will write to you as long as I am single, I will not when I get married. My mother is trying her best to make this soon, but I need time to adjust to the pace and privileges as well as duties asked of me now. Remember me always in the night we spent the warmer half of kissing at the door. Look in on Sally while you are there. You should go to her parties, they may cure your hunger of the body and reveal your hunger for the soul. Best wishes and love always, C'laragh.

The photographs showed natural colours of the fields and the dawn on weeping willows. One had an immense space of green, Claire was sitting near a knee-high ring of rocks arranged in an unsymmetrical manner, that maintained sturdily without any apparent cement, the shape of a wall. Her hair was carried by an invisible wind, blowing from behind her. The second photograph displayed similar characteristics.

Sally thought after a second letter that Claire was well adjusted now, much happier than when she first arrived. She thought Claire would get over her problems. This she knew from another photograph sent to her, where the wind was in her back again, and not in her face. She explained that that was the form of an Irish prayer. I realised that Claire had sent me a similiar message. I became more fond of Sally as time went by, became a regular participant in her parties, contributed to the atmosphere and enjoyed its floating worlds of uncommitted passion. It was a change and soul-safe sex.

My three months were soon over, it was time to adjust to the trip home, at least in an exterior mood and expression. I rang Claire the week before I left London, as she had asked me in the only note I received of her. She was not at home and I was asked to call the following week. It was a plain message of clean, planned severance, irreversible and with a minimum of discomfort to all.

We arrived back in Kuwait, my father was waiting to escort us to Basrah, a hundred and eighty kilometres across the border. The year's novel change had expired; it was returning to the ease of expected normality, gradual and painful to adjust to, after the total freedom and newly-acquired need for flesh without the hard effort of any commitment. That was unavailable, unacceptable and totally condemned by small-town minds seeking control and strict adhesion to social rigidity of unleashed will.

It was also the year where our American school was given its last twelve months of franchise. School education in Iraq was to become totally public, never again for any period to be dominated by 'foreign-brain-washing', the new revolutionary government was 'determined to close that gap through which it had neglected to retrieve the minds of young citizens from the incarceration of evil propaganda', as we were told on the radio. All of us, including Miss Walker and her band of missionaries, were condemned.

The new faces of power were exhibited from the start, autonomy from foreign influence, in a display designed for internal public consumption. My father never believed a word they broadcasted, especially their themes about the infra-structure of already-existing socialism needing harder injections of conformity, needing a public relations drive. He was uninterested in their intensive rhetoric and milder sacrifice of matters that were economically of no consequence.

New clothes for a style of fashion: this new revolution of public life had allegedly been precipitated by the Six-Day War a year or so before, by defeat and the publicly-motivated outcry of the populace. I was one of those who did not see it as a war and felt it was ludicrous to lose when the radio was announcing advancing, righteous armies on all fronts, for the best part of five days, to be told on the sixth day the war's over!

I remember it well. Shadows of Jessica tore at my allegiance to the Arabs, while shadows of patriotic feeling for a war I never understood tore at my pure allegiance to Jessica's memory and the warmth it still had. It was eventually the lie that broke on the sixth day, the will (of God!) that accompanied its unveiling, a chance of inadequate transport that the best regional army, ours, was supposed to have at its disposal; such an army was not more than fifty miles inside the Jordanian border when the unagreed-to truce took place and hostilities were cancelled.

For nineteen years or more, the spirit of hostile liberation had thinned with dismal preparation, and when the hour came, the gala performance drew back its curtains on the lazy actor, the stage riddled with woodworm, the director with his boastful shouts and the deficient playwright. The awakened audience lamented the performance and lack of standard with disgust, angry with the self-deception that resulted in more meaningless deaths and payment of ignorance with lost land.

Jessica was as non-aligned as I was, she no more believed in the blood-tainted homeland than I did in victory aimed at national recovery. Palestine seemed lost forever. When the time comes to end this problem of entity, of the 'Jews brought to order', it will not be a low-cost war, but may become genocide for either to win. No such price is ever comfortably acceptable.

I could not see my finger signing the order. Neither the Jews nor the Arabs seem sufficiently intelligent to accept margins of loss and gain: for both it will be all or nothing, it will always be thus. Both, who believe that they are God's chosen people, may be chosen again for the high altar. What of human waste, what of loss of mind!

What do I feel towards the Jews and the Arabs? A blanket of silence and an irrational need to escape the colour of my skin.

When Claire asked me about it, in one form or another, I decided to exhibit my intention and desire in life, to compensate for the world's abundance for wars, including the most recent. She did not ask again; she had her own pain to erase, I had my ridicule for our leaders, their loud promises and shallow employment of loose words. We both had an undeclared agreement to avoid the subject.

11

Preparations of Severance

In the few years that followed my trip to London, life in all its signs assumed a gradual dull appearance with the acceptance of reality. The politics of the country became more partisan and defiant and less progressive, moving instead towards reversion. The simplistic version of life, however, remained one of logistics. All those encouraged by the new shape of socialism were trying harder to demonstrate a passive outlook and become less involved in the process of change.

All those others who had been captured by the (secret) American backing of the new government were hopeful of an early turnaround and quite confident of taking the system from within; they were sleepers from a bygone day. The majority of the populace, in a self-induced trance, were in search of a better education for their children, better paying jobs for their future and a stability which was mostly desired to sustain the general choice: to eliminate the communist movement from Iraq forever.

All those were dreamers, they thought: If that was achieved, ninety percent of the people would find their backing of the new government unjustifiable and quite unacceptable. At the dawn of this revolution: there were two major powers apart from that of the previous nationalist government that was just unseated: one was the socialist party of Baa'th (re-birth), as it was called; the other was the communist party. After the massacres that were perpetrated in more than one major city in Iraq during the late fifties and very early sixties, the communist party seemed to have committed political suicide.

Freedom was supposed to be a celebration and hope of freedom to come. Insofar as politics were the object, the regime before this one had planted seeds of economic stagnation and discontent. The Americans (or rather the CIA, as my father specified) were faced with two alternatives: the 're-birth' or the communist party; the final choice was obvious and the population were entrancing themselves of revival, or so they thought, which helped matters further.

Their chants took on a strong version of national pride that bordered on war and averaged an orchestrated lease of confusion. The dilemma of the new, reborn state encompassed two objectives, neither optional, if the system were to survive. One was the elimination of opposition, this was achieved by 'cleansing' the army of 'old cobwebs', and the fast depletion of possible 'other' political movements. The crusade against the communist party was sufficient price for the appeasement of the Americans, to keep them from de-stabilising the new semi-socialist system (and even give it their blessings).

The other survival objective was a serious regeneration of up-to-date education, revitalised secondary school programmes and more spending on establishing three new universities. Grants for past graduates to continue their further education in the West and in the Soviet Union, aimed at a quick transfer of technology. Such transfers to Iraq were not without a hidden agenda: the band of the ruling council wanted military might, which could only be achieved by sending the country's citizens abroad and escorting the new technology home before adapting it to means of war.

The latter course had its hazards: some people like me who had travelled and caught the 'flower-power' revolution on its last legs were more influenced by such signs of the age as escape from social trappings and freedom for speech, expression of thought or simply higher economic drives. They brought back with them a vision of utopia that released its rebellious temperament often, invisibly, and with vigour for change.

I, for one, could not get used to the stringent instigation of 'proper' social behaviour, either by rejecting it or by accommodating myself to it, which was difficult and impossible at times. The first year at college was horrendous: the indoctrination of the new rulers was serious and full of phraseology which at the very least was pure rhetoric, and which most of the time sounded at best as if it meant caring for fellow humans elsewhere in the world as well as at home. The theme of universal caring was a captivating idea, especially when mixed with a minimum of inexperience of the shifting sands of politics and vibrant youth. The minds of many were easily steered towards this new idealism that had two dimensions of national and political identity.

The communists in college were the other end of the spectrum: the total rejection of any 'tattered' values, on the one hand and mixed-sex get-togethers, on the other hand, which were sufficient to attract those of us who could be won over, who were stifled with the suppression of thought and denial of activity free from responsibilities. Such were the hallmarks of a society that took youth as a mere stage towards maturity, no more than a phase to be controlled harshly, which was in retreat from any change in the world and were a peace-at-all-costs logo.

I should have been more attracted to the communist leagues, I, the free soul of London days, who had absorbed an anti-war way of thinking from that time and from my pen pal letters, which showed the inhumane face of war, the destruction of a nation so easily perpetrated by the Americans, (helped by Iraqi television coverage of daily bombing reports from Vietnam, designed to stem sympathy against both the Americans and the pro-Russians in a mass media cover-up of the real hands wagging those puppets in power, while assuring everyone how anti-American and how pro-liberation of Palestine they were!).

There was one formidable obstacle: the mention of the name communism always revived in me the memory of the street-riot rituals, of that old man whom I had never known but could never forget, dragged behind a speeding lorry past the point of mutilation. The communist 'youth' movement of those days of anarchy had made me anti-communist forever, not personally hating anyone who was associated with them, but abundantly repelled by the ideal and insufficiently motivated to merge myself in the movement. Irrespective of how eloquently the ideal presented itself on paper, I was sure even with my politically unsophisticated mind that such a group of people would never give you anything that was in common with freedom of the mind. The daily news bulletins on the Soviet troops on the streets of Prague, during the summer of 1968, when I was in London, had already revived and sharpened up that image of mutilation, immunised me against the onslaughts of this newly masked but ancient convention of a hieracy of thought.

The prevailing atmosphere of unequivocal conviction permeated as it was with laments and precautions was equated for me with uneasiness and created in me the wish to leave my life as it stood. I had decided unconsciously to leave Iraq, at as near a stage as possible in the future. This new drive to emigrate entailed severance from family and familiar abodes. The family that I always had a sense of duty towards, a duty that I had grown to accept and value, was the most forbidding sign forecasting probably impossibility. This sense of duty engraved on the character was not exclusive to Muslims, but was a format for all religions, across every different social spectrum. It was like circumcision which most people thought of as a Muslim ritual, but was a social habit of all religions in Iraq, originating from early Judaism.

Apart from the strong attachment to my father, who was a unique force in exposing the world's fallible modes of thought to me, and to my mother who was the luminous ideal of all self-sacrificing purity, warmth and affection of soul, there were my two younger sisters: I feared for their loss in such a society, if left behind unguided or unaided.

My parents were now in their late fifties, already worn out with responsibility and the hardship of managing their hand-to-mouth funds, which thinned past the second week of every month. My mother had worn the housewife's label all her life. Her family's land had been long confiscated, and she was like all of us, dependent on my father's take-home pay from the available court cases. My father was an honest solicitor, who only took on cases which he thought had a good chance of success; he always turned down cases which he thought weak or hopeless. He did not follow the practice of many solicitors of his day, who demanded unrefundable retainers, to be paid irrespective of success in defence cases or in the acqui-sition of claims. He had always paid for his policy of fairness with the casual, possible and sometimes truly threatened hunger of his family. He thought the consequences equitable to his clients and to his conscience; we had to accept it readily too.

There was also my grandmother, a lady who had spent most of her life in Iraq. She was originally from Turkey and had been brought 'home' to Basrah when she married my grandfather some sixty-five years before. He was on a trip to Turkey, on government business, when he decided to marry the fourteen-year old and bequeath her to her new family forever afterwards.

My father did explain once how Turkey was in total turmoil after the First World War. This resulted in her losing contact with her family, especially after the forcible drive to redistribute peasants and land, publicised as objectives to modernise the country and masked as trials towards making the agricultural system more efficient. In Iraq of the 1900s she was an immigrant who was denied her rights in a rigid society of total duty and commitment to her husband's offspring and the devaluation of any commitment to her own family.

I always sensed a dark-coloured guilt of despondency in her eyes, a dazed apathy which inhibited speech most mornings. She could not speak Arabic fluently, although she had been in Iraq most of her adult life; or maybe she found it subconsciously coercive and did not have the full intention of trying. This made her not so close to other members of the family who communicated with her in simple terms and only when necessary. I would have liked the contact to be more vigorous, there were many questions and queries I would have liked her to answer and clarify, but I found it difficult to establish such a tie.

Her warmth towards us children was, nevertheless, very evident and undisputed; it made our attachment to her almost umbilical, as it was accepted wordlessly and randomly. She was another dependant and in her seventieth year, a bond I could not selfishly sever in my prediction of the future, although any plans of such abandonment of home were still far away, at least until I had finished college. I would then be able to establish economic independence in a new country, wherever and whenever fate or opportunity deemed it possible.

In the immediate term of endurance there was college and the plain edge of interest in study and new friendships. The large mixed seasons, close and friendly, allowed me inauguration of renewed interest in some people.

Most of the boys were childish in their outlook on the girls in class, I found them immature in the first year and for most of the second year. I had one close male friend. We studied together most of the time and we talked less about anything else that was not in our curriculum, and especially politics. He had been long converted to communism, was gentle in persuasion and difficult to sway

intellectually. He was a self-educated man, intelligent and unthreatening in his self-chosen jaunt. But, as with friends I had made
before, sooner rather than later discussions of theology and politics
became more dominant. I could not persuade him to keep those
subjects out of discussion, while he felt he should be able to make
me 'one of them'. When that failed, he simply disappeared and
never came back to study with me again. Politics in Iraq were
always more serious with boys than friendship or brotherhood,
and always ended in discord.

I found myself alone again and without the impulse to fight for
that friendship. In the chemistry practical sessions in the laboratory,
I was teamed with May, a softly spoken, thin girl of nineteen. She
had a dark tan and gentle manner. May's interests did not include
sex, politics or sport. She was interested in chess, music, poetry
and in discussion itself as a means of understanding every point of
view and window of thought. She was slightly religious, but did
not allow that dimension of her character to affect her life or her
attitudes towards friendship or companionship. She was invariably
different from most of the girls in the class: a hard worker both in
study and in the acquisition of study materials.

Although we had been assigned the same slot randomly, I found
her of interest, simply because she was different. I seemed to be
attracted through curiosity or interest to girls who were not of
average personality or character; and seemed so consistent in that
direction. I had decided from the first day I set out to win her
friendship that platonic discretion of thought should apply only.
May was a girl who exhibited her puberty and age in the sequence
of her thoughts; led by words, not by her appearance: her legs were
thin, and her breasts were those of a twelve-year-old.

She was a woman whose womanhood hibernated until the spring
of self-activation, incubating itself merely beneath a surface of
quiet gratification and peace. We started sitting together, making
laboratory reports together, studying for tests and orals together;
every conversation listed a variety of words and sentences for
objective discussion, subjectively impersonal.

If love was a hidden venture, it was never explored; if it was
driven into hiding before a mob of social conventions, it never
made any pretence of rebellion or was sworn into secrecy; it was a
kind of love that promoted itself through a forthright mind and

enjoyed a semi-existence through comradely friendship, purged of bodily need and protective of its residence.

For the first three years of college, we were considered mere admirers of each other. Everyone expected a streak of behaviour that indicated sensuality of pose and purity of purpose; while we were innocent of guilt in any far-sighted plans, we were friends of unusual kind: not touching when we had the chance, not pretending or tricking each other's minds in spoken or gestured wickedness.

We had that year a private goal: to be among the first five in class. It would be half-way towards being in the same grading for the following final year in college. We were not swayed by either Eros or news of the third Arab-Israeli war. In October of 1973, while most were involved in either loneliness, sex or a regeneration of pride (when the Egyptians showed that Israel was vincible in war for the first time), we were deep in a demanding programme of reading on our three popular trends of enthusiasm: books of chemistry and other sciences; books of poetry; and the literate faces of humanity and philosophy, of convictions and reflection.

After Christmas, it was the new year: a time to start new habits and shed those that had terminated their purpose. One of my new resolutions in my strata of needs was to try to make my ageing grandmother feel the warmth I drew from her more dominant and more solid than ever before. She was estimated to be in her seventy-seventh year and unwell most days and some nights of any week. Her complaints, constantly discounted by her doctor, were alarming.

I tried to compensate for our unyielding exchanges of communication with extra hugs, long glances, and presents and mostly sitting with her more often than before. I was afraid to lose her, instinctively fearing a repetition of the past dashings of anticipation that turned terms of bondage into thoughts of guilt.

One night she came to my bedside: she had chest pains that had strayed down her left arm. I was so tired after an eight hour open-book examination in biochemistry that I wanted to believe in her senility rather than in the reality of her pain. I woke my mother and we called the doctor on the telephone. The dedicated man was not in his house. After three hours of waiting, he appeared half drunk and very merry having celebrated his daughter's engagement. He examined my grandmother with the speed of an alcohol-befuddled mind and decided she was not sick. He gave her a sedative (the new-culture therapy for everything) and hastily went home to bed.

After another hour, she came to my bed again and stirred me out of my dreams as if she knew she was dying to a point of hopelessness and in true confidence.

I brought her to her bed, sat at her side and wished to ignore her opinion. I must have fallen asleep, the clock struck at the arrival of four o'clock in the morning. I turned with a stiffened neck and cold limbs that were unrespondent in spite of my usual dexterity of youth. Her eyes were almost closed, still as her tired body and the age-broken spirit to maintain continuity of breath and senses.

I tried to wake her, she was almost unconscious. The hour of day was already ominous of death for me; it was the hour I had foreseen that Jessica was dead. My awakening almost as ominous also as that which resounded my past and resembled past slippage from all that was a life to me in Jessica. I woke my mother, again. She reacted as sadly as she was concerned at heart. The doctor was called for the second time; he arrived after fifteen minutes, more sober and only smelling of the alcohol he had consumed. He was more worried than he was angry for being sent for. As he was examining her, I noticed that she was of dull pulse and look, he spoke less than he usually did and moved less convincingly.

He uncovered her chest, his hands poised under her left breast. He started pushing downward in a rhythmic motion and frantic effort to revive her. Although he could not feel any pulse, he tried and continued relentlessly for about ten minutes. He then instructed me to do the same. I had had more energy and interest than he did, my motives were those of desperation and almost selfish enticement for my hope.

When we failed to produce any reaction from the woman's muted heart, he turned to me and asked me to leave the room, then closed her eyes with a gentle touch of one hand. I went out, conscious of her body's stillness and her soul's peace. He covered her with a green flannelette sheet that was on her bed. He passed me in the corridor without any significant measure of notice.

I went into her room, I stood in the dark. Her face was erect towards the ceiling, pushing the covering sheet upwards. I went to her, slowly uncovering her face. Her eyes were open again. I kissed her on the forehead, moved my hand across her face (as he had done a few minutes before), kissed her again on the cheek and gave her some of my tears. They seemed to stay where they were implanted on her face, hanging in silence. I looked again to her face; her eyes were closed, as if they were waiting for the final embrace and the closing of the curtains forever and for all time; waiting for the hand of not-a-stranger.

Her death did not cripple my senses immediately, as all previous losses had before. I was strangely saddened: I felt that she was free and finally at peace. Her life was surmised in her sons, in her total dependency on not thinking deeply of her past, dependent on the affection of children she had raised, without that touch of her childhood in her own immediate family. She had not seen or contacted her own for over sixty years. She remained that immigrant soul who refused to lose her identity to the point of not learning the day's language of communication. Her defiance was towards herself and inward within her ribs, a place where her hopes and wishes remained enclosed with every pulse of her beating heart while it had the will to declare its intentions and aspirations, unweakened or deterred by time and the mounting odds of failure.

Exhausted, finally out of age, it lay robbed of all essential initiative. Her egress was profound in depicting the second and only method of leaving, the single alternative to travelling home.

I was at home for a week, drained of interest. I did not want to go to college. It seemed so unimportant in purpose, so hopelessly worthless and meagre in its impact on oneself, set beside consideration of how one's life ended one's control and tenacity of existence.

I went after the week had elapsed, out of pressure and the need to talk to May. I stayed in the student canteen for most of the day. At the afternoon hour, when our lectures ended, I walked past my locker in the hope of seeing her. May was at hers, nine lockers away. She failed to recognise the despondency clouding my face in true reflection of any feeling.

She greeted me with a smile of longing, saying in her mild manner that she had missed me, without exposing any other intention of feeling or thought. I explained, as we stood in the middle of the fifty-metre-long corridor, the reason for my absence and, in the dual sense of the message, the apathy of awareness that had occupied my thoughts. The woman died an immigrant far from home, I emphasised, sure of my aching.

Her funeral was muted. Covered in a long white sheet, she was deposited in the sand as naked as the day she was born, clothed in the sadness of those who loved her and the white cloth, all that she was allowed to carry with her to separate her from the sand, the darkness and the heat of earth vault that would entomb her spirit and fragile body.

The family wailed for longer than she could hear, the house was full of tears and cries, desolate of smile. It extracted few words from all those who sank in sadness. There was no one with an identity that stressed her existence before she came to Iraq. May was not convinced of this: the woman had had her children in this country, she might already and many years ago have reduced the ache for her own people to mere memory; a woman lives for her children, a good mother always does, she gave as her definite opinion.

I saw the possibility, but my mind was not totally convinced of such a simple solution to eradicate the heaviness that filled me deeply. It alleviated some pain but did not erase all its remnants. May was adamant: I was a man, I could not think like a woman, no matter how thoughtfully I tried. She knew what women thought, she was a woman, she concluded. I agreed with her in one sense: I admired my grandmother, admired her Pied Piper calling, which allowed her an interest in children at the expense of herself and her life, when she married.

We sat in the little garden pathway separating the laboratories in the full February sun. She surprised me with a book, a present she had hidden for five days in her locker: she had remembered my twentieth birthday, when I had not. I never really celebrated any of my birthdays. It was not a common social practice in Iraq where only the elite and most materialistic families seemed to find it a occasion for boasting and a reason to brag.

The book was a surprise on its own: it was in English and its title, The Outsider, encapsulated a description of a man who did not belong anywhere, written at some length. It was by Colin Wilson, a young and complex man of twenty-four or so then. I took it and promised to read it in the time ahead, not committing myself to any deadline or period for report or discussion.

She had copied her lecture notes for me, for all the lectures that I had missed, and handed them to me as a present also. I appreciated her interest and valued her effort in word and gesture, touching her hand for the first time. She blushed. I apologised, as it had not been my intention to do so, but rather a slip of the mind. Her colour disappeared instantly. She did not speak of it and declined to extend any comment that might reveal her thought.

After two weeks or so I found myself accepting my grandmother's death simply. It would take almost my whole lifetime to forget her or stop thinking of her, at least on every birthday. Her spirit became within me. My plan to leave Iraq developed a sense of urgency, I did not want to stay there longer than necessary.

Her death seemed to sever a vital link that had held back my thought and my consciousness of being elsewhere. I did not want to die in a country where I felt I was an immigrant like her, detached from its customs in thought and conformity. Furthermore, selfishly, I did not want to witness the deaths of any of my family. I wished to leave and dissolve, intent as I was on disappearing, loosening contact, hoping that I would feel guiltless and free. It may have been a childish stream of thought, but it felt real and absolutely true in its hearty wishing and aspiration.

The fourth year in college saw us wrestling with harder demands on our time; studying was difficult and led to languid nine months. The shadow of military service was drawing clearer and closer with every passing day; but with it came also the feeling of paying one's debt to the state after such a service and of being qualified with a college degree that might bring further possibilities of financial independence from family and the old binding existence of home.

Apart from the approach of final examinations, the last two months of that decisive year in college, were riddled with an unintelligible mark of affliction: May seemed different, absorbed in a quite a tangible wordlessness, her eyes were expressing what seemed like a terrifying feeling of running out of time, something that was anticipating its death, something she would not describe or define in understandable logic, that logic which had attracted me to her since the first time we spoke seriously of life and thought. This enveloping sheath of silent petition was most evident on the last day of the exams. She seemed so helplessly saddened, so unaware of her words, so frail in looks, so uninterested in speech. I stood with her outside the exam hall, we compared answers as we usually had after each exam for the last three years. She was numb of word as I wished her well and started to head for home.

She extended her hand to stop my fleeing: she wanted to ask me something in the garden, in a place we had shared so many times before, in full view of the rest of our colleagues, open and frank as before.

She started her sentences in a low voice, looking away from me: 'Do you have plans to marry', she asked me bluntly. I denied having any intention that might bind me to anyone in the country, any motive to give away my soul within the bonds of social intimidation of 'settling down', or raising children. I did not want to breed any children, I wanted neither the responsibility nor the duty. I explained further that I felt no depth of physical or emotional binding to any one; I had become a loner, quietly content with my own company, seeking the flight of thought and release out of the darkness into total freedom of behaviour and action: I wanted my life to contain nothing permanent to an extent that demanded allegiance and commitment of life itself.

She seemed deeply sad, prevented only from crying by the anger of being unwanted. 'I may have to marry someone I have never met. My brothers are open minded, but not to the degree of understanding a refusal to marry a nice man, since I have not got a contender for my virginity and attention. I expected you might have been interested, a sultry lover whom I like and may even love. Have you not considered it ever?' she asked honestly.

Her personal appeal astonished me: 'I have not thought of it really', I explained, 'I had planned to go away from here and I did not plan to come back. You would hardly expect me to marry and leave, what would be the point? And if I did marry, I would have to come back, would I be expected to?' I was watching her anger overtake all the expressions on her face. It seemed to accumulate with every word I spoke.

I added further: 'We're of different sects, would your family accept me if I asked for your hand?'. I appealed to her logic to intervene. She replied with a stern question: 'Would your father come to ask for me, knowing I'm of a different sect to you? My brothers might wave this type of objection aside at my request.' She was certain. 'Your family would not be happy,' I rejoined, 'I know it from the experience of others. Mine would find it uncomfortable to accept as well. Religion is the worst divider of any nation, it sets social boundaries, demanding more perfection of its followers than God does; such a marriage would simply not be strong enough to withstand the pressure, the sniggering of old women and the jokes of old men in the crowded cafés on a summer afternoon.'

'We would be branded college dreamers, fools of distant imprac-
tical logic,' I added in full exhibition of what I thought life would
be.

She looked me in the face: 'Are you not even yielding enough to
consider a change of heart? I do not ask for much, a promise you
will think about it. I would be willing to wait for you as long as need
be, if you promise to return sometime to me, after days of roaming
have brought you home to a thought of me,' she said, trying to
explore a dark tunnel she had presumed already lit in her mind.
Her eyes were full of requests that bordered between tears and
disappointment: 'Remember you told me I'd be a very good mother
to my children; maybe when you think of children or need to have
them, you'll think of me,' she softly remarked.

I was left with re-evaluating my motives. I promised to think
about it, although the chance of my averting the choice I had
already made was near to improbable, if I was honest with myself.
She asked me to consent to the two weeks before we came back
to pick up our final grades as a time for thinking, for making
adjustments, for a change of heart. We agreed on it: a required
space.

The two weeks flew by indifferently for me with a minimal
affliction of thought. On the resolute day of finally receiving our
grades I went early. I had to explain myself to her: I did not want
her to transfer rejection, which was not personally aimed at her,
into some kind of dislike-filled emotion towards me. She was also
there early. We forgot the excitement of scrutinising the grades that
were already posted.

She was waiting in the same seating area, where she had reserved
a bench for us. The little garden was full of couples, who were
unlike us in the sense that they were either saying goodbye for the
summer or making definite plans for an arrangement of one sort
or another for future contact on more hospitable occasions. I
approached her, aware of the crowd and the sensitive atmosphere
that appeared to anticipate my serious purpose and my decisive
and truthfulness sentences.

I greeted her with a cordial manner and asked if she had obtained
her grade yet. She asked in return if I had thought of the matter
further, as if we had been together two minutes, not two weeks
ago. I confirmed I had, in a short sentence that accompanied my

serious face and uneasy look. I was silent for a short while as I rephrased my thought into spoken syllables.

'When I consciously wanted your friendship, I wanted it safe of any consideration of involvement that demanded more than sincere friendship utterly without strings,' I started to explain. 'I thought of the problem of our two sects from the beginning, of the conflict of such a following. I thought I was utilising it positively, to prevent possible seriousness in either of us, I thought you wanted to be safe, and I did also want that,' I added carefully. I continued further: 'When I met you first, some three years ago, you boldly expressed a lack of interest in boys as a serious venture. I took that as the positive sign you were showing me to set the rules of companionship and friendliness.'

She was silent. Her tears were trailing down her cheeks. Drop by drop, the wetness on her summer-sunflower dress was expanding from directly beneath her face, drops that were flowing anywhere the angle of her face was guiding them, on top of her thighs, on her flower stitches across her breasts, on her lower arm, in a noiseless sobbing that was penetrating boundaries of the sane logic that was my strength and my prevailing wind of decision. I stopped speaking for a short while; it felt like a whole morning.

She gathered her words hesitantly and in an attempt to block the floodgate that had been left open. She stammered: 'Yes, I thought like you I was safe, for the same reasons, but the logic we harboured was foolishly changed into something I did not want to accept for a long time. I finally surrendered, to my own unwise detriment. I have what I did not resist strongly against having.'

She continued, aided by a white handkerchief daintily embroidered with a neat, thin red, blue and purple thread that assumed its sensitivity from the care with which it was placed: 'Would you not reconsider, a promise will keep me in hope endlessly?'

I could not answer. I was silent. I did not want to lie, did not want to exaggerate nor to mislead her into the depravity of untruth and breach of promise.

I said goodbye. She stayed seated and motionless. I headed for the ferry, but on reaching it I realised I had forgotten to collect my results. I went back. I saw May at the main gates of the university. She had her black sunglasses on and looked composed again and indifferent, somehow.

She stopped at the gate, her face fixed on mine. 'I could not say goodbye, it was the hardest word in parting, a declaration of final separation,' she said simply and turned away, slowly taking herself to the gate and the mass waiting on buses for the ferry, disappearing almost like a shadow or a phantom that had made its last and availing apparition.

I had passed with second class honours, my name immediately under May's; our results were identical and symbolic of our most equitable effort together. There was an irony in this permanent fixing in time and official recording of data.

The next two months were spent in passive anticipation of military service. Such an unknown echelon of our lives invoked little thought and few gestures. Some were thrilled at the man's life to be encountered. I had mixed reactions of eventuality and absolute necessity. In one sense, the absence for months from home looked like a new test of will and a review of strength, not in pure endurance but rather in the ease of separation and severance from the familiar surroundings and a loving family.

I did not want to speculate, I simply wanted it to start and finish early in my life.

12

My Outward Self

In the summer of 1974, there was little left that could address the thoughts of all of us who had passed their final exams; life seemed to be passing by but with an over-serious mind and intention. In pause of youth's interlude, that had lasted four years of college, separating the still youthful outlook of secondary-school minds from that of boys ready to embrace arms; and the girls for the most part, to ready themselves in motherly womanhood. The four years were in a strict sense an ejection of fragments of youth and inno-cence in the trials of intent and an airy solitude that became a seesaw between present reality and that romantic betrothal of slow time free of true responsibility in its selfish solicitude.

Mothers were also burdened with the worry of possible deaths and the sadness of seeing their fledglings elude their character of children forever. It was a time of solitude for those mothers who, as was expected of them, had become by now totally and silently integrated into a dependence that made home a refuge from the outside world and a stronghold that nurtured seedlings in a safety that ordained its cleanliness of mind and left would-be mortals untouched by the decay waiting outside the dominion of mothers and high walls.

Mothers, who were at best unqualified statisticians except of life, had alarmingly calculated the fifty-fifty probability of recovering their sons after military service had elapsed and society had returned their remains home. Death may not simply mean stillness of body, it could merely be the stillness of mind and paralysis of will.

Mothers never shared the strength of martyrs as shown and discussed on TV, newspapers or radio. Their sons were not a negotiable exchange of someone's logic or drive, although mothers probably believed less in heaven, where defenders of God and country went, than in heaven being under the feet of all mothers, as the prophecies had depicted in their evaluation of mothers and their status in religion. The robust hardy and brawny reality of their lives indicated giving, with little appreciation.

Fathers were consultants of reality; they steered the sinking ships while mothers emptied out the taken in water. Their partnership was always based on the strength of fathers and the softness of mothers; their love manifested in different, yet truthful reflections: fathers wept in silence and away from their children, (an image that built itself beyond the third dimension of existence), while mothers showed their sorrow in public weeping, as if they had a contract on tears, a bargain for the allegedly weaker and sillier sex.

The bonds binding them to their children are somehow compatible and comparable: two different types of anchorage, two strengths of face and smoothness of belly. They lay their lives on the miserable one-to-one gamble of achieving the perfection that they failed to attain in their own lives by themselves. The cycle is eternal and may prove fruitless, but they must try it, if only to clear their conscience.

Their stance on military service may been tainted with obedience to the reality, passing uneasily and reluctantly into clear acceptance that is calmed slightly by the notion that not all draftees are singularly, badly affected; yet daunted by a random choice of the gods and their envy of others who with less effort secured a better posting to nearby camps, exclusion on the grounds of medical ailment or through fixing medical tests, or even shortened periods of service because of secondment into civilian jobs of lower standing by some lawful or pay-induced arrangement. These intricate feelings went on almost endlessly, ending in confusion over the call of duty.

The indelicate awakening of new college graduates such as us started early in army style: on the day of the provisional medical screening the sergeant commanded the attention of the newly conscripted and unwilling troops with a loud voice that aired his authority and impressed his superiors, listening approvingly, in the next room. The sergeant's demeaning attitude stemmed from two facts that he recognised as essential, necessary and almost visionary in the strict moulding of his charges: graduates were soft-bellied toys, who were required to render service in the days of most pressing exigency.

This was masked against a hard, unfeigned background of near-hatred of these 'spoiled' and privileged few who were 'here' for a short while, exposed for the most part unwillingly to such 'wonder-ful' order of things. The college degree was another incitement for envy and disrespect of the system. We were paraded naked from one examining room to another. We were asked to cough as hard as possible, as the medical officer held our penises, angled at a concave eight-inch mirror, (the army way to detect gonorrhoea and possible homosexuality at the same time, as he watched you and the object he held simultaneously).

As for long hair, it was the worst point the sergeant could encounter, as he was pleased to use it as an ultimate excuse for humiliation of 'girlie impotents', pouring his hard-earned vocabu-lary into ears which were stretched to a true measure of indignant emotion for this duty they had legally inherited. Long hair was a warning sign of corrupt ganging-up, of disruption of conformity and a breakdown of order, illogical and unintelligible to those minds that had known the maps of the stars or the depth of philosophy, nuclear fusion or management, the detection and microscopic recording of devastating disease.

But the disguise of anarchy in us could be an intelligent and deeply kept matter, not as they claimed, advertised on top. For moments like these and more to come, the four years preceding assumed the form and soul of utopia; more and more every day and on every occasion, we were tinged with a longing for our previous supple and clear friendships and the hours of book-entranced existence. Although they were early hours yet, college had, alas, already shown signs of failing us in our understanding of or reaction to army life.

Between the medical examination and the draft move to training camp, were two months of waiting in lazy and idle thought. We thought little about the training and even less about our indifference to the time to be spent away from home or about the drastic changes that were expected to ensue, irrespective of our will or worry.

These changes, although expected, could not be defined; genuinely unestablished variables.

September came early into this dragging time. We reported to the train station as instructed. The military police were in charge of us all, as inhumane as they were efficient in herding us into carts of which the air conditioning had been turned off or was defective, (they were building tolerance of hardship early). Drinking water on the fourteen-hour trip was also scarce.

It was a new discovery: the army was not as homogeneous as one had thought. The worst arm of the machine was the military police – the MPs. No one in the army, irrespective of unit, rank or organisation, had any respect or appreciation for them; we could all of us see the reason.

The sergeant in the draft office, whom we had thought tragically harsh, was a lamb compared to these wolves. They had so many heads counted and to be delivered; that was all they car�d about, not how they did it. Their batons enjoyed mistreatment and unnecessary force. The only people who found them and the trip fascinating were psychology graduates, who watched, complied and analysed during the whole trip. They found it interesting to watch us, deprived of dignity and water, locked up in carriages whose doors were only opened when the military-designated train stopped to pick up more unfortunates, or at the end of the journey.

The trip welded us to each other and designated us definitely as the property of the army. We arrived in the capital, Baghdad, about five in the morning. We were separated into groups here and there in uniform numbers, each destined to a particular camp. Lorries were waiting for us at the station. The operation proceeded smoothly, bolstered by the reputation of the MPs this morning, rather than their ferocity.

Biology and medical graduates were lucky: they were allocated to a main base that housed medical services and the main military hospital, Al-Rasheed hospital, named after a famous caliph of the ninth or tenth century AD (if I still remember my history correctly). We were sent with physics and mathematics graduates to a camp about eighty miles away from the capital, on the edge of the desert. Sand for miles had built an intentional wall around the camp.

We were assigned the new barracks, a set of four large shed-like rooms, furnished with beds that were exactly two feet apart and metallic lockers a foot and a half square, to accommodate our essential T-shirts, combat and parade gear. These lockers had to be positioned exactly in the middle of the space between every two beds, leaving three inches' space from each bed. The sergeant used to measure one or two arbitrarily, on inspection.

The eyes of the sixty-year-old Kurdish man, ten stones and fitter than any of us, would find the offending locker by a slight look, with a minimum of energy and stare. He had been in the camp for the last thirty years, he told us. Every grain of sand that shifts in the night and sometimes during the day knew his name and bowed to his footstep. This mountain man was at home in the desert heat, although he originally came from a village half a mile away from the Turkish border, in one of the most northern parts of Iraq, where snow accumulated for nine months of the year.

Although there were beds there when we arrived, they consisted of regular-issue three-inch mattresses. The metal frames that formed the bases of the beds arrived a week later. We slept on the concrete floor for the first eight nights. Although this was not particularly unpleasant, it was hazardous: we killed three scorpions the very first night, as they hungrily trod the floor in search of warmth, we were told. They were pale yellow and not easy to see in a dim light. After we reported the find and kill, we were given an anti-scorpion shot once a week for the first two months, which felt probably worse than the actual bite.

The water in the camp was also tainted with a strange smell. We found containers with the chemical symbol for camphor near the water treatment unit of our division. Camphor was added to the drinking water in minute amounts, as was evident in the taste and faint yellow colour of the water, to quell any abnormal sexual drives amongst us, or so we were told once.

The basic (parade) training lasted ten weeks, for twelve hours a day from four in the morning until six in the afternoon, every day, with a break of ten minutes each hour and half an hour for lunch. Sometimes we would get extra hours, if we had failed the morning or evening roll-call inspection with a lax shoe string, or a beard that had felt smooth to the hand but had not passed the roll-call attendance sheet test. (This was pressed against the beard and rubbed; if the slightest sound resulted, the verdict was that the soldier in question had not shaved that day, a verdict unswayed by any assurance or trial of explanation.) Boots, belts and 'dog-tags' were usual inspection targets.

Other violations, apart from the untidy locker and when put away things in sequences that were not in accordance with the rules set out in early drills, were not as frequent, the commonest inspection was dropping a coin, the size of a fifty-pence piece, perpendicularly on to the blanket and stiff sheets of the bed. The coin should bounce upwards about six inches above the drop when the tension in the bed was according to regulation.

On weekend days of the first month in camp we were not allowed leave or into town. On those days, if the sergeant-major passed by and on inspiration of thought decided we were bored, there was this pile of oven-baked yellow and red bricks. It awaited our attention regularly. The bricks were piled at a particular point and we were asked to move them to another designated point about fifty metres away. The next weekend we might be asked to move them back neatly to original point. This was a regular exercise. There was no time to stay idle in the army, we had to be doing something irrespective of the time of day or night. Relaxation might 'breed anarchy and laziness'; it was not army policy, ever.

The training unit we were in was part of the chemical warfare division, a formation newly established three years before. It contained laboratories for the making of different chemical warfare weapons. The army had learned the need of these and their 'tactical value' during their previous confrontations with Israel, which had had this type of weapons some two decades earlier.

The hardship of training was soon to become a customary, usual effort. We were shedding our college skin, and hastily. The uniform had a captivating character that assumed a life of its own when worn. We thought differently, acted differently and were more compliant in that suit of warrior conviction and aggressive tone. This was specially noticeable to me when we were given our first weekend pass to go to Baghdad.

We hit the town like a tornado of children on their first outing on to the streets after a long period of being kept at home locked up. The presence of girls on the streets was amazing. Their smiles were so inviting that we followed one or two home before we realised that we were being led on fruitlessly.

I went for a nice lunch and to the cinema. The afternoon was refreshingly different. We called home, the first contact in five or six weeks. Mothers cried and fathers were anxious to know where we were and how it was with us. After an early supper, it was a trip to the cinemas again, (disco-type cabaret halls were out of bounds, as we were not allowed to wear civilian clothes, or drink in our military uniforms).

At about eleven in the evening, we went to some cheap hotel, where every four or five of us shared a room, (we did not care about the impersonal treatment, at this stage we were already used to it), and were asleep faster than we could anticipate or ever imagine. We woke up early, all five of us in the room and went out each on his own to find a café for breakfast. At seven in the morning it was long walks, then cinema, lunch, cinema and supper, before heading to camp early in the evening.

I arrived at the barracks earlier than any one else and went to bed without a thought of the starry night or anything else. The world had already stood still, again.

The cycle continued for the best part of four and half months: basic and then paratroop training, chemical laboratory work, week-end (day and a half) breaks and barracks again. The cycle of suspended thought and routine compliance had sustained itself smoothly without much resistance or the slightest hesitation, calm and uniform in texture and the way it blocked reflection, without the scheme of war, played down as a light skirmish, between the army and Kurdish 'separatists' in the northern regions of the country.

The genesis of the fight had not overtaken any intentions of survival to the extent of encouraging either hatred or enjoyment of fighting. I was learning to survive, but at the expense of my life, not any one else's. We were to be sent to the north when a change of plans had been implemented: some of us, picked mainly at random, were chosen to attend the reserve officers course. If we passed, we would be commissioned officers, reserve core, on active duty. There was no real sense of volunteering for this list of named 'volunteers'.

We, all twenty-five of us, chosen from this selection, were moved to a different camp. More training followed, more lectures and better accommodation. We lived high for the next six months. I enjoyed studying again; the technical lectures were less than aver-age, but philosophy and strategy of war, my favourite two subjects, were discoveries of intrigue. They really exposed man for the vain, violent, soulless and greedy creature he was; his cunning was evil, his reality was always destructive, his faith in himself almost frightening, he was profane.

The difference between infamous men over the centuries lay in knowledge and technology. Their immoral intention was merely to use whatever means there were to achieve the most in the short expenditure of effort and time. Progress seemed to be an enthusiasm for those discoveries which made destruction easier and more complete, injury and killing practical and invention profitable in devising illegal tender whereby paper values were exchanged for life itself. They made man worthless.

I had an aptitude for passing examinations, well developed in college and used at this time bleakly: I was, again, expressing on paper the right answers, but feeling unrighteous for them, I simply wanted to pass.

After the ceremony, a ritual of speeches and false inducement of values, we were given a chance to select our new units by lottery; it was the most hazardous yet cleanest distribution of choice, dependent at least on luck and the will of the gods, rather than on corruption and human assignment.

I drew a major placing in the capital. I did not want it. I exchanged the posting with another man, who lived in Baghdad, and I was allowed to take up his in a little desert town a hundred miles from Basrah. I needed to get home, I had not been home since I had been drafted, nearly ten months ago. We were allowed three days' leave, a prize for passing the grade and an illusion of allocation, of freedom within the discipline of duty.

The three-day leave was a heaven of indivisible hours when life regained some slight significance, a touch of warmth and a fundamental implementation of sanity. It was moments of unutterable and priceless worth of the pleasure of familiarity and the health institution of love; it was home.

I spent the time at home, around my father, accompanying my mother or talking to my sisters. The world was sanely plausible.

A year passed after my posting to the desert camp, passed without much hesitation and with even less pain. I found the rule of discipline attractive in principle and had adjusted to the concept of a tiered pattern of command. The life had an unacceptable side: the subordinates (non-commissioned officers and privates) were only a means for strict control and the sadistic presentation of 'human' nature. I felt their almost blind hatred and mistrust of their commanding officers. We, the reserve officers, of whom there were four in that unit, won the admiration of the underdog. We were as strict but with a humane face of compassion. We asked them to trust us and they were not disappointed in us, their problems fell on us; it reached the stage where we were consoling them, becoming their friends rather than their higher-ranking ordinates.

This was not acceptable to the 'real' or career officers, some of whom were of the extreme opinion that we were showing an imaginary understanding to achieve favouritism at their expense. We were not deterred, we represented the new idea of 'soldiering': obedience with dignity and understanding, order with compassion.

It was rumoured that May had been assigned a post in the same town I was in, teaching chemistry in some secondary school there. It was a town of eight square miles and five main roads, two bazaars, one cinema and less fate, we never met on the street, although I was there for five months.

The cinema was not a reliable refuge for me, as much as I had liked going to see films. It was an unusual cinema; the seats resembled those we used to have in our garden, thin-framed and light to carry around, unriveted to the floor. People used to rearrange their chairs casually according to the seating of their friends. The intermission between the trailers and main feature was irregular, dictated by the volume of sales that the wandering sandwich-man achieved in the designated time. Sometimes he complained loudly and offensively if the projector man started the film before he had sold at least half his batch of food. He was a nephew of the cinema owner and thus demanded his royal rights. These humorous events nevertheless added a cheerful flavour to the tattered films shown, which in an average showing might contain randomly stuck-together clips of as many as three movies, all on the same roll of film. Unrelated events, dialogues in different languages and different plots of different actors seemed to mix easily without any objection from the audience.

At the beginning of February 1975, a new insurgent front was 'characterised'. My unit was moved north as part of a 'conceived plan' to cope with it. The unit with its four hundred men was packed in two hours and on the move in little over that time. We were sent to an area not more than sixteen miles from the Turkish border. The scenery was captivating though the still nights, accompanied by days noisy with bullet and shell-fire were hard to live with at first.

The Kurds were an attractive people, whose elders shifted their politics with the prevailing wind. One day they were told by their tribal chiefs to fight the Iraqis; a week later they were fighting with Iraqis against a faction of their own people financed by either Iran or Turkey. The common man's life was the paying price for the privileges of corrupt elders.

It was a vicious war, based on slight consideration of life and guided by those who lived some three hundred miles away on either side of the border. The villagers were experienced politicians, whenever possible, though this could not always be achieved: the army used chemical warfare when some of its units were cornered and about to be annihilated. The children of the Kurds bore the scars of defeating the army on any given day. Those villagers who were neutral in war were hunted by their own people, their women were raped and their children hung by their feet until their rotted bodies were either discovered or fell apart from decomposition.

The prisoners of war of either side were more or less fortunate, depending on who was in command on the day and in what area they were captured. Both sides were interested in any information that the prisoners had, but were not worried how they got it out of them. Life had become almost fatalistically unmoving and uncaring.

Death, after a little more than a year in the army, had lost its primal significance, its fear and meaning. Death was a rabbit out of a conjuror's hat, of continually fading interest. If death came, it came as simply as that and as painlessly as that. A sense of loss that carried its own significance of longing and sorrow, as experienced in previous deaths in my youth, was almost illogical now. Burial, whether bodies left behind in the snow, or the ceremonial flag-veiled rituals, was similar in its effect on the now unmoved memory. Missing in action or fly-covered, dead personnel were equally listed absent and crossed lightly from attendance roll-call sheets.

War made us uncaring in surviving our own nightmares and thought.

During the passage of nearly three years many faces once known had disappeared or had never came close enough to allow you to know their distress, or to exchange casual impressions.

The succeeding weeks replaced the ones before, until the next in succession replaced them in near-rigid order of eventuality, in their deep incarceration of will and little thought of anything else. All those who were important had either died or were discharged for one reason or another, friendships neatly forgotten with the next bottle of beer and the first bar around the corner.

There were no attempts to fashion any new friendships after the first year and a half in the army: the implications of an ideology of imminent loss, separation or death were true and total. The need or new friends was not essential, the bond of arms took the place of the finer integration of thoughts in true friendship: we fired in the same direction. It was a new format that assumed closeness of fate to a degree of mutually dependent existence.

Although all of us, men of the hour, friends of destiny and comrades of fortune, were left closer with every battle, brothers after missions, we disappeared into towns or cities on leave; only those who drank together on short-time furlough and lived within staggering distance, were pleased to announce it true friendship. Everything else was a necessity of the moment and prudence of the day in action.

Loneliness was a mythical overtone from a childhood of no consequence, which vexed us little; we had grown up the second time with amazing gratitude to the gun and the political unwillingness of our elders. We tasted a solitude in the silence of the kill and in the pure reference of the storm, we had been evicted from thought beyond the momentary need to stay alive and earn leave in minimum attempt and with least cost to ourselves, (get it done and think not of the killing later, omit anything between furloughs and alcohol that's unreal and unimportant).

Mothers did not ask, fathers probably knew, but did not attempt judgement, sweethearts were either enticed by the hardship and 'best proof of manhood' or attracted by the colossal need their men revealed to them in search of the warm shoulder, the forced joke and the drive for sex: not that of deprivation but of much needed serenity.

In February 1976, the war was cancelled and suddenly silenced. The government had made concessions to Iran. The agreement left the Kurds without the across-the-border support and agitation. A 'practical' solution had prevailed. As before, some Kurds joined the Iraqi side, some stayed in stalemate of confusion and were disarmed in Iran. At the end of the conflict, the used Kurds were, again, dispensable and had to 'make the best of the circumstance'. The pawns of destiny were again bereft of hope and purpose.

An officer who served with us once spoke of his mother's people:

the Kurds were locked out of their destiny, still presumptuous in their claims that they could forge a state (although throughout history they had been in control of their lands for a period no more than forty years). In Turkey, they could be shot on the spot they stood on, if they spoke their language or were accused of speaking it; in Iran, they had been forcibly moved to arid deserts in the south and dispersed in negligible clusters; in the Soviet Union, their spoken identity had been submerged and erased in new affiliations; they seemed to prefer rising against the one side of the four dominating forces, Iraq, where they had their principal residence easier in relative terms.

Alcohol mixed with his indignation in his attempt to show his allegiance (we could never tell where that lay, although we believed his version of events and description of his people). He agreed that 'these' people, for all intents and purposes, are out of luck: their situation in Iraq was not as bad as it was in the other territories, they were allowed to keep some of their identity, they had their own schools and autonomy of belief and could easily keep their heads above water (he was adamant); but they failed to see the impossibility of their goals and the never-ending manipulations of other governments. No other side had ever conceded anything to them, I thought, only they themselves. Their plight and self-urged dreams were caught in a blinding twist of fate: they were dying, content with the cost and the superficial gain of world recognition, which was worthless, as I saw it.

The claim that this war was sustained to impede an attempted partitioning of Iraq, was not totally untrue: the mineral rights in the northern territories of Iraq (and in adjacent areas in Iran and Turkey) had overridden the rights of those who wanted to impose rule on themselves.

In the end, the elders of the tribes were obtaining the spoils, irrespective of who had won or lost the war. Their 'royal' heirs were not those dying; others were.

We were not as promptly discharged as we had expected. Yet that morning did come with such worry and anticipation that I did not want to believe it until the order was officially signed and sealed.

As I went about saying my farewells to fellow officers, the word came that our unit and the rest of the division was to move and to the western desert, close to the Syrian border. A major multidivision exercise was ordered to test the readiness of the army at short notice. (The fact was that there had been a coup in Syria that morning. The exercise was a gesture of the government's readiness to send some troops across the border, if requested, a rumour quickly denied).

I took a taxi to the little town where I was to board the train home. I did not want to wait for the courtesy car of the military police, either to avail myself of it or to chance the cancellation of my discharge. The taste of freedom was making my mouth water, my mind was wandering again and my spirits eager.

I arrived home the next morning, worn out and anxious to listen to the news of mobilisation, half-wondering if I was to be recalled for service after eighteen hours of hope and anxieties. The coup must have failed. The radio announced news of bloody street fighting in Halab. The tone of the broadcast and the strong language of condemnation on Iraqi radio of the Syrian government, reporting that it had arrested hundreds of civilians, confirmed the flop was in essence a disappointment to 'us'.

I slept early that night after the excitement and the temporary uncertainty of tomorrow. As for the last two years or more, sleep was void of dreaming, or the latter was honestly suppressed from memory after awakening. I got dressed and headed to the university, on the excuse of obtaining grade certificates and such other papers.

I had been writing to an old friend, studying now in Ireland after his discharge from the army some four months earlier. I wanted a place in a college in Dublin, with the intention of continuing my education to attain a master's degree in chemistry. I could now write in better assurance that I was available to travel, as I had been discharged (and in hope of travel before the next war started, when I might be drafted again).

The university was empty of students and our sitting-spot in the garden unoccupied. The cold that struck my thoughts was as chill as that on the frost-bitten leaves of the few evergreens still in place in February.

I went to the bench that time had marked with indifference, I sat confronting time past spent and I remembered her laughter and her tears. I appreciated the solitude that was driving my senses to thought and deeper concentration. I was glad not to have promised what I knew I could not yield: time and an oath of keep.

Yet I had missed her, had wished we were still close friends and still free of commitment, that we could meet freely without the social or selfish assumptions of linkage and binding, without the need to explain or excuse our friendship. I wanted freedom but also wanted change and affection, pure of anything but simplicity. I was a man who had put away his childish things.

On the way home, on the battered ferry and within the ten-minute interlude between embarking and disembarking, I had left behind the prevalence of discontent and the wishing that things could be different. I had rested my hopes on leaving. The university graduate office was on the town side of the waterway and I went there as soon as the ferry had docked to start the procedure of obtaining the required documentary proof of my four years of study. On the way home I stopped at the shopping malls, at the little shops heavy with dust and spices, at the nearly-frozen river that linked my veins with my past school and the way home.

I had a cast of thought that wanted to store those images so early before departure. It was an earnest of my will to leave and the expectation of a last look.

I decided not to write to my friend in Ireland but to telephone his flat. It was Sunday. He was almost asleep when he was called to the phone, answering my enthusiastic voice with words muted by tiredness and interrupted by yawning. He had been to a party the night before and had barely slept for three hours when I called. The girl who answered the phone lived next door to him. She was just as sleepy. He was also feeling the cold which the main hall of the house, where the phone was housed, was forcing upon him. He was nevertheless delighted at my news.

It took the best part of ten months, before arrangements were finalised for my attending Trinity College and before I was ready to fix my departure from home.

I found part-time work as a demonstrator in college, in charge of the students' practical chemistry laboratory. Roles were reversed in that I was the one who set problems rather than solved them and attended examinations from the supervisor's bench rather than in a state of apprehension and the distortion of worry.

I used the time to examine my resolution to leave Iraq, to thaw out the silence of two years, to cry (if I had to) for those who died, and to propose absolution all those who had harshness of face and softness of illusion in demanding my levied pain upfront, in my now deep past. I spent more time at home than I ever had intended to divide it between walks and my memories itching for the here-after.

My mother had a balance to steady, a price to pay and an intuition to follow. The choice was between my being killed in war and my being away, of being partially lost but not forgotten and most likely dead in one war or another. Her heart favoured the obvious: set him free. It was a price she was not ready to interpret but would willingly accept, as fate and as God's will.

Her intuition was of an almost final, lasting release from the nest of dreams and the bosom of tenderness, away from herself and her eyes. Her pain directed the flow of her past indecision towards a lesser degree of loneliness and the greater substance of saving my life than having me for shorter periods, subject to the unpredictable whims of politics and false opulence of meagre patriotic aspiration.

Her hope remained: he could one day return in my old age; he could be the one to close my eyes for the last time; he could have children, those that were to be babies and those that were as tender respect and thoughts of appreciation for the sacrifices of his mother. He will never forget his heritage of love born out her heritage of willing and solitude in waiting for the return of her only son. He shall brighten my twilight, a thought of love, a smile of warmth and a heart full of longing and hard hugs; he may wander but he'll find me waiting in hope and in want of reunion.

Although we never spoke of what was to come a few years hence she knew these possibilities might be less likely to come about than she felt true.

I was cowardly: I did not promise to return, I did not boldly deny her future welfare more than an adventure. I discarded the comfort of loud statements of intention: I still believed I would melt away like the early winter sleet, traceless and unlingering, in a new land and newer dreams.

I had one more trip to make to the capital to get my travel visa. I spent three days in Baghdad, living the nights of less hurried streets, walking in the mist of the freshly dampened roads and river fronts, getting wet on purpose as if those clouds of home would not rain on me again. On the last day as I collected my visa, a day of small mercies and lighter afflictions, I saw Rhea. The accident was more than an uncommonly strange quirk of probability, a relapse of the impossible.

It was heaven and hell, bordering on the insanity of ignoring my thought and my sane wanting of touch her, the candid, lingering ache of deceptive purity and unselfishness. We stood in the crowd of the afternoon as if cloaked with passive will to prevent it happening, of it all being but a dream.

She had aged twenty years more than her years suggested. I had aged as much, although unlike her, my ageing was that of the body. The handful of years between us seemed to have been stretched to the point of deformity, as if I had failed to catch up with her or her body had broken away from her actual age. There were folds of skin under her eyes, her brown eyes, that expressed now the heavy-handedness of time and disdain of living in false contentment.

Yet I would have known her eyes calmly anywhere and acclaimed them loudly anytime. We stood with our words not daring to come out of hiding, our surprise untinged by belief, our hands paralysed and our faces still, lost.

She ventured first: Edmund? I replied with an emotional hug, discounting the social rules of public behaviour of the sexes, I did not care. I responded with my heart to long-lost want and the short-found hunger of the long summers and briefer dusks. She pulled away, in control of her emotions, her wariness hard earned.

I thought of her as a childhood friend suddenly found, almost sexless. I childishly asked her to go to a café for a cup of tea. She smiled and opposed the motion, outvoting my intention with her own: 'Let us go to my flat, we can talk there more freely, someone might see us in public.' I agreed, led by the breath and without a murmur of a thought, by her words, as she used to do so easily before.

We walked to her car, not too far away in the parking space in the middle of the city. She was driving a fast model that indicated her husband's success (if he was still with her).

She drove for less than twenty minutes, to a suburb of the city. She had a flat in a high rise building on the top-fifteenth-floor: on the horizon, the city lights performed for her effortlessly and without charge every night for as long as the night sky allowed or lasted. I stood on the veranda, taken by the view; inwardly I was debating what to say or to ask of her: twelve years had passed, or was it more?.

She suddenly disappeared for a span of ten minutes that seemed to me now ten seconds. She returned dressed in jeans and holding two glasses full of whisky. She moved in an aroma of cool-textured thirst, ignorant of the possibility of this being the last time we would meet, presuming there would be many more times in which to rout the loneliness of separation. I had readily accepted the glass with the look of 'how-did-you-know-I-drank' and 'thank you'. She did not ask if that was a drink I liked, she knew me again without a need to establish rediscovery.

The ice offered itself to me as it melted willingly into the alcohol and exchanged its dissolution for the fast disputed heat from my hand. The malt was as smooth as the thought of her on my lips. There was the silence to conquer and the word to find, the surrender to endearment and the wish to express beyond the moment of embarking on speech and awe.

I asked how long she had lived there. She confirmed: always. This was her temple, this was where she was herself. Her husband, the one I had known, had passed away a year or two after they arrived here. She had married four times since then, been widowed at least twice and divorced twice. It was an arrangement that kept her from giving away my body for free, she explained with solemn words of wisdom. 'I could never understand or accept an empty bed two nights in a row,' she added further. She asked me if I was married already. I shook my head in denial. She smiled as if she had won a wager with herself.

A man like me could not want to play at sailing a float that was beached on a shore of providence or force himself to push it to sea, ankles sinking in the mud, for the sole expectation of avoiding loneliness; such was my general thought but I did not speak it.

She refilled my glass, which I consumed almost greedily with eyes that watched the empty bottom of the glass fogged with intermittent breath, amid the noise of the remaining ice cubes hitting the abandoned space without compassion. I looked at her jeans which were pretty and unfashionably slender in the leg. She let slip a slight giggle: 'It's not a message of NO,' she said softly. I did not understand. She asked: 'Would you be more encouraged if I had a dress on instead?'. I now understood. She was not sending me a message that she was unattainable when she wore the tight jeans; they could unroll easily if I wanted them to. Somehow, I did not really want to sleep with her. I wanted to stay beached on her shoulder, unhinged from the flesh, in silent recollection as I sank slowly into velvet-textured dream.

She dimmed the lights of the room. I was unsure of her action. As her lips went to cover mine, I looked into her eyes as I must have done hundreds of times before. This time the hunger was displaced by a timed explosion of words rather than by unworded pleas of 'more'. I stoppd about an inch away from her face. I wanted to say: 'Talk to me first', but failed to command it sternly. We kissed, in peril of letting the solitude of want escape cheaply, we kissed again and again and again.

She asked if we could sit on the soft carpet, unstained and new of any display of pleasure or spillage; and of new life with its comfort. We sat where we could still see the sky from the glass door of the balcony. The night had grown darker with the lateness of the hour and the effect of the alcohol that now had an authority of its own. We kissed again.

I held her hand: 'Please don't make me sleep with you, don't renew the haunting craving again; please, I have only one night left in the city.' I had voiced my petition to her gentleness and sincerity. She held my hand still, looking at the floor, her satiny hair drooping over most of her face where it stood out in the distant lights. Her mouth seemed to form words that I could not understand fully. 'Was it not her ageing body that revolted me or some other fear of transmission of some disease that was making me refuse her,' she asked pleadingly.

I explained that in ten days I was leaving this country forever. I had said it so simply that she did not believe it instantly. She could not understand why I would not give her a last reminder, if it was true. I was not looking for a slide into small pleasures in exchange for what might be my last binding memory of home.

I tried to explain: being here with her was more wonderful than passing through casual sex. I supposed love had a new face, while she was its long past, forgotten face. Her body silently attracted me, tranquillised my own and allowed it its physical presence and some of its purpose. I was afraid of dependence again becoming its strongest aspect; I was afraid of slipping into the degree of need I had of her before when we were together; I was afraid most of all of the trivial caging of passion, I was afraid of a hundred and one other things I might not be able to control. I was afraid to have a newer seed that might not match its past glory when I was a virgin and she was my goddess. I was afraid of carrying away with me a final disappointment.

I almost preferred to keep her image as I had known it for twelve or thirteen years, with old impressions not dusted off, truly a safe harbour of undisturbed, reinforced memory of loss.

We had more whisky, more sentences, holding each other's hands. We finally either drunk too much or were too tired to stay upright. We went to bed, fully clothed and covered with an old sheet. I woke up at the break of dawn, as the yawning curtains left open earlier in the night stretched in the early morning breeze. The flat was cold, contrasting with her warm body and the chilly bed. I stroked her hair for long, uncounted minutes.

I made a cup of tea, just for me and I sat at the kitchen counter, watching her asleep with her dreams and still, childlike contentment. At six in the morning I went to her bed, kissed her on the forehead, told her I loved her always and left.

I rushed to the hotel. I had two hours to make it to the train station for the trip home. The taxi wrestled with the morning traffic, yet I got to the station fifteen minutes early. The day train was awaiting its mighty engine.

The thirteen-hour trip was inaugurating my farewell. I watched the passing shadows and tall figures of the land through the eye of a window and the fully opened pupils of my mind.

The intermittent stretches of golden corn contrasted with the wavy wheat alongside, the wet fullness of rivers with the dryness of the sand following, all within the span of an hour, the busy black-clothed women collecting hay for their cattle with the empty fields of scrap iron, with the burning, scaffolded giant candles of gas and the smell of oil almost within distance of the tracks.

The country side stood aloof from my goodbyes, the world did not expect my knock on its thick wooden doors thousands of miles away, enforced by a whispered wish and my will to make the effort, unchanging in its attempts, its forecasts of failure or success. I was an orphan of the testament of my thought; no one expected my lenten solitude, to accept it or to offer it refuge. With the encouragement of my mind and in the solace of despondency, I stood alone, obedient to the essence of my will.

13

The Promise beyond Babylon

In the journey so far travelled, I have held faith with hope and mixed loss with love. In times of softer hunting and lighter crosses, gains have been those of suffrage and peaceful lamenting of luck. In hours of animal scent and clad nakedness, I had fallen wounded with my blood a proof of destiny. Peddlers of indifference had laid me silent with their cosmetic laughter and worthless distance. I believed yet I spoke not.

Strange wants subdue me when I think of the past: I want to relive its warmth, abdicate its mistakes and repeat its stray surrenders of the will. Every breath that had crossed my own, lived its long significance affording lesser pain in truth; every soul that had crossed mine overcame its presence as it believed its insignificance regrettable and shattering into more pieces than the numbers allow its paste-together complete. What would I have been, but for those who taught me life, those who pressed hard to stop the bleeding and those who posed their smile to chaperon the blood-flow, unwilling to arrest its spillage.

In the distortion of twilight, a butterfly may restrain the fluttering pulse of its coloured wings among the lavender, a cry may reflect its preference for opaque brightness in the ensuing dance of heat with time and the selfless, restless drive between ground and sky. A questioning of purpose seems inadequate in times of leisure and tremor.

For the mother I left behind there were three things eternal and lasting: faith, hope and love. In the afternoon of life, love outlasted its parentage of giving and delayed taking, a dusk of sorrows loomed loss and confusion, as if it was but a magical distemper in allegiance of the fog, as if it was but the fragrant residue of promise and distracted will.

Yet all seems possible and had leased its unwanted probabilities to the wind, to scatter on the edges of a note torn in anger or disappointment, dancing on an air of distress: a mistress of life and a cleavage of the heart with hard closed eyes that laid its juice sultry with the strength of unalloyed pain.

For the mother I left behind, the gift of language should last forever, unbroken in its worth and dressed in the plain colours of summer, brought forth in the brightness of winter and furnished with a soul-cutting blade in autumn. Spring was, now, a myth of the mind and a desolate fiction in pastures that hid the edges of the quicksand and the hunters' near intention to kill. She had expectations, but I refused to pretend I could dismiss fate, put behind me in alm.

My mother had released me. I was willing and she concealed her decision undisturbed on the surface and with silent eyes, accepting all with a forced smile and a simple effort.

Although that day was my twenty-sixth birthday, I was not aware of it, neither did my mother seem to portray her usual words of glistening wishes and sincere hopes.

At the train station in Basrah we stood all of us like a family in a portrait of excited reunion, with silence randomly broken by trivial words or sentences that avoided above all the mention of goodbye and any reminders of past times. I thought it odd: no one had brought any memories along or spoke of them, as if all of us were determined to spend the time in looking in each other's eyes, in trying to smile and forget this was happening until after the whistle had blown, when the smell of diesel would become the sign for immediate severance and I but a shadow. The train journey was quelled with some degree of indifference which made the hours fewer than they had seemed. I found the darkness of the carriage befriended me with a void of mind and easily sleepless of remembrances. I could not think of my past, as if it had been erased or washed clean away in a clinical state of mind. My thoughts seemed to have been masked with an emptiness that for the first time in my life did not assume pain, as if leaving Iraq was the achievement of a lifetime, beyond which, now that it was now almost consummated, nothing was prominent any more. Nothingness seemed so natural and soothing.

I arrived in Baghdad the following day and headed for the hotel. I had to ensure my booking on the plane was still valid. I went shopping for a few traditional nuts and sweets, presents for my friend in Dublin. The afternoon passed easily, starting with lunch, then a cinema before going back to the hotel to rest.

I called my family from the hotel room, to inform them that everything was in order. It seemed strange that I was speaking with such formal language and military precision, as if I was reporting progress in preparations to senior officers. My mother at the other end had to interrupt her sentences often, handing the receiver to my father or one of my sisters when her tears threatened to deform the sound of the words and clutter the line, as it seemed, with an unclear tone that sounded as if it was going far away, then coming in near. It was as if she was talking to me against an inconsistent wind.

I promised to keep in touch as much as I could, as if they were children and I was promising them anything to overcome some mutinying: as if I had become an acquaintance.

I found myself in Paris on a rainy afternoon looking for a hotel and dragging my large case behind me. I found a hotel not far from the Arc de Triomphe. The room was spacious for one and had small windows overlooking a backyard which held no promises of scenery or tidiness, although it seemed attended to almost regularly. I sat in the room; I was alone and I felt it in the profound quietness and the scent of the newly starched sheets, crisp and white, as if almost virginal.

I went for a walk in the early evening, looking at shops and finally getting something to eat in an Italian restaurant. It was my first time at such a restaurant and I liked the food I was served, enjoying their recommendations as my command of any language other than English or Arabic was non-existent. We, the waiter and I, seemed to reach a mutually acceptable understanding despite the barriers of slight words and the hand signals to ensure the correct message in the choice of food. I was full and he was content to have pleased my taste in the menu chosen.

On the way back to the hotel, I passed a small cinema with doors slightly open. I went in, examining the film posters, and although I could not tell its content or style, I decided to go in. The film was about a woman with a child who was shown sleeping with her friend, also a woman. It was odd for me in the beginning as I could not understand the dialogue and the love scene was not shown until the near end of the film. The relationship did not survive, as the child woke up in the middle of his sleep and caught his mother with her lover; this seemed to put the mother in a corner, where she had either to defend her love-making or explain to her small child the truth of things. The mother seemed to decide on termination of the affair.

In my hotel room, I thought of the woman with her child and her lover. I did not analyse her decision so much as think of the biology of the relationship. I had not known of such activity amongst women although I had heard of it amongst men. It seemed so out of purpose and shallow without the penetration of their bodies, although it seemed from the acting more spiritual and deep, than if it had been between two men. The warmth of the two women, while it lasted, was evident and natural in expression. I found myself not thinking of its ethical implications although the teachings of my childhood and adolescence had insisted that it brought about the deprivation of the soul and destruction of all good deeds in one's life in the eyes of God, be it one single act of need, maybe even of chance.

It seemed I was already changing, becoming numb to my past and its clear, forthright thoughts of right and wrong. It felt quite undisturbingly far away as if I had been released forever from every restraint of thought.

I was awakened in the morning by the rustle of keys trying to open my door. I could barely focus on the smiling face of the girl who stood in the doorway asking in French if she could come in (I presumed). I could not answer, so she went away with the same smile she had offered in lieu of her question.

I was awake then and decided to have breakfast. I changed and was on the side street in less than a few minutes, after a short moment debating whether I should shave or not. The feeling was anarchic and I went down without shaving my slight shadow. After breakfast, I found the Irish airlines office was not so far in a taxi; I wanted to confirm my booking for the next day. The attendant was apologetic, but as I had not confirmed it the day before, the plane now seemed full. The next plane was in two days, he announced. I had to book a place on that one. I went to the hotel and with the help of the switchboard telephoned my friend in Ireland. He was not at home, so I left him a message that I would be late arriving in Dublin, on the third of March.

When I went up to the room, the maid had the door flung almost open was changing the sheets on my bed. I saw her tuck away my pyjamas underneath my pillow as I walked in. She smiled again; her face of less than eighteen summers seemed almost childish and almost welcoming in its wordlessness. She spoke to me in French and I in English, not replying to her remarks.

She suddenly changed to English blemished with the pronunciation of her mother tongue. Her command of words did not seem totally logical, and although I could understand what she said, it seemed oddly constructed and alien in texture, rippling abruptly from a question mark to a full stop at the end of a sentence.

Dominique, as she was christened, was from the country. Her father was American and her mother French. She was a university student in her first year, studying philosophy and theology. My immediate thought was how strange a combination; it must be hard to restrain one against the other. I had served a long apprenticeship in avoiding both and almost felt the words ridiculed their marriage as an impossibility, but was not interested in discussing the oddity of the matter. In my view she must make one conform to the other or else both would perish, as I had seen them perish easily before in my past when I tried to attenuate their vigour, to make them co-exist peaceably and be lines on the same page.

She was amused and astonished to understand that I was from Iraq, although I spoke English with an American accent. Her fragments of thought made her looks and her posture look almost familiar, almost like those of Claire. The resemblance was strengthened by her straight hair and warm look. She stayed talking to me until she finished her duties, then took leave of me and promised to come back after seven in the evening if I was still there. Her promise seemed void of malice and pure in intention, as if we were children and that was the time allowed to come out and play. She lived next door, the last room in the corridor, as close as a wall away.

At seven or so, she knocked on my door. I opened it and she came in, a bottle of wine in one hand and daisies in the other, the soul offering for the evening to come. We sat on the bed and drank the wine. Her voice was low and mine was hushed whenever it became louder than hers. She explained simply that she had a job she needed to keep. The manager would withdraw it if he knew she was in my room. I was receptive to her motives and her reasons.

We spoke little of ourselves and more of the world, what life in Iraq and Provence was like, our families and our books, without leading on intentionally to opinion or our terms of reference. After two hours, the wine had made our words hazy and our minds elusive of expression. For the next hour or so we sat looking at each other without a word traded in the silence of the room. We were in a trance, and neither of us knew what land lay on the other side of the fog, we were shipwrecked and suspended on misty waters. It felt somehow wonderful.

We must have eventually fallen asleep, I awoke as she was turning away, it was five in the morning and dawn was trying hard to overcome the darkness and the obscure sky. I kissed her on the nape of the neck, as if I knew that would be acceptable and favoured, as if she was Claire. Her head creased back and I did it again. She turned toward me and faced me, sleepy with the hour. We undressed without feeling the cold of the room and without noticing the time it took, almost an instant. Her body was tender and my soul was aching.

She took me, again and again, and I was but a child in want. Her eyes glittered in the light of the morning reflected in the large mirror and borrowed from the small, bright window. At eight, I lay robbed of energy and closed my eyes for sleep. She slipped away without a warning and more slowly than she had come in. She woke me at three in the afternoon, carrying a tray of food and announcing: 'Lunch, you ordered, monsieur?'.

We ate and stalked our hunger with more sleep that afternoon. It seemed so natural, as if we had lived together for years and had no need to speak none of promises or bondage to each other, as all that had already been said years ago and settled long before we had taken our bodies to an altar and shared them equally.

I marked the day in my pocket diary: Her name, the hotel phone number and the date, the second of March 1977. The opposite page had the flight number and time of arrival: three thirty in the afternoon, local time, Dublin. Three pages before and endless pages beyond these markers seemed fated desolate of intention.

Late in the evening we went out separately through the hotel door, I first, then she. The five minutes between us felt like an hour standing at the corner of the street, under a faint light. I felt we were like two homosexuals: forbidden to be together under a forceful warning from the company.

We went to a bar, then to a late-night cinema. I was not so slow in understanding the plot of the film that time. It was a Swedish film about two cousins who fell in love in their childhood and became lovers at the awakening of puberty. It was a simple film filled with warm colour and length of craving. She almost cried when the boy tried to kill himself, while I cried when the girl died of illness later in the plot. It felt real and lifelike, the fourteen-year old was so tender, with brown eyes like Jessica's. The film made me remember: gave me back the silence I lost not long ago, made me return empty handed and poor to my past.

We went back to the hotel, I first, then she; separately again as we had left. I went to my room, but she did not follow. I did not miss my companion in the next room, although I could not go to sleep until dawn was evident again. As if she had not existed; I neither thought of her nor wondered where she was.

In the morning, she woke me asking to make the room and change the sheets. I asked her where she went last night; her reply was cold and showed no interest in the facts. I tried to apologise, but it seemed useless. I sat her down on my lap and told her about Jessica. My life seemed to be summarised briefly in neatly chosen sentences that did not omit the truth nor mask the essence of loss. She was touched and I was forgiven. She kissed me in a sisterly fashion and I her. I went out briefly before lunch, to look for a present for her and found one, a crystal model of a butterfly, the glass refracting all colours of the rainbow as you turned the body towards the stray light of day. She appeared with an envelope in her hand and we exchanged our gifts informally.

In the musk-green envelope were seven or so flowers, expertly dried and evenly tempered. A note was folded like a smooth fence. A correspondingly timid hand had written on it: These are flowers, kept from childhood. I give them for you, for your butterfly (Jessica), may she accept them and release you to the fields, even if you were allowed to become the tare amongst the corn and the colour in the shade; at least you'll be free.

My gift had no note to express the reason for my choice, but she smiled as she unveiled it, understanding its reason and amazed at the harmony of its smooth soul.

She kissed me long and then left the room in silence. She had gained the attention of my soul and knew it well in honesty of innocence and truth of time. I had another land to reach and another peace to make. The day had been quite ordinary and yet unforgettable.

14

A Cross for a Beggar

It was the end of May 1977. We shook hands, standing under the yellow fog light of the street, obstructing the late evening breeze, casting darkness on the part of the path nearest to us, avoiding the final word as we stared into each other's eyes, catching there a look of intimate wishes and hard feigning any reason for retreat into yesterday. All seemed lost, all seemed but the past, nothing rigid or real but a faint moment.

Her eyes shone like a thousand stars on a summer night. Her tears pale like wax, dripping from the sacrificial glow of her silence, clung to her like a second skin unwilling to shed itself in brightness of the light and the darkness of intentions.

I stood, my eagerness stressed with hope, stamped with a strange bewilderment, sombre as if I was a broken up crest, casting a shadow shorter than my height and dressed in the numbness of the moment. I could hardly betray my will without failing it.

She leaned forward without slipping out my hand and surprised me with a whispered 'take care', followed by a kiss softer than her words, gentler than her voice and more wanting than her insistence. She pulled away a little, as if to see my face or to ensure I had heard her, to insist on a deeper silence or to instigate a reason for other words, now completely forgotten. She followed her stalling with another, softer kiss on my lips but added nothing that might demand an answer or supplant those last words spoken in strength, in the absence of my reply.

I leaned over her face, smelt her perfume, as if it was to be the last time I breathed its mixture of excitement and nuances sweet in their attraction. My lips found her neck and printed a light reminder of heat on her skin over and across the chain that held her cross to its value for her. My lips found the cold metal and crossed over it trespassing the crispness of her strength.

She paraded her instant reaction, hugging me and rocking me as my head found its familiar resting place on her shoulder and decided to remain there, even if it was for the last time. I found myself in tears, that followed on fast as I breathed her skin and led towards a flood of sighs and loss of control. I was a child again, holding his disfigured gift, broken in need of comfort, his will to stop crying lost as if forever.

She wiped the side of my face and with the same hand wiped her own, sharing the liquid pain, smearing her eye-shadow. She put that hand on my mouth as if to tell me: 'all tears taste the same', or to stop me begging for an end to indifference, or simply to push her mind to remain strong and her own lips wordless.

She looked at my face once more, kissed me on the eyelids and slipped her other hand out of mine without that earlier clear hesitation. It was time to release herself and drain the tears, as eager as the edge of a newly sharpened knife, as honest as the resonant confession of guilt, but as stony as a promise broken with intent.

I stood unwilling to say I loved her as she walked into the darkness at the unlit end of the street. Nothing was further exchanged, nothing relented, all trespassed in sadness: she came and faded like a butterfly in a short summer, which I had claimed it, pretended it a lifetime of spring.

'Oh, bless me father, for I have sinned'; my voice climbed the wooden barrier of the confessional, hanging on the little curtain on the other side of the low window and ending in faint words for the ears of the priest.

He was not looking directly at me, as if he was tired of routinely repeated sins; anticipating all the possible forms he had encountered, or was encouraging me to go further than that simple declaration, untrying my hesitation and bleeding me of will to stop spilling my honest realisations, wrongs undertaken for any reason. I stopped to measure his reaction, while he assured me of his wakefulness with three simple words: 'yes, my son'.

My confession was stammering. I had little intuition for what I should say and feared rejection. I was neither a Catholic, nor a Christian, either by birth or proclamation. Yet I had come to yield my worded intention and seek comfort. It had been a turbulence of such amplitude that it had already worn down the tranquillity of my soul to near apathy. I had not seen Andrea for two weeks. The last goodbye had never been the last thought of her, but I often found myself thinking of her in a peculiar mention of another name. The thought used the name 'Jessica' when I was reflecting on Andrea which was confusing, even to my mind which had always been clear in matters of sequence, until now.

There was also the matter of judging God. The loss of Jessica some thirteen years earlier had questioned the intimate gentleness of that absolute, irreproachable and uncompromising power, which most of us accept from childhood until death, through days and nights of laughter and tears. I wanted to hear God's miniature version of the world through the mouth of God's keeper of intent and the enforcer of his intention.

I wished I was allowed to smoke, in this dark, small corner of the world, where I was naked of all colours but those affected by the mind and the perception of the man in black, the two of us separated from one another by thin compliant timber and a harder barrier where thousands must have declared their regrets softly and I repented loudly and easily.

Under the sudden impact of this last thought I felt I was unimportant, yet privileged to a strange degree as my need to conform blended with my need to shed my pain with an ease that might justify my occupation of this meagre space amid the darkness, where one can only see a little square containing a window to the mind of a man outcast for his strict opinions and admired for his sacrifice; a man who stood to live aside from physical touch, while crowded with the declarations of those who represented the other side of behaviour: a human, sometimes humane.

He seemed a man of privilege as far as being proclaimed a chosen one, but might be lonelier than I was, thought more skilled in containing the monotony of his life. Yet I had not come to judge him, to compare his plain authority or to ask purely for advice. I had come to release my portion of dark contention into a vessel that might turn it into wine. I wanted this man to decode probability and make me simple, accepting, sympathetic to the world.

I needed the light shades of purple and red to emerge from the grey shadow of my eyes and become whole once again, not a figment of some enigmatic imagination. I was a man whose twenty-five years of being were already taking on black and grey tones; everything was that colour without discrimination of experience or intention. The priest urged me again to go on.

I started after a short pause: 'I have come not for absolution but for explanation'. I proceeded: 'Does it matter where I was born, who I am or what I have done?' I asked in contemplation of an answer that should be simply 'No'. He answered me differently: 'Not to God, my son'. It was acceptable to me.

'I have been in Ireland barely three months now, I have had a girl for the past two and half months and she has gone, probably forever', I surmised. The priest was silent, probably anticipating the climax. 'Is she dead, dying or pregnant?' he asked. Suddenly I was filled with a feeling of oddity. I corrected his questions to allow him to find out simply. 'No, our paths parted, two weeks ago, each to his wind and each to his sail, drifting when the sea's calm, riding the storm when we cannot sleep, weeping when we can'.

He was silent yet once again, before he asked: 'How do you know this, have you seen her or spoken to her since you've parted?' He had a valid point, which seemed to contradict my assumption that we had not met since. I tried to explain: 'I feel so, no, I know so'. I could feel his poor opinion of me gathering pace, winding up to boredom or even disgust.

I started again: 'She left me because I gave her an ultimatum: she had to choose either me or her drugs and she chose one.'

The priest seemed to hesitate, thinking hard; a good sign, I thought, for me, in place of unworded sceptism. He asked: 'Would you like me to talk to her and arrange therapy?' I answered in the negative, implying I did not want her exposed to the world. I went on to explain further: 'It's hopeless, father.'

The priest was disheartened, and quite easily, I thought. This had not been the first time I had lost someone to something I could not control. 'Andrea's image: Jessica, who some thirteen years or more ago (I'm feeling hazy about years now), had committed suicide'. I added: 'Again, now, I am going to lose Andrea, maybe in an overdose, it's still suicide to me.'

The priest's mouth seemed to move faster than his words: 'We must put an end to any trial like that, the life God has given to anyone is ours to shape, but not ours to waste or to destroy.' He was adamant.

I was one who did not carry such restlessness so far, for I believed that one cannot stop the march of another's will; whether it was God's gift or creation is irrelevant. My old argument, which always bewildered my father and my teachers, that if God wanted, he could have averted such like loss or sinning, but did not, such an argument was surfacing again. I felt it: 'God has let me down, he has chosen me to suffer for those who died: their suffering seems over, but those who were left behind with the cutting edge of memory, those were the sufferers, who pay the final fine and have to accept the alms of others' sympathy, irrespective of whether it was truly meant or offered,' I explained. The priest was silent.

He finally seemed to endure his curiosity no longer. Overcoming his suspicion, he asked when it was I had last gone to confession. I honestly answered that this was the first; I was usually a pagan. He was disdainful of this answer that revealed my obstruction of the bright consciousness of the God he saw as the light of the world. He stopped the questioning and asked if we could talk face to face. I did not deny him his right.

We emerged out of the dark cubicles, both covered with sweat, a sign of a hot summer starting already. He was slightly astonished by the tone of my skin, tanned by both long days in the sun and the heritage of far away places. We went behind the altar, into a room bright with the afternoon sun and with the reflection of its light in the glass covering the faces of giant portraits, which looked half hand-painted and half photographs, of different saints and scholars. On the first instant, the room seemed to me deeply soaked with utopia and its tranquil air.

With a certain look of curiosity, he started asking me whether I was a Catholic, a Christian or what. My head shook in denial everytime. He offered me tea, which I accepted silently. He sat back in an old chair, facing me as the sun shone on his face. I told him I was troubled.

He asked me about my family and whether they were happy; I was living away in a culture artificial to their way of thinking. I did not ask myself that ever. My mother, understood the world but had no intention of expressing her understanding or revolting against her fate of simply being a woman in a world owned by men. In any case, she definitely wanted me out of Iraq. To her mind, being away, obtaining an education of the world and being alive was better than being drafted into another man's whims of war. She was a classic mother first and a woman second, in a country that seemed to graduate college students and its own war victims in equal numbers, and with the same frequency.

He was listening, but no comment came forward from the long look of intense thought reflected in his silence and the slow lifting of the cup of tea to his mouth, which he drank as if it was a ritual. He suddenly asked again if I wanted him to help Andrea, hinting that he needed to know her full name and address, to try effectively. I yielded without thinking. She lived around the corner from the church.

He guessed with satisfaction: 'That is why you are in this church', satisfied that he had started to understand my motives for the confession: I wanted to be close to her at the same time, as close as it was possible without being with her. I conceded with a soft voice, like a schoolboy who had been caught and could not but admit his hidden reason.

He promised he would never tell her that I had gone to see him, though I did not know whether I could truly believe him. He added further: 'You should not complain of God if people take their own lives as if it was his will. He would never instruct any of us to do that, we have to make our own choices. You also have to live your life with someone who will be there for you and you only. Anyone else who could not make this promise and keep it, would be the wrong person to mould your life for.' He ended his long sentence abruptly.

'Your mind should learn to acquiesce experience into the wisdom of reading people's fate with you or without you. Country roads have many a small pebble lying in wait for the beggar's bare feet, yet neither his blood nor his pain shall make them pity him and move out of his way.' He added: 'All of us have a cross to bear, it may be hard, invisible or the cause of our bleeding, it will be there whether we wish it away or throw it to the wind, it is always with us and for us to carry forever, we can only let go of it when we are buried and forgotten, never before that that we could become faint to others.' He soothed my soul, almost in a hypnotic fashion, ending my insurrection with a few words and calm attention.

Probably, the strength of physical similarities between Andrea and Jessica, the way she looked at you with her brown eyes, or by contrast smiled suddenly with sheer enjoyment after you had looked back as hard at her, or the way she gave you the world in twenty-five minutes, sharing her breath when she was so close to you, or when she spoke so little but so concisely, relaxing only when you had understood or agreed, or her skin that felt like the end of the sky captured in a velvet touch, or this or that, . . . I haven't found out the end of things yet.

I was now, as I was once, without pain, poised to seal tranquillity of mind into a glass jar, ready to lease my courage to conquer the universe without comprehension or hesitation over what might follow. Childish, perhaps, but life was feeling enthusiastic in its aperture away from any despondency, it was mine to give away and no one's to question its lead or its correspondence of faith. Her eyes then, as always, were the point of meeting and the end of waiting, nothing else ever mattered or existed when we were together. I will always remember her eyes, even in my senility and unto death.

I came out of the room and into a dark, cold hall that smelt of unblemished polish. I walked for about an hour before I realised I was at the door of my flat. The white swans on the edge of the canal seemed as vicious and uncaring as ever, although the afternoon was warm and the sky was still lit with an orange glow of clear, soft existence.

June started the next day. It seemed doomed to be already a month of hard decisions and long-drawn-out heat. I almost felt homesick, when I saw the pictures of old Basrah on the television, in the eyes of Sinbad the sailor. It was not the same town I grew up in, as this was allegedly some thousand years earlier, I could smell the spices and feel the damp air as the camera went on capitalising further on every possible second of the expensive Hollywood set. It did not look real although I felt it real. It recalled for me the nursery rhyme my mother used to tell me about Sinbad, who could only achieve fame as a sailor and as a mischievous prince. She must have seen the same script played out, and as simply, by different actors. I preferred her rhymes to the lengthy killing of imagination.

The night was longer than the day it inherited. I could not easily sleep. Being a Saturday, the next morning was as heavy. I decided to go to the beach, to my favourite secluded spot, a fifteen minutes' climb from the terminus of the 31 bus route, which started from the city centre, utilising the best part of almost half an hour to reach its destination. Howth was a place where the wind never stopped throwing the waves against the rocks, or sending them foaming against the dried seaweed on the lower reaches where the shallow waters only lay lightly before the next tide. It was always more beautiful than the map could ever reveal with its lines hedging the green and the different depths of sea shore.

I stood for hours watching in silence, my mind resting from speculation or analysis, bare of thought and willing the time to slide by gently unnoticed. It was heaven.

On the way back, I stopped at the small church that was uphill from the bus terminus. Its stained glass glittering in the afternoon sun, its doors forecasting willingness to receive any one who needed to enter, its cool interior heavy with lingering smells of molten wax, all in silence now that the small organ was stilled, hinted at anticipation and quietness; all that silence, replacing bodily hunger with service for the soul.

The bus journey seemed longer than it really was, the six or so miles slowly accumulated before ending sharply at the terminus. I passed a man sleeping in the late afternoon, smelling of cheap wine and quite happy not to endorse the world or fulfil any of his duties towards it. I looked in my pocket; I had ten pence left in the folds of my jeans, which I readily forfeited to him. I had a feeling, or perhaps more than a feeling, I hoped I would never become like him. My compassion to the beggar was self-motivated. I was afraid, as if I was forecasting my future, that I would be like him. I was a man who felt his life not his own, who felt far away from home. Homesickness and apathy combined to lay layer after layer of sadness without resistance from me.

For a moment, when he was waking up to accept the coin, I was that beggar, clad in some hope and about to forsake the world. The penalty was there in front of me, yet I felt drawn to become like him, willing to be orphaned of ties I had initiated and respected, ties I once wanted and almost begged to have. The choice, if it was a choice, of cutting loose was not real most of the time. I felt I was almost him, or at least was in his early stages of decision. His body and odour of cheap wine did not disturb me, to my surprise. He asked me to drink some of his wine, handing me a bottle that had dry mud-like fingerprints on its neck, as if freely offering me something that seemed to have been held tight to his chest for most of the night before, that he was defending from others or had fought for dearly.

His tanned skin was a select mark of that sun-dynasty of all street dwellers, who displayed a toned-down impression of enjoyment and of time passed in the heat, rather than a worship of the sun's rays. I felt as if privileged to belong and be there. I drank some of his wine, a liquid that in its pale texture and taste had more in common with vinegar than with wine. Still, I drank some of it, without a thought for the burning in my throat that developed instantly.

I sat cross-legged and irritable of the hard pavement, uneasy at the possible permanency of such a decision, which dictated what seemed like an equitable trade between apathy and tranquillity. It was as if an intention to become a drifter was about to manifest its character as the lethargy of intent's stucco.

Although I did not welcome it, it had an unfamiliar spell about it. I was half-way to becoming a fellow of the cardboard camps and within hours of accepting the test. I drank again from his bottle, taking the container without being requested to or being offered it. For a moment, I was no different from him or any of his compatriots; I was learning. The wine took its toll on me and I fell asleep, crossing my arms on my chest and folding my legs into my groin. I felt strangely safe, peaceful and without worry.

By the evening, I was feeling hungry. My tutor told me not to worry, he knew of a place that left good food to waste every night. After eleven o'clock, we went to the back entrance of a restaurant serving pizza. In the half-lit alley were tens of cardboard boxes, most of them half-filled with food. It tasted almost like leather, but the teeth complained little.

We were full and he signalled to me his intention of getting a bottle of wine. I searched for any money I might have left. There was none on me. He was looking at my watch. I felt it was not mine and offered it to him to quell the almost hysterical joy he was exhibiting. He promised to share the wine with me.

He disappeared for ten or fifteen minutes, coming back with three bottles that had the same label on them, printed in black on light red, a label that said 'Paradiso' and some other Spanish words which I could not decipher and did not care to investigate. It tasted a little better than the afternoon batch. He gave me one and kept two for himself. We shared a corner of a barricaded door that smelt of mould and oblivion. I found the wine pleasing and the darkness of the street soothing in its privacy.

He murmured some indistinct sentence that ended with the name on the label. I was astonished that he could read or understand it, as if I had already judged him as ignorant of mind. I asked him what he had said. He returned with a stern voice: 'This is the poetry of Paradise.' I could not comprehend what he was saying. He looked at me with a long gaze that preceded his next sentence: 'If it was that peaceful in heaven, why would they offer wine freely there.' He expected me to answer or maybe laugh. His consonants and their vowels seemed so far removed from our cold seats and so intimate with philosophy that I found them troublesome. Although he made a hard point, I felt his soul as soft as the wink in his right eye. I could not carry his argument forward, so remained silent, feeling almost drunk but conscious of him.

He finally accepted my silence with some of his own and ushered me to a pile of cardboard boxes lying barely moving in the night breeze at the end of the street. We used them to cover our faces. Sleep came swiftly to the glassy eyes that reflected the light from the sign board high above our heads, which confronted us with its glitter of colours and the vibrancy of the electric currents gushing through its thin glass veins.

We were awakened by the muted scream of a young voice from across the street. A tall man dressed in white and black was leaning over a blanket inhabited by someone. The effort persisted. The tall figure pulled the blanket away and the small build of a girl stood up and went to regain it. There was a brief struggle. She gained her blanket and ran towards our abode. The figure followed.

The girl flung herself between the two of us and held on to my right arm, hiding her face behind my shoulder with her eyes closed to all of us. The tall man, who was in his early thirties, stood watching. He asked her to come away, showing her his fat wallet. She spat at him (and presumably at his money). He tried to kick her in the leg. My companion growled and pulled a thin, shining blade from his side. The glint deterred the attacker more than the gesture of his readiness to slash the man's face. The attack was beaten off with hardly a word and even less choice. The girl was crying. She could not have been more than sixteen. She sat upright, covering herself from her shoulders downwards with her valuable blanket. Her hair was matted on one side, a sign of sleeping predominantly on that side of her face. Her eye on the opposite side swollen. She made a gesture that she was going, without expressing any words of gratitude. Neither of us, the original occupants of the site, tried to stop her. She got up and then sat again, changing her mind without being either persuaded or asked to stay.

She leaned against my arm as if it was a pillow and seemed almost instantly to fall asleep. I fell asleep before long and like her without saying anything. I could hear the sounds of a wine bottle emptying into the hero's mouth at regular intervals. Apart from the effort to lift the bottle to his mouth, he was motionless. The girl did not seem either disturbed or awakened by the sound, as if it lullabied her to deeper sleep.

Sunday morning arrived earlier than we wanted. The police were on the streets before anyone else. We were awakened by one of 'them' and asked to move away from the door which had housed us for the night. The three of us got up without visible resistance. In the early morning sun I looked in her eyes; they were marble-coloured eyes in their sorrow. We all drifted into another back street and another until we reached the river Liffey. We sat by the bank in a togetherness that was complete and undirected, as if our minds were one and our bodies moved by the same will and muscles. It was too early to speak and too late to introduce ourselves. We were inhaling the morning mist and welcoming the heat of the day with equal acceptance.

After an hour or so, we threaded our way to the back alley where we had fed last night. The girl followed without asking where we were going. There were no boxes left nor any evidence of food. The prized loot had either been removed or been raided by others like us overnight. The end result was the same, we remained hungry. We walked on to O'Connell Street, filling its barren pavements with shadows.

Later that morning, I was drawn to the loud voice of a woman, emanating from the middle of the main street. She was dressed in a black suit of skirt, jacket and beret. She held a hand-painted plaque of Jesus across her chest and a large copy of the Bible in the other, raised high above her head.

She was shouting more loudly than she needed, since the streets were still half-empty. I went closer to her. She almost stopped her words at my approach. I stood, with my other companions behind me, watching her. The preacher continued with greater vigour

before her newly formed audience. She paraded her thick Bible in
front of my eyes, mellowing her loudness gradually. She looked at
me with large eyes that seemed to have swallowed the world. She
asked me to receive the covenant of God with open arms and purge
my soul of its dark corners. I was not committed to her cause. She
asked me if I was hungry, and I replied strenuously 'Yes'.

The lady put her plaque down carefully against a lamppost, still
holding her Bible hard against her chest riveted with her elbow.
She then reached and opened one of the three chains she had
around her neck. She handed me the chain which was weighed
down by a small golden cross. She kissed it and asked me to do the
same. I did, without either conviction or mistrust. The sheen of its
cleanliness and the bright yellow light it reflected against my skin
captured my eyes in a trance, only broken by a fragment of thought.

She asked me to keep it, wishing perhaps I would promise to
keep it with me always. My companions were watching me with
eyes that pressed me to say anything to have it in our hands. I held
it gently in the palm of my hand, between a thumb and first finger.
I was debating with myself whether to keep it. The ease with which
I had proposed changing my life into that of the man who slept on
the street was now being challenged with equal ease. I still had a
place to go to, a life to resume if I wanted it, but I did not want to, at
least for the moment, for the day, for the year. I was thinking of
other times in my life, inevitably of my mother.

I also thought of pawning it, but then I did not feel I could do
that. To keep it on me would be hazardous, my companion's thirst
was nearly dry and his last bottle almost empty. To keep it carried
also a promise to believe in it. I wanted neither to give it away, nor
make promises I might not be able to keep. I was on the thin edge
between honesty and the wish to please my new found friends. I
gave it back, as slowly as I was handed it, as if it was a fragile,
expensive crystal the value of which lay in its intact body and the
light reflecting from its inner edges.

The lady took it back, accepting my rejection, but her face sowed
little seeds of anger on her lips. She put her cross on again and
continued with what she was shouting, disregarding our presence
and walking in a circle of a few yards back and forth. Both her
hands were now holding the Bible as high as they could stretch, the
portrait of her saviour was still leaning against the lamppost, in a
contentment without regrets. She was voicing with transparent

loudness a prophecy, a plain acknowledgement of the coming of her Lord that was not so much a warning as an emphasis of fact. She had already forgotten about us or had at least decided to do so.

I retreated to where the other two were standing, barely a yard or two from where I was. The girl looked at me with a look that told me she was thinking: a bet on this horse is a lost bet, this is not what I want. Our other companion was even more honest in expressing his feeling; he told me I was a fool, a gold cross would have given us wine for days, all three of us. I had acted against the interest of the clan. I was a fool, whose honesty was near its value in stupidity. He simply walked away, followed by the girl. I followed after some slight hesitation and more confusion.

At the edge of the street, we all sat down, sharing a small entrance to a condemned shop. The man took out a bottle I did not know he had. He offered the girl a drink, which she took. I was waiting to be offered one, but was not. The bottle made successive journeys between their mouths, bypassing me. I was being punished for the misfortune of not practising deception.

I had never gladly accepted reprehension since I had been five years old. I was not going to think he would succeed where my father had eventually decided to use logic instead of coercion to make me conform. I decided to go to sleep, leaning against the door riddled with woodworm, with my eyes closed. I could hear the girl's sick laughter and the man's propositions of kissing get louder and louder. They were near a point of drunkenness where anything was possible and anything permitted. I turned my face away from them and fell into sleep.

I woke up some few hours later to find my companions had abandoned me to the midday (or even later) heat. They had disappeared like dust-drift in the wind, without a mark as to where they had gone or which direction they had taken. The streets had erased their being as if they had never been there or had peopled my imagination and I had woken up from dream.

I walked in the hot city air until it was time to give up looking. My body ached with stiffness, my head ached with the wine and I myself ached with the odour of my body. I walked out of the city centre and towards my flat in Rathmines without being guided or thinking of where I was going. I was like a dog finding its way home by instinct and with minimal thought of direction. I found myself at the door of my flat, looked for my keys and found them without further delay. I was as if home again.

I took off all of my clothes, peeled them off as if they were saturated with time I wanted to forget, as if they could not be cleaned ever. I discarded them in a heap in a plastic bag destined for the refuse collection. I did not care that some of my clothes had been worn for the first and last time, they were to be shed for ever.

I felt newer blood in me after a shower. I was thinking of Andrea, Jessica, my mother and the priest. I belonged to my old world once again. I had been retrieved from suspended time, unwillingly but perhaps fortunately. I was 'me' again, regardless of faults or miscomprehensions; I had been found after the fog, alive and as well as could be expected. I was with that soul again that I had known best and longest – mine.

15

Rainbows

There are those colours of the rainbow that defy the rules of physics, in shades that are not allowed in concept but are easily seen with the naked eye and the open mind. Such are the colours of love, such are the prophecy of friendship, the ecstasy of hope and the long dependence of the soul.

If one was to open a chapter for every heart one encountered, every quiver one moulted or every sunset to which one shared the dawn, the words would demand a second language that perceives emotion in different shades, where love and pain stood on opposite fences, divided by the sense of time and provoked by the sensitivity of light to tenderness at the breaking point and beyond. The choice of seeing the additional colours of the rainbow remains at all times a personal contention of one's past, a reflection of its delicate store of memory and its threshold of pain. Nothing simpler, nothing more complex, nothing in between.

That Sunday afternoon it was as if I had woken up to find that I had not put away my childish things: they were all around still. The previous day was best forgotten as a dream; nightmares might not be as easily forgotten. I had decided that and on an early night. Yesterday had been long past my bed time. A cold shower was needed too.

The night was to pass easily, without the usual trend of waking before morning. Monday was placid, as compared to other Mondays endured before. I made my way to college, collected my mail from home off my bench and read the two letters I had received while smoking a cigarette in the hall before trying to start an experiment that was long overdue.

The college rag week, which had started that day, did not increase one's enthusiasm or devotion for work either. Free open-air lunch-time concerts, sitting on the short-cut grass and drinking beer, the heat of the sun and the free feeling of being a student: everything combined in that sweet, suspended time and the long hours of peace with one's soul. It was the most wonderful time in all our lives, where the only two complaints seemed to be not being millionaires or absolutely, passionately being in love.

The evenings were long that year and this one was no different. I walked from the college to my flat, passing lovers kissing at bus stops in the full heat of summer. After cooking myself a light meal, I was ready to go to the bar. I was about to leave when a light knock came on the door, announcing someone's arrival. Even before opening the door, I could guess from the light impact of slim fingers that it was a girl. It was Lelia.

She was a country girl from Galway. She had spent most of the last ten years in Dublin, although her accent did not suggest the length of time she had spent there or how far from home she had come to live. She was a civil servant, in a comfortable nine-to-five job with minimum antagonism and hardship. Her other life could not be outlined with such ease or comfort, I was sure, without knowing why. She was of slim build, with straight auburn hair, fair skin and light freckles.

She was a girl whose mind and words would make any man into a friend if she wanted, and without effort on her part. Her acceptance of people was simple: accept them unless they hurt you. She lived in the first floor above me sharing her flat with Peggy, a well-built girl who wore round glasses all the time and flaunted her long red hair, which always seemed uncombed from the tangles and kinks in it. Peggy had matching freckles that filled her face with a childish look that always gave a false impression of her age. Lelia was one year younger than I was, while Peggy was possibly older, I never inquired nor was told.

Lelia wanted to borrow some soap, or so she said. I lent her a new bar I had, without asking her to come in. She looked curiously at me as she was always asked in. Her eyes had that question mark that never failed to appear whenever she was thinking of something or questioning it, looking half-away from you.

She took the soap in one hand and was about to close the door behind her with the other when I seemed to surprise her by asking if she wanted a cup of tea. She accepted, after the usual, almost formal query of it not being too much trouble. I assured her it was 'one on the pot', in bad English, indicating with a simple gesture that her question was unnecessary.

We sat facing each other at the small table, set up near the window, a foot or so away from my unmade bed. She took a cigarette when I offered it. I asked her if Peggy was in. She smiled, implying that I was interested in Peggy. I assured her that I only wondered if she would like a cup of tea too. Lelia assured me 'No', in a hurry. I noticed the speed of her answer. She then asked how college was and advanced from that to ask if I was going out tonight. I said: 'Nothing planned, just going for a drink, alone'. She smiled again.

I wanted to ask her if she would like to go out with me for a drink, but I was not sure if she would interpret that as a date, which was not my intention or reason in asking. She had been in my flat many times for cups of tea or a chat, nothing more serious or romantic, nothing but a shallow, platonic exchange of light conversation, mostly analysing the weather. I finally asked her, after two cups of tea and an hour of casual exchange. She agreed easily, commenting she was ready as she was, without the need to 'go upstairs' to change her clothes.

We walked a short distance to the main street in Rathmines. At the bar both of us soon settled with our drinks, she with her mineral water and I with my pint of ale. She hesitated, rubbing the condensation off her glass, before she finally said: 'May I ask you what you did over last weekend?. Let me explain first,' she interrupted herself and my words before I could reply. Last Saturday night last, she had had a dream she could not explain to herself. She was walking through a wide street in town when she was attracted to a man sleeping under a cardboard box on the other side of the street. She had an impulse to go and see who he was. She crossed the empty street, slowly stopping at his feet. After she had been shading the midday sun from him for a few minutes or little more, the beggar finally lifted his face from underneath its cover, wondering why the light was less than it had been some minutes earlier. Lelia and the beggar gazed at each other, each trying to identify the face revealed.

She had a feeling, she thought in her dream, that she knew him. He looked as if he was debating the same issue with his memory, either of them could confirm the feeling. She asked him 'if he was alright'. The tone of her voice seemed more familiar to him. He complained of this or that before asking for her money; he was an experienced beggar who was not about to miss a chance sent from heaven.

As she was taking out her purse, his voice suddenly matched a name which appeared in front of her eyes. She had to ask: 'Edmund?' The beggar, taken back, could not hide his shock. He was silent for the first time in his life, in the midst of his begging. He automatically went to brush his jagged beard, but his hair did not respond because of the coating of dust, dried up food and liquid that stiffened his hair for days and weeks.

His astonishment was that some one knew him. He acknowledged his name with somehow slacker enthusiasm, unsure of what was could follow. 'I am Lelia, I used to live in the flat on top of yours, what, ten, fifteen years ago. Do you remember me or Peggy?'. She thought she had assured him.

I was getting uneasy about her tale. She had dreamt of me in the same night I was 'down-and-out', with the final twist that it was some ten years or more on. The implied future tense of her sentences was troubling me. She noticed my uneasiness and asked me not to interrupt her, although I had not said anything. She read my expression of distress; my face was paralysed, showing pale disquiet.

She continued: 'You had a beard at least ten inches long, filled with a grey colour. I could not determine what it was, whether it was age or some other matter.' I managed a smile at her disgust, her mouth was shaped like a deformed 'O' and her hands were holding her breath, as if she could still smell the beard.

She had asked me in her dream how I had 'ended up' like that. I had answered with many unconnected details; or she could not remember exactly. It seemed that I had started this trip when I decided to experience the freedom of the world for one night. I was knifed the next day by one of my street companions. I spent the next six months or so in hospital, nearing death more than a few times. On coming out of hospital, I had lost whatever money I had, lost my flat and my place in college. I must have been put on that road when the turning point had already been passed, for ever. I was on the streets longer than I could remember, or so I had told her, and she had simply believed.

She could remember herself almost thinking in the dream: 'That's why he disappeared, suddenly one day and never returned again to the house'. She took a gulp of her drink, as if there was more, harder details or as if she was debating whether she should tell the rest. I was waiting too.

She had asked the beggar if he was planning to go home. He confided in her that such a project would require a large sum of money. Lelia turned back the collar of her blouse to reveal an old golden cross. 'I was going to give him this, but I could not be sure he would pawn it for a ticket home. I was afraid he would drink it instead.' She was explaining logically her inaction in that dream in terms of 'him' rather than 'you'. I understood her reasoning and assured her that I appreciated the thought and that after all it was only a dream. She looked away, as if disregarding the latter part of my statement; as if I had ridiculed her prophecy.

I was not without doubt, not without worry and not without interest. I wanted to know more, but the dream seemed to have ended abruptly. She had woken up and the tie was broken. I bought both of us another drink. I decided to confess to her where I had been over Saturday and Sunday. She listened with a silence that implied interest and an active comparison of her dream with the actual procession of events.

I did not want to elaborate my reasons for cutting arbitrarily all the strings to my life. I was driven by something more lethal than apathy, more invisible than a thought and more pervasive than a loss of will. I had merely drifted into a code of not thinking of myself more than in defence of my depression. I could not explain my drift any more than she could explain her dream. I had already forgotten, or at least was not consciously taking any stance on my action; the question was, would she do the same with her dream?

I asked: 'Do you always dream such events that come closer to prophecy and tread on foretelling the future?' She was silent for a while, then started her sentences in a fashion that reminded me of stories ominous with 'once upon a time'. 'In the village of Spiddal, about twelve miles from Galway city, I lived with my two sisters who were younger than me. I was the unlucky one of the three. From the age of six, I could dream of events that were out of the ordinary, and these would happen. Some I could not speak of, some I would let slip, some would keep repeating themselves concurrently until they happened. I was blessed with a vision which bordered on insanity. It was unwelcome to me, like carrying a curse too far into a distance beyond one's soul. People would look at you with that wordless look as if you had a skin tainted with gangrene or leprosy.'

I took advantage of the temporary break in her thought to say: 'You mean, people treated you as if you were a banshee?' Her hand extended to cover my mouth before the very last word was out, but she was too late. I felt her anguish over the use of the word and I kissed her hand and apologised softly.

She was almost tearful: 'When we were children, I used to look forward to the rain falling, but quickly get impatient if it took hours to stop, I liked to see the different colours of the rainbow that were born afterwards. Rain was always a small penance to pay for the thrill of the colours that was my reward for feeling cold and impatient. There was at least seven additional colours I could distinguish, more than any of the other children saw.' Her eyes could break through the lines that separate the rainbow colours, penetrate the fragile divides to where the other invisible colours lived in sanctuary of pale obscurity. Ever since she was sixteen she had wanted to be like those colours in her own refuge. She had to leave Galway, wait for people to forget before she could return, if ever someday they did.

I asked: 'Why did people think you had direction of your dreams, why did you have to carry a cross you had not chosen to carry but were born with, like a hand, a look or an expression of thought?' She was not sure what the answer was, but produced a point of view that was as logical as it was possible: 'It's much easier to condemn something we cannot understand or have than to try and accept it as a matter of fact'. I agreed with her without saying anything, my eyes expressing our consensus. Her mind was finer than any I had encountered in a long time. She was intellectually balanced.

I had had similar experiences of visions like hers. I could be more accurate in points of death and loss than she could, but my vision was limited to those two aspects of foretelling. I did not have the extensive power to see most things as she did. I was more fortunate than her in that I could keep silent about my dreams. I had trained myself to keep thoughts where they belonged: in my mind for my mind and not for other people's ears. I was also less fortunate than her in that I only dreamt of things I did not want to dream of, deaths and the loss of those whose lives were so valuable to me that my dreams were simply nightmares, unforgettable and imprinted for years on the thought, until memory tended to fade out its instruction, to ease my pain.

But like her, unfortunately like her, I had no control over my dreams; they came always unexpected, although my will rejected them on the best of days. My choice was limited to acceptance of their happening. I was her nonidentical twin-soul and she understood my predicament as I confessed it. She was happy she understood.

We walked home in the warm evening breeze, her skirt brushing against my jeans, our hands unlinked and our souls untangled. At the door of my flat she leaned to give me a kiss on the cheek. When I asked her to come for some tea, she accepted. As we sat around the same small table for the second time that day drinking tea, a noise was coming from her flat, like that of a rusty gate opened and closed deliberately and in fast succession by a child's hand. She was smiling, I too. It seemed that Peggy was entertaining a friend seriously.

I was getting tired and so was Lelia. Peggy was not exhibiting any lessening of her jovial enterprise; the sound got quieter before starting again in an endless cycle. I offered Lelia my bed. She hesitated until I explained it was for her alone, I was planning to take to the floor. She made my bed on the carpet from the supply of blankets and one extra sheet left after making hers. She wanted to sleep on the floor and give me back my own comfortable bed. Though she offered many times I refused.

She turned the light off before undressing. I undressed too in the room, warm with the heat of the day and the damp summer air. I left the curtains half-open, letting some light and 'air' into the room. I turned towards my bed when I noticed she was looking at me. I had forgotten I was naked, and there was sufficient glow in the room to expose at least the outline of my body. Her eyes shone in the darkness, reflecting the soft light. It was a timid brilliance and a flicker of a look.

I woke up to the smell of fried eggs and bacon. She was making breakfast. After we had eaten, I was asked to make two promises, that I would not tell Peggy she had spent the night here and that I would not talk of her dreams to anyone. They were easy promises to keep. She took her cross, fastened its chain around my neck and asked me to wear it and never to pawn it. I promised to keep it on me, not to pawn it and hoped never to lose it. It was a pretty cross, the heat of her body still within it. I could feel her warmth through its touch on my skin and easily imagine the paler shades of the rainbow as the morning light shone from the window on the cheering gleam of the cross.

The day swiftly started and ended with equal speed. In the late afternoon I went to see Bird on a wire. The collection of Leonard Cohen's songs in what was a short film depressed me. I was never a fan then of this singer, who was at his height in the late sixties, the other side of Bob Dylan. It became fashionable to downgrade anyone who did not have a record of Leonard Cohen. He was not the only singer I later became an avid listener of, some ten years or so after his songs had declined in popularity. In the sixties, when Beatlemania was a creed, I liked the Hollies and Elvis Presley's late fifties or early sixties songs. Then, in the first half of the seventies, I seemed to discover the Beatles all on my own. I liked music as it represented for me colours of the seasons, although I seemed to be some ten seasons behind.

Many a time in a man's life he has found what he was looking for but lost it for sheer hesitation. Lament drags the soul along by its edges, behind the speeding dust, the penalty of the debating mind. I was always that man, not pretending, most of the time to be any different.

Yet my regrets always fell like summer rain, seeped through my hands and dried with different degrees of hardship. As my life matured, it ultimately concealed the cuts made by pebbles in the healed foot, dissolving that pain with other sorrow, mixing it into experience, until all was but a pale reminder and faint scent of something somewhere else, familiar but not strongly recognisable as true. It was the only humane way to put a soul to sleep lightly.

I once asked Lelia if she was going to introduce me to her boyfriend. She chuckled and pretended that her tea had gone down 'the wrong way, to her windpipe'. After further cups of tea, she admitted she was a virgin. She was quite a sophisticated girl in mind and manner, attractive in looks and spirit; it was really startling to see her quite so unattached, so vestal.

The thought travelled through my mind like a storm. I was always a man who valued the flesh as much the soul. I could never imagine myself being without either for long, especially when one was young, so racy for life and for the intimacy of the words uttered in darkness after the body had been shared and the edge of the soul exposed.

Lelia explained her declining of offers simply: she found the reason for chastity in being not dependent. She would give it and herself to a man if she could be sure he would remain with her for the rest of her life. If she gave herself to any man she really liked, when she was not sure of the immortality of the relationship, she would become hooked on sex, dependent in time and accepting even the most transitional relationship. She fell hard always; she had already known that in her teenage years. She might not be able to live with her loneliness in between relationships, so she was willing to wait until she would find the ever-constant man and fill his life with a lilac of children. I could understand, yet disagree with her.

I was one who did not want children, not out of refusing to accept their responsibility, not out of disliking them, not out of pure selfishness, but out of despair of the world. Ten years earlier or more I had decided not to leave additional legacies in a world I of which had already condemned the soul as irreversibly decaying. The world had long passed the point of no return. No saviour, no religion or fate, I thought, could avert the outcome.

Lelia asked me once if I would find it easy to take my own life. I honestly replied: 'I haven't yet tried. I am either too much of a coward still, or I have not yet reached my true breaking point.' Simply, I was still living my life not because I really had to, but because I had not reached a personal threshold of pain and loss of will.

I was truthful to the degree that I did not claim never to have thought about it, rather truthful in confessing I had not yet tried it. I further declared that when I reached that point, I would not soften the impact or prolong the lingering. I was not ever into drugs. Alcohol was as near as I had got to unleashing my sorrow onto myself, relinquishing my ordered mind onto winds of silence and impairment. I had also a more powerful reason for not taking my own life. When Jessica had taken hers, she had assumed ownership of my life for ever, until the last throb. It was her way to possess someone until eternity.

I had no wish to become the hardest line to cross in any person's life. I wanted to bequeath nothing that would last as long as a lifetime. When I die, I simply want to be forgotten, to fade away like a grain of sand shifted with the ease of a passing breeze, mixed unidentifiably with other grains of sand. I wanted neither children nor memories of me to survive my life; it would be enough for me to have lived freely for as long as my life lasted.

Lelia, as I remember, had commented then: 'Jessica is still etched on your soul. She seems to be the cross you'll always carry within you. Hopefully she'll always keep you alive, unwilling to take your life on an impulse or at a point of breaking.' I agreed: 'Yes, I do not live my life as freely as I think, do I?' The paradox was so visible, yet so unreal, like those other colours of the rainbow, always there, always in being, always a refuge of sanity.

In my silent weeping for Jessica, I always seem to dream of her eyes, a tear hanging at the edge of her eye, stopping for minutes before slowly falling, like a dew drop, lost forever amidst a soundless whimper. I lift my palms open, trying to catch the tear; I catch it but briefly before it trickles past my will, out of reach always. I invariably try, but the dream will not repent in its repetition of my trial and failure. She has been always my elusive dream and my far away mirage at the end of a rainbow, mine alone, mine alone, always and everlastingly there. She may only release me at the end of my life.

16

Flaws of Birthright

As much as Lelia was a refugee, I too was a refugee of sorts, for I was an immigrant; my soul lay divided between past and hope. My passage, although thorough in its learning and detailed anticipation, will and failure, love and distance, remained not mine. My past made me belong forever to the people I had met and known, to whose ways I ascribed, unintentionally or with a full expression of values.

I had brought to my new world a collection of memories of the old. I had brought the spirit of my father, the tenderness and pain of my mother and sisters, the colours of my past. I could not implant all these in my stride without remembering the people I loved, while others I denied a word or a thought, even in passing. Every morning I thought of my mother, my father, their lives together and apart, the converts of mist and dew, complying in the early morning sun, becoming mere vapour invisible to thought, only to return and be converted again and again every day until eternity and infinity whichever came first.

I was not removed from the strange equity of events, I can still remember everything as it was or sometimes made even better by hindsight and imagination. I, Edmund, was but my father's essay and his pride above all pride. He lived in me and shall live forever. In his words, repeated so many times, lay stories and many a thought, I remember them and always see him at the back of my mind, continuous as a film, honest as a vision. I always stood there and he was transparent for me.

Amongst all joys, the joy of a son, the uncompromising outcome of ease of life and the slowness of time for the past nine months, the affection for positive gatherings in good health and celebration, face both parents with a tolerance of noise, a softly quiet anticipation, all quite unprecedented in complexion and simplicity, yet different from that of the end of pregnancy and one that releases the sin of pride.

Nothing could at the end of any stage be as wilfully wonderful as a first-born son, after a miscarriage, a lost son and three years of waiting, they both agreed. My mother was at her upper, entwining, thin end of her thirties, consolidating hereafter worries of oncoming infertility.

My father had cloaked his moody disbelief of life for the day extended his right palm to a few and honoured his unstained pride with the occasional smile, appreciation and deep thought of the years planned ahead.

His life has not been anything but years of slight possibilities and the erosion of his most outstanding hopes. Having to attain a degree in law at the age of thirty-five, twelve years after abandoning education after leaving school in a tantrum, after knowing what life had for the unfortunate and the generous, the deals of letting one's soul go in exchange for co-existence, and suddenly learning classical morality all over again, these all seemed as an inevitable diminution of a full life by one's own motives for such a profession that delayed all judgement on paper and contributed slowly to the progression of demanded goodwill and righteousness in a fashion that only conveyed the uniformity of an acceptable life.

It was a profession that assumed nothing and accepted the bare minimum of mankind's costly experience. The choice was certainly his and it ultimately revealed itself to him as uncompromising as it was forceful. Yet at heart he was as simple as he was clean, accepting and faithfully trying for all purposes of achievement and inquiry, a man who was neither impaired by disillusion and inequity, nor iridescent with the fashionable will of the gods of power.

It has been a while since he took on willingly and unintentionally a mood that created both his faith in himself and his endurance of life at a time of vivid turbulence in the country.

The social changes in his small town were enamelled with the veneer of an imported ideology and tinctured with an erupting dread of doom. He was neither a capitalist nor a communist. He was a man who thought of himself as an intellectual: boundaries of strict loyalties lay sharply at the foot of the common good. He might accept the logic of those for whom poverty was a mere shadow, once education and tradition were blended not to make rebellion but into conformity.

His other criterion was infringement of the class divide: a man from a well-known family entrenched in tradition normally holds good, even if he is poor, provided he does not cross the threshold of agitation without the backbone of insincerity. After all that typecasting of people, at the end of the day he took the value of a man from his stance on morality and on upholding the common values of the rejection of good by evil.

Yet he held his judgement on any man private or revised it when he needed to without the least indication of showing it to be the case. He restricted his politics to a self-motivated and self-contained debate of a resilient opposition to the regression of most mankind (and fewer women) to what the world was that day. He kept all this to himself and for his own satisfaction and depression. It was not time to quit dreaming, yet the onslaught of losing grip of hope to the wind was threatening in its closeness and deviousness.

At the same time, to his alarm, he, the not-so-long qualified solicitor, found the terminology of his profession very close to begging, yet far removed from the nervousness of failure. People came to him to ask him to take on a case, fathers broken by the demise or failings of their heirs. They, who could not understand it if my father declined to take their thirty pieces of silver on the excuse that the case was unwinnable, after all other solicitors did it anyway, win or lose, these people found him odd.

Furthermore, other people found him uncooperative in contentious cases of divorce or custody of children. He always found himself encased in his piety and he felt happy not affecting other people's lives in such a manner. It was not for him to declare a preference in fine-line tugging, though he was hungry sometimes because of it. The persistence of such worldly gravities beyond points of law and of future excellence or lengthy depravity as a result of such court actions installed itself uneasily in his mind if he was to be involved. Yet he was still intimately acquainted with hunger and its hidden, driving ability to force acquiescence with the reality of everyday needs, for the provision of basic living and beyond that of wealth.

But before he would be tempted, he would look at his hands and would instantly pull away from an deviation by a swift mental erasure of thought, followed by acceptance of whatever was available, in a mentality that was always cost-effective on sorrow and pride.

He drank when that kind of debate took a heavy toll on his dreams, or when the latter loomed cord-strangled or caught between the gears of their wheels. The following day offered a hangover and wit always, mixed with forgotten bouts of low spirits of the night before.

His father before him was regarded as an absolute monarch, at least to his own people, who feared him, loved him, admired him and sometimes hated him, all in a space of a day or in a distance short of a lifetime. His father dabbled in politics and had more aspiration than he could contrive to achieve. His golden rule was over-confidence and a simplistic view of the world: I ask and I shall receive amply. The new rulers in his day were effective in sending him into exile twice, oddly with the same ploy: an invitation to a boat party, where he was made drunk; by the time he woke up the next morning, he was far from the reach of his body guards, too far away at sea to protest or force a reversal of his situation to his advantage.

My father could explain this in his mind in an uncomplicated fashion. His father, entranced by a woman, went on the boat on those two occasions for two reasons: the first time to see the woman, the second time to ask her why she went along with what happened the first time, secure in the thought that it was improbable it would happen a second time in the same way.

He further thought the strength of his father's position was such that he personally was never afraid of assassination; the new people in power would not think of that as he had a popular following. His father might be put aside but would never be put down, even ruthless people had their invisible line which they would not cross, and probably his father knew this very well. In some other, darker corner of his mind was another view of the event: even powerful politicians could be trapped with invisible nets and the miscalculation of overconfidence.

His father left him when he was merely two years of age and

again when he was thirteen, both times with the grandeur of thought that others would look after him; at neither time did he feel but abandoned. Some years later, he acquitted his father of the charge, finding him not responsible and giving him the benefit of the doubt for his guilt.

He himself had a son now and it was easier to accept his father's absence, following a tortuous logic that culminated in the argument that his son belonged to him and not he to his son. His father must have had felt the same. At the same time, that other feeling of the power to shape or write history with his initials in bold letterings, must have shone like a comet in the night sky: indestructible, unreachable, yet captivating, forcefully overriding every solitude, dragging soul and body in its intrinsic passion for endeavour, its ardent desire to quench its thirst, its demands and impulses.

He could try and successfully come to understand that his father had what many men only dream of: a constant drive towards what looked attainable and plausible and yet was impossible. He still felt he had to attempt its hopelessness with a will that only matched his determination with devotion and his disappointment with harshness.

On the morning of the twenty-eighth of February 1953, now that he himself had a son, Edmund, he thought for a moment about his father again; he could still understand him as he did a few moments before, but the new situation tells him he felt differently, as if it was possible to see both sides of thought at the same time and feel at ease with both faces of the paradox.

A sense of achievement overcame all his past disloyalties; a son, a wonder of an item that affects you by its mere physical presence without a word or act. He rested his unbalanced books of past accounts: a new opening, a beginning, a sudden gush of breath that lightened his senses, a change of role and outfit, a change in expectations to a thought of love and a notion of duty, the two mixing passively and willingly as if in a jar of homemade honey brightly-enamelled goodwill.

When all the departing guests had left the quietness of sound as a gift behind them, as the last one closed the front door tightly, the day seemed as long as it took to run its course, long but bright with its loud happiness. It was time for a short chat and for expressions of pleasure in the achievement, to renew the glow and to further the tender feelings. He and his wife now had a new being to address and a new dimension to acquire.

The child was a day old and the bedroom still kept its birth odours: sweet, discreet and illogically enchanting. It was not a difficult birth but one that had plastered anxieties over every wall and within every sheet crease, one that was restless with sheer anticipation but also with forthcoming relief and happy gestures of pride.

It was time then to speculate on the future, to divine dry deserts and entrench motives of welfare and devotion for the child. Sometimes it seemed for both of them a validation of superior reason and holy method, but the marriage was never as justified and at the same time never as fragile as it was now embracing their lives in a union of fruitfulness and anxiety.

In one sense he feared the gift borne from the gods, though in another spirit it was a practical motive for assessing and tackling realism away from the pure preserve and the shining order of the world's judgement.

By another reasoning, she was happy in the same tense to be alive and still have a healthy boy, not merely for her own life but more for the baby, that it had a living mother. She felt her satisfaction of being more than just a woman who had expended her usefulness or logical being by giving birth to a baby, as her own mother did when she was born, her mother, whose warmth and pampering she had never felt. It was the dissipation of something she had always feared and expected to happen, that she would die on giving birth like her own mother. She had that fear not out of any social or culture rule or education in the belief, but out of gut feelings and misguided instinct. It was refreshing to disprove it.

As she held her baby for the thousandth time that day, she felt as relieved as if it was the first time. She said nothing and fondly let herself lose her tiredness and the mere expediency of time; she silently smiled and forgot about the world.

Sitting on the edge of the bed, he lit another cigarette and watched the grey smoke flow around his fingers and contour in the light like mist on top of a mountain peak swiftly unfolding in a westward wind. He had followed more in thought as he watched and touched the child in the warmth of the unintentional silence.

She commented without being asked, 'My father likes his baby grandson.' 'Why shouldn't he like a lively, good-looking child, a first born of his eldest daughter?' he replied softly. She continued the sentence in her mind: especially since he may see a likeness in the baby to his first wife, of whom I'm the only daughter.

She thought further of her father: he had never let her down, had always intervened when she was sad or when her half-sisters were harsh, even when her stepmother mistreated her, or simply when he was away for even a short time and she wondered whether she should tell him she missed him; there was always the hug and the sad but warm look in his eyes whenever he stared at her without a reason.

It was surprisingly easy to play the rewind-fastforward button of memory in a ten-second exposure of an endurance span of thirty years. Yet she did not want to dwell longer on that part of the memory, which still boiled with sadness and smelt of levied sulphurous indignation. She selfishly wanted to remember her father's face on those occasions and fade out the rest. The unfavourable parts reminded her of other, later, times when she felt that she had married to escape the endurance course. Although she never believed that she had married by such design, the thought of such subconscious motives made her at times relentless in resenting life's ground rules of fate.

One look at the baby's complexion and placid temperament told her that all fears of a second motive for marriage other than love, were irrationally baseless. The baby toyed with his newly found mouth and agile, closed fists. Her silence was smothering his, while that of the father was hovering faithfully over both of theirs.

He had gone out of the room for a short period and by the time he re-entered the mother and child had already fallen asleep together. The sense of such early unity was unmistakable and almost as if still umbilical.

He sat drinking his alcohol in the half-darkness of the room, as a faint silver-blue light from a nearly mature moon filtered through the clean glass of the window. The rented house was shimmering with tidiness and devoted attention. His wife took her duties seriously. He welcomed the slender glass with his lips and its contents with his satisfied throat.

He always drank more than a little, but never ended in drunkenness or a bad mood. It was a long-standing companion in his solace, called upon when the world passed him by forgotten. The thought of the child sleeping so near was soothing. He was ready to defeat the ungrateful, distrusting world with just a look and mere thought. He was ready to undo all that which only yesterday was justification for despair. It was a new feeling and a refreshingly new-learnt strength, something he had lost and as if accidentally found. The honesty of his feeling worked his soul into a temple of hope.

When he opened his eyes again, it was already the next morning. The milkman had left two extra bottles of milk and, methodically, the bill. This simple impression of uninterrupted habit told him that the world by this morning regarded his new child as a common event, one of thousands in the everyday running of life. He was slightly uprooted from his early morning optimism. Added to that the child was awake and already complaining for a feed. He felt suddenly that subtle changes had to be made in his life, or that at least he should not resist them when they were coming anyway.

He made some tea for himself and boiled some milk for the child. He decided then to wake mother; he preferred to call her 'mother' rather than 'wife', and for the first time in two weeks or more he called her by her name.

He thought of this in a deep and logical manner: the absence of people round them prompted the one-to-one conversation, where the words seemed linked continuously even over days, and for that one did not need to call the explicit name.

She woke up with a contented smile, tired from her stretch in bed. She did not seem to notice that he had just called her by name; it was the softness of his breath that instigated her alertness to a full sense of his need.

She noticed momentarily in the same eye frame that he had not slept in the bed and that there was an empty glass by the end, where he must have fallen asleep on top of the new bedcover. She said nothing, felt surprise that she had thought of it, then discarded further reflection; the day was just beginning and the baby needed feeding.

Thursday was the gateway to the weekend in many of the Middle East and Muslim countries by law. His first thought was that it did not feel any different from any other Thursdays, except that it was the third day in the life of his child. This made it somehow feel different and more exciting as much as it made it thought-worthy.

The year of 1953 was neither ominous nor prosperous, but carried within it a restless fostering of uneasiness, a secret promise, unpredictabilities, lighter-hearted waiting and a thread of pure anticipation for indeterminate change. The turmoil in Egypt the year before, the unrest in Eden the month before, or the silence preached in Jordan in the past week, were all overflowing, an agitated mixture clinging to the neck of a pot often heated and deliberately cooled.

In Iraq, the days were numbers of slow time, a casual reminder of quiet living; yet there was the occasional riot, the feared-instigators with their label of 'communists' and the absolute McCarthy-like effecters of policy, who were true believers in that they were nothing less than implementers of law. He thought how amusing it was that the groups were a driving force against each other, but yet depended for their full existence and justification on the actual survival and strength of the opposing group.

He had stood for parliamentary elections once, got bullied by government agents who saw him as a loyalist drop-out on account of his family affiliations and vast farmlands, and heckled by new-left protesters as a reactionary who at best was either a government candidate with a change of face or a narrow-minded nationalist who took his aspirations from the new system in Egypt.

These agitators, as they were called, seemed to him like a swelling, fed by the throbbing torn vein of discontent and aggravated by the swooping arrests and false labelling of anyone whose views did not match those of the official politics of the day. He was neither happy for such stacking of the cards, nor a believer in the doctrine of looming fate.

The new king in Iraq was merely fourteen, still in his early political adolescence; his guardian was an ambitious man who thought of power as the initiation of the means; the country was more rural than urbanised in its area and people; the same prime minister had been in office for more than twenty years, except for the eight months of insurrection during the second year of the Second World War.

For my father, the country was edging towards silent eruption. Many felt that it was time for more stabbing and less noise. A revolution in such a place, he thought, would in its most peaceful face be a thesaurus for premeditated and violent change. He told his friends repeatedly of his brief experience in those sixty, short pre-election days. He told it with command of thought that showed his failure unblemished and consoling in its tones. He had to rescind his effort in a spirit of serious realism. It was not worth the fear of detention had he won and then abstained, or the fear of loss of his life had he won and conformed to the politics enshrined by power and greed.

His moderation in his political contribution was in a strange sense in conformity with the unworded guidelines of both edges of the razor's blade. His two-month-old withdrawal now seemed sensible and infallible, looking in the light of the moment less harsh in its passive appeasement of its old sense of purpose.

He knew for one thing that he was radically different from his own father and although it saddened him as he felt himself failing, in some aspect of pride, his own birthright, he felt he was accommodating reason and was logical in his assessment, something that assured him of his strength in himself. That strength he had thought was slipping far away from the grip of his tightly clenched fists in his drive towards self-betterment. He concluded that only strength bid for sacrifices; weakness did not even allow for consideration of such a thought.

On days of small misconstruction and mild degrees of assumption, the quietness of the backyard and the chilled pint-glass of beer assumed the ease of living and required nothing that the self would have to explain or defend. The common man was not so common, he would mind others as his own children, disadvantage only himself and detain nothing in his mind that was not generally pleasant or sentimental.

But there were others who would gamble the day's takings of trust and conscience, hide their voids of honesty, dread only the roll of the cheating dice and walk away when all had lost its value, thinking that they had survived. He was a man who took only what he was offered in good faith, a man who found softness in rock and warmth in the chilled glass of alcohol, tenderness in the February wind and complained not when his pockets echoed his deprivation of means.

He could only feel pity for those of his friends who took him on cunning escapades and pride in those who stood by him and asked nothing in return. Both sentiments were qualities that he failed to erase or even discreetly discard for all the years of his life.

All the same, he was a man of discipline, a bold-line character. His choices were easily made. Many times he thought that was the way it should be done, as if the choice was not really a choice but rather a test to see whether he would deviate or bend. He had always acted thus: made his choice without a doubt and with the minimum of time for decision.

One topic that always troubled him was his lust for love in his life and the implications of a continuance of feeling after the taking. He used to think that once a man bedded a woman, it seemed pointless to try again. Love in his teenage years had to be without touch; the heat of the body would dissipate the warmth of the soul tragically and irreversibly. It was not that he felt a woman was cheap to allow him to divert his desire from his thought into his body and then into hers, as probably most men in his day thought; but a feeling he could not explain or define usually followed: he simply lost interest, and preferred to file the first encounter as one needing no adjustment on his part and hid it so deep, so that he could not retrieve it even if he wanted to.

He never used to mention any names when the boys and later the men of his age used to gather and deposit in competition their memories of past takings on a score sheet of boasting and as proof of manhood. He felt then as he always did: such a flow of names and addresses exposed the woman to tribulations of scorn and torture that went further than condemnation of the act which the boys enjoyed and relished, as if the complicity of the boys was not criminal while that of their partners was unforgivable and punishable.

When he offered his lifelong friend Drake this view for consideration, his friend told him that he was taking Greek philosophy too seriously and applying it further than the sexual identity of man deserved: a man was more important than a woman, even in the religion in which both men were inscribed and which was stamped on their birth certificates.

He had no quarrel with religion, any religion, as he found it a prerequisite of character, and although he was not a practising Muslim, he found a clean conscience an effective threshold for honesty and a good basis for soft, untroubled living. He felt it was enough that he had that bright-glowing attribution which actually allowed him sound sleep and in a strange way made it unnecessary for him be strictly religious. He thought of his drinking, for most of the time moderate; he would have to give it up if he decided to follow religion strictly by the book. That somehow did not seem a choice he was willing to make right away and was happy to reach an instant impasse.

For most men of his age and temperament, the efficacy of life lay
at the margin of laughter and beneath the day's encounter with
their jobs. The loud jingling of their pockets at the end of the month
was the sound of success and the ultimate sign of pride, with which
to clothe all attitudes.

For him, money contributed to his prime feelings, to the strength
and health of his conscience; it was an essential and elementary
factor. He felt his trouser pocket and was not surprised at the result:
a few coins asleep in inertia and apathy. The day after tomorrow
was payday, he told himself, wait and it will arrive.

He spent the rest of the morning listening to the radio, roasting
his well-lined cigarettes on top of it and smoking them warm in a
leisurely absence of deep thought. Then he went into the back
garden, carrying a glass of chilled beer and a plateful of peanuts,
sat down and drank a little under the shade of the tall datepalm. He
fell asleep and woke up half an hour later, drank more from his
glass of beer and fell asleep again. After lunch, he did the same.
The end of February was mild and sunny, encouraging long occupation of the well-groomed garden with its tall trees and low shrubs
that smelt of spring and radiated colours of regeneration. In the
middle of the afternoon, his wife went to bed taking the child with
her. He felt lonely for her silence and her presence, finished his
drink and decided to go inside to be near her while the radio was
playing low.

Most of Thursday night and the whole of Friday passed in normal
fashion: quiet, with very little said, both parents watching the new
baby when he was awake, watching him briefly when he was
asleep and watching each other in silence, without either of them
disturbing the continuity of ease.

These days set the pattern for the week to come. But the following
week was not a good week at work: three clients whose cases were
won could not pay right away. He did not find it in him to force
them and accepted their promise of good faith. At the end of that
week, he was anxious, angry at himself and despondent. The
child's presence was driving him to feel he was stupid for not
demanding his fees at the beginning of proceedings or at least more
forcefully at the end of each case.

This sense of new reality was mixed with an impression of
disheartening loss and fear of not being paid ever for services

rendered. For the first time in his adult life he felt taken in, like a child of six.

Although the days brought few disappointments among many triumphs of winning and within those victories payments of labour, the ones who did not pay kept coming back to offer explanations which he felt were true, though a few, he felt were mere deferral of debt. As he came to accept the good with the indifferent, the reputation that he had built in the small town came to accredit him with shrewdness and equally with compassion.

The small town people learned how to plead with him when they were without means, while those who were trying to use him as a legal aid without paying came to understand that he knew about them. After all he was a smart lawyer, with good intentions and aptitude.

This kind of approachability worked against him when the big merchants realised the same. In their view he was kind but labouring under a degree of illusion; he was wasting his time with small fish, earning less and accepting some of his fees as bad debts which he wrote off without hesitation. Slowly, gradually and then wholly these people, who could have given him the means to be rich, withdrew from contracting him and eventually forgot about him. He felt sometimes that he was a lost soul, out of its class by choice, but not fitting into the resulting affiliation, which was neither of his birthright nor his true sentiment.

He was not vain enough to refuse to undertake cases without fee or to demand the going rate or higher of people who could pay it and found his fairmindedness leaving him living from one month to the next, from one case to the next with only slightly more than enough to cater for his family's expenses.

The rented house was at the end of a dockyard area; it was nice, comfortable and best of all had a bedroom window on the second floor that viewed the incoming ships as they docked, the ton upon ton of golden, shining wheat stalks that were crunched, the wheat germ that was milled and stocked in the departing ships.

Every time he watched the ships, big and small as they came empty and left laden with the prizes of the land, he wished he had a passage on one of them, not as a stowaway from reality or unhappiness, but as someone who wanted to see the world, feel its breezes and sample its colours.

Yet it was always a dream and not anything he contemplated

seriously. The watching of ships and dreaming were to be forgotten soon: his young son at the age of three months was found to have asthma, contracted from the waves of wheat germ that hung over the dockyard like flies over refuse. He decided on the advice of the doctor to rent a house elsewhere, pay a higher rate and forget the thought of ships and powered carriage along with the lock of his rented house. He missed it a lot at first, but then decided to concentrate on something more practical and probably more urgent: making more money.

The next year, 1954, saw many changes: his father-in-law, who was also his father's last surviving brother, had died of a heart attack, or heart failure as his daughter called it in her grief. He had liked the old man, as it was he who had sponsored his college education and helped him financially to achieve the law degree. He could not forget him and when the man consented to his marrying his favourite daughter, it was an added portion of admiration and liking.

The father-in-law had also seen to it that he could in his professional capacity offer advice in any legal problem or venture that the old man or his sons were exposed to in the routine and daily run of things. Their financial support was appreciated by the now-experienced lawyer, who regarded the small fee as unimportant as it was all for the family.

His cousins, who were also his brothers-in-law, then asked him to keep the duties undisturbed for a while when their father died. He showed a degree of reserve when he expressed an opinion or advised the old man, not because of the age difference but rather because of his respect and deep admiration for the man.

The father-in-law was rich, mixing with high society but also simple and caring for the problems of the poor and above all immaculately honest; qualities that he would have expected and imagined his own father to possess, if he had lived long enough for him to know. The death of his father-in-law did bring an unexpected wind of change for him. His wife inherited from her father on his death only a few pieces of land; the rest she was made to sign off to her brothers.

The latter were working with the full confidence of their father in the last years of his life and were allowed to have power of attorney on his behalf. Mere weeks before his death, when he was ill, they changed the holdings of the most expensive pieces of land to their own name, without his knowledge.

When the man died without leaving a written will, the time was opportune for them to perfect their plans. He, the resident lawyer, has suspected as much but could not bring himself to mention it to the father. Two of the three boys were lawyers themselves and did not need a counsel to act in their personal matters of business; they neither wanted him to deal with it nor included him or asked his advice in such arrangements.

On the day when all the immediate family gathered to discuss the division of land and inheritance, a harsh exchange of opinion and expressions of desolation detached the boys from the girls. He sat there as someone who had come with his wife for the sole reason of safeguarding her interests.

He sat and listened to claims and counterclaims, as the boys told the girls of lands sold last year, properties auctioned the year before and so on, all the deals accompanied by perfectly produced documents and stamped papers proving the exchange of deeds. He sat amazed how the boys could have planned for this years ahead, how they could deny their sisters the claim to their father's estate and more astonishingly how they could have done it legally.

He thought of all the people present as immature children who wanted to steal each other's marbles and fight about it, pushing and pulling as children did, thinking that what they wanted was so important, so justified that they were fighting for it and that no one else mattered. He, personally, did not want any of it, it was not his and that removed it from being his goal. On the way home he fought with his wife, the woman he loved, and felt that he could lose her as she thought he was not protecting her interests.

He tried to explain to her his position in the matter with soft-worded confirmation of his love and duty to provide for her, in words that tried to comfort her, such as that they did not need the money that badly. Ultimately he tried to explain that in reality he felt the only way out of the situation and for her to gain her rightful share of the estate was to take her brothers to court.

She concurred, but by that angry stage, he refused to represent her or support her in court, on the grounds that such action would muddy the family name and might result in branding her brothers as thieves if not simply as dishonest men who would have to live with such a reputation for the rest of their lives. He thought furthermore of his son in the school years ahead and of himself branded as a greedy husband who, people would speculate, was the driving motive behind his wife's court action. All the possibilities seemed to promise worse and to cut deeper and deeper as they were unfolded.

His wife saw it as her birthright, her inheritance, and tried not to dwell too long on the financial reward of such motives. She thought that it might hurt him, as if she was telling him that his provision of a livelihood was inadequate. It was like a minefield, where every step might mean an explosion and confrontation with a loss of limb and resulting in deviation off the course of the discussion into a backward retreat or loss of ground.

For an experienced lawyer who had a duty towards her as his wife, she also found his logic too passive to accept. He was too hard in not speaking loudly for her, too naive and accepting of the fall without a gesture of fighting back. Her half-sisters saw it as a sign that he had personally made a deal with their brothers. They wasted little time in telling her that and went to make slanderous representations of the truth as they saw it. He was simply and truly disillusioned, he felt hurt and to his mind the sooner he forgot about it the better.

The turmoil of a lack of choice for him and the option of choice within his wife's mind produced a conflict of instincts that extended to their manifestation in words and mood. He thought that the small town would live on the rumours and devour the family; she felt that she had lost many chances during her younger and adult years, things she would have attained if her own mother had been alive, mostly the focused attention of her own father rather than any materialistic gains.

She had worked hard all her life to conform to and please her half-sisters and -brothers. Her father's life seemed wasted now and she wanted physical proof that it had not been so: some piece of land to build her new house on, where the continuity to her children would flowing from her own mother's womb and be held in heritage for her own children. She kept looking upon her young baby of just under a year: he deserved an inheritance, a birthright of physical dimensions.

Self-claimed birthright did not mean so much, she went on to think; look at my own husband, so honest, so passive and landless. Nearly fifty years after his great father's death he had but a memory and a discreet hesitation; people always remembered his father, but would they remember him? The honest man may lie forgotten a day after his death; he had neither land to bequeath nor power to install in his heirs; a great common man with the birthright of a deposed and self-exiled king, a wasted stature, a wasted lifetime.

The papers dividing the inheritance came the next day. The arguments raged once again, were blown-up and flattened before rising and dying in repetitive fashion; he was not convinced of his wife's dialect and she had two obstacles to remove: to convince him and to fire a fight in him. One was difficult, the other seemed almost impossible.

He felt more and more coerced with the passage of those slow hours, reacted more sharply and became more resistant to new logic or newer pleas. The 'legal' papers remained on the hallway's dainty table, distasteful and besmirching the atmosphere with tension.

He had decided to try and forget they were there. She had decided to leave them in place to remind him of the affair everytime he went to work or came home. The papers became a draft for a trap rather than simple legal papers. He seemed unmoved but yet disturbed, she was disappointed but still had some hope of remission.

Eventually, after the passage of some weeks, she signed them in deep silence and with cutting resignation and sent them away to the brothers' now newly appointed legal representative. The spoils were cut to size unfavourably and she accepted her defeat with lingering stares and ever more frequent silence.

She was offered two small pieces of land in the city out of hundreds of acres of prime investment and not more than a handful of coins in cash. After a period of two years and a miscarriage, she decided to leave it to God to drive home her feelings of injustice to her brothers in the hope they might feel some remorse, and forgot she had lost so much from weakness of resolve.

Soon after her last miscarriage, the idea of a second pregnancy in six months worried her, but she was proved wrong. The new baby was progressing larger in size and mood than she had ever before experienced, it felt different and in the cold January air more like a seven-month carriage than the five months it was.

In March, she seemed to lose a little at the waistline, while in May, when she was accompanying her husband on a shopping trip

to the capital, she seemed ready, in energy and breath, to conclude
the nine-month wait. This state of readiness subsided somewhat
over the next few days and she decided to wait and not raise the
alarm. But the next night she knew it was arriving undeterred and
she was taken to hospital to deliver her newest offspring.

The new baby was a girl, placid, open-handed and particularly
quiet. The memory of her first-born baby boy, who was now just
under three years of age, was in striking comparison to her new
baby. The earlier experience seemed far away and vivid. Looking at
the baby girl in the cot and thinking of her son, she felt a mixture of
happy expectations and slight worry for the future.

It took her longer this time to arrive at the birth, and she felt that
her earlier experience did not comfort her or make her less agitated
as she approached the moment. She remembered something that
no other woman had told her she would experience: with every
pain and effort of labour, the face of a woman kept telling her she
was her own mother. It was a peaceful face limited to two colours,
black and white, as if taken from an old crumbling photograph.

The midwife was amazed at the premonition (none of her women
had told her anything like that experience amid the long hours of
pain), she was excited and pronounced that this baby would be
caring, motherly and the most wonderful of all her children. She
even foretold the auspicious length of the baby's avoidance of
hardship: it was to be a very lucky baby, heartening in life and to its
mother at the same time. The proud mother slipped gently into
sleep with the satisfaction of believing the interpretation.

He had decided at the end of the week to go home to his small
town, accompanied by his wife, son and daughter. On the way to
the station in a taxi, his thoughts were of asking his mother to come
and stay with them for a long duration. Although he had asked her
before to do so, she had not jumped at the opportunity. His mother
was a gentle woman who after nearly forty-five years in Iraq, still
had trouble with the language, could not speak Arabic freely,
insisted in an indirect way on stumbling through her conversation
and always threw more than a handful of Turkish terms and words
into the bouquet of her opinions.

He was still thinking of his mother when the train started to
gather speed amid clouds of white smoke and the smell of burning
coal. The overnight train stepped cautiously through the vast farm-
ing heartland of its course. The journey had become monotonous

after the first hour; all around was green and fertile by nature rather than design. He looked at the sunset; the eventual contrast of bright yellow-orange against a dark green background, framed in the middle of the window, was enchanting and for once he did not mind the slow pace.

An hour later, he looked again and was amazed that the sun was still dominant in the withdrawing sky; the light was still the same colour radiating inside the compartment. When he looked closely, the sun was nearly disappearing into the bed of the horizon, just under a sheet of darker shade: the golden colour of maize and wheat was reflecting the illumination of the sky. The support of endless fields of shining stems and grains was more wonderful than the background light.

The farmers in their last hour of labour seemed disenchanted with the passing train. Their grain, however, was accepting and happy to show off its natural character, calm and unpremeditated though it was. He calculated that the train schedule would not allow him to see and compare the pose of these crops with the waves of the rice paddies, as it would be almost dark when they passed by, a few hours later.

It was that time of the year when the long stems of the rice, bleached white and fragile in their thinness, would cover the high-water marks of the over-drenched soil and make its dark brown colour ambiguous to all those who could forget it was there underneath. Only the farmers knew all the time that it was there. Onlookers always seemed ready to judge the efficacy of the moment as it unveiled itself and had very short memories, he thought carefully.

Although the land was almost always rented from year to year, to the same tenants, under the same conditions and with the same hard work by the majority, the overseers seemed to get the benefit of not gambling on the output of the harvest. They were paid in crop by the farmers and in cash by the landowners. The latter were undisturbed by floods or drought; at the end of the year, a third of the harvest and the lease fee would come in as predictably as sunset or sunrise. Their guarantee lay in the deeds and the 'I O Us', the demonstrated successes of the overseers and the plentiful offers of others to replace the debt- and register-stricken tenants. The new people would usually clear the debt of previous tenants, either with the promise of a higher cut to the owners or in scheduled cash repayments. Those who defaulted sometimes ended up working for the new leaseholders for a meagre number of sacks of grain and a place to live on the same land for the next year or more.

The land was the complete assurance of both status by birthright and the dominance of fate, especially when fate was on your side. He had strong feelings about the farmers and the landowners: they exploited each other, although, he had to agree, for different reasons. But he could only feel apathy for the overseers; these he thought were a training ground for the system in imputation, harshness and brutality, iced with hypocritical loyalty, tinctured with disregard to anything but the leaseholders' rule.

He thought of a farmer who had walked fifty miles once to complain directly to the landowner, a foolish man who must have known that the system had existed far longer than memory and survived better than honest outcry. The man was evicted without notice, and he, the lawyer was powerless to contain the outrage or plead the morality of the man's case successfully. Ever since that day the overseers classed him as soft, undignified and unworthy of attention. He had to defend himself every time he had dealings with them, he had to remind them of his name every time there was a confrontation and worst of all he had eventually to deal with them in the third person singular, indirectly through his clerk. The rule of law made provision for precedents but did not really make it easy to override the established sequence or result.

He felt then as he had since: the law was only as honourable as its implementers and faith-carriers, but above all as its care for continuous justification and change; the law had only the conscience of those who wrote it and the will of those who stood by it, disfigured it or beamed its impartiality on to all who resided in its spirit.

He often thought of the beautiful, blind figure, embodied in cold marble, of the goddess of fair conclusion: her stiff scales always even; she did not seem to care for change. Laws seemed divinely absolute on paper, their print authenticating the wisdom that had to last forever. In a way, fairness was an implant that had forsaken its own rights towards the whole bold body of equity, while the net of law, unlike the fisherman's tool, was in its strength fragile to time and its anonymity untested.

After the baby and her brother had been put to bed, aided by the rocking of the train, their mother, pale and tired, was unable to resist what her babies found most soothing and most natural, and fell asleep to a rhythm which was like that of a heartbeat, occasionally missing a beat and registering small tones of a soft track and the nailed-fixture of forty or so years.

He made his way to the bar compartment, separated from the first class by scores of long second-class carriages and at the end of the train, as if the management were expecting trouble after closing time. The bar was too crowded for his liking, so he decided to buy a few beers and take them back with him to the sleeping compartment.

Entering carefully and without waking the other three occupants, he sprang the beer from the first bottle and toasted his new daughter. The first bottle was emptied fast and without much thought. Half-way through the second bottle, he thought of his mother again and suddenly felt the strength and length of her homelessness. The faint yellow bubbles, small and elegant in their energy, that seemed to reach the surface and abruptly lose their vitality and attracted his attention and slowed his concentration for a short period, until the next batch did exactly the same; all seemed set on repeating the same purposeless pattern.

Solitary drops of rain on the window flickered and distorted the light penetrating at intervals from outside with the passage of a distantly lit house. Something was missing from his fingerprints: perhaps it was the fullness of belief that he had done everything he could for his mother; perhaps the suspicion he had not really done so.

Many a time he had asked her what was it that left her crying in the middle of the night but, as little children do, the threshold of adult pain always eluded total comprehension and the least, shallowest explanation made all understandable and comforting.

It was not until his fourteenth year, when she told him she was homesick, that the tall Turkish woman started to unbend with the passing of time and admit to not being happy. On those nights, the stillness of the air and the thick mahogany doors, could not conceal the sobbing or the trivial trick of stopping briefly before the next wave of wetness seeped on to the suspecting cheeks, contracted with pain and in anticipation of the oncoming flood of wordless desperation.

The alcohol in the darkness of the compartment and the shadow of the rain drops on his face stimulated a few real tears when he pictured his mother's.

He remembered the first time his mother told him her maiden name. It struck him as that of an Armenian, which did not fit her Muslim religion. Armenians, he knew, were Christians, stringent orthodox and living by a strict code. His father told him once that his mother was the daughter of a humane and famous Turkish field commander who had asked him personally, when he was on his death bed to look after his only daughter. That was when he brought her with him from Turkey and married her.

Turks in those days, he knew, killed Armenians simply for the joy of hunting down a man in flight, in a spirit of 'sport'. They certainly would not make them army commanders, would they? The two stories did not fit together into a reasonable version of the truth.

Then one day, when he questioned her about her maiden name, she told him a story; she was reluctant to but told it in the end. She was a young girl of twelve when a battalion of Turkish militia rode into their village of about eighty inhabitants. They questioned the village headman about a particular vigilante, but he was adamant the villagers neither knew him nor of him.

The major in charge was not convinced, or did not want to be convinced, and because the village's alleged help to the wanted man or because they had not reported his presence, five boys and four girls between the ages of nine and fourteen, were gathered and taken from the village to the nearest government outpost four hundred miles away, to be held until the man they were looking for was surrendered to the authorities.

She was a girl of twelve then and that was the last time she saw her parents or her sleepy village. Some of the older boys reported they had heard the soldiers saying that they were not returning ever to the village. She remembered a sergeant taking one of the boys away into the woods one night and returning him to the makeshift stockade bloodied all over the back of his thighs. When the boy persisted in crying, the sergeant shouted at him to accept his situation as their village was no longer within distance nor in existence.

The girls were not touched or beaten, while the boys were flogged regularly until they no longer complained or spoke any sentiment of any kind. The preferential treatment of the girls seemed illogical at the time and was certainly not due to respect for their sex. When the convoy reached the garrison town, the boys were separated from the girls. The latter group was put on a donkey-drawn carriage and sent to Azmir, some seven hundred miles away, a journey of infrequent meals, requiring much patience.

The eldest girl, who was fourteen, was flogged once and did not survive the journey, but she was given away because of her inflamed feet and whip-marked face to a farmer who got her for a sack of grain and a handful of copper farthings. The three remaining girls were surrendered to a fat, oily-moustached man of fifty in Azmir. On changing hands, this man instructed his oldest house-woman to tell them about their new religion, their new names and language. They were taught Turkish and were not allowed to talk amongst themselves in their native tongue; but most importantly and firstly the name of the fat man was carved into their memory, followed by the word of respect, as if it was one word.

He was a famous ex-army man, who had fought and was injured in the groin once in a battle with the Greeks, whereupon he was released from the army with full honours and relative privileges. In time he became the court supplier of new flesh and serviced pleasure, setting high standards of true value-for-money and unblemished transactions. All his imported merchandise was guaranteed disease-free and virgin, and had the reputation of being so proven with time. He himself, the dealer, paid high prices for such quality and once killed a man for deceiving him in such a transaction.

This supplier of humans kept her in his house untouched for two years. He did not have any boy heirs and she was safe from spoil. One day a friend of his he had not seen for years called to visit him – the honourable Turk – and in the excitement of the moment the fat man offered his friend drink, food and a girl of fourteen to take home.

After a month, the visitor called to the house again and told the Turk he was on his way home, so in the space of two hours the two men exchanged conversation and hearty assurances of maintaining ties and said their goodbyes, while she, the young girl of innocence, was told to fold her clothes in a wide silk scarf and leave with this man for a place, at an unspecified distance, which was to become her second home in just over two years.

That was how she became a new wife, in Iraq, some thousand

miles away and at a moment's notice. The Turk did not even say goodbye or wish her luck; she was a mere virginal hand-me-down, and if she was lucky, her husband would give her the security of a home, long possession, children and goods.

Remembering the brief story of his mother took a hard toll as he finished his second beer and started on his third. He tried to console himself with thoughts of some admiration for his father, who had treated her well, told no one that she was given to him. More than that, his father told everybody that his new wife was the daughter of a famous general, who trusted him with his young and only daughter and married her to him moments before he left this world, contented and assured of the best for his offspring.

Furthermore, would her life have been better if she had stayed in Turkey, most probably to be sold elsewhere or end up in some brothel, or as part of a death settlement be inherited by someone else, inherited her, just like an item from a closing-down sale? Yes, she was lucky, she was not soiled en route from her village, was kept untouched until her marriage and final departure to Iraq. Her life even after his father's death could not have been that bad, considering the other possibilities. Had she not ended with his father, a mother he loved beyond words and further than he could express?

There was one thing he could do now, a friend of his was going to Azmir, emigrating to Turkey to join his great uncle's family and taking over the family business in that city. He could ask him to inquire about the Turk, whose name he still remembered; it was etched on his mind from the day she told him the story, as deeply as it was on his mother's sanity. Maybe his friend could find out more about his mother's village and see if it still existed. If that was achieved, he could think of sending his mother to visit her folk, although fifty years or more had elapsed.

This thought calmed his unsettled, anxious conscience. He was happy he had reached the tranquil plateau of a decision to try to do something to ease his guilt over his failure to alleviate his mother's pain.

He could understand and appreciate the heavy-handedness of loss, being forgotten in time, the loss in being rootless and without the means to appease one's longing for the framed picture of one's own family, for a wholesome and healthy life amongst one's own people. The idea gave him the will to sleep until sunrise, at peace with the world and all those who made the world for him.

The train arrived at Basrah an hour late, predictably slow in letting out the last shriek of steam, with which it always announced arrival at the terminus. The taxi journey was tolerable, with one of the children still asleep and the other engrossed with the pictures that slid past through the tightly closed window frame of the taxi.

He found he was telling himself that the boy was just adjusting to the new location, comparing it with the capital they had left behind the day before. Was the boy starting to recognise the shapes of buildings and design of particular streets, or was that too early for a three-year old boy, he asked himself. Anyway, the child must have some degree of observation even at this age, his silence could only mean that his mind was really engaged. It continued until they arrived at their own doorstep, when the boy made some show of noise.

As his wife was making breakfast and later changing the babies, he found himself on the phone to his emigrating friend. The request was made, details were given and the friend agreed without hesitation to find out as much as he could in the shortest possible time, as he understood the significance of finding out any connections remaining still in Turkey.

The two men bid each other goodbye. It was fortunate he had rung his friend that morning, as the man was leaving for Istanbul that afternoon. He thought maybe luck had intended he should think seriously about the matter the night before, otherwise he might have missed the chance. As he did not know the man's new address in Turkey he would have to wait until he was contacted by post and given the friend's address after the latter had arrived, settled in and then instigated the search.

He was more anxious than any one to find out, unreasonably anxious and impatient. Unlike the night before, when he was tranquil and pleased to have reached the threshold of instigation, his initiative in the bright light of day, made him uneasy. Such days were always so. To reach a barrier and know how to gather one's will to cross it did not mean that the longest or the hardest part was already travelled.

My father confided my grandmother's story to me after she had died. I was told not to tell it to anyone. And although I was at college, a fully grown man, I was reminded of the harshness of society as it stood watching to strike any one down with least reason and mercy.

I had kept her secret, inherited it with my memories of her, with everything I owed her, with the essence of loyalty that needed no reminders.

17

Diary to the Wind

In the post, one day in June 1977, I received a parcel which, when unwrapped, at first felt unimportant: a package of brown paper enfolding a small booklet. I opened it slowly. My father had sent me his diary, to Dublin. I was unable to interpret his intention, although I was fascinated with it. No letter or even a note of reference accompanied it. His handwriting inside it gave his identity away immediately, in words written with care and almost as if drawn.

The first page of the diary read simply:

December 15, 1955: Not enough information as to the actual existence of mother's home village, the letter confirmed the impossibility again. Trying to get the search going again: sent more money for hire of another man to investigate. Hope is low, six months of waiting is too long. The year may end soon without news that would retrieve faith, faith in telling my mother some good news. She does not seem unhappy here, but I can see the disguised sadness in her silence and forced interest in the children.

The wife is pregnant again: another boy would be welcome, a quieter boy than my eldest even more so, with pride and joy in having another son. A girl instead is also nice. Trouble in my gut: I must stop drinking so much. Have to regulate my other desire after the next child is born. Today I marked case-file number 2001 with a good result, case closed, verdict very favourable and fair. The new house has passed the foundation stage. Big gardens, full of lemon,

orange and datepalm trees. I hope. And an olive tree for a blessing
of good-luck, I must remember to get one. Hedges of sweet-
smelling plants, rows of rose bushes in four colours: pink, white,
red and yellow. I must have them all, a garden with high walls to
lock away the world, privacy of thought and voice, hope of gain
and achievements for the new year. In another year the house will
be finished, and in its wet, infant gloss, I feel it now, a new
beginning for us; a true visual image of our contentment.

Egypt is in the news again, a failed military coup, more unrest
and less contentment. After the nationalisation of the Suez Canal
and the triple-front assault by the French, English and Israelis, we
all thought the might of armies was tested against the will of
the people. For months now, nothing about the role of the fair
Americans had been in the news. Nasser must have wanted to
cover it up, imagine the Americans saving the Arabs from their
national fervour, Nasser victorious but only with their help, when
he could have demonstrated the genius of his plan and the true,
inevitable eventuality of Arab unity. He had probably hoped for a
euphoria of nationalism when the West reacted to his well-timed
nationalisation of the canal, he probably did not expect an act of
war.

The Americans must have new markings for the division of old
territory. I knew it somehow, their support was for the clean
surgical removal of Nasser, they snuffed out his initiative by stopping the triple-force assault, followed by a planned coup. The
insurrection, however, was too well mapped and was put out by
Nasser's league of secret police. It does not stand to reason that a
revolution of the people, by the people, for the people, requires an
army of secret police to protect it from itself. Egypt seems like a sea
of silence and corruption again.

The Suez Canal is not won yet and may be lost forever; all those
who relinquished their lives for it must keep the satisfaction of duty
and reality in separate jars. It is not fate that has won, but futility of
time. All wins may carry a price when they should be prize enough
when righteous, they may be worthless when inhumane, totally
unattainable when bent by force into out-of-shape injustice.

Democracy is for people of mild temperament, who respect
values, the world is not ready for democracy, not ready for the
dream but ready for the utopia. Even in countries where elections
are held regularly, wins and losses are usually marked by a fine line

of leaks to the press of file contents marked: 'For the rainy day'. When all is done and not lost, the people will vote on the sharpened edge of a sword or in the play-around vocabulary of strong voices, romantic in their remembrance of times long gone by and the longing for a return to past-rejected pasts. All of us are blind-folded and breast fed; they do not seem any different from us in the 'free' world.

The other side of the dark window: in 'common-man states' life looks worse: desolation of the soul in the drive to save it from the greasy materialistic claws of exploitation and into a bigger exploitation. Stalin is the father of such costly games, he may have encouraged the West in his success in Hungary a few years ago, he could be secretly blamed for today's Suez, except the West was not united, which evened the odds a little.

The will of divided nations is a mere lesson in the historical facts of failure. The man with the thick stick who treads softly is the model for power. If you have got it, you would be stupid, it seems, not to use it in your own perfected self-interest. For the dreamer and godly good, the same as ever: utopia, feasible although man has reached his limit in being human.

It seems that neither the acquisition of pure knowledge nor the defection to slight, unremoulded philosophy, offers factual or real answers to questioning the history of man. The only time we seem to learn, is when the branding is tattooed, unremovable, beyond the skin and beneath the tongue like that on sold animals, when the pain of words deter their waste and when the need for a virgin start is beyond the will to commit mistakes that are insignificant and more merciful when error occurs, when all seems lost and everything must be re-cycled to the beginning of its existence, avoiding the sharp bends in the flat-race for all precious time; even when it becomes evident and necessary to slow down a little, to actually stay in the race. Oh, such seems the universe a paradox of puzzles and a colourful maze.

Oh, how nice it was when others had explained the world flat and coloured ignorance with simplicity, shaded the strong light with soft glass, when confidence made everything acceptable and everything was covered by the wisdom of others, when glass gave out a solid ring as it was tapped by the finger, or properly supported its fragility by shattering as it bounced off the hard earth; not when it looked like clear glass, but tapped dull, and was the unbreakable, unreal and totally deceptive new-fashioned plastic in progress now.

A fever of excitement-fever in favour of the bright future of humanity can be a sign of slow sickness or simply a greater mark of that childish anticipation. The latter is usually true when a simple impossible is boldly seen as believably plausible. Is it not ridiculous to call the fine-conscience oath of doctors as Hippocratic as if it was an anagram of Hypocritical? Or is it implied as the truth of their nature? I have seen very few who were worthy of their true oath and its spirit. It always seems that we express the truth in oddest of ways; only children and those of us who prefer senility to sheer madness appear clearly and softly confident of our step. All of us who are critics, are either disillusioned or confide in ourselves nothing but our failures and there lies the fine line, which may not be always seen or felt as a division.

Leaving room for hope, I keep my sanity to feed my children in silence, those that are here and those whom I may beget and unintentionally dedicate to the soil of time, to flower in the world which I have long doubted and to which I have debited my exist-ence, lived purposefully or reservedly. Control is in part inhu-manely and regressive as much as it is in part compelling for survival.

The intricate balance between staying in play and cheating to win, seems neither easy nor puritanical, as a roll of the die is also neither of these. I seem to be part of a universe I cannot control; yet I believe in myself and want to be its Phoenix.

The diary also read:
December 18, 1956: I find myself again in a maze of thought as I give more thought of the newly conceived, unborn child: I welcome it with apprehension for its sanity. A thought like that never entered my improper wishing before. I always felt more hope when I learnt of the conception of the last four, the two who survived as well as the two who miscarried in sadness: all of my wife's and a little of mine. Yet this child seems to give me a feeling of sadness of which I cannot foresee the origin, although I don't know the child even by sight: it is still to be born.

The price of success is not always as high as many acclaim its true value to be. Certainly it does not fit with the theoretical Greek ideal. Once my philosophy teacher in law school told me that Socrates was condemned for claiming that material sacrifices made to the gods, either in thanksgiving or as vows, were in return for favours or wishes granted, pay-offs of kind.

He made me accept that such things were, legally, trade-offs and bribes, and as such were immoral, as the gods should be of higher standing, should not require this purely materialistic want or need; they should be spiritual and always beyond greed. Since that day I have found it hard to accept that gods of any kind require of us something in return for success or achievement: our failures and sufferings, past or to come, must be enough to balance what we have taken in the form of gifts to ourselves. Also, a conscience is enough payment of penance for the trip. Those who travel through life without it, are people who pay less than others.

Maybe I'll enjoy success in work, in harmonious relations with less mental pain, throughout this year. My worries really make me think of my new child's conception. I pray it is only a momentary disillusion, not a feeling that this child will be my tax on the good year I had so far. If punishment was due, it would be so unfair that it should be exacted on a pure soul, while those who sinned were fined on the surface.

December 19, 1956: I had a nightmare last night. I was standing on strange ground that arid and waterless, my beard touching my sunburnt chest and blown out of shape by the dust-laden wind. I could see no one who wanted to ask me what I was doing. Instead the few passers-by were driven by the heat and the strong sunlight into hurrying on.

I had no reason to stand there, yet still I stood willing the silence into unquestioning tolerance. After a while, a man, well dressed and seemingly gentle, offered me some water from a clay jug. I had not seen such pottery since I was fourteen or so. I accepted it in a smile of gratitude, although the dryness of my mouth was making me suffer as I smiled.

When I lifted the jug to my mouth, it was empty. The man was surprised it was empty, looked long at my face and then walked around me with his head towards the ground. A few yards away, he stopped, looked again and said a few words which I could not catch. He turned away in disgust, as I did not answer him. He disappeared into the distance without casting a shadow which I could follow with my eyes and by which I could predict his position against the sandy lines of the horizon.

Everything in the dream was either black or white, even the usual grey colour of the pottery was more black than grey. The man's eyes were black, his clothes were the white of linen and the sand took on the air of a fine white sprinkle instead of the golden-sandy texture that I know from the waking world. There was a distant sign, which simply stated 'Iraq' in desert-tarnished black letters. I could understand neither the message nor the hidden content of this dream. I can neither believe it essential that I should take heed of the spartan length of its hostile language, nor ignore it. I simply dread its apparent truth of prediction, which suggests especially being a refugee and in need of charity, more than the actual immobilisation of thirst. The unrecognisable background in the dream may indicate that the dream itself is false process, imaginary and best be forgotten.

Two empty pages followed before the diary recorded:
December 25, 1956: The registered letter from Azmir bears an unbe-lievably dark summary of news. Mother's village had been found: the remaining occupants are Armenians. The letter confirms mother's story: the troops carrying children away, the same number and age as reported. Furthermore, a man in his seventies remem-bers the incident, his children and grandchildren are still alive. His relationship to mother is not clear, but he is related closely. The man in question got overwrought at the mention of mother's Christian name, he was most likely to be her younger brother or cousin. He spoke in sorrow of the loss of those children and others taken away, as if it was known that they were dead and buried, describing those years of slavery in thought and body.

When he was faced with the possibility of mother's being alive and maybe coming for a visit, the same man tried to change his story, denying he knew of anyone of that name. He clearly did not want the missing woman to return. A few nights later, the new-found relative confessed that she would not be welcomed in the village again, especially since she had a new religion, had married outside the church and had those children outside the beliefs of her birth. He was no longer interested in letting her join the flock, even if it was temporarily or for a visit.

He also threatened, as a headman of the village, that if she did so anyway against his wishes, she would not be welcomed by anybody in the village and that he would see to it personally that the rest of the women treated her as if she was a cheaply-paid prostitute, returning after all bridges had been burnt to acclaim her purity, regardless of the fact that she did not willingly become what she is today. He suggested that she forget her birth and life before adolescence, and wisely accept her life as it stood, as the only one she had, with everything else a bad dream she should erase from her memory.

My friend, therefore, does not recommend that she should make such a journey. The news is disheartening for me; at last, I thought, reading through the early part of the letter, I can wipe her silent tears with some joy and ease her memory with the gratification of finding her long-lost family. I have to make a decision soon, whether to tell her of the finding or fold that letter in my diary for ever, filed unread.

It is hard to apportion the worse blame either to the Turks or to her own people. Her innocence and blamelessness for all that has happened seem casualties of that age and unfairnesses she had to carry within her unknowingly for the rest of her life. Even the meek seem heartless when they shed their falsely submissive skin and play ruthless when they can.

The humbled man retracts his teeth in humiliation. In the face of a later forceful exhibition of strength, he elevates the point where pitilessness parades again in a cortège of might, almost forgetting past weakness or inflicting his true taste of power on those that he can manipulate or degrade.

In loss and gain of power, all of man is criminal, all is of corrupt soul, all is not what we show as the truth; while those of us in the middle ground are onlookers, dreamers and maybe disguised faces of either extremes of the human condition. It is better, I think, if she was not to know at all of her new-found relative, her link to her early life. I can't tell her of it, she may not believe it. Or if she did, she may become irredeemably broken into small pieces of lost, shattered crystal. I may never mend her heart again or soothe her affliction into forgetfulness, ever. I would rather she simply did not know or feel it possible for her to find her own childhood. She may accept it in time as lost and never found, misplaced in the noise of today and the tones of tomorrow. I shall tell no one of this find, they can all assume there was no living link to her beyond us, her children.

The last pages of the diary, hanging off the spine of the small pocket-book, read: (undated) This is the last occupied page. I have torn the others out and fed them to the fire. I neither want any one to feel I am a reactionary nor want any of my family dragged in the dust because of some statement I have advocated. I have checked the contents, I hope I have not missed anything that may give the wrong impression. It seems to me, somehow, feelings no longer matter, living through these years could be a triumph. Whoever said war was hell must be understating the cost of peace. I find myself angered and yet hopelessly void of expression. For my son and his two sisters, who have not seen power exploit a man's soul. I hope they will live their lives with the eyes of simpletons, undreaming and accepting what they can get out of their lives. My father was lucky. He died when his world was alive, when he had left his aspirations on a shelf still designated 'possible'. The seaweed also has days when it covers the golden sand and subsides, but retreats only slowly, more slowly than the rise of the tide, more slowly than the fall of the waves, mocking a confident, clean-spirited beach with dark residues that refuse to melt away in the morning sun. If my life ends tomorrow, my children, I hope, will remember me as now, with honesty and warmth, nothing less; I want nothing more.

Kept with the diary were pages untidily folded together in groups, as if to divide the time or spirit in which each was written.
The first section was dated twenty-first of September 1958 and written on sun-faded paper that seemed to have been kept where rain, wind and earth had had their share of it. It was written in a hurry of strokes. It was not easy to read, but the sentences were audible to the mind. 'I had to burn my collection of father's photographs and private papers, all the ones taken with dignitaries and events of the past. I had to burn my wife's collection of photographs too. Today I feel like an orphan, no, worse, like an illegal immigrant. My son watched the coloured flames, probably enjoying the spectacle, he does not realise, it makes him a child with no past to redeem when he "needs to find himself again",' (the faintly inked lines constituted the only paragraph).

The second page was similar to the first and was dated May 1961. It read as headlines:
The land is deserted, the farmers now own the land they always wanted, but forsake it for the city. Which one of them shall plough it wearing Italian leather shoes, when they are used to do it with their bare feet? Their sons earn good wages in government employment, they will take care of their parents. The price of the American rice, which has two hands held tight on the canvas and the slogan: 'A gift from the American people (to the Iraqi people)', (in Arabic), is flooding the market. It is sold for one tenth of the price that the farmer needs to grow his own. The similarly clothed sacks of wheat are similarly destructive. The farmer does not need to toil a whole year to find his crop stacked in the stores and rotting in the shade, feeding the rats rather than the people. This revolution, which had a banner 'For the farmer', must have had the word 'Not' censored out of its text, wilfully.

The words on the third page looked more crowded. Lying next to the first two, this page had a clean background and was written in black ink with ample time, it seemed, and refinement of language. It was dated twenty-first of March 1963. It started like a manifesto:

'It has been ten days since the coup took place. The shreds of the nightmare, of the past five years have already been folded into the fire. No more demonstrations on the streets, no more dragging of old people to their deaths with government cars, no more persecution of a man because his father had given him a name the mob did not like, no more cutting out of organs and gouging out of eyes, no more intestines eaten in public by sickly teeth and bizarre appetites, no more 'peace trains' travelling armed to any city where there was opposition to the mob, to kill children in front of their parents, no more proverbs like smack the runts and the big head will conform. No more slaughter (if we ever learn)'.

The second paragraph started with:
'My children can forget the 'popular resistance songs' that they had to memorise whether they wanted to or not. Freedom tastes strange after the bland taste of years of fear. I am not tearful or out of hope yet, though I fear it may not be over. But it is better now, anyhow. I hope the farmers can feed us again, instead of the imports driving us to future hunger'.

The fourth folded paper was short in content and dated October 1964:

'Another coup, another change of face, another attempt to fill different cells, another change of heart. Is this a nation or a set of poker cards? Nasser tried to invade Syria, to cause a coup, 'to reform (conform) her rulers'. Five hundred of his best special troops killed in the air, none of them got on the ground. Who had already informed the Syrians? What talk of Arab unity, we are busy killing each other and then trying to rehabilitate the corpses to fine ideals of rhetoric. This nation has not got a soul, it merrily has a body that stinks of cigarette burns and seemingly accepts its masochism.'

The final portion of papers, folded and added to the diary, were two pages stapled together, written in a form that looked as if it was intended as a letter. It was addressed on the back to 'My son' and dated 'July 1968 and further'. It started formally: 'My son'.

If you ever leave your heritage of uncertainty, your inherited sense of belonging, your past cut away clean, your faith in man cautious, if you ever leave here and decide not to come back, I bless you for your insight and will. I bless you with my love and pain. I shall bless you until my dying day. I bless your mind, your intention and your thought spared always for us, who remain behind the wall of ignorance and beneath the heel of stupidity, who still have hope for this country despite its past and its people.

The next paragraph was self-explanatory:

I have always given you a thought for the opposite, an open mind for both sides of the statement. Let your education keep you from slipping into anything that is not aligned to events and to the force of logic. You had a glimpse of the West in your American high school days: in books I brought you home, had a taste of the East in living here and in the education provided by this country's governments. The choice is yours, as it was never mine. I wish I had hopped on a ship and sailed away from here to see the world with my eyes, to feel the world with my finger tips, to die happy in the declaration that I had seen and done anything I wanted to. But such a utopia was never realistic for a man with a heritage and children, a man with a wife and mother. The smaller dreams were more costly at the end; satisfaction is always tainted when the big dreams stay unforgotten, when the reachable dreams are uneasy or take longer to attain.

The second page, written in different ink as if the latter had been laid aside for some time, started:

I am not sorry for having had you or your sisters, you were all the best I got in my life. Do not take this wrong: I release you, from your promise that you made me some ten years or more ago, when you said you would always take care of me and your mother until you died. Although children in this world (to us Easterners at least) are the insurance policy of their parents, when these get older and are unable to care for themselves. I do not expect this of you and insist you forget your promise, as if never spoken.

The page ended with a smaller paragraph: 'God bless your ship. Love will bind you to us forever, even though only in memory or fate'. It carried no signature beneath, but a note: P.S. 'I shall give you this diary (or whatever is left of it) the day I feel you're sailing away. Do not judge me harshly, I always loved you. DAD.'

18

A Trespass on Older Times

My father had sent me his diary, his private time and thought; he had lent me its fields and access. I wondered if I was allowed to be in it or simply watch it from the fence of words he had built to safeguard it from others. I would trespass if I was to judge his intentions or choices; I would trespass when I do the same with my own past.

I folded the travel-tattered diary. For days I have carried it with me like a Bible, held it to my lips like a cross, read it over and over like a confession. It was most of what I have with me of my father that is not mere memory. He would not look into my eyes when we said the last goodbye, as if trying not to haunt me, untying the last rope for the current to take the boat away on its own merit and chance.

Of my mother I had with me, the look mothers give their sons on departure to faraway places, the hug they give them as if they were not returning from battle and the trickle of small, lightly spread tears, for their sons to remember and never to forget, like a promise of lilac on a summer's day or the fragile butterflies once upon a season.

The room had become dark. When I had started reading the diary again, in early evening there was ample light coming from the window of the flat. Now, past eight, all was dim, all was formally night. I sat with my now cold cup of tea, trailing childhood days without the intention of serious retrieval. I softly recalled the infancy of thought free of the prejudice of current nonsensical appraisals or foolish, wounded feelings. All that had passed in childhood stood deep in musing, nothing more, nothing less.

I lay in bed, not caring that the day had passed uneventfully in an unpretentious lull. Days of soft shades have their own character too. At dusk, all would be forgiven, all would be laid like a single template, all would pass into a distant recess of time, none of it would be judged as demeaning its silence, none of it jolted out of its serenity, none of it laid anywhere but in ease of the day. I wished all my days were like these. I wish they were all stamped with a firm destiny and an image of heat-gathered breezes amidst the evening call of birds returning home. I was at peace with myself, once again, once upon a night. I wished my eyes would close in like passion to pass a dreamless night.

A knock on the door woke me up. I went to the door in a trance, I had few clothes on but felt unashamed. Lelia giggled as she told me 'Some one on the phone for you', turning away, yet without blushing (at least I did not notice her blush). I was awake again. I took the dressing gown from inside the door and put it on with subdued haste. The lateness of the hour had already told me it must be Andrea, the irregular breath on the telephone merely confirmed it, without a necessary introduction.

I had been expecting her call for a few nights now, but had not received it. She was nearly unconscious, nearly bereft of thought, with every sign of a near overdose. Without further inquiry I asked her if she could get a taxi and come to the flat, if she could manage that without being caught or sent to the nearest police station. She was as nearly sure as she could be that she could manage it. I told her I would wait at the door for her, as I knew that most probably she would not have any money for the cab.

I waited for nearly fifteen minutes before the taxi arrived. The driver was showing signs of agitation. He let her out of the taxi like a queen, opening the door for her and escorting her to the house, anxious to have her out of his taxi. He must have known she was not simply drunk and wanted his fare. I paid him whatever he asked and a little more.

I was opening the main door when the taxi driver came back and flung her coat in her face. She at least smiled sincerely and thanked him loudly.

The taxi door was shut angrily, as I tried to close the main door quietly; it was a lost cause. Lelia was at the top of the stairs, watching with a smile. She looked at us and then at me, murmuring: 'You have your cross to bear too?' She retreated into the darkness without further delay or comment.

Andrea could not even walk past the flat door, she found the bed blindly and precipitated herself on it. I went to the small refrigerator, retrieving the unopened litre of pure orange juice I had bought some days ago, in anticipation of such an emergency. I liked neither it nor what I associated with it since I had started dating Andrea.

The first two glasses were consumed after some stern persuasion, the third glass was refused, drunk and spewed out. The toilet, which was just outside my flat door was not in use, blessedly. White-coloured, undissolved tablets came out with the refused juice. It was starting to work. By the fifth glass and the repeat of the cycle I did not find it essential to hold her as she went to the toilet, now for the sixth time. The therapy was followed with three cups of strong black coffee. She was waking up to depression, as she usually did after such an episode.

She curled up on the bed, facing the wall that bordered a full length of my small bed and started to cry. I undressed her as far as she would let me, covered her almost naked body with a clean sheet and lay down beside her, trying not to make her feel cornered or pushed into a fix. She shied away from me.

I stroked her hair until she was looking tired enough to attempt sleep. She lay on her side, facing the wall. I shared my pillow and my compassion with her. I was no longer sleepy. After an hour or more, she started dreaming. I stroked her hair again. It seemed to ease her pain, even in her sleep. She had the turbulence of a thunder storm in a desert, loud but harmless.

I was not asleep but remembering how we met the first time, as if I was dreaming it all over again, or if it was happening now. I was barely three days in Dublin when my friend, whom I was staying with, suggested we go to a disco. I had just arrived via Paris the previous Sunday, and after three days of recalling army days in Iraq and my short but warm remembrance of Paris, we got bored that night. His suggestion was immediately agreeable.

The disco, 'Lord John's', in the middle of a small street that got its life and pedestrians from the main street in the city centre, was not quite open for the night. It was an early nine o'clock. The Sackville Inn next door seemed livelier and yet not too crowded. We went in for a drink first at that bar, a regular habit of disco-goers in Dublin, I was told. We simply conformed to the custom and had time to kill any way. I was not disappointed in the choice of bar, neither was he.

As the view of the bar unfolded, I had the strangest feeling I was seeing someone I already knew, without seeing her face. I was as if guided by a premonition or drawn by the heavy hands of fate. I could neither think nor know what it was, but my eyes were lured directly to the bar. There were four empty stools. A black-haired girl had occupied the end, fifth, stool, her back to us. I was staring without meaning to or consciously trying to.

My friend was smiling as he saw my state of almost silence. He asked me something (if I wanted a drink, I presume). I could not clearly hear him. He approached the barman, asked him for two pints of beer and returned to find me still motionless, as he had left me. He murmured something about my being like a torpedo, I was neither listening nor conscious of the joke.

I stood beside her, waiting for her to turn round, waiting for the unveiling of surprise and unconsciously ready for a shock. I kept saying in my mind: 'now'. She turned towards me in almost a full circle, her eyes had a smile that softly said: 'Hello'. I heard it, in my thought I replied: 'Hello, again'. I stood like a mountain of ice or a sheet of fractured glass, about to crumble. Her face was not the face of any woman, her smile was not the smile of mere friendliness, her eyes were not the eyes of any goddess; it was as if Jessica was alive again, as if she was the woman in my mind me, out of me and facing me. I could not express any word or take a breath. I had been transformed into a thin cloud of thought, waiting for her to say: 'Yes, it is me'.

I wanted to wake up from it, sure I was dreaming, but I could not cease looking at her. My friend pulled me by the arm, saying something to the effect that I was being rude. I neither cared nor was willing to stop staring.

The girl kept on smiling; she was probably flattered without knowing why and probably did not care why. It may have looked like instant infatuation to her, but to me it was like being in heaven, fearful of being sent to hell or worse of waking up to find it was all only a sterile extension of my imagination. I stood breathless, again like a school boy, conquered by his first crush.

Her mouth was moist with a smile and a devilish expression that formed itself into words: 'Take this seat, it is complaining of being empty, the wood's quite solid and the surface is welcoming'. I was not expecting the warmth of her voice or its clarity in that almost whispering sound. The similarity of tone to that I could easily remember of Jessica's threw my already dispersed concentration into further chaos of thought.

She was about to turn away, discouraged by my silence and the almost unrepenting mood of stillness in my eyes, when I sat down without trying to explain my action in bridging the gap between us. She smiled again, almost childishly expressing 'I've won'.

My friend pushed my pint that was perspiring in front of me, tempting my mouth with promises of coolness. I took my pint in my hand and put it to my lips, forcing a continuation of my silence. She was watching me, looking at me with eyes which were not ashamed of making the first brave move. My courage was less uncertain as to whether I was day-dreaming or in possession of the truth.

The alcohol was refreshing my memory, taking me away from speculation over her interest to the assertion of my own and releasing my words into a medium that had ceased to move as that coordination of mouth and tongue that children learn to use to express need and disguised opinion. I wiped the dew off my glass of beer, but it resisted my will and formed again in minutes, disregarding my fingers and achieving a wetness matched only by that of the soul.

She drained the last of the coke-colour of her cocktail, drawing the slice of lemon to its fate: she ate it with planned relish, separating its tender insides from the alcohol-softened skin, swallowing the segments and extracting the unwanted left-overs at the same time out of her mouth. It expressed experience that was coupled with will and enjoyment. It was my turn to watch.

The empty glass stood without an opinion as she moved it further away from her hand and in clear view of me. I recognised the implication: she was asking without asking, waiting for the offer without pretending she might not accept it.

I was slower than usual in offering, partly through not clearly understanding her motives, but mainly through fear of being refused. I decided to gamble and throw the dice with closed eyes, awaiting the voice that would throw out a reaction to inform me of the result. I was like a child: wishing hard entailed closed eyes, fists clenched tightly one against the other, restricted breathing.

She said 'Yes, thanks', without waiting for my sentence to finish its carefully formulated sequence of words. It was Kiskiddee and coke, with ice and more lemon. She waited for the barman to serve us and for me to pay for it, before speaking again, as if unsure of the offer or the obligatory terms of reference it imposed.

She asked first where I was from and not my name. I did not receive this with great enthusiasm and would have preferred her to reverse the order of asking. I introduced myself and she then did the same. We shook hands with ease and gentility of interest. She did not seem surprised at either piece of information and had no problem in repeating my name. I was startled and yet unconsciously expecting it, thinking of Jessica, a spirit who knew all of me that was to be known or had.

She looked at my new trousers and matching tie and assumed my next destination for the night correctly: 'Going to the disco, next door.' Her words were more of a statement than a question. I confirmed it with a smile which implied that I was not so much a lover of music and dancing but had another motive: to find a girl. She smiled back and proceeded with an intelligence that had me easily deciphered. 'You don't have a regular girlfriend, then', again stating rather than asking.

I had to defend my celibacy as if it was a condemnation of ignorant social behaviour, as if I was useless with women. 'I've barely got here, are women in Dublin that easy?' I replied in a tone bordering on belligerence or intent of war.

She retreated hurriedly to avoid answering, looking away and asking me in retaliation whether I had brought any of my 'four wives' with me. I smiled, taking her words in a spirit of pure conjecture and disinformation. 'Very few men in Iraq nowadays have more than one wife, my father only had the one. I am not married, not yet any way.' I finally declared all previous vows and promises to any girl null and void. She looked unconvinced and yet untroubled.

She looked at her watch, announcing it was eleven o'clock or near it. 'The disco is open now, are you going too?' she asked. My pint was two-thirds drunk and my friend's drink was long over. He was talking to a girl who must have come with her three friends. I had not noticed the four girls until now.

All of us streamed out of the door of the bar in single file before assembling outside the basement door of the disco. The queue had at least twenty people, including us. The sky was clear and the air was crisp with cool anticipation. We were all expecting good things to come, fretting little and wanting more.

Two boys were refused admission, then it was our turn. I wanted to pay for her; she smiled and dug out her free passes, gave me one and offered another to my friend. We both accepted. He paid for his new acquaintance, while her friends paid separately for themselves. No one complained, no one entered the door with any thought of apprehension, our faces were those of old friends, come together as a party of hunters united in will and excitement.

The dark interior was intermittently lit with flashes from the laser-like light that danced to the beat of all the songs played. The walls were decorated as if they were old dungeons, chains and metal armour suits hung every where and stood in every corner, opening on to a maze of corridors and three bar-service counters that assumed the maceration of the clients if not the age of the place to be fake and superficial.

There were two dance floors, one on the ground floor, where we had entered and a bigger one in the floor above, linked by a spiral staircase and another flight of stairs, wider and more slopping, at the back of the cellar, near the fire exit. The latter stairs were used by those who had consumed more alcohol than their legs could support or who were helped by such consumption to overcome their inhibitions over kissing or further moves in that direction.

We ordered our drinks and sat in a dim corner. Andrea and I were quiet. My friend and his companions were trying to talk, but were often beaten back by the drowning sound of the loud music. Sentences and opinions were repeated more than once before they were received, understood or accepted.

The mood of all those there was as light as the heart-beat music piped through the large and already suffering loudspeakers. The exchange of silent glances were getting more frequent as Andrea and I continued our slow consumption of alcohol. No words had been exchanged since we sat down in the darkness, we were like old lovers who had already said everything to each other over a long period; we looked like old acquaintances with years between us and within us, as if we had had each other long before, and were not on a first date.

I stretched my palm under the table to meet hers, brushing her thigh accidentally. She did not complain but, as if she knew I wanted to hold her hand, complied calmly.

Her hand was moist, surrendering with a gentleness that showed she was not sure in which direction my fingers were travelling as I fondled her slim, almost guileless finger tips. She suddenly leant her body closer. I responded without thoughts of shyness, uninhibited by the newness and slightness of our acquaintance. I could feel her heartbeat through her skintight blouse and she mine through my thin summer shirt as we sat still, in silence.

She gripped my hand as it reached her wrist, folding her hand firmly as if to pull my whole being closer. In less than a second I lent my lips to her mouth; she was expecting the kiss and I seemed to want it more. After some sad songs we started dancing. The fast accentuation of the music restored the bright lights to the dance floor, directing the need for movement straight to the mouth and bodies with it. I had been taught well that summer in London, which had opened its arms to me and in brief encounters. The enthusiasm and energy lasted longer than the hour seemed to us short. The punctuation of the beat eventually slowed down to allow a closer attachment among the dancers; it was kissing time again.

In the midst of the second song a strident siren and flashing lights left me full of amazement. It was just past one o'clock and I did not understand the instant change to harsh brightness. She smiled as if now she found my surprise amusing. 'It's a police raid,' she stated simply. The bar-barriers suddenly came down and their spotlights went out with equal speed. The beat of the music speeded up again. 'They are not supposed to sell alcohol after one o'clock.' she added.

After a few minutes, the siren sounded again and it was back to business as usual, the bars re-opened and the music returned to its slow pace, playing the same song that had been interrupted. 'It's over,' she confirmed with ease, 'now you can order again if you want to.' I was partly amused and partly undecided over what the event signified. I was expecting the police to dash in and walk through the place in great numbers, as my American film memories demanded. Instead, it was like a game of 'cops and robbers', swift and childish like the death of a player hit by the fast squirt of a water-gun, that brings about the end of the game.

At the end of another hour it was time to evacuate the dance hall; the strong bright lights and the silence of the music announced it,

while the movement of people to their tables and the louder tones
of voice that everyone was using turned the earlier soft shades of
the disco almost into a market.

It was evident from the outburst of conversation that most people
were trying to make a last effort to speak, to make up for the past
hours when few words had been exchanged. It was also time for
most of the guests to make other plans or arrangements to meet the
next day, or to try and make the night last longer in keeping the
same company discovered on the dance floor.

I had thought that being with her without the expression of any
particular aspiration was enough, until I found myself wrong. She
was looking at me silently, resting her elbow on my shoulder,
exposing her bare underarm to the light and the finely shaven hair
to me; her blouse smelt of anticipation and delicately scented
wanting that was more enticing. I asked her if she wanted coffee
elsewhere. She agreed without inquiring where that elsewhere
was. We left with the crowd, slowly and undistinguished from the
rest. We found a taxi with its driver almost asleep, awakened by
our asking if he was free. The journey to my old flat in the cab
shared with my friend and his companion was quick; we hardly
noticed the time.

The half-house that I was temporarily sharing with my friend
stood dark and as if sleepy, the dampness of mist and old wood
hanging lightly over it, collected over the years. With its large
rooms and rattling windows it suited the name we had already
christened by: the 'Castle'.

We climbed to the kitchen on the top floor, all four of us driven
by the need for coffee and the expected fulfilment of promise that
we had made the girls, of having a cup to quench the thirst. The
electric kettle cut the formality to a minimum. After the coffee, my
friend and his companion disappeared to the second floor where
we had our sitting room; we stayed in the kitchen listening to music
and nursing the remainder of the coffee and a hope for something
more.

The words distilled slowly first as she asked how long I had been
in Dublin and other trivial matters. I answered reluctantly before
an urge overcame my silence and I kissed her. All questions were
then set aside, discarded, as she held me and I held her. Kissing had
a new meaning, it brought the pure drop of honey and marvelling
heartbeat that did not rest until re-enforced by further cycles of

mouth over mouth and affectionate breathing in between longer spells of total but willing dissolvement of need.

I felt her skin of nineteen summers; it was lace and soft velvet, as she lifted her arm to cover my shoulders. My hands slipped into her blouse from the space of her underarm, touring her left side, her breasts were timid and her ribs were pulsating. My fingers had found the heat of time and touching was again the strength of craving. I wanted her more than I had wanted any one for a long time. I was bewitched, hexed as if to eternity.

After an hour of embracing we lay on my soft bed and undressed each other. Skin to skin we lay motionless, neither of us knew how we got there, nor did either of us question it. She melted in my arms and I melted inside hers in fair trade and exchange of intent.

Dawn woke us with its last breath like children and we exchanged the gifts of our bodies again. It felt as if once again it was the first time.

That summer was at best interludes of restraint and hunger, followed by nights of gluttonous warmth. I came to know her and allow her both time and distance. She would choose when she would go out with me, when she would sleep with me and when to be absent for days without explanations, excuses or thoughts of how I felt for her. I was like a man whose life was not his own, a man with a weight of gratitude for the least of alms, a man who had asked for little and received less without complaint or the sombre nutrition of revolt. I was happy, unpossessive and almost content. yet I felt most wanted when she would ring at four o'clock in the morning, sobbing over her misfortunes in her past life, crying, asking to come over without giving the impression that that was the purpose of her call: she was stranded in town without a fare home and without a friend's warm bed to keep her until morning. Many a night I woke from dreaming of her to hear the telephone. It felt sometimes like a premonition of her call and most nights like that she would call, late or early.

She never understood time or a body's need for sleep, her mind was the hour-glass, her eyes were the sparkling sand filling up and turning over to start again. Nothing else seemed as convincing or as real as touch or the kiss she had given me. Nothing else was important.

She had one nightmare that repeated itself, of her first boyfriend, a man whose heart was in motorcycles and whose pictures she carried everywhere she went. There was also the brother whose life she claimed was wasted one night when her father had let him take the car out for a drive; in the midst of his depression he had rammed the car into a wall and given up unresistingly his will to live. Yet another day she would confess that she grew up in a house of girls, with no brothers with whom to share teenage rambling or secrets, the perspective of the other sex's point of view and funny memories of teasing.

I asked more than once, probably twice, if she still saw her old boyfriend; the answer was always the same: 'He'll never return, he's away for ever.' I came to accept that the boy who committed suicide was her boyfriend. I also came to accept that his loss of will was aided by drugs, something that seemed to have cured his depression for ever. At those fences, I came to understand her reluctance to accept his death, inventing a brother she had never had and assuming her loss was less if the dead boy was imaginary.

We were both tied to those thin shadows of people whose death seemed somehow intended as a link and a trap. She had her nightmares of the boy in leather, forever on his motorcycle, she sitting behind. I had my unfading memories of Jessica's death always inside me, clearer than any photograph. Tied to her life were the worthless years that afterwards were no longer mine.

We were both controlled by addictions to memory, soothed by other addictions: Andrea's was drugs, mine was silence and quiet grief; every time we trespassed over that private land, the mind was assured of its penance in pain.

There were times when I wanted her mine, totally mine and all of the time. But Andrea was not the girl to be kept either by promise or by habit, she was always the spirit which could not settle temperately. Hers was a flock of thoughts that only knew how to migrate, rejecting all attempts to possess them undivided. Sharing time and people were essentials of her life and its wonderful paradox of need and longing, which transcended each other, daring the other to independence.

She showed her interest in renewed contact to the man, whoever he was. Her body was a temple of many prayers, her mind a thought shared with a few, her time a balancing of shares for all those chosen. She was faithful to all those whom she liked and the lesser number she loved, without any comprehension of unfaithfulness to anyone, without any understanding of being owned, of accepting the age-long ideology of possession.

She was born without the guilt of worry or the restraint of conforming, since her thought had no social pretence at all. I accepted her self-proclaimed vows of independence with difficulty sometimes but with ease at other times: when I was lonely it seemed not the best part of life to be apart; when I had just seen her the night before, I seemed able to respect her opinion. The dual attraction and withdrawal tolled and knelled, least explicable to me in thought and intricately chafed by the fear of losing her should I demand more than she would promise. I felt most of the time I was to lose her as I found her, in undaunted storm of chance. I was sad sometimes even to consider it.

One night, at the beginning of May, she telephoned me at seven in the evening. Such an early hour that was not her usual time of calling. Her voice was broken by silences interrupted by small sentences of formal, almost shallow, inquiry of how I had been. I had not seen her for over a week, I was almost sure that she was engaged with a new discovery, a new island under the sun or a new thought of prime significance. She had been ill, she told me, without specifying the medical reference. She had a voice that was suspicious of the telephone, as if suspecting someone was listening and she had resolved to take a vow of silence against a confession of some kind.

I asked her without expecting a refusal to come over to the flat. I was alone and had no plans to go out. She suggested a bar, local to me. I agreed to the compromise.

It was a strange windy evening, although warm enough to predict a hot summer to follow. I walked down the small street of Castlewood Avenue, after passing the almost deserted tiny green area at the centre of Grosvenor Square where I was living, a square whose name implied a class intransigence from former times of distinction; our 'Castle' stood at its corner, bleak and damp.

I walked to Upper Rathmines Road, a road never empty of passers-by irrespective of the hour of day or night. Most of the shops, as well as the small H. Williams supermarket, were still trading. It was flatland in reality, effervescent with people who did not hoard food or other essentials, for whom going to shops was a major method of passing the time, justified by lesser reasons of the low wages that most of the young population earned in the area. I caught myself thinking thus, struck by the small plastic bags they always carried, inhabited by one or two items at most. Yet it was a busy and peaceful community.

I went into the Lancer Bar, it was full of compulsive drinkers, even at that early hour. I found her already there, talking to a group of girls who disappeared as soon as I sat next to her, as if prompted by a prior agreement of sorts. She was drinking gin and tonic, and faster than she usually consumed her alcohol. I did the same while casual conversation flew back and forth, full of artificial hesitations.

After two hours or so, she wanted to go home with me. We walked out of the bar holding hands, but giving the impression that it was a first date: our hands were held lightly and loosely. She stood outside the main door of the house, until I had gone inside and turned on the lights, then stared at the flat with a weary countenance as if she had not been there ever before. She accompanied me to the kitchen, where we sat for the next hour drinking tea.

The verbal exchange was left to a few articulated thoughts.

I asked her if she was tired and if we should go to sleep. She agreed without that anticipated hesitation that had marked our time that day and which I was expecting. We undressed in the bright light of the room: we were not shy and it was as if we were back to the normal posture of intimate acquaintance with each other. The small single bed accommodated us with ease, once I held her and she me, unaware of the calm into which we had settled simply.

In the darkness of the room, I kissed her forehead, stroked her hair and whispered I loved her, all three without any complacent thought of deep affection, without strictly planning to do or say what I had done or said. I felt it and my mouth awarded my feelings voice.

She reacted without direct monitoring of thought or word, inherently. We kissed for a long time, huddled in a space where only the two of us existed and not another thought mattered or had any significance. She said nothing more and I said nothing further.

Her skin tampered with my intention of sleep and her lips gave me everything I ever wanted. I was at last at peace with my mind, over any barrier I had felt earlier in the night, when I could not decide from the tone and content of our superficial conversation if this was to be our last date or a civil ending of our relationship.

She withdrew her mouth suddenly from me to whisper: 'Make love to me.' I felt I did not want to, immediately after confessing my love and dependence to her, afraid of her interpretation that sex was the reason of my proclamation and the essence of my confession. I had entered a spiritual plane when I told her I loved her that held me still in a trance and left me somewhat unwilling to have sex post-haste.

My hesitant reaction drew from her an exclamation: 'Do you not want me, will you always not want me?' The two halves of the sentence, laid side by side, were stiff with wondering and a distinct sadness. I did want her, I always would, I promised. She was contented with the reply and her sensuous body showed it. We became gluttonous for each other's bodies, we made love five times, smoking in interludes of passionate words that inflamed the next surge of desire. I had never seen her so happy nor so eager for love.

Dawn came early at four in the morning; the light-violet of the clear sky was pouring through the small window of the room. We went to the kitchen to drink tea, to sustain our tired eyelids from closing in a dream: the dream had already happened. .

As we sat naked in the kitchen, she looked at me with almost shy eyes. I presumed it was my nakedness and the new form of thought that was exchanged earlier in the night, for she had felt different in my arms that night, as if she had given me her virgin body for the first time. I glanced down at my thighs, my groin was slightly tainted red. For a moment I thought my notion of her virginity was true before I realised that it could have been her period.

She apologised profusely, she was not expecting it to come for another two nights. It must have been the final time we made love, since the stain was small and thinly spread. She asked if she could wash me. Under the shower, we stood kissing and washing each other. I stood under the jetting water after it had turned slightly cold and she had abandoned it shivering. I felt cool and clean. She was dressed when I had got out; it was already five o'clock in the morning. A taxi came shortly afterwards and she disappeared swiftly into the newly born morning after a quick kiss and a promise she would call soon.

It was nearly a month since that last night of confession and promise. I had not seen her, she did not call nor could I reach her by telephone at her mother's house; I dug the number out of the telephone directory. I tried to reach her more times than I could remember, but she was always out, I was told. She neither answered my messages that I had left with her mother nor called back.

I saw her one day in Ranelagh by accident at about six in the evening. She was walking out the small off-licence, carrying a large pack of beers. She stopped briefly to smile and promised again to call soon.

I did not ask her for an explanation or where she was going with beer she never drank, but showed my utter amazement that she was in the road next to the flat without calling over. My face was expressionless with surprise as I walked on to the flat, where I spent the night sleepless, stricken with sadness.

A week later she rang me and asked to meet in town, in the middle of O'Connell Street. She was early and I was on time. We went into Burgerland and had something to eat, drowned by coffee. I asked her where she had been. Her answer was slow and timid, the expression of someone who was about to seed conversation with anger or cause it, afraid at the same time of its getting out of hand or loud. She looked around as she put her answer to me.

She proceeded cautiously: 'I am carrying your child.' Her face looked away from me, watching my eyes out of the corner of her eye. I was stunned, not expecting such a claim from her nor one so simply put. I was silent for about five minutes, though it seemed less. My mind was chained to surprise and endless possibilities of confusion.

I could no longer hear the clatter of the place as I looked at her with dreamy eyes that were softer than the tone of my voice. I was happy in a sense at the physical link to her which was implied, a link that could not be disputed and required a lengthy period of time from me. I had not a doubt it was not mine, I knew it was not mine, yet I felt the softer points of commitment and was ready to accept it. I was still in love, I did not allow the notion of her unfaithfulness to me, to make me angry, I wanted her more than I could have ever imagined. My placid face and warmth of smile was legitimate, something that seemed to disturb her.

My next sentence was half expected: 'Are you going to keep it? Please do.' She was not quick in reply. I could tell from the look on her face that she had not anticipated the second half of my state-ment. After a pause she answered with shallow breath: 'No, I will not, I am too young and impatient.' Her next sentence felt harsher:

'I need fifty pounds to go to London and . . .' She stopped at the edge of 'get rid of it'.

I almost condemned her, almost got angry, almost felt like screaming. I retreated into myself, measuring my words before my mouth could open and fill the silence. She interrupted my thought: 'I don't expect you to do anything more, it's a loan, I have my plane fare, but the expenses of the clinic I really need, it's all that I will ever need.'

I tried to dissuade her: 'I want to marry you.' She was silent, once again taken back by the unexpected. Her reply was a smile. After a further silence: 'Will you always accept it as your own?' she asked in low voice. I felt I had to be honest with her and assure her of my sincerity: 'I know it's not mine, the last time we slept together you had your period, but it's not important whether it is or is not mine; it will have my name; I want you as much as I love you and will love the baby, but I will not contribute to your abortion,' coming to the end of my breath with the end of the sentence. I was expressing the sadness I felt with a tinge of anger.

She was thinking hard, but said nothing further. She stood up quietly and looked into my eyes, gave me a kiss and left. As she passed the glass window on the outside, she had a smile that I could not interpret, warm yet shallow. I stayed seated; my mouth said 'call me', without the voice, she nodded 'yes'. I was confused at the abrupt closure of the subject, as if it was but a trivial exchange of words. My sadness was painful.

Whenever I thought of that afternoon, when she told me she was carrying my child, I was visited with utter confusion. If it was a test, then I may have passed. If it was an attempt to make me dislike her, then I have failed. Whatever the intention was I wanted her to know I would always want her, or so I thought unconditionally then.

She did not telephone for a month or more. One day I received a call in the laboratory at five to six in the evening: it was Andrea. Her voice, mysterious, did not project her lively personality as it usually did. She told me she was getting married, not specifically, but in the course of conversation. She was going on her honeymoon and should be back in a month or so. She then asked if I would like to see her after she got back.

The terms of my surrender were opaque with shades of contemplation and stains of dishonesty. I felt let down and my feelings totally disregarded, she had refused to marry me but opted to do so with someone whom she had met long ago but was not deeply in love with (as she explained). I could not comprehend the logic now, not her logic. I did not tell her, I could not tell her that I had already bought wedding rings, which I carried with me for weeks in my pocket, dreaming I would stop her one day on the street and tell her again I loved her; I would give her a ring and we both would wear them. I had been stupid and melancholy. I could not tell her I did it because I loved her. I was taken as if to the edge of a cliff and left hanging until the winds came. I had bought the wedding rings from a jeweller that proudly advertised: 'Jameson's, the lucky ring house'. I felt it was definitely a lie to me.

She was an unusual girl. No matter how one got to know her, one could not tell what she was thinking or doing next. I was unusually attracted to her, and the hurt would subside the next time she rang me or held me in her arms. Love was more than blind, it was soft to the point of breaking and strong to the point of mending with least words and warmth. It was like an evident addiction, but more than that: it was illogical in its withdrawal.

When I think of her now, some years on, the eyes have not aged, the smile has not been quenched, though the feeling is masked with the uncontrollable debris of time; but the ashes nonetheless contain her phoenix. She still lives on inside my mind like a breath of memory that refuses to subside, like a need that has traded my innocence of one sort with another, like a myth driving the wind on a cliff.

Yet time allows me to trespass always without refusing me rights of passage, looking on delinquently at my distemper and treating me like a lost child. I and time do not differ on the image, yet it guides me towards remembering whenever I turn towards my past. Its kindness finds me worn at soul and heavy at heart, its fallacious permission to visit, past the 'No Trespassing' sign always seeming open and dreamy, but biased to the point of wanting me to forsake her; but I cannot free the soul that was marked with liberty of wanting and passion of need, re-marking the distance like an albatross for a sparkle of sand.

19

Final Length of Passage

I had wakened in the silence of dawn, one morning in July of 1977. I had barely been in Ireland four months or less. My father's eyes were like his words, crammed into the orphaned pages of his diary. I saw them lit like sticks of incense, like shattered pieces of brown crystal glass, like a journey's end hastily gathered and thrown to the seas. I looked at the diary, as it sat closed, half over the edge of the dinning table, hesitant, yet willing. Its threads were lengths of a passage, its mosaics suddenly opened and more suddenly pulled down shutters, entwining in unrelated colours and wasted design. He seemed to stand alone watching the waves, his hand extended to release his life as it went floating down and away, while he stood unable to make the mark or be on the last boat out.

The distance seemed of too little length, the pain too passive in its complaint, the words too light of imprint; he and I both stood facing each other, the silence too prominent in its lasting. Both of us looked on without the gesture of a breath.

I watched his eyes, those shining stars of bright will and regrets. We were both unable or unwilling to fit the words to our mouths. As if forbidden to trade on the sabbath, we remained in an impasse, our fond thoughts a warning shot over the length's longing and the providence of the extended, open hand with its sense of let die rolled; with its anticipation, half-believing and half-wondering other possibilities, other lives unknown, unmatched and undivided in myth or will, uncordoned by forceful omens, those that leave to the last choice the freedom of its decision.

I looked through the thin, flat frames of the windows: the gut glass was thinner than I had thought, made more fragile-looking with the lifting mist and the sun which, as it gained its forcible entry, looked as if it had been helped almost incidentally, almost passively by the uncomplaining glass, to which it warmed in silence of the morning without a word exchanged. The sunlight and its glass seemed so familiar, so much like my father and me, so alike the both of us in the morning.

Yet all those issues remained unforgotten and unresolved; undenied, maybe, but unwelcome in thought or stance of the light.

I walked down the alleyway in the back of the house, all the way to Harold's Cross, passing by the hospice that stood as it had some sixty or more years, its gates wide open, its gardens empty, its caretakers still asleep at this hour and its occupants whispering words I could barely hear from the distance of the high wall. Their whispers sounded almost like a premonition, like a shadow on the mind, like a prayer of forgiveness loudly belting a soul that was thought to have been lost for its own salvation; a will leased to waste.

I went into the garden uninvited, but unopposed and unquestioned. There was a bench that seemed to have just been evacuated; it was dry while most of those in view were wet with the morning mist. It did not feel cold or hard; its polish was worn out and its wooden surface smoothed by use, as if it was the most favoured of the collection scattered over the green patches and avoiding the concrete walkways that threaded the whole area as if holding it together as one in a spirit of polite resolution and natural arrangement.

This bench was almost like an open-spirited confessional box. The small shrubs covered immediate view of it and it was slightly fleshed with flowers and long-stemmed, thinly extended twigs. Its privacy might explain its frequent occupancy and the preference shown it even so early in the morning.

I sat in its silence. Alone with myself. I held my own hands and my mind calm, as if safe in the wind. The birds were filling the quiet day with noise. Occasionally they flew quickly past the lines of clumped shadow. I sat appeasing my resting thought, not wishing to awaken it, almost fearing an implied loss of battle if I were awakened suddenly. The mind and I had an agreement: live and let live. The peace felt fragile and I battle-worn.

After some time that felt like an instant, a car drove on to the main pathway and headed towards the main building. It stopped where it was supposed to, limited by the end of the concrete stretch and a wide door that opened almost automatically, in machine-like precision, as if the operator had been forewarned and was already on the look-out.

A slender girl, looking twelve or so, got out. Her hair shone in the sun. Her face looking down at the concrete, investigating its craters and its finish. She was in empty-handed and empty-spirited obedience to the instruction to go through the open door. I was but ten yards from her. I did not think anyone could see me as I looked on through the tangled shrubs and their small windows of spaced branches. The girl stood at the doorstep and looked in my direction before her face moved as if to scan the whole garden. She did not seem ill, as she walked upright and there was no sign of any physical pain, but her eyes were dazed and her limbs easily directed without any form of thought, questioning or rebellion.

This interruption almost awakened me, the sun was high in the sky and I felt hungry. I walked back to the flat, the tea I had made in the early morning and not drunk, was now undrinkable. I lay in bed, sipping fresh tea and playing my tape recorder. I had forgotten about it for a few days and it seemed as if I had suddenly found it. I put an old tape of Demis Roussos on without any particular thought in choosing it.

The tape flooded my mind with memories, all those I thought I had buried and all those I had forgotten. My soul seemed to break out of its sleep with the impact of glass shattered by the casual toss of a stone from a playing child. All seemed hard to ignore, nothing remained but the sharp colours that volcanoes spread into the air and over the ground far distant from the point of seepage, first avenging, then slow and then avenging again, uninhibited, unrestrained, unstoppable.

I felt as if all the images were in conspiracy against my mind while I sat there overwhelmed, unable to voice my need for it to stop, to call on my sanity to prevent their illegal and almost illogical presence. The tape was a gift from Rhea, a parting gift of sorts, a farewell link unsevered and still the hardest words to music I could ever remember, as if a masterplan to retain the past unerased, with the future to be discarded but not with any ease, a reprisal hard-meant and elegantly dispensed in the mellow rhythm of memory.

On realising I had found Rhea's name, my mind seemed to rest its raging storm a little before Tamara's face appeared, her smile almost like a vision and her silence, almost like hell. She only stayed a little before the black voids swallowed her from my sight and the emptiness hung forever bare of incidence and colour; time had grown into nothingness.

I was awaiting the visit of Jessica; I could almost swear it, bet on it, know its coming; I had never been so sure in my life. But it never came, the blank screen lifted into grey, followed by colour. The sun still shone into the window and the brown-coloured carpet kept its usual shading of clean and spilt patches, clear and distinct.

I could not determine at first thought whether I was grateful or disappointed for her absence. It was the first time she had ever failed me in a long time of remembering and with such a short time of trying. I had felt her there but she had not come forward, although I felt she had seen me standing in the darkness riveted by its deprivation of light.

A knock on the door broke my wondering without my having to end it. It was Lelia, she wore a questioning face and an inquiring look. I smiled at her. She looked as if she either had just awakened or was about to fall asleep. She came in without a word of invitation, she neither waited nor seemed to ask for it. She sat at the little table where she always sat, without being directed to it, looking half towards the window, half away from me, without any intention of shying away from my eyes, it took her some time to establish the first word, although she did not look dazed or as if wearily debating a decision to speak. She simply seemed to be trying different forms of what she was about to say.

She started with an introduction: 'I think I am going to lose you soon.' A short silence elapsed before further comment. 'Are you going home?' she asked me, almost wanting me to deny the rumour. I had not thought about it much, I admitted in a superficial sentence that could not have increased her confidence in a denial, since she asked the same again, adding the word 'really' to the earlier question. Unmoved, I thought about it and offered the same again, coupled with a question of why she thought I was leaving.

She looked into my eyes, trying perhaps to assure herself that I was being truthful. 'It's my dreams again,' she tried to explain, I was curious: 'Do you see a voyage in my future, is it a holiday or is it settling away for good?' I had to ask. She could not confirm either, or did not want to. I tried silence, to flush out a motive or a description. The attempt was futile. She tried my silence and seemed to be gaining ground on me. I offered her tea, which she accepted easily.

I was thinking about my father that morning, my deeply hidden past before she came in and nothing as she asked me, I said in submission or report of fact. She seemed to have expected that somehow and believed me without further questioning. I lifted her right hand and slowly touched the left side of my face with the back of her hand, which she withdrew even more slowly. I was touched, surprised and flattered by her warmth. I kissed the back of her hand as it drew away. She smiled and almost stopped before her hand left my face, willingly taking in the whole length of the gesture.

She looked down at the carpet and then hesitated before saying: 'Do not run away into the depth of darkness if you're afraid of the dark.' I found the contradiction hard, her choice of words extraordinary, and the mind was tempted to seek clarification. I asked. There would be a moment soon for me to poise at the fence for the last time, to 'commit' a decision, as she put it. I thought of her last words; she seemed to equate my decision (as if she knew it or had heard it) to something criminal. I thought of her words but stayed silent, awaiting the end of the sentence; it was not volunteered, I had to ask for it. She touched me again, repeating her gesture and extending her flaunted inner calm further than before. Her hand stayed longer on my face, as if waiting for a confession. It seemed as if I was sworn to secrecy and was consciously keeping my promise. I looked away without wanting to confirm these suspicions she had now written on her silence and which had now filled her stare.

She stood up, and asked: 'You will let me know, before you do decide?' She did not wait for the answer and by the time I looked at her, she was already at the door. Her tea was left undrunk, neglected like a confirmation she had sought but left behind without its essence being defined or proclaimed.

I thought of her: 'singular'. I thought of her again, more loudly: 'exceptional'. Without taking a decision I reached out and drank her tea as if it were a thought she wanted harvested. It was not wasted.

I woke up as if I had slept for a short while. The clock was four in the afternoon and I must have slept since lunch time; the hands had moved four full circles since I had noticed them last. Eyelids down and mind closed, the world had leased me silence and tranquil deviation from thought for a few sparkle-grains of time, unmissed from the sand dunes of eternity, insignificant like a forgotten tale of no consequence, like a buried word. The sun had already weakened and its light now fought the edge of darkness, though not yet feeling its toll, rather the gradual and fatalistic loss of ground.

I went for a walk, having decided to before leaving my flat. The summer air was crisp with youthful wanting, the mild heat was laden with the voices of children and lovers' heartbeats as they walked each group to its purpose. I was almost lost amidst the reasoning of summers gone by drifting away like paper boats at the edge of a long unvisited river, taking with them everything intended as a purpose and keeping nothing given to me to keep like promises or thoughts of daisy chains and delicate butterflies fully focused just behind the eye like the photographs my father burnt or the look in Jessica's eyes every time I dreamt of her laid silent.

I passed the little bar Lelia and I had sat in more than once. Its doors were open but its spirit dull at this opening hour, so early in the afternoon, when most of its life lay elsewhere, its devotees either at work or at homes they inhabited until the darkness drove them to this refuge, moved by need or instinct. Most of us refugees came in here for the chance of letting the mind sleep away time herded to drunkenness and probable laughter. All of us vowed to retain sanity against thoughts of our lives or of the world through the edge of alcohol as it painted that world for us in colours of failed prominence.

I sat at my favourite stool, the street at eye-level and the sun away from my face, hiding and watching the currents of people cross or walk about, each in a world unrelated to mine. After the third pint, the sun became unthreatening and I could look at its tail-end in the sky. It was time to order stiffer drinks, it was time to cripple the mind as if started to stir and time to disable the will as it started its trial of pertinent dominance.

At eight in the evening, the daylight was visible but drowning before the striding dark. I had drunk about ten gins in the last hours and the sun had not yet set. My face determined to remain as blank as when I entered the bar, but my eyes were unable to show the same resolve; salt leakage was slowly filling up the small space guarded by the eyelids, all of it without my feeling the sadness that my eyes expressed so simply and with such evident liking. The mind was asleep but the heart was feeble, the hands crossed over the coolness of the glass stealing the life of the ice inside, the face calm.

I closed my eyes thinking they would take back the tears, control them, but the eyes refused and the salt trail dripped into my drink, where it disappeared without tainting the alcohol, leaving the eyes glassy as if I was drunk.

A soft-skinned hand, fingers stretched as if begging, touched my face, as if knowing the secret trail of tears without looking for it. The wetness of my face did not seem to surprise the hand, as her face directed a look of recognition to them.

Lelia came in front of my face and took my hand without a word. We walked out of the bar, she holding my hand and I almost without a will or a questioning soul.

We walked past the gate of the hospice, where I stopped as if seeing something, though I could not relate its significance to the sudden halt I had made and she with me. I looked into her eyes; they were crystalline and warm, as when she smiled some days. There was something magical within the gates, something indefinable, and luminous at heart. I did not know it, could not feel its pulsing centre; it was there, but I could not see it, my heartbeat could only announce its presence, my eyes failed to string its shape, guess its name.

At the private bench a small body sat at the edge of its realm in the quiet of the early evening. Lelia and I were almost at her side before we saw her. Lelia's hand over mine stiffened suddenly as if she tried to pull me away, but I was attracted to the bench, my eyes were on the small girl and her eyes on mine, looking at me with an invitation to sit. I sat without being verbally asked. Lelia, almost unwilling, stayed upright, defending her intention not to stay.

The girl smiled at me and said nothing I could hear. Lelia held my hand tightly with both of hers as I sat to her left and between her and the girl. Her eyes were suddenly full of a sadness that was impeachable of harshness. A sadness I had not seen in them before, as I turned suddenly to look at her face.

The girl sat herself up properly as if to assure us she was not a child. 'You were here, in the morning,' she asked me with a confidence that suggested that the question was more a statement than a question. I nodded without thinking. 'I thought I saw you. I came here before with my mother about five years ago, my grandmother died here, now my mother had come with me, I am to die here with the summer flowers and butterflies, better than in the winter, don't you think?' Neither I nor Lelia seemed to be shaken at the length of the statement or its ending; nothing separated us from the girl but the silence of nothing thought or said.

After some time spent with each of us looking at each other, the girl got up and started to walk on, as if she had made a decision or had reached the end of her stay. I got up without meaning to do so, so did Lelia. My only thought that moment was pity not for the girl but for myself. I seemed to have gone cold-spirited, the girl's acceptance and contentment for her death seemed to pass within me without an echo or a single bereaved feeling or word of sympathy, as if I was complimenting her, as if her life was worthless and she stood ready to erase its last trace without leaving anything disturbed in a place she had occupied for those years of her life.

She turned as if for the last time, her smile; evidence that her spirit was at ease and her eyes sparkling as if to catch the last reflection of the sun. 'My friends call me Jessica,' she almost whispered before turning away into the shadows of the tall entrance of the building, waving as if sailing away forever. I slumped onto the bench, Lelia covering my face with her body, her arms holding the back of my head. I wanted to cry but seemed unable to be human this once when it was the one time I wanted to so badly. The coincidence was almost unbelievable, almost illogical, maddening, almost spiritual.

She released the grip of her arms and felt my closed eyes with the tips of her fingers. Their shadows danced in the filtering light, their warmth almost moist with the heat of longing and the soft colours of the rainbow, vendors of her soul offering a trade for my pain. I accepted her hands and kissed the inside of her palms; once I gathered them together like two wings of a butterfly, wounded and seeking the gentleness of time.

She said nothing and I added nothing to her silence but more silence. We walked the way home to the flat, holding hands and slowly treading the pavement. At the door of my flat, she gave me a kiss and said goodbye. She had never said 'goodbye' before, it was the first time. I kissed her and turned away to the darkness of my room, closing the door behind me as if I should not open it again, ever.

The room spread its darkness untouched by the sickly yellow light of the street, not yet in full luminous strength. I sat at the table, the light wind of the evening playing with the aged lace-like transparent curtain.

My life lay before me barren, my thought childish and my purpose of being fragile and worthless. I suddenly wanted to go home. I wanted to go home, nothing else seemed of any significance. One thought persisted: my father would be disappointed, I had not achieved what I had come here for, a degree to justify my claim of being an intellectual, to show I was hard working, show the world in my little home town I was serious and had not spent my time here chasing girls. My father's face was in front of me, it was silent, expressing his will that I should stay. Failure would mean time unliveable and a sin unforgivable.

The thought of the mob's ridicule was bitter and displeasing to my mind. It was the hold of such thought which I had dreamt escaping, had planned to loosen its grip on me forever. Yet I had not been feeling at home here either; it seemed like a dream or a something out of an unreal world. My will to belong here seemed often shaken, I had lost the ability to become the man or the mind that was to live here easily. Visitors from the old world came to me almost every night I slept when I was sober, every night I stayed awake when I was drunk.

At four in the morning I was still on the same chair as some eight hours earlier, my eyes fixed on the window as the purple dawn replaced the yellowness of the street light. I was sitting without a tear offered in sacrifice for a sanity I felt to be becoming cloudy with words that broke the sentences which were its emphasis.

I sat lost like a homeless man without my cardboard, without my bottle of wine, disarmed by silence and feeling the razor blade, its sharp edge pressed against the soft edge of my soul as at the wrist veins, those that seem to rival my intention with a hardening pulse and coward compliance, bending easily under the downward press of the metal, while Jessica seemed waiting in my mind. One thought competed now with going home, being with Jessica (if my childhood promises of an after-life were true). Thoughts of indiscriminate length passed in my mind: I could not make the decision, at which of the two destinations I should arrive.

My father's diary sat like me at the dining table, sat like me passively awaiting some decision. The light breeze of the new-born day turned its pages, one at a time, as if designed to allow my reading of each page before the next one was exposed to light; but I had read it and was familiar with its lines, with its intransigence and soft breaking at the spine. The final page arrived: it was empty and unlike the rest more inviting, more turned-away face and less demanding. I took up my pen and directed my fingers at its surface. The words seemed crowded at the point of impact and I felt the conversion of thoughts into words almost futile.

The first lines read: I have reached a point of thought where a man's curiosity had dissolved the dotted line and all has become a page of a background colour, where the puncture of a man's soul is an everyday commonplace, where the seepage of will is beyond prayer and beyond stealth, where the lease of intention had become worthless, as has the will it always had and the passages it has undertaken in search of that religion called goodness, the bright warmth of man and promise of all those who wait.

There was a pause, a gap of three empty lines, easily unoccupied. I wrote the last sentence that made me one with my mind, it read: 'Jessica, I'll love forever'. At the full-stop of that sentence, an old poem I had written some fourteen years ago came back and flowed my lips:

> There are those ways of love
> of dependence quandary
> treacherous and bilateral,
> forsaking the world
> for other children
> other than one's seeding
> bidding courage against rain
> bleeding humour out of a storm
> faltering beneath desire
> when the tremor stains
> distant skies with purple shade
> in imminence and forecast.

Jessica lays her faded towel
on her bed and prays hard, hard
wishing the will in her hand
to deny the begging of her mind
retaining some logic magic wand
listing the moment unmanned
as a call of a hunger-awakened owl.

Her thighs still wet of her passion
dripping towards the shine-clean floor
anticipating dryness from its spent core
and humming tenderness beyond its score
while her lover slept-out of her store
of nightmares and destitute-look fashion.

Her gifts: her body and soul-alms
given with ease of her calm wanting
as shed years in summers of panting
every trend serious of her planting
red flowers, colouring her haunting
scatter-scent on black hair psalms.

When it is time to colour the bed red
soak-full of promise-binding thread
peaceful of the knife beside her head
looking for strings of dawn to be led
whispering God goodbyes, as she bled.

There are those ways of love
common with butterflies
and seasons of dispute
when a pauper's mind
denies him but his hunger
appetites for forbidden grape
restless upon crossing of late
threshold and posthumous hope
passionate without alcohol or scope
like thin plaits of a hanging rope
or the shine of a friendly blade.